FULL FORCE

A MASON SHARPE THRILLER

LOGAN RYLES

INKUBATOR
BOOKS

Published by Inkubator Books
www.inkubatorbooks.com

ISBN (eBook): 978-1-83756-554-2
ISBN (Paperback): 978-1-83756-555-9
ISBN (Hardback): 978-1-83756-556-6

1

I was headed to confront another man.

Maybe not physically—that choice was his. I hadn't brought any weapons, and I didn't need any. He was in excellent shape, a track runner in his spare time, a gun-toting federal agent during the workday. None of that concerned me. The only thing that mattered, the thing that had brought me all the way across metro DC into the heart of Petworth at nearly midnight, was what he had done.

And the fact that he wouldn't stop doing it.

I parked my pickup in a metered slot on Kansas Avenue and walked the final mile. Even in late spring, Washington was cool, barely sixty degrees. Humidity rolled off the Potomac River, sticking to the windows of parked cars and glistening on freshly paved sidewalks. The streetlamps were bright and evenly spaced, the storefronts freshly refurbished, the townhomes an even mixture of brand-new construction and historic builds in various stages of restoration. This was a money neighborhood, the latest winner of gentrification roulette. Young buyers, hot out of college and ready to leave their mark on the nation's capital. Business-men, lobbyists, political aides.

And creeps.

The address I wanted sat on Delafield Place, only blocks from Sherman Circle Park. The West Coast development money hadn't quite reached this district—the houses were well-maintained but old. All the power lines ran above ground, tangling over the sidewalks. Each light post was adorned with a "Drug Free Zone" sign.

And it was dead quiet. No pedestrians. No dogs sleeping on front porches. No patrolling neighborhood security or DC cops.

Nobody to challenge my approach.

I turned the corner onto Delafield and slowed, my gaze sweeping each iron-fenced yard and street-parked sedan. The houses were all townhomes, those on my left resting atop an eight-foot berm with concrete steps leading up to their front porches, while those on my right sat at street level. Untrimmed trees lined the sidewalks, wispy limbs casting long, inky shadows.

And my target address lay directly ahead. A blue town-home with a Clemson Tigers flag hanging from the porch. The grass was a week overdue for a trim. The exterior paint was faded and starting to peel, the flowerbeds a little over-grown and unmanaged.

And on the second floor of the home, escaping through the cracks of tightly closed blinds, soft yellow light leaked out. It was fourteen minutes past midnight according to my wristwatch, but the man I'd come to confront was still awake.

He would answer the door.

My jaw tightened, every memory of the past three months replaying in my mind at triple speed. The memory

of all those dates and times, all those innocent locations—
each marred by his unwelcome face. There was no deliberation in my mind, no second-guessing what came next. I
hadn't made this choice—he had.

But when I saw the woman, my focus faltered.

She approached down the righthand side of Delafield,
opposite me, and headed in my direction. Two hundred
yards, passing just beyond my target address. She wore a
jacket wrapped tight around her body to block out the chill
—she leaned low, ducking her head beneath the clawing
tree limbs. Not quite jogging but pushing the category of
walk to its limits. There was a purse slung over her shoulder,
pitch-black hair swept over one ear.

She wasn't looking toward me. She was looking at the
house—the same house I was headed for, and that was
enough to give me pause. To break my stride, if only for a
moment.

What happened next brought me to a complete halt. Not
one additional player, but two materialized from the shadows. Both men, both trailing the woman by one hundred
yards. The first walked along her side of the street, moving
directly behind her at an easy lope that kept pace with her
near-jog. The second closed from my side of Delafield,
weaving between cars and avoiding the brightest pools of
streetlight. Just like the woman, both men wore jackets. Both
had black hair, and as the three of them drew closer, I
noticed a final detail—a striking coincidence.

All three of them were Asians.

I stood motionless on the sidewalk, the bulk of my body
sheltered by the thick black shadow of a maple tree, my gaze
flicking between the woman, the man behind her, and the
man across the street. She hadn't seen either of them—she

was fixated on the path ahead, shoes clip-clopping on the sidewalk, arms wrapped tight around her body. The first guy kept his distance, still matching her pace.

But the second guy had drawn level with her from across the street, his body sliding into shelter behind a parked SUV. His back pressed against the vehicle's side, one hand dipping beneath his jacket. The woman was still a hundred yards from the blue townhome with the Clemson Tigers flag—I was fifty yards farther on, apparently as invisible to her as the two men who trailed her.

And as that second guy—the one hidden behind the SUV—withdrew his hand from beneath his jacket, all thoughts of my purpose in coming to this place vanished in an instant.

"*Run!*"

I shouted the single word at full volume, catching them all off guard. Their gazes snapped in my direction, and for a split second all three of them froze in place. The world descended into slow motion, the mist hanging static all around us.

Then the woman finally did the instinctual thing—the thing she should have done long before. She looked over her shoulder. She saw the guy behind her, an apparition in the darkness. She screamed.

And then she ran.

2

Everything that happened next was automatic. From the righthand side of the street the man trailing the woman from directly behind broke his cover and sprinted after her. On my side of the street the second stalker pivoted toward me, one hand still wrapped around the silhouette of a pistol, his gaze locking on my position. I looked dead into his eyes. I saw something there I had seen before—many, many times before.

And I knew exactly whom I was dealing with.

I threw myself behind the maple tree just as the pistol fully emerged. I hadn't got a good look at it, but the first muted snap of a gunshot told the story. It was a suppressed small-caliber. The report was little more than a loud click, but the whisper of the bullet was far less innocuous. It tore into the maple, spraying bark over the sidewalk. I scrambled backwards as the next shot ripped into unprotected earth with a spray of dirt.

I didn't give him time for a third shot. Launching myself back to my feet, I found better cover beyond the nose of a parked minivan. A brittle smack signaled the impact of a bullet slamming into one of the van's windows, and I covered my head as little cubes of glass rained down. Lying on my side against the asphalt, I saw his feet beneath the van's chassis. He was sprinting toward me, a flash of black dress shoes. I could picture the handgun held at the ready, suppressor leading the way.

I rolled just as he arrived, and the next bullet sliced past my arm and ricocheted off asphalt as I scrambled behind the front wheel of the minivan. His shoes thumped from the curb to the street. I jammed my hand into my pocket and clutched the only weapon I had on me—the oversized Victorinox Swiss army knife with a three-inch locking blade.

There was no time to flip it open. No time to stab. Only barely enough time to draw, cock, and fling the Victorinox like a baseball. It caught him dead in the face just as he circled to my side of the van. He stumbled back, blood spraying from his nose, the pistol cracking another near-fatal shot. The bullet cut past my arm just as I lunged to my feet, shoving away from the van.

I hit him dead in the chest, hard and sudden enough to send the handgun flying from his fingers. It spun through the air and clattered to the asphalt, sliding straight into a storm drain just as he crashed backward into the maple tree.

I struck him in the throat—open palmed, driving the web of my hand into his windpipe. He never had time to gasp, never had time to shout. The force of my blow crushed his trachea, terminating his airflow. He couldn't breathe, couldn't speak, couldn't scream. His eyes bulged and he flailed for purchase against a whipping tree limb, fingers shredding at late spring leaves.

My next blow obliterated any chance of him breaking his

fall. I hit him with my knee straight between his legs only a split second before my left fist landed in his right eye. He went down like a felled tree, stiff and helpless. His spine struck the curb, his skull slammed into the sidewalk. He was lights out and limp and I was turning. Back toward Kansas Avenue, back toward the last place I'd seen the woman running.

Just in time to hear a frantic scream followed by a gunshot.

I ran, hurling myself across the street toward the noise. The sound of the shot was like the others, little more than a loud snap, but the scream that preceded it served as a homing beacon. I was locked onto the spot—a darkened turn off Delafield one hundred yards ahead. I crossed the street and skidded around another parked SUV, reaching the mouth of a wide alley. It cut behind a slouching Chinese restaurant on my right and another strip of townhomes to my left. Concave concrete, about twice as wide as a car, with puddles from the latest rain shower still gathered in its middle. Only yards off Delafield, the alley was consumed by darkness, but there was just enough ambient streetlight for me to detect two vague figures.

One sprinting away from me, down the alley. The other lying in a crumpled heap on the concrete.

Lights blazed in the windows of the nearest townhome as I accelerated into a run once more. By the time I'd reached the first figure I had clawed my Streamlight Macro-Stream from my pocket, clicking it on and jamming the barrel of the flashlight between my teeth. I hit my knees, bright white LED light pouring over a black jacket speckled with blood. I grabbed her by the shoulder and rolled her body onto her back, blazing light into her face...

And knowing in an instant—she was dead. Shot straight through the forehead, right between the eyes, both of which were frozen open. A beautiful face, a young face. Mid-twenties, maybe, her chocolate-brown gaze now misted over with death. Her body still warm.

Her murderer escaping into the night.

"Police!" I spat the flashlight into my hand and shouted at the sound of approaching footsteps. Gasps. Civilians caught off guard and petrified by unexpected violence. "Call the police!"

Then I was gone, headed down the alley. Stretching my body for every ounce of speed it could produce, the flashlight beam bouncing over the concrete ahead.

Giving chase to a killer.

3

Beyond the Chinese restaurant the alley was lined by additional retail buildings to my right and residential chain-link fences to my left. I passed an intersecting alley and looked down it, but I didn't see him. I sprinted onward to the edge of Decatur Street and caught myself on a light pole just before falling in front of a rushing city bus.

A horn blared. I looked right toward Georgia Avenue and saw nothing but traffic lights and surging cars—no pedestrians.

Then I looked left, farther up Decatur. This time, I saw him. A blur of black clothing headed up the sidewalk on the opposite side of the street, temporarily visible behind a row of parked cars before vanishing behind a tree. I didn't think, I didn't look backward for oncoming traffic. I simply exploded out from behind the bus, throwing myself across Decatur and onto the sidewalk. Turning after him, stretching my legs as the darkened figure ran at full speed, jacket flapping. Arms pumping. Looking once over his shoulder. Running harder.

The breath was burning in my lungs, heart slamming in my chest as I poured on the gas. Every slam of my boots against the concrete unleashed tremors up my spine, but my spine was well accustomed to the abuse. Liberated from the seventy-five-pound rucksack I had hauled through the mountains of Afghanistan, I was unperturbed by the aching in my left leg or the protests of my mind. I'd done this before, and much more.

There was no *way* this guy would escape.

Crossing 9th Street, we approached 8th. We were moving east, and I was gaining on him. As he scrambled around the hood of a honking Honda, I was leaping a fallen tree limb, crashing through a mud puddle and approaching the same intersection. The Honda was gone. The Toyota behind it ran fifty yards to my left. It was just enough gap for me to explode across the street as the Toyota honked.

My target was barely fifty yards ahead. I could make out details of his attire, a snug business suit matched with a white-collared shirt. His hair was long, reaching down past his ears and running slick with sweat. Shorter than me, but built with similar bulk, he ran well but lacked the benefit of my thirty-two-inch inseam.

He was losing ground. I was seconds away from body-slamming him to the concrete.

Then he pulled a hard right just past 8th Street. Not across another thoroughfare, but into another alley. Fences and low brick walls lined either side, trash cans set out, shabby houses overhung by tangled power lines. It was dark, the pavement uneven. He had slowed a little, head moving on a swivel, searching for a route of escape.

But there was no escape. The walls were too high, the fenced backyards nothing less than dead ends. The houses were built together with no passage between, and at two stories tall he couldn't hope to scramble onto their roofs. His only possible route was dead ahead of him, and now I had him at thirty yards. Breath whistling between my teeth. Legs stretching for every available inch. He was out of time, out of room.

And at the last minute, he knew it. Fifty yards from the end of the alley, he turned. Jacket snapping, hand dipping. The concealed handgun appeared, a long black suppressor screwed onto the muzzle. He faced me head-on, and for the first time I could clearly see his face, fully illuminated by a nearby streetlight, vivid in the midnight mist.

Piercing eyes—not dark, but bright and brilliant blue. Pitch-black hair slick with sweat. Jaw clenched, the twisted white snake of a scar running down the left side of his face all the way from his temple to his chin. A nasty, tangled mark, strikingly vivid as he leveled the gun and the world descended into slow motion once more.

Then I was throwing myself to the ground. The pistol snapped, spitting a subsonic slug in my direction. The bullet missed by inches as I slammed sideways into a brick wall. I found myself behind a trash can—one of those large, modern plastic bins on wheels. It was full, the lid propped open on a compressed bag of trash.

Full, but not heavy. I knew that the moment I collided with it and the bin scraped sideways six inches. He fired again, the next bullet striking plastic but failing to fully penetrate the household garbage packed inside.

Then I was charging, grabbing the bin by its hand grip and rocking it onto its wheels. Shoving ahead, closing the

distance between us. Bullets smacking plastic as he
continued to fire, maybe frantic or maybe enraged. Frag-
ments of the bin's lid stung my face, but the garbage was an
effective bullet stop. I was ten yards away. Five. He started to
turn.

I released the bin and hurtled from behind it, striking
him from behind like a lunging defensive end. The handgun, still clasped in his right hand, was locked back on
empty. It flew out of his grip as he fell, my falling body
colliding with his pelvis and driving him to the ground.

Asphalt bit my elbows. He shouted and rolled, legs flailing. One knee caught me in the gut, and I grunted as the air
vacated my lungs. I clung on, managing to roll on top of him,
kneeing him in the groin just like the first guy. He grunted,
those brilliant sapphire eyes growing wide, the facial scar
glistening with sweat.

In that moment, he didn't look human. He looked
possessed, like a savage jungle cat, consumed by blood lust.
A blue-eyed, mutilated Bengal tiger just writhing with
muscle, desperate not only to survive but also to rip my heart
clean out of my chest.

His jaw was clenched. His body shook. He wriggled right,
one leg hooking my left calf, his left arm snapping up and
encircling my neck. The move was lightning fast, so unexpected and forceful that I couldn't resist. I couldn't
compensate.

The tiger threw me off like a ragdoll, releasing my body
as I tumbled to the concrete. My head struck the ground,
and I saw stars. I saw him flipping upright like the rabid cat
he favored, landing on his feet with perfect agility. He
twisted on his heel and wound up a plunging kick to my
face.

But I saw it coming. I snapped my head to one side, completing a roll of my own. By the time he realized he would miss, it was too late to withdraw the attack. He was off balance—I was back on my feet. I spun on him just in time to catch a lightning strike to my sternum, flat-palmed and horse-kick hard.

More air rushed from my lungs. I stumbled back. He followed up, closing the distance and pressing the assault. They weren't punches, not like American boxing. This was some kind of Asian martial arts style—quick and snappy strikes that kept me reeling, knocked me off balance. I drew my hands to my face and ducked a sweeping blow to my temple, but the move was just a fake.

The real strike was a kick to my exposed right side. An arching swing, a smack of his shin against unprotected flesh, just above the pelvis.

The pain was immediate and overwhelming. The last of the air rushed from my lungs. I crashed sideways into a privacy fence and began to topple. Even before my knees reached the ground the tiger was back on me. Right foot catching my collapsing calf, left foot sliding between my legs, knee driven against my spine.

Then his arm was closed around my throat, yanking my head back. I choked for air, but there was nothing to breathe. My lungs were already empty, and my windpipe was compressed just as I had compressed the first guy's.

The blue-eyed tiger pulled me closer, his knee counteracting the pressure of his forearm and doubling the choking power. I couldn't move. I clawed at his arm and twisted on my knees, fighting to shake him loose. Each time I fought to scramble to my feet he drove down with his right foot, locking my leg to the ground. I attempted to throw him forward, but the pressure of his knee against my spine worked as a fulcrum, making it easy for him to wrench my head back.

He had the leverage. He had the lock. All my developed muscle and raw desperation were useless. I blinked, and the sky over DC began to fade. I choked, and I saw a face.

Not a tiger face. This one had strawberry-blonde hair. Brilliant green eyes. The gentlest of smiles.

Then darkness closed in.

4

I never heard the gunshot, nor did I even feel the release of pressure. The first thing I knew I was slumped to the ground, body splayed across the concrete, breath passing in ragged bursts through a bruised windpipe.

I still saw stars. I still saw green eyes and strawberry-blonde hair. But I also saw shadows and grit, moldy bricks and grimy concrete. I tasted blood and muddy water. I heard footsteps and a shout. Running shoes slapping the pavement. The wail of a distant siren.

Then a voice.

"You alive, bruh?"

A hand grabbed my shoulder. It rolled me onto my back, but I could see nothing save streetlights and a dark sky. I was still choking for breath. Then a face appeared only inches over mine. Black skin, wide and concerned eyes. A skull wrapped in a durag, teeth flashing bright white, almost luminescent.

I blinked, and the face came into slightly better focus. It

was a young man's face, creased with concern but also indecision. He glanced over his shoulder, away from me. Then he was back, shaking my arm. I felt something pressed between his hand and my skin, and I twisted my head, glancing down.

It was a pistol—a snub-nosed revolver. I could smell gun smoke.

"Hey," he said. "I gotta split. You gonna make it?"

I met his gaze again, still gasping. There was just enough air left in my lungs to voice a half-question.

"Where is..."

"He's gone, man. I fired into the air, and he took off. Look, I can't hang around. Take care of yourself, you hear?"

He squeezed my shoulder. The gun disappeared into his jacket—black leather printed with a Washington Commanders logo. Then he was on his feet and he vanished from my wavering vision.

I collapsed onto the concrete and continued to pant as the sirens grew louder. Blue lights reflected against the nearby privacy fence and feet pounded—a radio crackled.

Then the first cop was there, and a song and dance I'd endured so many times before began yet again.

To the credit of the Washington DC Metropolitan Police, they ensured my own health and welfare prior to unleashing their predictable torrent of questions. I was helped to my feet and allowed a few moments to lean against the privacy fence and recover my breath while a pair of patrol officers searched the ground with flashlights, growing agitated as they recovered the first brass cartridge casing.

It was small, about the size of an ink pen. Nine-millimeter maybe, but the cops didn't offer me a closer look, and I didn't ask. While one officer marked eight casings with little yellow tags, the other kept his eyes on me, one hand on his gun. A radio exchange alerted other cops of the scene, and additional sirens rang.

Then, at last, the questions began. They came in a predictable flurry, all the whos, whats, whens, and wheres. I kept my story clipped and to the point, not adding any embellishment or unnecessary detail. I told them about Delafield Place. About the woman and her two stalkers. I recounted my attempt to intervene. My flight down this alley, and the garbage can I had used as a shield while the killer frantically dumped lead at me.

And then I told them that he had knocked the wind out of me and escaped. Vanished into the city just as the cops roared up.

The officer taking my statement made notes on a tablet with deft strokes of a stylus—the twenty-first-century version of a pocket pad, I guessed. When I was a detective back in Arizona, I had preferred pen and paper. The old-school method. But even though that had only been a few years prior, it felt like ages, and not just because of the change in technology.

"There was nobody else?" the cop asked, looking up from his tablet.

"What do you mean?"

"Nobody else was with you?"

I hesitated, sweeping my gaze down the alley. I noted all the overlooking windows, many of them with lights now shining behind blinds and curtains. Inside one of those houses somebody had dialed 911. Somebody had witnessed a one-sided gunfight, followed by a one-sided martial arts beatdown. Not my proudest moment.

Had they also witnessed my savior? A nondescript Black guy in a Commanders jacket?

I can't hang around, he'd said, and I thought I knew why. Firearms in Washington DC are highly regulated items. It's just about the furthest thing from a gun-friendly city in America. The fact that this guy had discharged a gun, even in an effort to save my life, could bring trouble for him. At the very least, it would bring questions.

He didn't want to answer questions. Maybe that was because he was a criminal, a drug dealer or a pimp. Who knew?

The only thing I knew was that he'd saved my life, and one good turn deserves another.

So I simply shrugged. "It's kind of a blur."

The cop grunted, making another note. Then a series of police codes I didn't recognize—further updates of the new age, I guessed—crackled through his shoulder-mounted radio. He answered. He called to his partner and jabbed a thumb at the patrol car behind him, the engine still rumbling.

"You mind riding with us, Mr. Sharpe?"

"Why?"

"We're headed back to the murder scene. Detective's on site. He'll want to meet you."

I turned my head and spat through my teeth to prevent a curse. It wasn't an unreasonable request. Certainly, it wasn't an irrational one. If I were the one standing in uniform, I would have asked the same thing. If I had been refused, I would have stopped asking and maybe reached for handcuffs.

But I wasn't the one in a uniform. I hadn't worn a uniform of any sort in several years, and during that time I'd learned to avoid government entanglements whenever possible. It wasn't that I disrespected the system—I simply hate headaches, which left me wondering whether it would be more aggravating to argue or to simply comply.

In the end I circled to the back of the cruiser and sat behind the bars while the two cops drove. They didn't handcuff me—probably because they wanted me to feel less like a suspect and more like an ally. We drove up Decatur. We reached the first alley where I'd turned off Delafield—the one where the woman lay dead, her body growing stiff and cold.

Gone was the misty solemnity of the place. The alley connecting Delafield to Decatur now looked more like a carnival, with blue and red lights flashing. There were DC patrol cars, a compact fire engine, and an ambulance. One unmarked sedan that must be the detective. A lot of people in uniforms.

The cops left me caged in the back of the car while they departed—a legal risk, on their part. With no door handles on the inside of the car, I was technically being detained. Nobody had read me my rights.

I dismissed the Fifth Amendment concerns with a sigh and resigned myself to wait. It wasn't easy—I was aching from head to toe, with concentrated pain in my windpipe. The blue-eyed tiger had worked a number on me in a brutally short period of time, and I wasn't too proud to admit it. He was light on his feet. He was well trained.

And he'd been armed with a suppressed weapon, the same as his buddy. An assassin's weapon.

By the time a greasy-looking guy dressed in a stained

white button-down and a wrinkled blazer finally approached my door, I'd already decided that whatever this mess was, I didn't want any part of it. It could be a would-be gang rape gone wrong. It might be a family dispute, or one guy helping his buddy to eliminate a pesky ex-wife.

What it *felt* like was something much more sinister. Something orchestrated, maybe political. The suppressed weapons and the advanced hand-to-hand combat training all substantiated that theory. Whatever the case, I hadn't come to Delafield Place to involve myself in the machinations of an espionage conspiracy. I'd only intervened in the first place to save a presumably innocent woman's life.

And I had failed. Completely. The reality of that failure hit hard every time I thought of the young woman's wide, haunted eyes—but the time to save her life had long passed. The only thing I could do now was to accept my failure and extricate myself from the proceedings.

Get out of the way.

"Mr. Sharpe, right?" The greasy guy leaned against the open rear door of the car, chewing gum like a cow chewing cud. "I'm Detective Dickens. Mind answering a few questions?"

I didn't think it mattered whether I minded or not. I simply grunted, and he proceeded, taking notes on an iPad the same as the first guy. The questions were predictable. I confirmed my name, I gave him my story. I omitted the guy in the Commanders jacket, same as before. I answered every question directly, and with as few words as possible.

Not because I wanted to make his job hard. Because I wanted to make his job easy, and because I didn't want to be a repeat character in his investigation.

The detective seemed to appreciate my directness. He

looked very tired, like he'd just been clocking out of an eighteen-hour shift when he got the call about a murder in Petworth. Now he would be working another six hours, minimum.

I'd been there.

"So what brought you to Delafield, Mr. Sharpe?"

I didn't answer. My gaze was fixated on the paramedics who had moved the woman's body onto a stretcher. They were covering her with a sheet. They were not attempting resuscitation. What was the point? A bullet to the forehead at point-blank range is a pretty permanent condition.

"Mr. Sharpe? I asked what you were doing on Delafield Place tonight."

I looked back to the detective. He stood with his eyebrows raised, waiting. Maybe growing slightly suspicious at my delay.

I shrugged. "Taking a walk."

It wasn't true, but there was no chance I would be honest about what had actually brought me to Petworth. It wasn't the kind of thing you tell a cop, even if he was inclined to understand. It wasn't the kind of thing you tell anybody.

It's just the kind of thing you deal with. Man to man. Over and done.

"A walk, eh?"

His tone told me he didn't believe me. The red in his eyes told me he was too tired to press much further.

"Am I free to go?" I said.

The detective sighed. He made another note on his iPad.

"Yeah, okay. Just let me get your number. I'll likely have more questions."

Of course you will.

I had to dig out my phone to give him the number. The

device was pre-paid, only a couple months old. Just one in a long chain of burner phones I'd bought over the past three years. It wasn't a habit of secrecy or security, it was simply a growing distaste for modern technology. I used phones until they broke, or I lost them. Then I picked up another at a drugstore when I needed to make a call, and the cycle started over again. New phone, new number. I never memorized it.

I read off the digits and the cop took them down. Then I exited the car, stretching worn muscles and considering the walk back to my truck. It was a mile, more or less. Then a thirty-minute ride back home.

Or, better put. Back to my current address.

"Get some rest, Mr. Sharpe. You've had a rough night."

The detective smacked me on the arm. He was just turning away from the patrol car when fresh lights flashed from the end of the alley—the Decatur end, where cops had not fully blocked off the entrance. Hot white LEDs flooded the pavement and gleamed in my eyes—high beams, and I lifted my hand to block them out. One of the patrol cops shouted and waved an arm, calling for the driver to stop. An engine surged and I retreated a few steps toward the nearest townhome as a bulky vehicle raced into view.

It was jet black—a Mercedes panel van without any windows behind the driver's compartment. Brand new, shiny clean, and unmarked. It squealed to a stop on the far side of the patrol car I had just exited, and then the doors popped open. Men bailed out.

Asian men.

5

They stormed the scene in a knot of four. Two from the front seats, two from the rolling side door of the van. All were dressed in black business suits exactly like the one of the blue-eyed tiger I'd chased from this very same alley.

And they were all *pissed*. That much was clear long before they collided with the line of cops that rushed to block their access to the sheet-covered stretcher. In an instant, everyone was shouting. The cops were extending open left palms with their shooting hands resting on holstered firearms. Three of the newcomers were falling back into a protective diamond formation behind their leader, jackets unbuttoned, dark eyes darting from one face to the next.

And the leader—the guy out in front, storming straight toward the line of law enforcement as though they were naughty school children begging for a lashing—snapped out a black leather ID wallet. It flicked open, displaying a white ID card.

I was too far away to read it, and I wasn't interested in taking a closer look. I kept the bulk of a police cruiser resting between me and the four newcomers who, for all I knew, might whip out suppressed sidearms at any moment. Call it the prejudice against similar appearance, or the simple context of the situation; I wasn't taking any chances.

And besides, I didn't need to read the ID. I already had a pretty good idea what was printed on it, and if I had any doubt, it was quelled by the leader's first declaration.

"We are from the Chinese embassy. We are here to collect this woman's body. She is a Chinese national."

He spoke with a heavy accent, thrusting his ID wallet into the nearest cop's face as though anyone standing between himself and the corpse actually cared about his credentials.

"Sir, you need to *back off*," one guy snapped. "This is a crime scene."

"This woman is a Chinese citizen from our embassy. You have no right to take her!"

It was an absurd claim—we were miles from the People's Republic embassy, and even if we hadn't been, any crime committed on the streets of DC was just as far outside the jurisdiction of China as it was outside the jurisdiction of Mars. These guys, whoever they were, had no authority in Petworth.

But issues of jurisdiction and authority didn't interest me. As the shouting continued, one thought alone played on repeat through my mind: *How did they know this woman had died?*

It had barely been an hour.

Still sheltered behind the police cruiser, I watched as the diamond formation of aggressive newcomers closed. The leader pressed the line of cops even as a DC police captain fought his way to the heart of the confrontation.

"We are here on behalf of the PRC," the newcomer snarled. "If you wish to avoid a diplomatic incident, you will surrender the body of our countrywoman."

His cutting demand might have worked inside a dictatorial nation-state like China, where citizens cowered under the bullying demands of their governing officers. But this wasn't China. This wasn't a dictatorial society. And I couldn't deny I greatly enjoyed what happened next.

Without hesitation, the DC police captain drew his sidearm. Falling into a perfect Weaver stance reminiscent of green camouflage uniforms and firing ranges at Fort Benning, he lowered his head to align his point of view with the iron sights, finger hovering just above the trigger guard of a Glock Model 17.

And just like that, the Chinese was staring down the mouth of 9mm American defiance.

"Back. Off."

It wasn't a request. The Chinese weren't given an opportunity to debate. Buoyed by the bravado of their commanding officer, the DC cops kicked into gear. More weapons were drawn. The Chinese were herded back to their van. A perimeter was established. Folding barricades were deployed from the trunks of patrol cars, and additional DC cruisers roared in even as the first news van arrived.

Word had gotten out. This whole scene was becoming a circus, right in front of my very eyes.

"Hey! Get him out of here!" It was the captain, his sidearm now riding next to his thigh as his flushed face glowered at me. The detective I'd spoken with earlier now stood calmly nearby, one hand cupped around a cigarette.

He indulged in a long tug, enraging the cherry to supernova-orange before breathing out between his lips.

It sounded more like a sigh. Like he was contemplating a new career in digging ditches.

"Come on, bud. You don't want to be around for this."

He wasn't wrong. I followed him away from the still-shouting Chinese to the barricade at the opposite end of the alley—the end I had originally entered via. The detective stopped there and extended his cigarette pack toward me.

"Smoke?"

"No, thanks."

He smiled. It was a very calm, very knowing expression. "Stick around town, bud."

Then he turned away, and I watched him go, shaking my head in disgust. Not at him. Maybe not even at myself. Just at the whole rotten situation—the entire degradation not just of the stiffening corpse under that sheet, or of the men who had killed her, or even of this city.

Of the entire human race. One balled-up, sordid, vicious mess. A mess I was so familiar with, had confronted so many times in its very worst attitudes that I barely gave a second thought to the shock of stumbling upon a lifeless corpse with a hole drilled through its forehead.

It was horrific, yes. It was disturbing. I was just numb to it, and there was nothing I could do regardless. This was the problem of the DC police, now.

I had failed.

Pocketing my hands, I retraced my steps back up Delafield to the trigger point of that night's drama. The space on the sidewalk just yards down from my target address...the blue townhome with the Clemson Tigers flag. That one particular individual, alone inside.

Only, he might no longer be inside. The upstairs light was off, and the house was silent. I approached quietly, sweeping my gaze down the street and still hyper-aware of the concentration of cops only half a mile behind me. I slowed, ready for anything as I turned behind a parked SUV to the spot where I'd fought the first guy—the guy I'd left unconscious on the sidewalk.

But he was gone—vanished without a trace. His pistol brass had been removed, also. The street was quiet and empty, the only sign of anything having transpired here being the broken glass of the gunshot minivan...some hapless third party's loss.

With a sigh, I dug the MacroStream from my pocket and used its dimmest setting to search for my Victorinox. The Swiss army knife-turned-nose-breaker lay half-buried in the mulch of a brick-bordered flower bed. There was even a smattering of blood on it. I wiped the stainless-steel tool clean with ease. The tool was unharmed, and I returned it to my pocket alongside the flashlight as I gazed at the van.

What happened here?

The thought stuck in my mind for nearly a full minute as I replayed each event like the action line of a stage performance. My position on the sidewalk, the approach of the woman and her two stalkers. The resulting fights, scrambles, and ultimate fallout.

How the woman had died. And how very close I had come to joining her.

It was odd, but even on full review I barely considered my near-death experience, or allowed myself much time to decide how I felt about it. It wasn't my first such brush with death, and knowing my proclivity for throwing myself into ill-advised situations, it likely wouldn't be my last. Nobody is invincible.

Actually, what stuck with me most about the entire encounter wasn't the precipice of eternity, but how I had been snatched back from its edge. That gunshot cracking through the night. A good Samaritan—or, perhaps, a less-than-good Samaritan—intervening, just as I had attempted to intervene on behalf of that woman.

Only he had succeeded. I had failed.

My shoulders sagged and I closed my eyes. I breathed a short but heartfelt prayer, not only for the soul of the recently departed, but also for the guy in the Commanders jacket. I didn't need to know anything about him to understand that a guy walking the streets of DC in the middle of the night with a gun in his pocket has problems, and divine intervention is health and salvation for all men.

At least...that was becoming my experience.

Concluding the silent invocation, I cast only one more look toward the blue townhome before departing Delafield Place for the one-mile walk back to my parked pickup. The man who graduated from Clemson University might still be inside that house—he might simply be asleep.

Whatever the case, this night had seen more than enough violence, and with so many cops nearby the opportunity for my planned confrontation had passed regardless. I would have to circle back to that issue at another time.

For the moment, I was ready to call it a night.

Resting next to the Kansas Avenue curb with twenty-two minutes remaining on the parking meter, my 1967 GMC pickup was undisturbed, its crystal-clean headlamps reflecting a bit of the streetlight. The engine fired up without protest, settling into a glossy-smooth idle that always made me feel better about life.

Casting one more glance back into Petworth, I bottled everything that had happened that night deep into the back of my mind. I archived those events, by force, alongside a catalog of just-as-bad and somehow worse events that spanned my personal history from the grungy streets of Phoenix to the rocky mountain ridges of Afghanistan.

I accepted the reality. I let it go, as best as I could.

Then I dropped the truck into gear and turned for home.

6

"Home" for me was a five-hundred-square-foot former motel room converted into a pre-furnished studio apartment in the southeast corner of DC, amid a neighborhood called Anacostia. Not a premium establishment by any means, but Anacostia wasn't a premium neighborhood—far from it. It was the sort of community that realtors described as "developing", politicians described as "economically challenged", and cops referred to as a "hell hole".

Poor, with elevated crime rates, shabby homes, unwashed streets and sidewalks, and convenience stores with bars mounted across their windows. Not a family place, not a tourist place. And yet I, as a relative tourist to my nation's capital, had established a short-term address here. Not only because the rent was cheap—at least, cheap for DC—but because in a strange way I felt more at home amid the potheads and street grifters than I did amid the posh and polished high rises of Alexandria.

It took me by surprise, but it shouldn't have. I'd spent the last three years living out of the back of my pickup truck, camping under the stars, renting grungy hotel rooms and drifting at my leisure. Never claiming an address and never feeling shortchanged by the lack of one. I'd made a home on the lowest rung of society above prison...and perhaps to my chagrin as a former cop, I kind of liked it.

Nobody asked questions on this rung. Nobody held any expectations beyond those basic concepts of justice that we're all born with—that you don't steal, don't lie, and do your best to treat others the way you'd want to be treated. The Golden Rule. But you don't have to dress fancy, speak fancy, drive fancy, or generally live fancy on the bottom rung. You didn't have to leverage credit and manipulate your appearance to *be* something that nobody wanted or cared about in the first place.

And I liked that, even if the harder edges of poverty were sometimes difficult to stomach.

Rolling into the parking lot of the U-shaped former motel, I lifted a hand to a neighbor who was kicked back in a lawn chair two doors down from my unit, a stack of crushed beer cans gathered next to him. It was nearly two a.m., but here on the lowest rung, one hour is pretty much the same as the next. At the end of my wing a couple was squabbling. Somewhere from the second-floor music played. As I stepped out of my truck, I smelled tobacco and pot smoke. The asphalt was pitted and flush with standing water, cigarette buts littering the sidewalks, an Oldsmobile resting on blocks a few yards away.

Welcome home.

"Out late tonight," my drunken friend mused, belching over a can of Miller. "Want a draank?"

I lifted a hand. "Gotta clock out, Rex. Save one for me."

He lifted a can in salute. I reached my door and slipped the key into the lock. The brass numerals read 107. The door itself had been painted half a dozen times with half a dozen colors visible wherever it had been scratched. It was dented and gouged, a bullet hole puncturing the metal near the jamb.

Just par for the course in a place like this.

Inside I locked and chained the door, kicking my boots off. I scanned my compact living area featuring a sagging card table, a dusty kitchenette, an AC unit that whined when it kicked on, and the entrance to a bathroom barely large enough to turn around in. My duffel bag rested on the table, clothes strewn around it. My violin leaned in its case in one corner. On the bedside table a worn leather Bible inscribed with my deceased fiancée's name was illuminated by lamplight.

And that was it. The items in my pockets. The worn camping gear in the back of my truck. One pair of keys.

A life in a shoebox. But it was my life.

My bruised ribs protested as I dragged the shirt over my head. The flesh where I had been shin-kicked was inflamed cherry red, and I suspected that my windpipe was also heavily bruised. Certainly it stung to breathe.

And I hadn't saved her.

I sat staring at the stained carpet for a while, picturing the dead Asian woman. Her bright, young face. The fear in her eyes when she'd first witnessed her stalkers—when I'd yelled for her to run.

What was her story? Why had she been walking alone down Delafield that night? And why had she been murdered?

My thoughts drifted down a twisted path of curiosity,

guilt, and simple exhaustion even as fresh sirens rang in the distance. Not headed to Delafield. Those rushing squad cars could be headed anywhere—to this very complex for all I knew. The couple at the end of the wing was still fighting, and she had resorted to throwing things. Empty beer bottles, by the sound of it. This wasn't the first time. I heard sirens almost every night—gunshots, sometimes. Random burning buildings. Stolen cars. Muggings.

More denigration of mankind—those harder edges of poverty.

I settled back onto my bed with a grunt, pain ripping across my battered ribs. My head landed on a flat pillow, my mind finally relinquishing the violence and failure of the night...and I saw the face again.

Strawberry-blonde hair. Bright green eyes. A smile that could thaw an ice age. That *had*, in fact, thawed an ice age. At least, a metaphorical one.

Just picturing her was enough to relax my mind. To make me forget the throbbing pain in my side or the burn in my throat. Even to forget Delafield Place and the unfinished business I would still need to resolve. To forget the sirens and the persistent screams from five doors down.

No, this wasn't a nice place. But I had a great reason to be here.

7

D espite my late night I was up at sunrise. Stiff, sore, and irritated to discover that my neighbor's domestic dispute had finally resulted in the arrival of law enforcement, but equally gratified to discover that I still had some instant coffee left in the bottom of the jar.

Hot water heated on the two-eye stove. A quick shower and a travel mug. No breakfast—I would catch that at the mission. Then I was outside lifting a hand to Rex, who apparently had never gone to bed. Firing up my truck and backing out behind a police car, simply shaking my head to the exhausted cop who caught my eye.

It had been a long night for more than one of us.

Back on the highway, I kept the Anacostia River between myself and downtown as I headed northeast. It wasn't a lengthy drive, but it was a slow one thanks to the perpetual congestion of DC traffic. I elected not to feel rushed and relaxed in my seat, sipping instant coffee and admiring the river as it reflected the sunrise—an unbroken current of natural peace amid a city consumed by the tumultuous chaos of democracy. There was some irony, there. Some metaphor maybe.

I just admired the water.

The community of Deanwood was little better than Anacostia in terms of wealth, crime statistics, or general cleanliness. With CSX rail lines cutting across the neighborhood and into Maryland, and various fabrication and light manufacturing facilities built along its perimeter, Deanwood had an overall industrial feel. A smoky, dusty, working-class town with a handful of good blue-collar jobs and not much in the way of white-collar interest. Another "developing" neighborhood that was too far from downtown DC to draw much interest from wealthy political operators looking for townhomes to remodel.

Deanwood was old-school DC—the part you never see in the movies. The part where real people live.

I parked my truck on the street across from a two-story brick building topped by a weathered plywood steeple. The sign out front read: *Grace Church of Deanwood,* and it was also weathered, the wooden letters peeling black paint. I made a mental note to refresh them when I was finished pounding shingles, then collected my tool belt from the back of the GMC. Down the sidewalk, around the front of the church sanctuary to the sprawling lot next door. Overgrown with weeds, occupied by a compact apartment complex not unlike the one I now called home.

Only this complex was unoccupied, surrounded by work trucks and stacks of building materials, most of its windows and doorways nothing more than empty holes. Piles of ripped-out carpet baked in the sun, the music of hammers pounding against the roof. It was barely eight in the morning, but work had begun. I was late.

"Brother Mason!" a cheery East Coast voice greeted me as I reached the top of the ladder. The speaker, a muscled Black man in a skin-tight tank-top, straddled the roof's ridge-line as he swept his hat off and mopped sweat from his forehead.

He was mid-fifties, slender and strong, and perpetually grinning ear to ear.

"We was about to send out a search party. You oversleep?"

"Long night, Sol." I caught the water bottle he tossed me.

"Not at the club, I hope."

I laughed. Shook my head. "I wish."

Sol—short for Solomon Washington, the foreman of this remodel and the long-time handyman of Grace Church—cut loose with another chuckle.

"I know all about dem long nights at the club. Nothing but bad memories and empty pockets at the end of that slide, let me tell yah. The Lord got better things for you."

I ducked my head, accepting the counsel and not over-thinking it. I wasn't going to explain my nocturnal distractions from the night before. The bullet scar on Sol's shoulder and the prison tattoo covered over by a cross on his left forearm told me that he would probably understand, but some things don't need to be said.

Some things simply need to be sweated out.

"Grab a hammer, Mase," Sol called. "Shingles ain't gonna nail themselves."

I tucked the water bottle into my belt, and without another word we were back on our knees. Myself, Sol, and two young men from the church's prison outreach program.

Both Black, both recently released convicts with petty felony records that made traditional employment a pipe dream. Both lost souls just needing a guiding hand.

Sol Washington was that guiding hand—I was friendly company. With a tool belt full of roofing nails and a sixteen-ounce claw hammer, I began dragging asphalt shingles one at a time from a plastic package and aligned them over brand-new sub-roofing, driving nails with a tap followed by a slam. One after the other, the sun blazing and sweat soaking my shirt. Water bottles for rehydration, homemade sandwiches from Mrs. Washington eaten on the tailgate of Sol's battered Dodge for lunch.

Then more shingles. More sun. More soulful hymns sung *a cappella* by Sol, punctuated by the pound of the hammers and the occasional muttered profanities of the two work-releases—always followed by a "Sorry, Sol," whenever they caught the older man's side-eye.

It was good work. Hard work, a day full of it. I made twelve bucks an hour, which I only accepted because I had to make rent. I believed in what the church was doing with the recently purchased apartment complex. When the remodel was complete, they would open the facility as a rehab center for ex-cons. A home where those who had fallen off the ladder could at least ascend to its lowest rung, inspired by the gentle love of Sol and his fellow parishioners.

It was a good place to invest my sweat.

We'd covered half of one wing by the time my watch read four-thirty, which wasn't bad for amateur roofers. I slid down the ladder and helped Sol to pack his tools into lock boxes in the back of his truck. He paid the other workers in cash—the same twelve bucks that I made, joined by an obligation to attend church on Sunday and to abstain from drugs, alcohol, and prostitutes.

Then he prayed with them. He gave them each a hearty hug. He waved them off and turned back to me.

"Dinner? Ms. Sally's got dumplin's."

Just the thought of Ms. Sally's steaming-hot chicken and dumplings—joined, usually, by homemade french bread—was enough to make my mouth water. The sandwich was long gone.

But I had other plans. Plans I'd been daydreaming about with every swing of my hammer.

"Can't tonight, Sol."

He arched his eyebrows. "Off to the club?"

I rolled my eyes. "What if I told you I had a date?"

Sol snorted. "I'd say she could do better."

We both laughed. He waved. I started the truck and turned south again, back for my apartment. A quick shower, a nicer shirt.

I was still smiling.

8

L ogan Circle was *not* the bottom rung of the social ladder. Just north of downtown, only a hop, skip, and a jump from the White House, the collection of Victorian-style townhomes was clustered amid shopping and dining options. Everything was walkable, everything was very safe and clean. With elegant streetlamps illuminating parks and outdoor cafes, and poodle-mix dogs on leashes as common as pedestrians themselves, Logan Circle wasn't quite posh. It wasn't quite elite.

It was closer to the "wannabe" status of elite—a mini-Georgetown. I always struggled to find parking for my GMC, and usually had to hoof it from an adjoining neighborhood, fighting my way down sidewalks packed with business people on phones and political aides who mistook themselves for full-fledged senators. The smell was all cologne and freshly cut grass. There was no trash on the streets.

It *was* a nice place to live.

I lucked out and found parallel parking only three doors down from my destination. Leaning close to my rearview mirror, I ran fingers through my hair and straightened my collar. The shirt was pressed white, some boutique brand I didn't recognize and wouldn't have bought for myself. It was a gift, just like the Citizen watch that replaced my Casio, or the khaki slacks that replaced my work jeans. Everything was scratchy, a little stiff. But I didn't mind changing. I didn't mind paying twenty-six bucks for parking, or battling the throngs on the sidewalk with a fresh bouquet of lilies tucked beneath my arm.

The air smelled good. The skinny redbrick townhome I was headed for gleamed in the sunset. As I mashed the bell, my heart rate escalated. My swollen throat tightened, and I subconsciously pinched my collar together to obscure the faint bruising.

My mouth went dry. I swallowed. I was smiling again.

The door rushed open, and there she was. All strawberry-blonde, bright green eyes. She was in my arms in a moment, the plastic flower wrapper crinkling against her back as I pulled her close. We kissed, and she smelled amazing. Like a lottery win in the Caribbean. Like the first spring after an ages-long winter.

"Hi." Evelyn pulled away from me, eyes shining as she returned my smile. Really, it was more of a grin. She squeezed my arms, and I resisted a wince. Those muscles were sore, as much from Sol's roofing hammer as my fight in Petworth. But I didn't care. She could squeeze me all night if she wanted.

"Hungry?" I asked.

"Starved. Let me get my purse."

Evelyn took the flowers and ducked back inside, leaving me in the summer breeze. A moment later she was back, locking her door and taking my arm down the steps. Her grip felt good against the crunchy cloth of the dress shirt. It felt natural.

I started toward my truck. Evelyn hung back.

"Why don't we take my Coop?"

The "Coop" she referenced was a Mini Cooper S two-door—a turbocharged little psychopath that was only a little larger than an average refrigerator. I had to bunch my knees up to my chin to cram my six-foot-two frame into the passenger's seat. My head hit the ceiling whenever Evelyn powered across speed bumps...which was as often as she found speed bumps. She cackled every time.

"What's wrong with the truck?" I said.

Evelyn wrinkled her nose before she could stop herself. She rocked her head. "It smells like sweat..."

Sweat. Well, I couldn't deny that.

"Come on. The Coop is just around the corner."

She shot me that sunshine smile again, and I forgot all about speed bumps.

THE RESTAURANT WAS CHIC. That was Evelyn's word for it, and I wasn't quite sure what the term meant. All the tables were small, the lights low, the dishes fine china. Everyone drank out of wine glasses regardless of whether they drank wine. The prices were...not recorded on the menu.

In the four magical months I'd spent dating Evelyn, traveling from Iowa to DC to pursue our relationship, I'd learned quickly what a bad omen the absence of prices was for the health of my skinny wallet. Nailing shingles at twelve bucks an hour was enough to cover my rent, fill my truck, and fill my stomach.

At least, the way I was used to eating. Canned beans and lots of eggs. Working man food. Most of the items on the menu I had never heard of—the names of dishes included a lot of accents and foreign words. A lot of fancy, flourishing script.

"It's French," Evelyn said, beaming. "I've been *dying* to try this place. Everybody at work is talking about it. Took me three weeks to get a reservation."

I forced a smile, shifting on the narrow chair. There was a button in the cushion, and that button was becoming intimate friends with my tailbone. I couldn't seem to escape it.

The waiter came—no, he was a *sommelier*. He was here to talk about wine. I shot Evelyn a sideways look, and she hurried to save me, recommending a pour of something exotic. I nodded.

"Sounds great."

He bustled off. The actual waiter came and asked about an appetizer. Evelyn bubbled about escargot, which was a word I *did* recognize.

Snails.

My gut tightened but I kept the smile going. One glance at Evelyn was enough to erase any of the awkwardness I felt, any of that fish-out-of-water, country-bumpkin-in-the-big-city discomfort. It was a strange thing—I'd grown up in a big city, one of the biggest in America. But then, I was also poor. A nice meal in my eyes was any place where you didn't order your food at a counter. French dishes and sommeliers were way beyond my depth.

"I know it's different," Evelyn said softly, wrinkling her nose in that semi-grimace, semi-smile way she did whenever she really wanted me to like something new, something outside my comfort zone. I'd memorized that cue months ago. I appreciated it.

"It's great," I said. "It's really nice."

The sommelier came and poured. I guzzled, then caught Evelyn blushing. Several people were staring. The sommelier looked ready to faint.

Evelyn leaned across the table and whispered, "You sniff first."

Right.

A three-course meal. Snails. Duck with cranberry sauce. A dessert that wasn't sweet. None of it was very tasty, none satiated my blue-collar appetite. I was already contemplating a pit stop at a drive-through on my way home...but I was content for that to wait. For hours, if necessary.

Just being with Evelyn was the best part of my day. Watching her eat, listening to her jokes. Asking sincere questions as she recounted work stories—the prospect of another promotion with the Centers for Disease Control. Her staunch disinterest in returning to Atlanta. Her concepts for developing her department and soliciting increased funding from Congress.

Evelyn talked like a waterfall—one steady, endless, stream-of-consciousness gush. It wasn't how she'd been in Iowa. It was more like I remembered her years before, when we first met in Africa. I was an Army Ranger; she worked for the World Health Organization. We met under gunfire and became mutually infatuated beneath ocean stars. Lots of late nights on the beach when she talked and talked just like this.

Her family. Her work. Her favorite TV shows and travel ambitions and deep desire to one day foster children from orphanages. All the personal, intimate things.

I hadn't known it in Africa, but I knew it now—the

endless chatter meant that she trusted me. It meant she wanted me closer. I loved it.

The waiter brought the check. I reached for my wallet. Evelyn waved me off.

"No, no. My treat!"

I flushed before I could stop myself—not because I had any sexist objection to a woman paying, but because I had some idea *why* she was paying.

Before I could stop her, a credit card appeared. The waiter was off. Evelyn relaxed in her chair and just smiled at me.

It was a good smile—dimpled cheeks, a little rosy with wine flush.

"I've talked all night," she said. "How are you? How was work?"

I sipped water. "Really good. We're almost halfway on the roofing. Another week and we should be replacing windows."

"You've installed windows before?"

"Sol has. He'll teach me."

Evelyn fell quiet. I rotated my wine/water glass. The seat cushion button was biting my butt again, but I didn't want to shift. I didn't want to make her uncomfortable.

"You know..." Evelyn started, then stopped. I raised both eyebrows.

"I was talking to the facilities manager today," Evelyn continued. "At Constitution Center." She lifted her wine and took a long sip.

"Oh?" I already knew where this was headed.

"He says security will be opening a hiring cycle next month. They like ex-military. Pay starts at sixty a year, plus benefits. Just forty hours a week."

Forty hours a week.

I knew what Evelyn meant when she said it, but she couldn't have any clue how it landed. Not like work-life balance. Not like moderation. More like the slam of a judge's gavel as he pronounced a sentence.

Forty hours a week...for the rest of your life.

I worked well more than forty hours now. Six days a week, sometimes as much as ten hours a day. It was hard, grinding work. There were no benefits, at least not the corporate kind.

But I could leave any time I wanted. I could quit any time I wanted. And the thing of it was, I didn't *want* to quit. Because the work mattered—it was work I chose, not because of the compensation package, but because I believed in what the church was doing. I liked being around the people.

For much of my life, I hadn't lived that way. The Army told me what to do, and I did it. As many hours as they demanded. The Phoenix PD was much the same. I believed in those jobs as well...

But now?

"I just thought you might be interested." Evelyn sounded apologetic.

Apologetic—and maybe disappointed.

"I appreciate it," I said. "I really want to finish the rehab project...we've got a few months left."

Evelyn nodded. She smiled again, and it wasn't as bright a smile as before, but just as sincere.

"Maybe later this year?" she said.

Maybe.

I killed time with my water glass while Evelyn signed for the waiter's tip. I shifted to combat the button. Sweat trickled down my spine, and I thought every eye in the place was locked on me. I could feel them, boring in. Identifying me as an outsider. Ridiculing me for it.

"You wanna...get some ice cream?" The moment I said it, nothing on earth sounded better.

But Evelyn didn't answer, and when I looked up, she was no longer looking at me. She was no longer smiling, either. Her mouth had dropped open half an inch. Her cheeks flushed.

I followed her line of sight, and my own gut tightened. My heart thumped two beats faster. My muscles bunched, already commanding me to rise out of the chair even as my gaze locked on my target.

He was twenty yards away. Tall and slender, a swishing black government suit, dark hair and dark eyes. A gentle smile.

He was the man I had driven to Delafield Place to confront, and he was headed our way.

9

"Evelyn!"

He spoke with a southern accent. Not the country boy, light-beer-drinking, football-loving sort of accent I'd become so comfortable with during my tours of the South. This was a different sort of drawl, much gentler and more refined. It spoke of lake houses and yacht clubs, box seats at baseball games, private predatory schools, and elite colleges beyond.

It was *money* South. The sort of heritage that had propelled Alex Parker Hudson from his Buckhead childhood into track-star fame at the Clemson University, and then on to Quantico. Because he'd always wanted to be an FBI agent. He'd always wanted to carry a gun and do some good.

Or so Evelyn told me. And she would know—she had been married to him.

I tugged the napkin out of my shirt collar and stood as Alex approached. Evelyn did not. She whispered "Please don't" and reached for my sleeve. It was too late to stop me. I didn't say a thing, just staring him down as he glided right past me and stopped at the table. Still smiling, albeit a forced, semi-sad smile.

I wasn't buying it, not for a moment. I knew a lot about Alex Parker Hudson, more than Evelyn had told me, and more than I would tell her. Whatever he thought he was doing here, he wouldn't be staying.

"Of all the gin joints," Alex said. "How are you?"

His voice softened when he spoke. There was that inflection people use when they want to convey sincerity—genuine concern. Not just "how's it going?" but "how *are* you?"

What a crap sandwich of a question to ask.

Evelyn's lips parted. She hesitated. I spoke first.

"We're great," I said. "Alex, is it?"

He didn't immediately look my way. He stared at Evelyn a beat longer, his smile gone. His mouth closed. Then he slowly turned—and the smile returned. Much softer.

And much less sincere.

"I do apologize—where are my manners? Mason, right?"

He shouldn't have known my name, but it didn't surprise me in the least that he did. He extended his hand, and I didn't take it. I didn't answer, either. I just stared.

The smile on Alex's face expanded, just a little. It became something more like a smirk, a very knowing look—like he knew *exactly* who I was, just like I knew exactly who he was.

And why shouldn't he recognize me? He'd seen me before. We'd never spoken. But he'd seen me.

And that was the problem.

"I guess I'm not the only one short on manners," Alex mused, dropping his hand.

I still didn't answer. Evelyn broke the silence.

"Alex, this is Mason Sharpe."

She didn't tag *"He's my boyfriend"* to the introduction, and I didn't mind. This wasn't high school. Alex Hudson knew exactly who and what I was. If he was smart, he wouldn't challenge the status quo.

Alex rocked his head back. "Sharpe?"

"That's right," I said. I wasn't ashamed of it.

Alex's brow crinkled. He seemed momentarily confused. "Mason Sharpe...wait. Were you...in Petworth last night?"

The question landed like an artillery shell. My gut tightened, and Alex nodded.

"Yeah...I recognize the name. My office received the police report this morning. Nasty business. I'm so glad you're okay!"

My face flushed. I could feel Evelyn's eyes on me. She didn't speak, but I knew what she was thinking. It made me want to ram my shin between his legs and terminate his family name. To slam his face into that stupid little table and make the wine/water glasses jump. I didn't care that he was an FBI agent. It hadn't made any difference the previous night.

Only, now Evelyn was here.

"We were just leaving," I said.

I circled the table. I pulled Evelyn's chair back as she stood. I took her hand, not giving Alex a second glance. He wished her goodnight, and she mumbled a goodnight in return. She was flushed, like a schoolgirl. We stepped into the cool May evening, a gentle breeze carrying down broad Georgetown sidewalks. Women in nice dresses, men in premium suits. A lot of open-air dining joined by boutique shops closed for the evening. No parking, just valet.

Evelyn handed over her ticket at the stand, but still didn't speak. She'd dropped my hand and when I reached for her, she didn't reciprocate. She subtly turned away.

The valet brought the Mini. I tipped him but Evelyn took the keys. She got in before I could open her door. She slammed it before I could close it for her. I glanced over my shoulder, back toward the French restaurant.

I couldn't see Alex Hudson, but I could feel his eyes on me. I wanted to punch those lights out.

I folded myself into the car and Evelyn slapped it into gear. The turbocharger went to work, and we hurtled down the street. Through a light, around a bend. Navigating back toward Logan Circle, a twenty-minute drive with traffic. A miserable, long time.

I glanced left. Evelyn wouldn't look at me. She was still flushed, her eyes rimmed with red, but she didn't cry.

"I'm sorry," I said. I wasn't sure what I was apologizing for. Maybe for the fact that I hadn't already buried Alex's feet in concrete boots and dropped him in the Chesapeake Bay.

"What was he talking about?" Evelyn demanded.

"What do you mean?"

"*Last night*," she said. "A police report?"

I looked away, not answering. I'd spent most of that day forgetting the events of the previous night. Not thinking about the dead Asian woman, or why she was dead, or how I hadn't saved her.

It wasn't that I didn't care—I *did* care. Too much. I just couldn't do anything about it.

"What happened?" Evelyn pressed. "*What did you do?*"

There was a little accusation in her tone. A pre-loaded sense of suspicion, probably a residual effect of our activities in Iowa. All my vigilante activities.

"I didn't do anything," I said. "A woman was attacked. I was there. I tried to intercede. That's all."

"Intercede? Intercede *how*? Did you kill somebody?"

Again with the pre-loaded angst. It was getting under my skin.

"No."

"So why the police report? Why did Alex hear about it?"

"Because she *died*." I spat the words before I could stop myself, and instantly regretted them. I was still angry—not at Evelyn, certainly. Just at myself. She was jabbing at an open wound. She didn't even know it.

"What?" Evelyn said.

"She was shot. I didn't get there in time."

The car fell silent. I looked out the window at the passing Washington neighborhoods. All the townhomes and apartments of Georgetown. All the addresses of senators and congressmen elected on shoestring campaign budgets, and now inexplicably wealthy.

More crime.

"Why didn't you tell me?" Evelyn said.

It wasn't what I expected. I looked sideways. Opened my mouth, but didn't answer. I didn't know how to answer.

"Why, Mason?" Evelyn was still red-eyed, still flushed. But now she looked more angry than stunned.

"I..." I stopped. Inhaled. "I didn't want to alarm you. It wasn't a big deal."

"It's big enough for the FBI to be involved!"

Sure, like that's true.

I thought it, I didn't say it. I had as little clue what had really happened in Petworth the previous night as most, but I seriously doubted that Alex's office—whatever office that was—had been consulted with regard to the crime.

No. However Alex Hudson had learned of the murder, his interest was much less in the victim, and much more in the witness. The man dating his ex-wife.

The ex-wife he was still obsessed with.

"I was upset," I said. "I got there just after she was shot. The cops interviewed me and then I went home. I went to work. I just...wanted to not think about it."

It was closer to the truth. I wasn't sure if Evelyn bought it or not. She sat with both hands clutching the wheel, her foot planted into the brake at a stop light. Staring straight ahead and not speaking.

"Talk to me," I said.

Evelyn shook her head as though to herself. She looked out the window, avoiding me.

The stiffness in her posture, so far removed from the joyous bubbliness of only twenty minutes prior, cut straight through my chest. It was like a bullet, like a knife. Plunging and twisting. It made me angry. It made me want to take a sledgehammer to whatever wall she had thrown up.

But I kept my voice calm. "Evelyn, please."

"Why?" Evelyn's face snapped toward me. "Why should I talk to you, Mason? You never talk to *me*."

"What does that mean?"

"What do you *think* it means? Good grief, you can be so thick sometimes."

The words flew like buckshot, but they didn't sting. They simply left me confused.

"Is this about last night?"

A snort. Another shake of her head.

"Evelyn..."

"It's about *everything*, Mason. You never tell me anything serious. It's all surface-level with you. No past, no depth, nothing real. I've bared my soul to you again and again, and all I get in return is appetizer chitchat and sports commentary. For heaven's sake, you were involved in a *murder* last night and you didn't even think to mention it!"

I stiffened. I wasn't sure why. I retreated into my cramped seat as we reached the highway and the Cooper accelerated. It was a manual and Evelyn was grinding through the gears, stomping the clutch as though it owed her money.

"I wasn't involved in a murder," I said. "When you say it like that, it means I was implicated. I was just a witness."

Another snort. A shake of her head.

"What?"

"Exhibit A, Mason. Exhibit A. You're not hearing me."

The Cooper bounced onto an off ramp, and Evelyn turned for Logan Circle. Only seconds remained until we reached her townhome, and it didn't take a relational psychic to know that I wouldn't be invited inside. I was running out of time to fix the situation—to connect, to break through.

I *did* hear her. I'd heard her before. This wasn't the first time we'd struck this roadblock. And yet...

And yet I didn't know what to say. I dropped a bucket into my mind and the well was dry, just like my mouth. I looked into her squinted, pained eyes, and I felt Evelyn's hurt as much as her anger.

I just couldn't break through.

Evelyn surged past a parallel-parking space, then threw the Cooper into reverse and deftly slid into it. The parking brake clicked. The engine cut off.

She didn't reach for the door handle. She didn't unbuckle. The motor ticked as it cooled, and she kept her head twisted away from me. She was looking out the window, but the glare of a streetlight turned that window into a weak mirror.

I could see the tears running down her cheeks. Silent streams, no sniffing. No sobbing. Just pain.

And I knew it was bigger than me. It always had been. Old scars, catastrophic trust issues.

Alex's handiwork.

I placed a hand on Evelyn's arm. She didn't recoil. I squeezed gently. In the reflection her eyes closed. Her body seemed to calm.

"I'm sorry," I whispered.

It wasn't a fix, maybe not even a patch. It was all I had.

Evelyn reached one thumb up and gently brushed her cheeks. She breathed deep. Then she turned and forced a smile.

"It's late," she said. "I've got an early meeting. Call me tomorrow?"

"Of course."

She leaned close and kissed me on the lips. It wasn't a passionate kiss. It wasn't a lengthy one. But it was sincere.

Then we both got out. Evelyn went to her door, I went to my GMC and gave the engine time to warm while I watched her townhome. Watched the second-floor light click on. Imagined the shower hissing, steam rising. Evelyn kicking her heels off...maybe crying again.

My own knuckles tightened around the wheel, and I backed away from the curb. I turned south and crossed the river. I returned to my shabby little motel-turned-apartment. I parked in front of my door and fumbled with my keys, still thinking of Evelyn's real heartbreak.

And thinking about how I was going to fix it, permanently.

I turned the key. I pushed the door open, my gaze catching on an envelope resting against the door frame—a bill from the front office. Rent come due. I stooped to collect it as the door swung open.

And then the first gunshot cracked.

10

It wasn't a detonation—not the full-throated blast of a .45 ACP only inches from my face. This was a snap, a clean and crisp pop dampened by the application of a quality suppressor but nonetheless menacing to my trained ears. The moment I heard it I converted my stoop into a diving roll, abandoning the envelope and lunging straight for the floor.

There was no time to retreat, no time to second-guess. The second bullet was already on its way, hot lead ripping through my jeans and brushing my leg. I couldn't see my attacker, but I could smell him—a sour odor of sweat and cheap cologne. It flooded my nostrils just as I was driving myself back off the floor, heart pounding, adrenaline pumping, body kicking into gear. Training and desperation and instinct taking over all at once, screaming for self-preservation.

And then I hit the bed like a charging bull. One shoulder down, legs bunching and driving off the floor. It was my only chance, the only possible bullet stop that stood between myself and the shooter, someplace farther inside the apartment. I didn't grab the mattress, I grabbed the entire frame. I launched myself off the ground, powering the bed along with me, flipping it toward the ceiling and converting it into an instant shield.

More gunshots popped. Bullets struck the mattress and one broke through. It brushed my ribcage just as I smashed into the underside of the mattress. I was crashing ahead, driving the furniture into the dark. I couldn't see a thing—mere seconds had passed since I opened the door and already everything that transpired since was just one domino falling into another. An inevitable sequence that could only end with one eventuality—death.

Mine, or the shooter's.

A cry broke the darkness as the bed surpassed its upright axis and crashed forward. The mattress broke free of the frame and fell. It struck a body—footsteps thumped. Somebody was stumbling.

No, *two* somebodies. I differentiated voices even as I drove one boot into the underside of the bedframe and scrambled up it. I was climbing, clawing the Victorinox out of my pocket. Activating the three-inch locking blade with a flick of my right thumb. Crushing down on a writhing, struggling body as the mattress slammed face-down on the floor.

And then I found the second body. He was trapped against the closet wall, one leg caught beneath the mattress. Twisting, fighting to bring a pistol to bear on my position. Muzzle flash lit the room, and I detected a snarling face.

An Asian face, male and shrouded by black clothing and a black hood. His shot ripped over my left shoulder. He snatched the muzzle around, sweeping it toward my chest.

Then I was on him, shoving the gun aside with my left

forearm even as I slashed with the knife. Steel bit flesh and the gun cracked once again. Glass shattered somewhere behind me—the bedside lamp, maybe. I kicked off the bedframe and drove him against the wall, pinning him in place. I tasted blood—his blood. My knife had bit. We toppled sideways in a writhing mess of arms and legs, crashing toward the floor. I swept again with the blade, cutting maybe his side or maybe his hip. Whatever it was, I bit deep. I drove with my right shoulder, roofing muscles bunching and powering the blade through his clothes. He screamed. He jerked.

We both rolled. My left hand found his right and I grasped the gun by its slide. His arm was yanking—he was trying to fire again. Next to us the bed frame was jerking, the mattress heaving beneath it. His companion was fighting to dig his way out, and I could only imagine there was another gun in play.

I needed my current adversary neutralized—immediately.

I rolled left, landing on my side and trapping his gun arm. He kicked off from the wall, yanking to break free. I tore the knife out of his side, the polished steel blade gleaming momentarily in the ambient light of outdoor streetlights. I saw his face—burning, hateful eyes shrouded by shadow. He snatched his gun arm again, striking desperately with his left fist. Jabbing at my eye. Going for my throat.

Then I plunged my knife into his neck—one sweeping thrust up to the hilt. He choked and blood sprayed across my face. The body jerked and I tore the knife free. He was choking, no longer grasping for my throat but now grasping at his own. Fighting to stop the blood flow. Fighting to get away from me.

And from somewhere behind me his buddy was fighting out from under the mattress. The bed frame was crashing against the wall—I was out of time.

I rolled right, landing on my back, and dropped the knife. My right hand slapped the floor, sweeping desperately across my bloody living-room rug just as the second shooter emerged from the shadows.

I found the first shooter's gun. The second shooter raised his. I saw the weapon in silhouette form under the glare of the parking lot lights—a long, tubular suppressor. A slim, lithe form. Glaring, hateful blue eyes, a snake-like scar running from his neck to his temple.

My hand closed around bloody polymer, my finger curled through the trigger guard. His suppressor arced toward me just as mine arced toward him. He saw it coming —I detected the flash of uncertainty across his face. The momentary indecision. I clamped down on the trigger and the pistol bucked.

But he didn't return fire. He threw himself toward the wall at the last possible moment. My bullet missed him by inches, striking the ceiling instead. Then he was turning. Throwing himself through the door, out into the parking lot. Sprinting away, just a black shadow on the run.

But not getting away—not this time.

11

I reached my feet just as the body next to me fell still—the last of those gurgling gasps fading into the clutches of death. Over the bed frame, around the displaced mattress. I exploded through the door with the captured pistol held at eye level, sweeping the parking lot.

I saw him as a shadow exiting the entrance of the apartment complex and turning right. Jacket snapping in the breeze, legs stretched into a full sprint. The tiger was there and then he was gone.

But I was after him. I launched off the sidewalk and hurtled past my truck even as lights flashed on from apartment windows on all sides. In true ghetto form, nobody was stepping outside. Nobody was offering assistance. Sheltered behind the safety of their walls, they watched in terrified silence as I reached the exit and turned after my prey.

Finger on the trigger, hurtling at full speed, I saw him a hundred yards ahead. With every stride my legs ached, the pounding in my head matching the thunder of my pumping heart. But I was gaining on him, very slowly. He turned a corner, and I followed. He crossed the street and I was right on him, deftly sliding between parked cars and gaining another precious yard.

We passed a club, a convenience store, an overgrown and empty lot. Puddles on the sidewalk and a stray dog that darted for cover. No cops, no other civilians. He was down to fifty yards away—I could have shot him in the back. I dug deep into an evaporating reservoir of energy, already tapped dry by a long day of nailing shingles, and lunged ahead.

If he turned, I would fire. No hesitation. No second thought. Two shots to center mass, one to the head. Lights out.

But the tiger didn't turn. He sprinted on, not even glancing over his shoulder. He headed straight for a T-shaped intersection—he would have to turn, left or right. One streetlamp glared down amid a spray of slowly gathering rain, and I closed to within fifteen yards. I felt more than saw the tiger slow—a psychological uncertainty, a mental pause. I thought he was deliberating which way to turn.

But he didn't turn at all. The car burst out of the shadows instead, a flash of jet-black. It was a sedan, a Mercedes. Heavily tinted windows, no markings. It cut dead across his path, squealing to a stop. The back door popped open. I ground to a halt myself and lifted the gun. Ready for a blast of rifle fire. Finger tightening around the trigger.

No rifle fire came. My prey dove instead, plummeting into the back seat. Tires squealed. With a howl of German horsepower, the car was gone, and I was running again. All the way to the T-intersection, hanging a hard right. Finding the sedan already at the end of the next block—squinting to identify the license plate.

There was nothing, just a blur. The car hung a hard left and then it was gone, melted into the night as quickly as it had appeared. Leaving me standing alone beneath a developing rain shower, panting and dripping.

12

I stood in the rain for five long minutes, just catching my breath, clutching the gun, and staring at the intersection where the car had disappeared.

It all happened so fast that there hadn't been time to think, and now that there was time, I realized that there wasn't much to consider. I had recognized the second shooter—the survivor—the moment parking lot lights glared against his snaking facial scar. Those hate-filled eyes, that tight-lipped sneer. I hadn't recognized his friend, the man I had knifed to death.

But that didn't matter. The only thing that mattered as my heart finally calmed was the inevitable question: What the *hell*?

I looked over my shoulder, back down the street the Mercedes had raced out of. I looked up the street I had chased the tiger down. Both spaces were empty, the glow of that lone streetlamp broken by a now-steady shower of rain. Already I was soaked, cool water running down my arms and washing the blood splatter away.

And rinsing the would-be murder weapon.

Stepping closer to the light, I rolled the handgun to properly examine it for the first time. The grip felt semi-familiar in my hand, a touch of checkered polymer with an enlarged trigger guard suitable for a gloved shooter. Not so dissimilar to the feel of a Glock or a SIG, but on closer inspection this weapon was neither.

Not striker-fired but hammer-fired. There was also an external safety. A small engraving on the lefthand face of the slide read *CF98-9*, and a quick dump of the magazine confirmed the caliber—nine millimeter.

But the most notable thing about the weapon—other than its six-inch attached suppressor, anyway—was the symbol embossed onto both sides of the grip. About half an inch across, impossible to miss. Made famous by the Soviets and appropriated by nearly every so-called people's republic since.

It was a five-pointed star inside a circle. A subtle, innocent symbol that said so little while saying so much. This wasn't an American weapon. It wasn't any kind of weapon I'd ever encountered before.

But what did that matter? I had a pretty good idea where it originated and who had carried it. I also knew for a fact that this pistol had been loaded and chambered with my extermination in mind. That was detail enough.

Driving the magazine back into the well, I press-checked the chamber to confirm the presence of a round locked and ready. Then I looked once more down the street, daring the scar-faced man or any of his thug counterparts to reappear. Daring them to make a stand.

Nobody did, and I twisted the suppressor from the muzzle off the pistol, tucking the can into my left pocket and the handgun into my right. I kept my fingers wrapped around the grip, and then I turned back the way I'd come.

I started for my apartment, fast-walking and reviewing the events of the last twenty-four hours in my mind. Everything from the first appearance of the Asian woman in Petworth to the moment that Mercedes sedan screamed up... just the way a Mercedes van had screamed up the night prior, Asian men with diplomatic IDs bailing out to collect the body.

Asian victim. Asian killers. A potentially Asian pistol.

It wasn't a difficult riddle to solve, but I wasn't interested in solving it. I wasn't interested in doing the Washington Metro Police Department's work for them. I was only interested in the fact—infuriated by the fact—that yet again I had a secret. Something I felt obligated to conceal from Evelyn for reasons I couldn't explain and couldn't overcome. Confused protection instincts, maybe. A simple jadedness to violence and danger. I didn't know.

I'd faced these problems for weeks, but riding back to Logan Circle in her Coop was the first time Evelyn had cried about the disconnect, and I wanted to kick myself for every tear. For every faltering accusation she had made, all of which were justified.

Curse these guys—curse them for making my life complicated when I was fighting so hard to keep it simple. No, I wasn't dealing with this, whatever it was. This wasn't my problem. I'd come to DC to rebuild, to nurture something new and hopeful. I was calling the cops, I was making a report, and then I was moving out of Anacostia. I wasn't dealing with this.

At least, that was my strategy until I reached the apartment. I didn't have to call the cops; one of my neighbors had already done that for me, and multiple patrol cars were already on site. DC officers were inside my apartment, stepping in and out with flashlights sweeping the parking lot. Everyone's doors were still closed, but lights shone behind the blinds of each occupied apartment. Louvers parted, wide eyes stared out.

And something was wrong. I could feel it from the moment I reached the apartment complex entrance. The cops were there, but the energy felt...flat. There was no sense of emergency, no sense of animated focus. The officers were alert but not alarmed. They inspected the apartment grounds with curiosity, pointing and shining lights, but half of them stood with their hands in their pockets.

No weapons drawn. No crime scene tape, or radioing for backup, or marching down the length of apartment doors, interviewing witnesses.

It was oddly calm. Complacent, almost. Entirely the wrong energy for a bloody crime scene occupied by a throat-slashed Asian man and multiple bullet casings.

I stopped a hundred yards out, one hand grasped around the concealed pistol, but slowly releasing it. My gaze swept past the cops, past my truck and my apartment, down the length of windows. Catching an eye here or there but finding nobody outside—not even Rex with his customary six-pack. Nobody was talking to the police. Nobody was explaining anything.

Then I noticed two of the cops moving my way. One in uniform, the other dressed in a cheap black suit. Bald-headed with a mustache, ducking his head to light a cigarette. Slowing to a stop ten feet away from me.

It was Detective Dickens, the guy from the previous

night. His buddy stopped also, one hand resting on his sidearm.

"Well, Mr. Sharpe," Dickens said, exhaling gray. "We meet again."

I didn't answer. I simply looked to my apartment door. I looked inside to the floor beyond.

I couldn't see much, but what I did see was bare. Clean. No displaced bed or mattress...no blood spray.

"Out for an evening walk?" Dickens said.

I still didn't answer.

"What's in your pocket?"

My gut tightened...and I thought I understood.

Slowly, very slowly, I eased my hand out. Empty. I let both arms hang by my side. Dickens grunted. Inhaled a long drag, then breathed out through his nose. He lowered the smoke.

"I think you better come with us."

13

I t wasn't a suggestion, and I didn't argue. The cops patted me down and stripped away the commie handgun, the suppressor, my phone, keys, and wallet. I kept my mouth shut as they loaded me into the back of the detective's car, expecting a storm of questions at any moment.

But they never came. Not one inquiry. It was as though they already knew what was going on. Or maybe it was just the opposite—they were so confused that they wouldn't even bother with questions until I was back at the station. Whatever the case, I wasn't afraid, but I was reasonably concerned.

DC is not the kind of place you want to be caught with an unregistered, unlicensed firearm. Especially with a matching suppressor in my left pocket, an accessory heavily regulated by the Bureau of Alcohol, Tobacco, and Firearms. I hadn't ditched either item prior to returning to my apartment because I still half-expected to be ambushed by the Mercedes sedan.

Also, I expected there to be a body in my living room. A

crime scene. A litany of physical evidence to substantiate my story and assuage the concerns of law enforcement.

Why wasn't there any crime scene tape at my apartment? Why wasn't there an ambulance—a body bag?

I had an inkling of an idea, and I didn't like it.

The ride to the Washington DC Metro Police Seventh District Police Station was a short one. It was located on Alabama Avenue, only a couple miles from my apartment. A funny-looking, misshapen building with lots of windows and a diner-car-style facade that ran across the face of most of the first floor.

The streets surrounding it were dark, but the building was not. It was fully illuminated, fully active. Lots of cop cars, lots of cops. I was removed from the rear of the detective's sedan, still not cuffed, but escorted at both elbows by armed officers. Up the sidewalk, through the door. A metal detector and another pat-down. A winding hall fresh with the smell of a lemon-scented cleaner. Into Interview Room 4.

White floors, white walls, white plastic table, white plastic chairs. A coffee pot that was half-full but turned off— also white. A camera in one corner. No two-way mirror, no windows at all.

"Have a seat," Dickens said.

I stood in the doorway, hands at my sides. I glanced side-long at him. "Or?"

He cocked his head and raised his eyebrows, not saying anything and not having to. I took my chair. The door shut and I noted that there was no knob on my side. No fresh coffee near the pot, and no cups.

That was too bad because driving roofing nails is hard work, and exhaustion was finally catching up with me. This was my second rough night in a row. My second inexplicable collision with murderous thugs with whom I had no personal beef.

And yet, they hadn't arrived at my apartment by accident. They hadn't waited in the shadows for anyone else to arrive home. They wanted me dead.

I just didn't know why.

The detective left me with my watch, and I checked the time only every fifteen or twenty minutes, well accustomed to the routine of softening up a subject by leaving him to marinate in a stew of his own thoughts. It was the same dog and pony show I'd implemented myself at the Phoenix PD. You leave a guilty guy alone in the quiet for long enough, and some of the weaker ones will practically beg to confess. To explain. To justify.

But I wasn't guilty, and I wasn't impressed by base inter-rogation tactics. So I remained calm, reviewing each detail of the home invasion in my mind. Every visual, every concrete clue. Anything that might be applicable in substantiating my defense.

Then Dickens returned, exactly one hour and twenty-one minutes after he'd left me there. He brought coffee in Styrofoam cups for both of us. He carried a notepad and appeared legitimately finished with life.

Settling into his chair, he sparked up a cigarette despite the No Smoking sign hung on the wall, inhaling deep and breathing out between his teeth. Leaning back and rocking his head until his neck popped. Letting his shoulders sag. Not even looking at me yet.

Tired. Beaten. Fed up.

"What did you do?" I asked.

Dickens cocked an eyebrow. Thumped ash straight onto the floor.

"You didn't start here," I said. "Or maybe you did. But a guy who responds to targeted assassinations in Petworth shouldn't be kicking rocks in Anacostia. This place has 'career graveyard' written all over it."

I made air quotes. Dickens still didn't comment. He sucked on the smoke again. Then he smiled.

"I thought I was the detective."

I didn't answer. He flipped his portfolio open and held the smoke between his teeth, rustling through print-offs. Making a show of spreading them across the table. Taking his time, squinting, grunting. Messing with me, I thought. No doubt hoping to goad me into talking about any one of the documents he'd collected off the internet.

News stories. A DOD file. Even a personnel file from the Phoenix PD, which was admittedly impressive, because I knew the old crow who ran the records division back in Phoenix, and her turnaround time for interdepartmental requests ran something between four years and never.

All the documents involved my past. It was an impressive collection, much too comprehensive to be assembled in the eighty-one minutes he'd left me alone in this tank. If I had to guess, I would say that he'd begun assembling this stack the night prior.

Right after Petworth. Right after that woman was murdered, and he collected ID from the lone witness.

"If you've got a question, you should ask it," I said.

My tone was a bit terse. I wasn't sorry. The last of the documents the detective scrutinized was a print-off from *The Arizona Republic*, a headline that had followed me from state to state like an invisible billboard.

Proclaiming my past. My loss. My heartbreak.

Dickens looked up. He exhaled smoke through his nose.

Then he simply swept the documents into a pile and slurped his coffee.

"Okay, Mr. Sharpe. I guess we both know how the game is played. Why don't you just tell me what happened?"

I squinted, momentarily evaluating my options, my odds. The potential risk. As a former cop myself, I knew how astoundingly stupid it was to speak to the police without a lawyer. How it only ever helps the boys in blue, and never the suspect.

But then, lawyers are expensive and nailing shingles barely paid my bills. Besides which, I hadn't done anything wrong. I was innocent. It's the same rationale that lures all men into the trap of blabbing, and yet here I was, falling for it myself. Maybe I was more tired than I thought.

I told my story from the start. Everything that happened since I'd last met Dickens in Petworth. I told him about my job swinging a hammer. About my date in Georgetown. My trip home. The letter by my door that had saved my life, and the resulting fight inside my cramped apartment.

I told him how I knifed one guy in the throat and pursued the second on foot, wielding the first guy's handgun. I described the tiger's piercing blue eyes and his snaking facial scar. The jet-black Mercedes sedan he had escaped into, and the walk back to my apartment.

I told him that his coffee was bad, and he should stop smoking before it killed him.

Dickens smiled a little at that last comment, promptly lighting up another cigarette. He slouched in his chair with sweat gleaming on his bald head and regarded me, unblinking, for a long time.

He'd taken notes, but he didn't consult them. He'd finished his coffee, and he didn't call for more. He just stared and smoked until I rolled both hands palms up in a *"Well?"* motion.

Then he grunted. "It's a nice story, Mr. Sharpe. A pretty good explanation for committing a Class C felony."

"Is that what they're calling the Second Amendment these days?"

Dickens snorted. He stabbed the cigarette against the plastic tabletop, putting it out. Then he withdrew his phone and tabbed across the screen. A moment later, he laid it on the table where we both could see it.

No comment. Just a video playing. I scooted forward and leaned over the table to block out the glare of the overhead lights. I recognized the sidewalk outside my apartment—my pickup truck briefly visible in one corner of the frame.

Then my door, unit 107. My linoleum floor and...

And nothing. The room was perfectly, flawlessly in order. Better than I'd left it before my date with Evelyn. The bed was assembled, right where it should have been. No sign of damage. The mattress was there, and the comforter was neatly stretched over it. The floor was free of debris or shattered glass or bullet casings.

There was no blood, either. And *no body.*

I shook my head. "That's not how I left it."

A grunt. The video played on. The camera angle pivoted, looking back toward the door. I squinted, searching for bullet holes in the walls. Dents in the sheetrock from crashing bodies.

Still nothing. The walls were dingy, as they'd always been. But there was no sign of a struggle.

"That's not right," I insisted. "There was a rug with blood on it. A lamp that was shot. They're both missing."

Dickens remained quiet. I looked up to find him ignoring the video, watching me.

"I was gone barely twenty minutes," I said. "Somebody must have cleaned it up. Taken the body."

Still no answer. Dickens was like a stone figurine.

"Did you interview my neighbors?" I pressed. "They would have heard the struggle. There were lights on when I left."

"You mean when you gave chase to this supposed intruder while illegally armed with a deadly weapon..."

I closed my mouth. I crossed my arms and settled back into the chair.

I wasn't saying another word. I'd already said much too much. I knew that to some degree Dickens had to believe me. He had to know that there was more to this story than he had found in my inexplicably clean apartment.

Maybe he *had* spoken to my neighbors. Maybe Rex had corroborated my story. For all I knew, maybe the cops themselves had cleaned my apartment before taking that video.

No—that wasn't logical. They wouldn't compromise evidence. Maybe that video wasn't recorded in my apartment at all. Maybe it was a neighbor's, maybe it was an empty unit.

But I'd seen my violin case in the video, leaning up against the wall. It *was* my unit, and it was clean...which could only mean one thing.

I wouldn't be the one to say it.

Dickens closed his portfolio. He stood, tucking it beneath his arm.

"Would you like an attorney, Mr. Sharpe?"

It wasn't the question I expected. Cops—even good ones—aren't usually in the habit of volunteering counsel to their witnesses. Still, I said nothing. I didn't even look at him. I just sat until Dickens grunted for the third time.

"Okie-dokey, then. That's all from me."

He departed the room. The door closed. A long few minutes dragged by while I chewed my lip and processed, then re-processed the facts at hand.

Two Mercedes vehicles. Multiple Asian males, all in similar dress. A murder victim who was also Asian. A Chinese national working at the local embassy, if those men in the Mercedes van were to be believed. A foreign, suppressed handgun that might also be Chinese.

And finally, my apartment. Scrubbed clean in *minutes*. No hint of a crime.

What did that add up to?

I was pretty sure I knew, and I was just beginning to calculate what I was going to do about it when the door opened again. A dress shoe slapped the floor. Another figure stepped into the room.

We made eye contact before he crossed the threshold, and already I was out of my chair. Already my right hand was clenching against the tabletop, my blood boiling even as my better sense shouted for me to remain calm. To hold back. To keep my fists to myself.

The newcomer was tall and lithe—a runner's body. He was dressed in a cheap black government suit, and he flashed an FBI badge.

It was Alex Hudson.

"Hello, Mason."

14

I remained standing as the door clapped shut. Alex approached the table and laid his badge face-up on the table.

I hadn't so much as glanced at the ID. I hadn't taken my eyes off him at all. I was just standing there, my conscious mind replaying a drum-beat warning while the subconscious animal grumbling inside my chest fought to be let off its leash.

"You should sit," Alex said. "Did they offer you something to drink?"

I didn't answer. I kept staring. My eyes burned but I didn't blink. Alex stared back, looking almost as tired as Dickens. Then he unbuttoned his jacket and scraped back his chair.

"*I'm* sitting down."

He reclaimed the ID badge and tucked it into his jacket pocket. He produced a notepad and a pen, flipping through a series of pages and preoccupying himself with a single note.

All the while I stood, mind still racing. Still caught off guard.

Alex looked up. "Really, dude. Junior high was like two decades ago. *Sit.*"

The polished southern accent—all that money drawl— was still there, but the good-natured charm he'd projected at the restaurant in Georgetown was long gone. Alex was all business.

I sat, one fist resting on the tabletop as Alex watched me. Then he looked back to his pad. He shuffled notes. He clicked his pen closed and leaned back in his chair, much the way Dickens had.

"Okay," Alex said. "I'm going to make this as simple as I can. I've already made calls to the police commissioner and cashed in some favors. They're going to drop the gun charges and dismiss you from further questioning. You can collect your personal effects at the door. Then you're going to go back to your apartment. You're going to pack, you're going to fire up that old jalopy of yours, and you're going to do what you do best. You're going to hit the road. Capisci?"

I blinked, so caught off guard that my thought train completely derailed. It wasn't at all what I expected—whatever I expected. So calmly delivered, so matter of fact.

And yet, so completely logical.

"Excuse me?" I said.

"Consider it a gift," Alex said. "A second chance. Whatever. Just get your crap and get gone—before I change my mind."

The animal was back. Trembling in his cage, shaking at the end of a chain. I felt it in my chest, I felt it boiling up and heating my blood. Roaring in my mind, making me crazy.

And I'm not a crazy person. I'm not a wild, irrational

person. I'm generally good at managing my own temper. But this was something else.

"Did you do this?" I hissed.

"Do what?"

"Did you set me up?"

A snort. "You're way out of your depth, Sharpe."

"I was *jumped*," I said. "I was nearly killed. There were two guys, and I left one of them dead on my living-room floor."

"So you keep saying. But there's no body, there's no blood. Just you and an unregistered firearm coupled with an unstamped suppressor. These are the facts; I didn't make them—"

"Penn Quarter," I snapped, cutting him off. "Monday at lunch. Greek restaurant with the red and green umbrellas, table by the fountain. A gray tie and a copy of the *Post*."

Alex froze, mouth half opened. His mind seemed to skip. Then his eyes turned hard.

"Foggy Bottom," I continued. "Saturday evening, the theater by the river. Back seat, a ticket to that Audrey Hepburn replay. Atlanta Braves hat and a box of M&Ms. Rock Creek Park, last Wednesday. Cross Trail Nine near Colorado Avenue. A blue windbreaker and a dog on a leash —*not yours*. Alexandria the previous Sunday, the farmer's market. Jeans and a Capitals t-shirt. Green backpack and an obsession with asparagus. Nationals Park, the Friday night before—"

"Enough," Alex spoke through his teeth. His face was scarlet, nearly crimson. Gone was his nonchalance, his condescending cool. He looked like a rubber band stretched to a breath away from snapping. He wouldn't blink, and he didn't look away. He was fixated on me.

"You've been stalking me?" Alex said.

"No, jackass. You've been stalking *her*. And you're going to stop or, so help me, I'm going to break your legs."

Alex's fingers closed onto a fist. His body tensed, and for a split second I thought he just might hurtle out of his chair. He just might let his own beast off the chain—set it loose on me, the same way I wanted to cut mine loose on him.

I wanted him to do it. Internally, I *begged* him to do it. Because for the half-dozen offenses I had listed, two or three more still lay locked and loaded in my mind. Definite dates, times, and locations. Instances I had confirmed in person but never told Evelyn about.

It wasn't her problem. It was mine, and if a random woman hadn't been murdered in Petworth the night prior, I would have already dealt with it.

"It's not what you think." Alex still spoke through his teeth. I was no more intimidated than I was impressed.

"It's exactly what I think," I said. "And this is how it ends. You're going to get back on the phone and lock in those favors. This circus—whatever it is—is over. The gun charges are gone, it's all gone. And then *you* are going to hit the road. You're going to ask for a transfer. You're going to land a cozy desk job at the FBI field office in Nowhere Montana, and you're going to stay there, because if you don't—"

I leaned forward, lowering my voice to barely above a whisper. "I will *destroy* you. Not just your legs—everything you are. I will end your career. I will bury you in a field. If you *ever* bother Evelyn again, if you ever *come near her*, it's over. *Capisci?*"

Alex swallowed. A trickle of sweat leaked from his forehead. It ran down his nose before he could wipe it. He still hadn't blinked. But despite the indicators of agitation, there was something new in his eyes that I hadn't seen before. Not fear. Not anger.

It was...

I couldn't decide. I didn't care.

"It's not what you think," Alex said again. This time his voice had dropped. The anger had melted. A tinge of defeat took its place...or maybe it was just extreme exhaustion.

"*I don't care,*" I repeated.

Alex stood at that, all in a rush. He kicked the chair back and snapped his jacket around his body. He buttoned it and turned his back to me.

But he didn't leave the room. He just stared at the wall while a slow minute dripped by. I gave him the time, seated with my arms crossed. Waiting. Knowing I'd played my ace, and whatever choice he made, it wouldn't end well for him.

Stalking is a serious crime. The kind of crime that would decimate a proud FBI career.

When Alex looked back, the sweat was gone. The flush of his face had calmed. He was still strained, still as tense as a bow string. But his voice was calm when he spoke.

"The woman in Petworth—the woman who was killed."

"Near your house," I said.

His jaw clenched. "Yes. Near my house."

"What about her?"

"She's a Chinese national. She works—*worked* for their embassy."

"So?"

"So you're a smart guy. You were a Ranger, then a detective. Why do you think a foreign national connected to the Chinese embassy was assassinated with a suppressed weapon by obvious professionals? Why do you think that I, an FBI agent, was immediately made aware of the case? Why do you think that those same professionals attempted to eliminate *you*, the lone witness to their crime?"

I shrugged. "No idea. Why don't you enlighten me?"

He approached the table again. He leaned low, two fists resting on its top, his face only inches from mine. "Or how about I just spell out the obvious? You've stumbled straight into a septic tank. There's crap all over you, and frankly, I couldn't care less. Drown in it for all I care. But what endangers you endangers Evelyn. My *wife*."

"Your ex-wife," I corrected.

His mouth was half-open, a retort ready. He stopped. His lips closed.

At last: "That wasn't my choice."

"I'm sure it wasn't," I said. "Just like it wasn't your choice to sleep with another woman."

His fists tightened. Once again, I saw the beast lunging against its chain and I longed for it to break free. For him to throw the table in my face and let me have it. It would be a short, brutal fight. I liked my odds.

But the beast retreated just when I thought it would charge. He withdrew from the table, shoulders loosening. Hands opening at his side. He breathed deep—just once.

Then he was calm. Totally collected. Cool again.

"If you really care about Evelyn you'll take your wrecking-ball life elsewhere," Alex said. "Whatever you think you know about me, whatever you think you have on me...trust me when I tell you, I can be every bit as nasty as any grunt in the Seventy-Fifth. You're not the only man who can dig a hole."

He stared a long moment longer. Then he simply turned. He opened the door. He disappeared through it.

Leaving me alone at the table, my own beast pacing at the end of its leash.

15

I was released an hour later.

No charges. No accusations. No apology for my detainment, either. The DC cops kept the five-pointed star handgun and its matching suppressor, and they made no comment as to my claims of carving a man's throat out in my living room. They simply returned my personal effects—phone, keys, wallet, and MacroStream flashlight. Then they walked me to the door and left me on the sidewalk of Alabama Avenue.

Free as a bird...and feeling twice as vulnerable.

I walked the two miles back to my apartment complex, arriving just past one a.m. to find many of the windows still illuminated, many of the blinds still parted to allow a view of my approach. There was still no crime scene tape, and when I entered my apartment I found it exactly as it appeared in Dickins's video.

Clean. Orderly. Almost perfect, except my rug was missing, and so was the lamp that had been gunshot. A careful inspection of the bed confirmed the presence of multiple bullet holes in the mattress, but the sheets had been replaced. The blood on the floor scrubbed away.

It was a quick job, and while obviously a professional one, it couldn't be perfect. A black light would likely still reveal blood splatter on the floor and walls. A more thorough interrogation of my neighbors would uncover the truth of my confrontation with two would-be assassins.

And yet, none of those basic investigatory steps were being made by the DC police. The apartment complex was as bereft of law enforcement interest as though the officers who had reported to the scene only hours earlier were responding to a petty domestic dispute—a naked drunk bashing cars with a baseball bat. The police were already gone, they were already disinterested. They'd made hardly any attempt at all to uncover the actual truth.

Why?

The question pounded on repeat in my head, a drum beat that made me want to put my fist through the wall. I didn't have an answer, but other, simpler questions were easy enough to resolve. Questions like what was likely to happen to me if I simply tore back the covers and climbed into bed, or hung around Anacostia for a repeat dance with my Asian friends?

I had to get out.

Cramming my clothes into my duffel, I packed my toothbrush from the bathroom and my shampoo from the shower. The violin case rode my shoulder—the last item to recover was Mia's Bible, which still rested on the nightstand. I reached for it, then stopped just as my fingers brushed the worn leather.

The nightstand's single drawer was open. Not far—just about half an inch. But inside I caught a glint of lamp light reflected on polished steel, and I tugged the drawer handle.

It was my Victorinox. Spotlessly clean with the blade closed. Resting alone in the drawer with a sticky note pasted to its grip.

See you soon.

My blood boiled. I snatched the knife out and tore the note off, checking the back. It was blank. I looked to the door, but nobody was there. The parking lot outside was as calm and quiet as I'd left it, my truck waiting for me.

They were gone...but they *had* been here. Whoever they were. I wasn't crazy.

I pocketed the knife and took the Bible. I slung the apartment keys onto the bed for the manager to collect. Then I departed the room, leaving the door unlocked. I climbed into my GMC and fired up the engine, half-expecting the truck to detonate at the twist of my key.

The motor rumbled as usual, and I dropped the column shifter into reverse. As I backed out, Rex appeared on the first-floor breezeway, shirtless in the night with his beer gut hanging over his waistline. He lifted a hand—just a two-fingered goodbye. Maybe a silent apology. I nodded in return, and then I was rolling out of the exit. Turning toward DC and monitoring my mirrors. Changing highways and switching back on my route. Making random turns, taking surface streets, and sometimes driving in wide circles. I conducted a full surveillance detection route, carefully searching for any form of a tail. Not just Asian guys in black Mercedes, but cops in unmarked sedans.

FBI agents in dark government sedans, lurking close behind.

Nobody followed me. Nobody aroused my concern. After

nearly ninety minutes of careful observation I was satisfied, and I drove straight out of the city. North to Bethesda, Maryland, where I selected a cheap hotel.

I parked in back. I paid in cash. I tore off my clothes and showered under piping hot water.

It wasn't until I lay stretched out shirtless over a new mattress, staring at the ceiling and forcing my mind to calm, that I finally approached the true heart of the problem at hand. Because despite my release, despite my survival of an assassination attempt, despite my safe haven in Bethesda, I *did* have a problem. It was the kind of problem that, not too many months ago, would have been easily rectified by doing exactly what Alex had told me to do—by hitting the road.

If DC didn't want me, fine. I was no great fan of DC myself. I could find a campground in West Virginia, a beach-side hut on the Outer Banks. Go about my life. Leave the FBI to their headaches and the blue-eyed tiger to his psychosis.

Only, that was then. Before Iowa. Before I crashed head-long with a force powerful enough, beautiful enough, magnetic enough to launch my nomad life right off its aimless trail and straight onto a pair of iron tracks. Tracks that led me to DC and were keeping me there.

Because I *wasn't* abandoning Evelyn. She was the best thing that had happened to me in three long years. Our relationship wasn't something I was looking for, it wasn't something that I completely understood. But it was good. Truly, magnificently *good,* and I wasn't discarding that. I wasn't leaving.

And that led me to my second problem. The problem that, much as I hated him for it, Alex had been right about. *Somebody*, for whatever reason, wanted me dead. Likely it had something to do with the murdered woman in Petworth, and my eye-witness encounter with her killer. Somebody was cleaning up loose ends, and there was little reason to think that they would stop. They would keep coming, keep stalking me.

And by proxy, that endangered Evelyn. Sooner or later, directly or otherwise. How much danger, I wasn't sure, but any amount wasn't acceptable. Not under any circumstances.

I'd lost love before. It *wasn't* happening again.

So, what to do?

I pondered the question for an hour straight, just staring at the ceiling with my fingers interlaced behind my head. Studying the patterns of the popcorn texture, sucking my teeth. Chewing my lip. Calculating angles, vulnerabilities. Options.

And arriving at something very simple, very elegant. Not a lethal option—that would be too messy and would result in too many ancillary complications. No, this was so much more discrete. And, if conducted properly, so much more effective.

I was satisfied with the strategy. Enough so that I inhaled once, closing my eyes and breathing out slowly through my mouth. Relaxing into the pillow. Accepting the work ahead.

And drifting easily into welcome sleep.

16

The dead woman's name was Rui Huang. I found it, along with a beautiful picture of her hugging a Sheltie on the Washington Mall, after a five-minute Google search the following morning. She was indeed Chinese. A clerical assistant at the People's Republic of China embassy to the United States—Washington, DC. Born in Shanghai. Living in the US for "the past few years".

That was all her brief obituary recorded. All the detail of an assuredly colorful, passionate young life reduced to just a few lines of vague script, submitted to the news site, no doubt, by a casual friend. A neighbor she passed in the hall.

Somebody who cared but didn't really know her. Nobody really knew her, it seemed. I couldn't find a Facebook page, I couldn't find an Instagram or an X account or any of those usual trappings of modern digital life. Rui Huang was quiet. A ghost, really. Not a permanent resident of the United States, but judging by the smile in that photograph, she had been a happy one.

And now she was dead. Why?

The question mattered, but it was beyond the scope of my current problem. The riddle I was more interested in solving was *who killed her?* And to that quandary, I thought I had an answer.

Departing the hotel, I drove my truck to the nearest Walmart and parked in the back, locking the doors and the camper shell. Then I called a cab. I directed the driver to the nearest major rental car dealer, where I secured the use of a brand-new, jet-black Toyota Camry. Just about as generic and forgettable a car as you could drive in a place like DC.

Behind the wheel, I headed south, back to Washington, and Petworth.

It took me nearly two hours to find him, but find him I did. Standing on a street corner lighting up a joint, looking half-awake and a little overdressed for the weather in his black Commanders jacket. Leaned against the brick with his head tilted back, green pot smoke drifting between his teeth, he never saw me as I parked the Camry and approached with my hands in my pockets. Shoulders loose. As non-threatening as I could appear.

"How's it hanging?"

It was the first thing I thought to say. I wasn't sure if it was something kids said anymore—I wasn't sure if I cared. I only wanted to gain his attention before I startled him, but I startled him nonetheless. He stood upright, dropping the joint and stamping it out. Wide, semi-bloodshot eyes turning on me. His body bunched for flight, already half-turned for the alley behind him.

Then he stopped. He squinted. He smiled.

"Whatdiyaknow," he laughed. "You survived, big dog."

I stopped ten feet away. I didn't want to crowd him, and

there was no need to draw closer, anyway. The sidewalks were empty this time of day. We were effectively alone.

"Thanks to you," I said, pointing my hand like a gun at the sky and curling my trigger finger.

He nodded slowly, and his smile faded. He looked suddenly suspicious, eyes narrowing. He stepped away from the wall.

"Well, good luck to you," he said.

"Hang on a minute. I want to talk to you."

He stopped—against his better judgement, it seemed. I could see the war in his mind. He was younger than I remembered, barely out of his teens. In excellent shape, but harder than he should have looked. The shine of youth was already dulled. The streets were wearing him down.

But there was enough empathy in his character to generate concern for a stranger. At least enough to pop off a shot in the dead of night and save that stranger's life. Maybe enough to hear that stranger out.

"Whatchoo want?" he said. "You a cop?"

I laughed. "I was. Not anymore."

I couldn't tell if the honesty assuaged his concerns or put him further on edge. His gaze darted to his right, to the street. Traffic was light. He could make a break for it if he wanted.

"I need your help," I said.

A snort. "I done helped you."

"And I'm very grateful. But that problem I had, that guy you ran off? He keeps hanging around."

I paused. He stood with his hands in his pockets, and I wondered if one of those hands grasped a snubby revolver. Maybe the barrel was already pointed at me.

"Sorry to hear it," he said. "I don't work protection."

"I didn't think you did. Actually, I was interested in my own protection. Something...portable."

Now he was really on guard, his body compressed like a spring. "What makes you think I know anything about that?"

I ducked my chin toward his jacket pocket. "Because you're already packing, and I doubt you have a permit."

He held my gaze another long moment. I remained calm, relaxed. I smiled, just a little.

At long last, he smiled also. He turned and disappeared down the alley without any further comment. He was gone half an hour, and I waited patiently the entire time. When he returned, he simply handed me a white paper card.

No name. No phone number. Just an address.

"Tips appreciated," he said.

I doled out a hundred-dollar bill, and he lit up another blunt without comment. Just a nod. I wished his Commanders good luck.

Then I was back in my Camry, plugging the address into the car's built-in GPS and following the blue arrow to a convenience store on the corner of two one-ways in Congress Heights. It was another "economically challenged" neighborhood on the eastern shore of the Potomac River, not far from Anacostia. The convenience store was abandoned, the front door barred and chained. The note on the card simply read "back door", which I located after jumping a four-foot fence and landing in an overgrown lot populated by trash.

The backdoor was covered in a tarp. The room inside was illuminated only by ambient light seeping in through a high window. There was a table, a notebook, and a pen. All else was empty. Just a blank concrete floor.

I flipped the notebook open and I found what I was

looking for. Makes, models, and prices. All printed in a shaky hand of blue ink, organized by weapon size, not caliber. I made three selections and circled them with the pen. Then I dispensed the requisite volume of US dollars onto the table. Nearly a grand in total. Most of what I had left in my wallet, and there wasn't much more than that in the lock box beneath my GMC's bench seat.

But it was a worthy investment. I left the cash and returned to the Camry. I kicked back the seat and dozed for half an hour.

When I returned to the back room of the convenience store, the notebook and cash were gone. A plastic grocery bag rested in their place, and inside that bag was everything I had ordered.

One Smith and Wesson SD40VE, fully loaded. One Taurus model G2C, also fully loaded. And one Kel-Tec P11 subcompact, only half-loaded. Just as it was described in the notebook.

All the guns were dirty. All of them had had their serial numbers ground off. I carried them in the grocery sack, avoiding any risk of leaving fingerprints, and returned to the Camry. Then I drove west, across the river and back into the core of DC. Past downtown, the Capitol, the White House. Up Connecticut Avenue to where the real gamble of my operation lay.

I found another motel—the Sleepy Days Inn, near Dupont Circle. Plenty old and moderately secluded. I paid cash for a room on the second floor and took my grocery sack inside. I used a hand towel as a makeshift glove as I distributed the weapons around the room—drawers and beneath pillows.

The last item I left was another burner phone I'd

purchased at a drugstore in Congress Heights. I'd powered it on just long enough to run a few incriminating Google searches, and also to save that picture of Rui Huang and her Sheltie to the phone's camera reel.

I wondered about the dog. I wondered what had become of it—if a friend had ensured its welfare, or if it had thirsted to death in Huang's apartment, another victim of her murderers.

They would pay, regardless. I left the phone in the night-stand drawer next to the bed, and I surveyed the room once more. Then I cranked the bathroom water on long enough to wet the tub. I left some lights on. I tossed a towel onto the bathroom floor.

Then I was back in the Camry. Circling out of the parking lot and onto Connecticut Avenue, driving three blocks across town to my final destination.

Another country.

17

Maybe it was Western bias or an influx of my own personal vendetta with the men in the Mercedes sedan. Whatever the case, on first blush, I couldn't help but think that the embassy of the People's Republic of China looked like something out of a dystopian film about authoritarian abuse.

Parked across International Place from the embassies of Ethiopia and Bangladesh, the PRC building was constructed of white blocks, both walls and roof, both polished smooth until they looked like marble. There were very few windows, and those were all covered in mirrored tint. An iron fence, about eight feet tall, ran across the courtyard of the embassy, and a tall flagpole proudly displayed the red and yellow Chinese banner as it snapped gently in the American breeze.

Or the Chinese breeze, depending on your interpretation of international law. Technically, that little postage stamp of land beyond that fence was no longer America. It was no longer under the control of the United States government. It was sovereign Chinese soil, and something about that thought sent a dull chill up my spine.

I parked the Camry across International Place and surveyed the embassy for half an hour—not because I really needed to, but because I wanted to double-check my homework before I dealt my hand. My logic was solid, and the diplomatic officers who rolled up at the site of Rui Huang's murder reinforced my strategy.

A Chinese victim. Asian—potentially Chinese—assassins. Chinese diplomats laying claim to the body.

I could be wrong, of course. This could be an organized crime thing, not a political one. For all I knew, Rui Huang owed money to the Triad, and they had grown impatient in collecting. But I didn't think so. I thought it was political for two reasons.

First, the elite nature of the covert operatives who had attempted to erase me. And second, the immediate involvement of Alex Parker Hudson, and the interest of the FBI. The FBI doesn't often care about women killed for unpaid gambling debts.

So, yes. I felt good. I was at least ready to roll the dice, and with my trap set, there was nothing left to do except to proffer the bait. And the bait was me.

I shifted back into drive. I cruised around the bend, past a row of American sedans parked in front of the Office of Foreign Missions. Right to the front of the Chinese embassy, a guard posted in a shack with glaring eyes fixated on me.

I slipped the Camry into park. I climbed out and removed my sunglasses. I looked straight into the nearest security camera and lifted my middle finger.

THE CHINESE DID NOT KEEP me waiting. Within seconds of my vulgar presentation the guard was shouting. I ignored him, keeping the bird flying for three long minutes. Then I simply climbed back into the Camry and buckled my belt. I sat with my window rolled down while the guard made phone calls. I studied the mirrored windows of the embassy and imagined what faces stared from behind them—what binoculars were being lifted, what phones were being dialed.

United States Marines guard United States embassies. I didn't know who guarded Chinese embassies, but it didn't matter. I only wanted to know if one blue-eyed, scar-faced tiger was hiding behind those polished stone walls, and I got my answer six minutes later when a flash of black drew my attention from the entrance of the adjacent parking garage.

Polished chrome. A circular emblem with a three-pointed cross reflecting the sunlight. It was a black Mercedes sedan, and it was headed straight toward me.

I dropped the Camry into sport mode—for whatever good that might do—and slammed on the gas. The front wheels chirped and I was off, swerving down International Place, making a lot of noise and catching a lot of attention. I blew the stop sign at the intersection. I set off down Van Ness Street NW, slowing just enough to ensure that the Mercedes followed.

He did—and he was in a hurry. In seconds we were clipping along the divided thoroughfare, hooking left onto Connecticut Avenue and blazing northwest toward Chevy Chase Village. There was a roundabout on the line between DC and Maryland, and I looped it twice, waving at the Mercedes as we came window-to-window, with the Chevy Chase Circle fountain blasting white spray between us.

I couldn't see him behind the tinted glass, but I trusted—
I believed. And anyway, there was no turning back.

I departed the circle, heading southeast again. Back into
DC and back down Connecticut, mashing the accelerator to
the floor and weaving through traffic. I wanted distance. Not
so much that I lost him, but enough for me to maneuver. I
gained three hundred yards and could barely track the
Mercedes among the congested traffic.

Every car was a black sedan, it seemed. We were
blending in. I tapped the pre-loaded address on the Camry's
GPS and a route populated. I checked the ETA, then lifted
my phone and dialed 911.

"Emergency services, what is your emergency?"

"I'm staying at the Sleepy Days Inn near Dupont Circle.
There's a Chinese guy here with a gun. Room two-seventeen.
He's beating a girl to death!"

I hung up. I pocketed the phone and rushed through
Woodley Park. Over Rock Creek. Straight through the heart
of Kalorama and on to Dupont Circle. Far from "economically challenged" but nevertheless a decided step down from
Kalorama, the Dupont Circle area featured an assortment of
older hotels and shabbier restaurants. One strip club and a
couple of liquor stores. The Sleepy Days Inn sat off the street
with only a narrow one-way drive providing access to the
internal parking lot.

The Camry glided through. I parked just beneath room
217 and cut the engine. I took the keys and hurried out.
Across the lot I vaulted a four-foot gate into a mechanical
alley with electric meters mounted to the walls, mud
puddles gathered on the concrete. I could see Dupont Metro
Station a couple hundred yards distant. Traffic was
rushing by.

I stopped halfway down the alley and turned back, squatting. I had a perfect view of the Camry, of room 217. As the Mercedes squealed in, my heart was just beginning to calm. The sedan parked next to the Camry and three men climbed out.

All Asian. All dressed in black business suits. All muscled and tough, with that military or ex-military bearing that kept their heads on swivels. They searched the lot but glanced right over the mechanical alley.

They couldn't see inside—it was too dark. They approached the Camry instead and peered through its windows. They swept the alleys.

Then they split. Two headed for the clerk's desk. One stood with his back to me, head pivoting as he inspected the motel's second floor.

He was drawn to it. His instincts served him well. His buddies returned two minutes later, jogging. They had a room key. They'd paid off the clerk, and the clerk had cracked, just the way I knew he would.

The three men ascended to the motel's second floor and approached room 217. The leader's jacket snapped open and his hand dipped down to his belt. His men stood on either side of the door, their own hands riding their hips. Braced for action.

The leader turned once to check his six, exposing his face for only a moment, but a moment was enough. It was *him*. The guy with the thick, snaking scar. It ran from his temple down his face to his neck, contorting one cheek. Giving him a wild, animal look.

My guy. *The tiger.*

He turned back. The door opened. The three of them rushed in, weapons drawn. They were inside, they were searching the room, perhaps locating the illegal handguns with serial numbers scrubbed clean. The phone with the photograph of Rui Huang.

And then the cops were rolling into the motel lot. Sirens blaring, it was a pair of DC cruisers. They clipped through the breezeway and raced right for room 217.

I smirked, rising to my feet and taking a moment longer to admire my handiwork. The patrol cops approached slowly at first, then kicked into high gear at the first shout of "Guns!" The room was taken, the Chinese were hauled out and thrown down, handcuffed with their faces ground into the concrete.

It was all very efficient. I had to hand it to the DC Metro Police, they knew something about securing a room. In seconds, they would also find the planted handguns. They would find the phone.

And that would be that.

I turned back down the alley. I walked across Dupont Circle and located a sandwich shop. I took a leisurely lunch, not returning for the Camry until ninety minutes later, by which time the Mercedes had already been towed. Room 217 was marked off by crime tape—attention to detail that my apartment never received. The desk clerk seemed very animated, but he shriveled as I rolled by, staring him down.

He knew what he'd done, he just didn't know that he'd done it for me.

I hit Connecticut Avenue again and glided back through the heart of town, just beginning to consider where I was headed, and what came next. I wanted some assurances, of course. Some guarantee that the problem was truly resolved. I might call the DC police later that day and pose as a crime reporter—see what I could fish out.

With any luck, Rui Huang's murder would be quickly solved, and my life would be back on track. I could take Evelyn for hot dogs and a Nationals game. Get a good night's rest, then be back to nailing shingles the next morning.

A job well done. I was satisfied.

But then my phone rang, buzzing in my pocket. I was stopped at a light. I fished it out, half-expecting to see Evelyn's face—that bright smile, those gleaming green eyes with a backdrop of the Chesapeake Bay. It was one of my favorite photos of her. One of my favorite memories.

But it wasn't Evelyn at all. It wasn't a contact at all. The number read simply: BLOCKED.

And the phone kept ringing. Four times. Five. The light turned green and still I hesitated. When the phone reached eight rings, I thumbed the answer button. I placed the device on speaker, but I didn't speak.

I waited, and what I heard first was a laugh. Subdued, sarcastic. Dry.

"I'm sure you thought that was terribly clever, Mr. Sharpe."

The voice spoke clear English with just a hint of a Chinese accent. It was humorless, like the laugh—and not at all agitated.

"Who is this?" I risked the answer.

"Diplomatic," the voice answered. "Diplomatic *Immunity*. Ever heard of me?"

The words fell like a kick to my gut. My intestines tightened. My fingers constricted around the wheel. The world around me faded, and I saw red.

A whole lot of it.

"How did you get this number?"

It wasn't a particularly smart question, or even that relevant. It was simply the first thing I could think to say, and I had to say something. I had to regain some initiative.

"Ah," the voice sighed. "China knows everything, Mr. Sharpe. Every small...beautiful...green-eyed *thing*. And we'll be seeing her very soon. Have a nice day."

And then he hung up.

18

The moment the line went dead it was like I sat frozen in the Camry. The traffic, the pedestrians on the sidewalks, the buildings and the flags flapping in the wind—all of it stood still, blurring out of focus. My body went cold. The phone fell out of my fingers and thumped on the floor in slow motion, my mouth turning instantly dry.

And I saw her. Standing alongside Chesapeake Bay, I saw her. Only the second woman I had ever truly loved. Turning in the breeze. Smiling. Strawberry-blonde hair whipped across her face. Rolling her eyes at a bad joke I had made.

And then pitching to the ground. Falling against a tile floor. Leaned against the utilitarian wall of a school hallway. Clawing her way backward, screaming my name.

Silenced by the sudden thunder of a twelve-gauge shotgun blast to the gut.

The vision was so instantaneously clear, so perfectly crisp in my mind, that it was as though I was already there.

Screaming in that hallway, fighting for another inch. Reaching out through the blood.

Just a little too late.

Just like before.

I blinked and a horn blared. The world began spinning again, and I slammed on the gas. Around a bus, blazing through an intersection as the light turned red. More horns honking, the blinking flash of blue lights as a cop attempted to give chase. He was lost behind a mire of DC traffic. I was headed the other way, bearing right as Connecticut Avenue crossed K Street and became 17th Street NW. I was passing Lafayette Square, and then the White House grounds on my left. Traffic was thick and I laid on my own horn, breaking through the gaps between an endless deluge of sedans and SUVs—all black.

And I was dialing Evelyn. A favorite contact in my phone, the only one. The call went straight to voicemail, an indicator that Evelyn had bumped it. She was probably in a meeting, maybe on the other line.

I dialed again, squealing to an unavoidable stop at Constitution Avenue. I was encased by black Suburbans. The intersecting traffic was flowing thick, the piercing bulk of the Washington Monument gleaming in the midday sun just a few hundred yards off my front left headlight.

And still, Evelyn didn't pick up. Once more the call went to voicemail, and this time I didn't dial again. I texted.

> Call me. Now.

The light turned green. I leaned on the horn. The snake of black slithered forward in a cloud of gasoline fumes, and I swung left. East on Constitution for one block, the White

House passing on my left, the Washington Mall on my right. Trees and monuments and joggers with poodle-mix dogs and so, so many cars. With every inch the Camry crawled, I was no longer in a Camry at all. I was in an unmarked sedan issued by the Phoenix Police Department—a car my partner and I shared. I was blazing through traffic with lights blinking. My heart was slamming into my throat, my hand was dropping for my sidearm.

I was blasting between the cars, hurtling toward that school. And I was quickly losing my mind.

Just as I hauled a hard right onto 14th, slicing across the Mall, my phone buzzed. I nearly choked as the Chesapeake photo returned. That smile, those eyes. I fumbled and dropped the phone. I dipped my shoulders to grab it, and another horn honked. I missed a collision with a black Cadillac by inches.

Then I had the phone. I swiped to answer. I was shouting.

"Evelyn?"

"Good grief, Mason. I'm video-calling with Atlanta. What—"

"Where are you?"

"What?"

"*Where are you?*"

"I'm...at work..."

"Downstairs, now. Meet me at the door. Black Toyota Camry—I'm four minutes out."

"What? What on earth—"

"*Do it*, Evelyn. Please."

I hung up, only two more turns remaining between myself and my destination. Left along the Mall. Right just past the Federal Aviation Administration. It was government buildings and government sedans and government people on every side. I honked at slow pedestrians and nearly knocked a woman's purse out of her hands as I screamed toward a ten-story, glass-faced office complex that consumed the heart of the D Street and 6th Street block.

The entrance was on D Street. A row of glass doors, a gate allowing access to an underground parking garage where Evelyn kept her Mini, and the name of the complex printed in bold black letters across its face.

CONSTITUTION CENTER.

I squealed up to the curb, lowering my passenger-side window and scanning the sidewalks. Looking to the windows. Thinking about snipers and suicide vests and car bombs—all the crazy, wild fears that years in Afghanistan had ingrained in me, and years in the United States had done little to assuage.

Was I already too late? Was Evelyn trapped in an elevator with a crazed Chinese operative and a short, sharp knife?

The panic was getting to me. I could barely keep myself in the car. I checked my watch and forced myself to wait another sixty seconds. Then I would abandon the Toyota and head inside.

But Evelyn appeared first. Stepping out of the main entrance, her laptop bag on her shoulder. Confused and anxious, gaze sweeping the curb.

Then stopping on me.

"Come on!" I beckoned. I reached over the passenger's seat and shoved the door open. Evelyn approached, stooping to peer in at me.

"Get in!"

She didn't argue. She pushed past the door and fumbled inside. Long before she had the door closed I was slamming on the gas. Tires spinning, we headed down D Street. This time I wasn't concerned with a destination—not immediately. I simply wanted the quickest route away from the heart of town. Away from Constitution Center and the CDC satellite office housed inside.

"Mason!" Evelyn cursed and fought with the window switch. I'd left the window down and the wind tore at her hair much like the sharp breeze that day on the Chesapeake, only this time she was pissed. Seriously so.

"*Mason!* Slow down. What are you doing?"

I ran the window up to block out the noise. One more turn and I had us racing toward the on-ramp of I-395. In the middle of the day, traffic was thick but not quite congested. In another few minutes I'd have us south across the Potomac. Into Virginia, away from DC.

And still I was scanning my mirrors, mapping every passing vehicle, pinpointing each Mercedes but trusting no make or model, and no driver.

"*Mason!*"

"Stay down," I said.

"What?"

"Just stay down, please. I can't explain right now. Fasten your belt."

Evelyn continued her grumbling as she clicked her seatbelt, the laptop bag now riding the floor. She was running fingers through her hair, checking the mirrors just as I checked them. Gaze still wide, her anger tinged with genuine uncertainty. Maybe a little fear.

I kept driving. Over the Potomac and past the Commonwealth of Virginia welcome sign. Weaving and gaining ground, still searching each passing car and each trailing one. It wasn't a surveillance detection route, not a true one.

But at least I was aware of the vehicles most closely pressing around us. More than black, they were now red and blue and silver. Some white.

We were exiting the Washington bubble, returning to something approaching normal America.

I breathed deep, forcing myself to relax. With every passing mile marker, the tension remained but I was regaining control. My heart was calming. The paranoid visions were fading into the back of my mind—not dying. Never dying. But I could mute them again.

I could look sidelong at Evelyn, and I could accept that she was alive. She was safe. She was *with me.*

"Mason," Evelyn said, her voice quieter than it had been only minutes prior, but still stretched. "What happened?"

19

I drove another five miles before I would answer. Off I-395 and into the town of Lincolnia, a little spec of a place engulfed by the urban sprawl just west of Alexandria. I'd never been there before. Nothing about the city was familiar. But I took Highway 236 past strip malls and fast casual dining establishments until we were lost amid apartment complexes and the entrances of subdivisions. I monitored my mirrors, but none of the cars I'd seen on the highway followed us.

At least, I didn't think so.

I looked to Evelyn and inhaled once. Then I ran a hand over my face, a growing headache pounding in the back of my skull. She hadn't spoken since voicing her question. She was calm—at least outwardly. She was focused.

She was one incredible woman.

"I was jumped," I said, simply.

"What? When?"

"Last night, at my apartment. Two guys from the murder in Petworth the night prior. They wanted to kill me."

"*What?*"

I held up a hand. "I survived," I said, adding a sarcastic smirk I didn't feel. Evelyn wasn't amused.

"Why am I just now hearing about this?"

I hesitated, knowing I was treading into shark-infested relational waters. "I was busy. I spoke with the police and the FBI. I was trying to clean it up."

It was kind of true.

"What do you mean, *clean it up?* Are you okay? Did they hurt you?"

There was genuine care in her voice. Too much for me to dismiss her inquiry with anything less than a sincere response.

"I'm fine. They didn't get me. But..."

Now came the moment of truth...or half-truth. How much did I really want to say?

"They called me," I said. "One of the guys from last night. He...he threatened you."

I glanced right. Evelyn didn't blink. She just frowned, brow crinkling, nose wrinkling. It was so cute that for a moment I forgot how painful it was to see her so stressed.

"Me?" Evelyn said. "Why on earth?"

"They're trying to get to me," I said. "I'm a witness. They want me gone. I...may have pushed their buttons."

"What?" Now her voice turned hard. No more tolerance for my ambiguity. "What did you do, Mason?"

I lifted a hand. "I tried to corner them. It didn't work. Look, it doesn't matter. I'm going to fix it. Right now I just need to know that you're safe."

"What did you *do*?" she repeated. "Did you kill somebody?"

I had, but not that day. Not during my stunt with the embassy and the Sleepy Days Inn. So I shook my head.

"It wasn't like that. I just flushed them out. I called the cops, actually."

"So?"

"So...the cops let them go."

I slid to a stop at an intersection and glanced right. Evelyn appeared more confused than ever—and more frustrated. She wasn't even asking questions anymore, she was just boiling, like she might be about to explode.

I had to level with her. Nothing less would suffice—so I did. I fessed up about the embassy and my stunt with the motel. I didn't mention the illegal guns, but Evelyn filled in the gaps. She muttered a curse and looked away, face flushing.

I drove again, this time in silence. A long two miles as Evelyn monitored the passing Virginia countryside, her jaw working.

Then she drew her phone.

"What are you doing?" I asked.

"What you should have done from the start. I'm calling the FBI."

"I've already spoken to the FBI."

"I'm calling somebody I know."

"Alex?"

She tensed. Her face flushed darker red.

"You have his number?" I asked.

Her fingers stalled over the phone screen. She swallowed and wouldn't look at me. With each passing second I felt my own blood rising, my face growing hot.

I was angry. I didn't quite know why—I wasn't even sure

whom I was angry with. Alex, for sure, but what else was new?

"I already spoke with Alex," I said. "He's useless."

Evelyn lowered the phone into her lap, but she still didn't speak.

"The FBI can't handle this," I said. "Whatever it is. These guys have Chinese diplomatic identification—diplomatic immunity. They're untouchable."

"Untouchable for *murder*?" Evelyn pressed, finally turning on me.

"Of course not, but there has to be *proof*."

"You're the proof. You saw this guy, right? You gave the police his description."

"I did."

"So now—"

"So now nothing," I cut her off. "It doesn't matter if they have his face and his name and his address. It's not something DC cops can touch. It would be like trying to arrest the president. You'd need overwhelming evidence before you could touch him. All they have is a single witness who *claims* to have seen this guy near the scene of the crime. I can't even prove that he shot Rui."

"Rui?"

"The Chinese woman, the one they killed."

Evelyn sat still. Another two intersections and three apartment complexes drifted by. I was physically silent, but my inner monologue was rolling like a film at triple speed.

I was thinking once more about angles of attack. Vulnerabilities. About cornering my enemy, ambushing him. Not to set him up, but to destroy him entirely. To resolve this problem once and for all.

Mostly, I was thinking about how to keep Evelyn safe.

"What are you going to do?"

It wasn't the question I expected. I looked right and found Evelyn sitting with her hands in her lap, staring directly ahead. She was very clearly deep in thought, maybe processing her own accelerated film reel. But she wasn't asking for information, and she wasn't telling me what to do.

"I've got to shut this down," I said. "I won't live like this."

A short laugh. No comment.

"What?"

Still no answer. We slid to a stop at another light.

"What?" I pressed.

"I'm just starting to wonder if you *do* live like this."

The words stung. I opened my mouth, then closed it. I looked ahead and heard the voice on the phone again. Gently accented, overbearingly condescending.

China knows everything.

"I'll fix it," I said. "I'll get it cleaned up. I just need to know you're safe."

"Safe?"

"Out of town. Someplace where they won't find you."

Another short laugh. "Virginia?"

"Maybe. Or someplace farther they wouldn't expect. Didn't you say your college roommate moved to Chicago?"

A third, final laugh. This one shorter and even less amused. "I'm not going to *Chicago*, Mason. I have work to do!"

I swallowed. Considered. Glanced to the laptop bag between her legs and nodded to myself.

"Okay. So maybe a hotel. Someplace discrete. You can work from there. Video calls, right? I'll get you some food."

"What?"

"It won't be long. A couple of days. I'll square it away and then—"

"Are you serious right now?"

"About what?"

"About stuffing me away in a hotel?"

"I'm not stuffing—"

"But you are. Who do you think I am, anyway? Your teenage daughter? You don't get to just pack me away every time you get paranoid."

"I'm not paranoid, I just—"

"But you *are*. You sound *crazy*."

"I'm not crazy. I'm—"

"I don't know how I keep doing this. One nutty guy after the next. For all I know you're making this up. You owe some bookie ten grand and you're splitting town yourself. I might never see you again. Now *I* sound crazy. We're all crazy!"

Her hands went up. My foot smashed down. Brakes squealed. The car swerved to the shoulder, biting dirt and spitting up sod. We ground to a stop, slamming against our belts. I shoved the transmission into park, already shouting.

"I'm not *crazy!* I've never been crazy. I *love you*, and I won't *lose you*. Do you understand? I won't let it happen."

My eyes burned as I stared at her. My throat was thick, like it was stuffed with cotton. I wasn't crying—I wanted to cry; it might have been easier. My fingers trembled around the shifter. Evelyn stared back, a little wide-eyed. Very still.

I looked away and ran my left hand over my face. My skin was slick with sweat. The interior of the Toyota suddenly felt like a sauna—like the crushing, constricting coils of an anaconda. I flicked the A/C on and stared out at the highway, watching the passing cars.

Still searching for that Mercedes.

"This is about her, isn't it?" Evelyn whispered. Her voice was soft—no more judgment. No more anger. Maybe a little hurt.

"No," I said. "It's not about her." I faced Evelyn. "And that's what makes it so very, very special."

Evelyn blinked. She looked away and did the thing with her thumb that girls do when they're brushing away tears while pretending not to cry. She gazed out her own window and sniffed and the A/C rustled her hair for a long time.

Then she reached across the console, still not looking at me, and took my hand. Our fingers interlaced. She squeezed.

And I felt alive again.

"Pick a hotel," Evelyn said, softly. "I can give you two days...then I need to be back in DC."

I squeezed back. I wanted to thank her, but the word stuck in my throat. I simply used my left hand to put the car back in gear, then drove with our fingers still interlaced, neither of us speaking.

Another twenty miles—way beyond Lincolnia, to the far side of Chantilly. There were lots of hotels there. Dulles was just a mile to the north and a steady stream of airliners streaked overhead, landing and taking off. An endless churn of travelers, and a good mask for somebody who wanted to remain out of sight.

I selected a three-story hotel with plenty of visible security cameras in the parking lot—deterrents, I hoped. I paid the clerk for two nights, holding my breath until the pre-paid debit card went through. I wasn't sure about the balance, but I knew it was low. I also knew I couldn't ask Evelyn to pay.

Back in the parking lot I found Evelyn right where I'd left her, watching an incoming 737 as it streaked out of the clouds on its final approach. I opened her door and squatted down.

She still didn't look at me. She was just watching that plane.

"You wanna go someplace next weekend?" she said.

"Like where?"

"Like..." She cocked her head. Smiled. "Africa."

"I know a nice spot on the beach," I said, returning the smile. "Quiet hotel...good food. Amazing sunrises."

"And booty?" Evelyn asked.

I shrugged. "Rumor has it."

She stepped out of the car. I wrapped my arms around her and leaned close, hugging before we kissed. The kiss was short and sweet. Very soft.

She smelled amazing.

"For the love, Mason," she said. "*Please* don't do anything stupid."

"Does that sound like me?"

"I'm beginning to think so."

I kissed her again and shut the door. Evelyn stood a moment fiddling with her phone, maybe shooting off a text or an email—explaining while not explaining why she had vanished from work.

She was way up the totem pole with the CDC, I knew. She was also a workaholic. Personal time shouldn't be a problem.

Evelyn finished the message and looked up again. Then squinted.

"Whose car is this, anyway?"

"This?" I glanced at the Toyota. "I stole it."

Evelyn flushed. She flicked her middle finger. I carried her laptop to her room and tried not to make a show of inspecting the bathroom and the closet—tried not to look paranoid. I kissed her again and returned to the Camry. I sat for a while and gazed at the hotel, envisioning Evelyn inside. Encased by concrete and glass with a deadbolt and a prayer.

Was it enough? I could only hope.

Powering back onto the highway, I felt my seat tremble as the jet wash of an Airbus exploded overhead. Maybe headed overseas. Maybe headed to Africa.

But I was headed to DC...and war with China.

20

Long before I reached the city I had a pretty good idea what I needed to do—and I even had an idea of how to go about doing it.

Evelyn had hit the nail on the head when she suggested that Rui Huang's murder should be enough for police intervention. I had further driven the point home with my illustration about arresting a president—how you need absolute proof to make it happen. It was a bullseye about half an inch wide and a thousand yards distant, a nearly impossible shot under even ideal circumstances, and these were far from ideal.

And yet, that was my target. It was my only logical way forward. I now knew for a fact that the men who had killed Rui were Chinese operatives working directly for the Chinese embassy. That was bad, but what made things so much worse was the fact that those operatives had so easily evaded my trap at the Sleepy Days Inn by claiming diplomatic immunity, a specialized privilege reserved for foreign diplomats working in official capacity for their home nation.

The key term in that description was *official capacity*. A foreign diplomat does not have carte blanche to break any law he pleases and then hide behind diplomatic immunity. His illegal actions, whatever they may be, are only protected when those actions are claimed to have occurred in relation to his or her *official capacity* as a foreign diplomat.

Put simply, the fact that the blue-eyed tiger and his buddies had escaped my trap meant that their bosses, the big cheeses at the PRC embassy, had covered for them. Had made phone calls. Had erased problems.

And that could only mean, in turn, that whatever sick and depraved operation these guys were involved in, the bosses were also involved. Not just with their attempts to murder me, but presumably with their original scheme to murder Rui.

And that made all of this—the whole bloody, corrupt enchilada—a much bigger problem than I had initially assumed. I wasn't dealing with some rogue embassy security personnel who had raped a drunken colleague, then stalked and murdered her to keep her from talking. I wasn't dealing with rogue operators at all.

I was dealing, directly or otherwise, with Beijing itself. Or at least with whatever branch of the Chinese government was in the practice of murdering its own people, then covering it up. It was a major risk for the Chinese to pull diplomatic immunity in a case like this. If the DC police or the FBI could ever *prove* that these guys killed Rui, the game would be up. The Chinese could still protect their people from prosecution, but the political fallout would be astronomical. A massive diplomatic crisis.

It was the kind of thing that could result in embassy staff, or even an ambassador, being declared *persona non grata* and promptly evicted from the Land of the Free. I couldn't imagine that was a corner China would willingly be backed into, which gave me some idea of how important it must have been for them to erase Rui Huang.

And it also gave me my opportunity. However slim, however minuscule a target in my metaphorical rifle scope. Still, it was an opening. Because if I could prove beyond any question that Chinese diplomatic officials hiding behind diplomatic immunity had murdered a woman on the streets of DC...it was checkmate. One way or the other, the game would be up. The FBI would *have* to act. The Chinese would be forced to pull their people.

And then my problem would be solved. The Chinese tiger would be recalled to China, his mission scrapped. Or maybe he wouldn't even make it that far. Maybe the Chinese would see fit to levy him with punitive damages, squashing a failed operator like a cockroach under a boot.

Authoritarian governments have been known to do that. I might get lucky.

First, I had to solve Rui's murder. And to do that, I was assuming a challenge that not even the FBI seemed capable of overcoming. Granted, the FBI was hamstrung by political pressure and legal protocol. I was concerned with neither. I wasn't a cop anymore. I wasn't a soldier. I was just a guy in a rented Camry with forty-eight hours of opportunity while his girlfriend hid in an airport hotel room.

I had to make those forty-eight hours count.

I began by refueling the car, then stopping off at my parked GMC to collect my lock-pick set—just in case. The next stop was a dollar store for my essentials. Dry foods, eight quarts of water, a notebook, and a mechanical pencil. I packed it all into the car then drove to a riverfront park in

Arlington, just across the Potomac from DC. Parked near the water, I spread the snacks and notebook over the hood of the Camry.

Peanut butter crackers and penciled notes. It wasn't much different than my days in Phoenix's homicide division, only I lacked my partner's keen mind and relentless lamentations about her beloved Phoenix Suns. The memory was almost enough to make me smile.

Almost.

I started with a clean page and recorded every individual fact I could think of, a catalog of evidence, before the details were distorted by time and chaos. I wrote about the guns, the cut of each killer's suit, the shape of the scar distorting the left side of the tiger's face. He was the leader—I knew that. Not so much as a fact, but as an instinct, and in my experience good police work is about fifty percent instinct.

Moving on from my targets, I retraced my memory to the original crime scene. Not my apartment, but Petworth and Delafield Place. Only yards from Alex Hudson's townhome, I placed myself back on the sidewalk and envisioned the three figures walking toward me.

Rui Huang. Two men trailing her. All of them walking fast, Rui leading the others by under a hundred yards, walking with purpose. *Headed* somewhere.

But where? What was Rui doing in Petworth, anyway? It was miles from the Chinese embassy—all the way across town, in fact. What had drawn her to this random stretch of street in the middle of the night? What had she been up to?

I caught my mind careening down a trail of cause and effect, of motivation and context, and I shook my head to clear it. It didn't matter why Rui was in Petworth or what she was doing there. That was all well beyond my interest in

solving her murder. I only needed to pin the Chinese operatives for her death, whatever the context that had motivated
them to kill her.

Focus, Mason. Relive the moment.

I breathed deep. I mentally returned to Petworth and
focused on Rui, saturating myself in her every subtle movement. Picturing her face. Her body language. Her animation.

She was moving fast, yes. And...was she huffing a little?
Was she out of breath?

I closed my eyes, and I thought so. I remembered her
hustling, but she hadn't yet noticed her pursuers. She didn't
notice them until I shouted. So...why was she winded?

The logical explanation was that she was in a hurry, and
she'd been in a hurry for some time. It was a lengthy walk,
which generated a further question.

Where had she come from?

I switched from the notebook to my phone, calling up
Google Maps and panning around the greater Petworth area.
I imagined how Rui might have arrived in that district,
assuming she didn't already live there. I didn't think she lived
there. It was a long way from the embassy, and not a particularly inexpensive place to live. I doubted that clerical assis-
tants working for the People's Republic commanded much
of a salary.

So I assumed she had journeyed to Petworth. Not via the
train—the Green Line ran along Georgia Avenue, only a few
hundred yards from Delafield Place. If she'd taken the train,
she shouldn't have been winded by the time our paths
crossed.

Besides, she wasn't heading west to east, away from the
Green Line. She had been heading east to west, *toward*
Georgia Avenue. So unless she had finished her business in

Petworth and was returning to the train, her route had originated elsewhere.

But she hadn't concluded her business. Everything about
her body language spoke to a woman on a mission—a
woman headed somewhere. She was on her way, not on her
way back. She hadn't driven because if she had, she should
still be in her car. There was plenty of parking in Petworth.
She could have found a spot right at her destination. For the
same reason, she couldn't have taken a cab.

No, it was indeed public transit. Just not the Green Line.
So what, then?

I returned to the map. I tabbed the transit button, and
Google obliged by highlighting every train station and bus
stop across Petworth. The vast majority of them were clustered along Georgia Avenue, but one lay east of Delafield
Place. Bus stop number 1002475—Sherman Circle and Crit-
tenden. Just about half a mile from Rui's eventual location
on Delafield, the point where our paths crossed.

Far enough to work up a sweat? To run out of breath?

At Rui's pace, assuming she was a little out of shape,
certainly. And that gave me a route, paved in a bold blue line,
compliments of Google.

I shut the notebook and collected my cracker trash. I
threw everything in the passenger's seat floorboard, just the
way I always had as a cop. Then I spun the Camry out of the
park and turned north.

Toward DC, and Petworth.

21

I thought I would need to drive Rui's possible routes a few times before identifying any useful evidence, but I lucked out on the first pass. Only yards from the bus stop, in fact, where I located a small convenience store with bars on its windows and a simple plastic sign swaying in the wind, creaking on metal hinges.

Bee-Gee's Package and Carry. A compact place, resting within sight of the bus stop. No fuel pumps, just snacks, household essentials, liquor.

And security cameras.

I stood on the sidewalk and glanced back and forth between the bus stop and either of Rui's probable routes. Both streets led toward Delafield, one only slightly more direct than the other. She could have taken either.

But both would have led her past Bee-Gee's. Both would have led her past the security camera concealed just above that creaking sign, staring down at the sidewalk and the convenience store's front entrance. Whether by peripheral or direct shot, if Rui walked past that store, she would have been recorded.

As would her pursuers.

I glanced both ways up the sidewalk as I approached the store's entrance, mapping a path overhung by oak trees and lined by waist-high brick walls. A blue USPS mailbox stood on the corner. Little townhomes were built together with political signs and sports flags displayed in their miniscule yards and on their porches. Street parking only.

I entered the store, triggering an electronic buzzer. The place was barely big enough to park a car inside. Shelves lined with miscellaneous hardware, cleaners, dishwasher detergent, and all the other domestic products I hadn't used in nearly three years were joined by items I'd used much more often.

Handles of whiskey and bourbon. Cans of beans and sausages. Candy bars and crackers.

There was one cash register encased behind bulletproof plexiglass with a narrow slot for payment and a cluster of small holes for verbal communication. The guy slouched behind it sat on a stool, his gaze fixated on a handheld gaming device. He glanced up when I entered—a greasy face with a scraggly beard. A dirty tank-top and uncut, uncombed hair.

He was white. Mid-forties. Overweight and decidedly irritable. He looked right back to his game as I stood just inside the door, hands in my pockets, surveying the interior but not reaching for anything.

"Can I help you?"

The accent was all Baltimore. He didn't sound very interested in helping anyone.

"Yeah. I've got a question, actually." I shuffled toward the counter, leaning one elbow on it. Appearing as nonchalant and friendly as possible. "Were you working two nights ago? Around midnight?"

A snort. The guy focused on his game, jabbing the buttons. Working on a wad of tobacco.

No answer.

"A woman passed by," I said. "Asian woman, mid-twenties. Black jacket. She was headed that way." I pointed northwest, toward Delafield. "She was being trailed by two other Asians. Men."

"And now she's dead," the clerk grunted.

"Say what?"

"I said she's *dead*." The guy looked up. "Shot through the forehead, right? I already talked to your buddies, pig. I'll tell you what I told them—you come back with a warrant, and you can see the security tape. But you better hurry. That stuff self-erases pretty quick."

He smirked at that. He spat tobacco juice into an empty bottle, then returned to his game.

"I'm not a cop," I said.

He didn't look up. "You look like a cop."

"Well, I'm not one. I used to be. I quit."

No answer. I glanced around the room again, surveying additional cameras mounted behind his cashier's cage. Plywood standing in place of glass in one of the convenience store window frames. A sign that promised prosecution to the fullest extent of the law against all shoplifters. A baseball bat leaning in the corner behind his stool.

It was dented and dirty. It looked well used. I thought I understood why.

"All bark and no bite, these cops. Traffic tickets and taxes...can't do much about real crime."

I said it like a drunk at a bar. Just one guy grumbling to another, bemoaning the realities of the world and rehearsing an assumed shared perspective. I'd done it before, many times, even in Phoenix. Detective or otherwise, if people hated the police, I wasn't above exploiting that. Why not? Everybody had a story.

The guy looked up, slowly. He squinted at me and stopped chewing. But he didn't answer.

"Let me guess," I said. "They were hours late when you called about that busted window, or about a shoplifter, and even then, nothing ever came of it. No arrests...no prosecutions."

"And yet I still pay taxes." He spoke around the wad of tobacco, more of a snarl than a sentence.

"But when some woman was shot in Petworth?" I said. "They were Johnny on the spot. Couldn't get here fast enough."

He ran a slow tongue over his lips, sweeping away tobacco saliva. He laid the game down, spat into the bottle again. Then he leaned back and folded his arms, suddenly looking very keen. Like a snake.

"Who are you?" he said.

"Just a guy."

"A guy, huh? A guy who used to be a cop?"

"Used to be."

"But not now."

"Nope."

"How come?"

I shrugged. No answer. I had a good reason and a good story, but when you're dealing with the prejudiced and small-minded, it's best to let them fill in the blanks themselves. They'll always default to spinning an imaginary explanation that justifies their own biases. And then, just like that, *bam*. You're an ally in their eyes.

Good police work is fifty percent instinct. The other fifty percent is dealing with people.

"Why do you want the security tape?" the guy asked.

"I never asked for the security tape."

"But you want it. That's why you're here, same as the cops."

I shrugged in a "you got me" way. He grunted, impressed with his own detective skills.

"You a PI?"

"No."

"So why, then?"

It was the opening I'd waited for. The moment when I threw my cards on the table—my real cards—and pushed him over the edge.

"Those guys who killed that woman think I'm a witness to the murder. They're coming after me, and they're coming after my girlfriend. I'm doing what any self-respecting citizen would do." I lifted my chin toward the baseball bat. "I'm getting proactive."

He laughed. Just a snort of a sound, accompanied by a spray of tobacco spit on his side of the bulletproof plexiglass. His gut jiggled behind the tank-top. He lifted a water bottle and chugged.

"You're a cold-hearted SOB, ain't you?"

"Some days."

He considered, chewing. Cleaning his teeth with his tongue. Then he shook his head.

"Whall, if you're a cop, you're a danged good liar." He twisted beneath the counter, producing a laptop. He tugged it open and input a password.

"All right. So what time did she pass by?"

THE VIDEO WAS GRAINY—BLACK and white, distorted by night and a low-quality camera lens. I was forced to watch it through the misted security glass. The clerk wouldn't come out of his cage.

But despite those inconveniences I found Rui. She was headed up the sidewalk away from the Sherman Circle bus stop. Jacket wrapped around her thin body despite the warmth of the night, legs moving in choppy little bursts recorded by the low frame rate of the camera.

She appeared and then she was gone, that quick. Certainly moving fast enough to be out of breath by the time she reached Delafield.

"There you go," the clerk said. "I found her the same morning the cops came knocking. They wouldn't ask nicely."

"Can you play the next few minutes?" I asked. "I want to see if she was followed."

An irritated sigh, but the clerk complied. I watched carefully, one ticking second after the next. I was looking for two Asian men in black jackets, flashing past the camera just as Rui did.

What I got instead was the front quarter panel of a Mercedes sedan. Just a blink, then it was gone. Gleaming chrome and dark paint.

Bingo.

"Rewind," I said. "I need to see that again."

The clerk didn't move. He cocked one eyebrow and spat into his bottle. I sighed and ripped out my wallet. A twenty-dollar bill slid through the slot in the plexiglass, and then he rewound the tape. I had him freeze it the second the car came into view.

It was so momentary that it was little better than a grainy blur. But it was there, unmistakably a Benz. I saw the hood and I saw one quarter of the windshield near the driver's side A-pillar. I thought I saw a hand on the wheel—I thought that hand was gloved.

But what really caught my eye was the sticker. Pasted to the bottom of the windshield near the dash, about two inches square. I couldn't tell the color. I could barely decipher the symbol of a mountain in silhouette, a river running through it. And just beneath that, a three-digit number. Nine-two-eight.

Nothing else.

I leaned back from the screen and chewed my lip, still fixated on that sticker. Still thinking.

"Do you recognize that symbol?" I asked.

"Nope." The clerk spun the computer around. He smacked it closed.

"Did you ever see that car before?"

"Nope."

He was back to the video game. Spitting. Chewing. Punching at the keys. I was forgotten, that quick. Twenty bucks made, amusement exhausted.

Right.

I stepped back to the sidewalk, back into the humid stickiness of a DC summer night. The air was thick, the mist hanging close to the ground. I looked down the line of cars parked on the street. Mostly black, mostly sedans. More government people. I didn't see any stickers of mountain ranges with rivers running down them.

What would that sticker be, anyway? A symbol and three numbers. An ID of some kind, perhaps? A permit?

What about a parking permit? A license to leave the Mercedes in a certain slot—say, slot 928—in some parking lot somewhere in the city. Or maybe outside the city.

It was a big lot, presumably. Nearly a thousand spaces, maybe more. A parking deck downtown?

But no. Parking decks downtown were generally metered. Pay-by-plate. They didn't usually offer regular, permanently reserved access.

So...where, then?

Residence.

I thought it, and I drew my phone. I began Google searches, combining various words for "rock" and "water" with terms such as "village", "community", "subdivision", and "apartments."

I scored on *Stone Creek Apartments.* The website loaded in full, vibrant color. The property was located in Arlington, just across the Potomac River. It featured several hundred residential units organized within three-story buildings. Exterior access to the homes, gated access to the parking lot. Reserved parking.

And the logo? A mountain silhouette with a river spilling out of it.

Bingo.

I headed for the Camry.

22

G ated apartments are silly things. I've always thought so. Not only does every pizza boy, every delivery driver, every flower courier in the city know the passcode—to say nothing of a few hundred residents and every friend they've ever messaged the code to—but the gate itself is a pretty helpless defense against intrusion.

It would stop my Camry, certainly. At least until somebody pulled in ahead of me, or the exit gate opened, and I slipped through. But why did I need the car? It would be stealthier to approach on foot, and to do that, circumventing the gate was as simple as walking around it. Down into the ditch, through some loose hedges and past a duck pond with a stone water feature.

Stone falls. Stone creek. How clever.

With the Camry parked at the drugstore next door, I slipped past the pool and the property office, hands in my pockets, gaze sweeping the premises. It was now past eight p.m., and most of the apartment windows glowed yellow with internal light. Occasional cars drifted by, mostly expensive, late-model sedans. Business professionals in suits with laptop bags slung over their shoulders bustled up and down sidewalks and stairways.

It was an upper middle-class community. Mostly mid-to-late twenty-somethings, it seemed. Mostly singles. Mostly childless. Very clean and very professional and very...stale. Generic. Ordinary.

I always wondered why people chose to live that way. Granted, I'd endured more than my share of the stale, generic, and ordinary during my years in the Army. Barracks are the very definition of stale. But the moment I was free of that lifestyle, I wanted my own space. My own color. I didn't want to live in a beehive.

And I still don't.

The thought occurred to me halfway through the 500 block of parking spaces, and I stopped short, my gaze catching on 505 as I thought of Anacostia. Of my breadbox apartment, just one room plus the bathroom. Dingy walls and noise from the neighbors above and beside.

A beehive lifestyle if ever there was one. Cramped. Uniform. Somehow...confining. I could leave any time I liked, but there was something about that key in my pocket that had felt oddly restrictive, almost like an anchor. Like something holding me back. I had tossed it onto the bed without a second thought. I had been glad to be rid of it, in fact. I had no idea where I would sleep later that night, and I was more than okay with the hanging question.

I preferred it. I was comfortable with it. I missed it.

My gut tightened at the thought, and I blinked at 505. I shook my thoughts free, re-focusing.

Forty-eight hours, Mason. She gave you two days.

I departed the 500 block and skipped laterally to 700. Each lot seemed to correspond to a numbered building, and none of them contained one hundred spaces. Each contained an even thirty-two, a perfect two slots for each of the sixteen units contained within each building. Two groups of four apartments on each level. Two breezeways. Two sets of stairs.

And best of all, there was a direct correlation between the labeled parking spots and the apartments they belonged to. It was almost silly—zero effort for discretion. All the apartments were even numbers. All the guest parking spaces were odd numbers.

So, slot number 928 corresponded directly to unit 928, and slot 929 appeared to be the secondary slot for unit 928. The guest slot. It was that simple, and slot 928, when I reached it, was empty.

I stood on the sidewalk and surveyed the second floor. Eight units were visible from the front of the building. Four on the bottom, four on the top. Seven of those units were illuminated by glowing yellow windows.

The eighth, the one to the far left nearest the empty parking space, was not. It was dark. Silent. The shades drawn.

Here goes nothing.

I took the steps to the second floor, fishing my lock-pick set out of my pocket as I went. I could hear music from one door. A TV from the other. A boisterous, inebriated discussion from the third. Women laughing, men shouting at a sports game. They were all the sounds of my own address back in Anacostia, minus the loud cursing. The crashing beer bottles. The stench of pot.

Many of the doors featured hangers or foot mats, but not

928. It was blank, just burgundy paint rolled over sheet metal. There was a peep hole, a deadbolt, some mud on the concrete depicting a footprint.

Nothing else. Just silence.

I glanced over my shoulder once, then approached the door. I began with the knob and tested it with a twist. The thumb latch was engaged, and I went to work with the picks, still standing. It would have been easier to work while squatting, but the silhouette of a squatting man in front of a door is a pretty suspicious thing, even from a distance.

Standing this way, maybe I was just fussing with the keys. Maybe I was playing on my phone. I could spare a few seconds.

The thumb latch clicked, very softly. I proceeded to the bolt, expecting and receiving a greater challenge. I maintained pressure with my turning tool and began picking each slider with my crook. One, two, click on three, nothing on four or five. I returned to the start and contended with a false gate on two before eventually obtaining a click. The remaining three sliders fell into place, and I twisted the turning tool.

The bolt slid. It thunked into the door. I withdrew the picks and glanced once more over my shoulder, then I was easing the knob and stepping over the threshold, fully aware that I could be shot in the head before I made it another yard.

It was a petty risk compared to the mental image of Evelyn collapsing against a wall, still so vivid in my mind that when I closed my eyes the vision felt like a real thing, like it was happening right in that moment.

I forced the image from my mind, and then I was inside the apartment. Off the concrete and onto hard tile, using the balls of my feet to minimize each footfall. The air was heavy with the stench of stale cooking oil—a lot of it, so pungent that I almost choked. The place smelled like a fast-food restaurant, a place that fries absolutely everything. I eased the door closed behind me with the lights off and dipped my hand into my pocket for the MacroStream.

I didn't turn it on right away. I stood listening, my eyes adjusting to the darkness. Sweeping the walls for any indicator of a security system, and finding none. Just an AC control unit, the slow blue blink of an internet router resting on the carpet, and the shine of a stove clock from the kitchen.

And silence. Near perfect. I thumbed the MacroStream, switching to its lowest setting, just fifty lumens. Pale blue glow washed over a tile path leading past a dinette to a kitchen beyond. The living area was to my right, paved in carpet. One couch, one TV set resting on the floor. Shoes discarded against the wall, a wall of vertical blinds blocking out the main window.

And cardboard fast-food trash—piles of it. Burger wrappers and pizza boxes. Plastic takeout containers and paper cups. But most of all, more than anything, fried chicken drums. Maybe two dozen of them, all KFC. They were stacked everywhere, nested inside of each other like leaning towers of Pisa.

It was the chicken I was smelling. The greasy bones heaped in the nearest paper drum, bits of rotting breading still sticking to them. It was enough to make me choke—and I love fried chicken.

Lifting my shirt over my nose, I scanned the Macro-Stream left across the dinette table, which was ironically empty and nearly spotless. The kitchen was visible over the bar, and as I approached I found more trash, more drink containers. A lot of soda cans, both empty and unopened.

But no dishes, no groceries. This place felt like a crash pad, like a weekend hangout. There were no pictures on the walls, nothing more personal than the shoes piled in one corner. The furniture was generic and cheap, and there were still stickers on the frame of the TV. Still tags hanging from the backs of the dinette chairs.

Men. That much was obvious. No woman had set foot in this place. But beyond that, I still didn't know. There was too little information.

I started down the hall, reaching a bathroom first. Towels on the floor, toilet paper on the counter. Toothbrushes and combs. A mess. On to a closet, which was packed with jackets and more shoes. No additional clues.

Then came the first bedroom door. It stood on the right side of the hallway, only a few feet beyond the living area. I used my shirt tail as a makeshift glove and put my hand on the knob...but it wouldn't turn. I twisted again to make sure it wasn't simply stuck, but it wouldn't give. It was locked.

Who locks a bedroom door?

Out with the picks again, this time on my knees. The knob was new, which meant the tumblers were clean. I implemented the same turner tool but forwent the crook pick in favor of a wave rake. It was a simple lock, and I didn't expect much resistance.

It was right. Four quick cycles of the rake and the knob twisted. I replaced the tools and rose to my feet, the Macro-Stream cocked in my fist like a pitiful weapon. I eased the knob as quietly as I could, holding my breath. Waiting for a stirring inside.

There was nothing. The door glided open. I stepped

across carpet, thumbing the flashlight back into low-power mode. I expected a bed, maybe more dirty clothes and strewn shoes. More cheap furniture with tags.

What I found was none of the above. I'd hit the jackpot, straight on the first bedroom, and the contents illuminated by my MacroStream confirmed every suspicion I'd had about the two men in that black Mercedes.

It was a forward operating post, nothing less. There was no bed, there was no cheap furniture. Just long plastic tables resting against the wall, all of them stacked with laptops and cameras, communication equipment and listening devices, black gloves and lock picks and a handful of grapefruit-sized drones. It was like something out of a James Bond film—all the spy tech a person could dream of, and that was just the perimeter tables. What *really* drew my eye was the table standing in the middle of the room, the one sagging under a heavy load.

It was the weapons table. Piles of submachine guns, pistols, and knives. Metal bins crammed with ammunition, a plastic container printed in logograms and loaded out with little square blocks wrapped in gold foil. Explosives—specifically, breaching charges, but wired together there was enough destructive potential in that box to blow this entire floor.

The guns were foreign. I only recognized the handguns, and that was because they were the same plastic-gripped, hammer-fired models as I had previously captured from my would-be assassins. A bold star molded into the grip, and an attached suppressor. There were four of them, all laid out on the table with accompanying magazines lined next to them.

Then came the submachine guns. A little like MP5s, but not really. They were also printed with logograms and also complete with attached suppressors. A row of five with accompanying magazines, red dot optics, slings and folding fore-grips.

It was a full load-out—a nasty collection of death-inflicting implements. And it was parked right there in Arlington, only miles from America's national capital. These were foreign guns—foreign operators. I stood staring at the arsenal in momentary shock, followed almost instantly by indignation. Disgust. Outrage.

Who was allowing this? How had these guys not been detected, detained, escorted to the nearest border like the dangerous intruders that they were?

Focus, Mason. The context still doesn't matter.

I left the weapons and began at one end of the plastic tables, borrowing gloves from the pile and examining each item. I checked the cameras for storage cards, but every slot was empty. I tried each computer, but they were all locked—no surprise.

I reached the end of the table and sifted through a small pile of cell phones. Far too many for the occupants of this apartment, however many they might be. This was clearly a burner inventory. I counted twenty-one in total, mostly cheap models, mostly smart phones but some flip phones too. Even the flippers required passcodes for access, and several were dead. I tossed the last back into the pile and was just turning for the door when something caught my eye—something non-digital, scribbled on the back of a KFC receipt. It was more logograms—Mandarin, I guessed. Or Cantonese.

I lifted the receipt and studied the symbols, but they were meaningless to my ignorant eyes. A pointless note, perhaps. A password that I didn't know how to use. Maybe nothing.

Or maybe something. I tore off a glove with my teeth and used my phone to snap a photo of the receipt. I returned the glove and proceeded to photograph the rest of the room, one angle at a time.

I was just returning to the door when I heard the footfalls. A thump outside, followed by a muted voice. It wasn't English, but it didn't need to be. The tone transcended language barriers, communicating surprise and concern all at once. I heard keys rattling, and then I remembered.

I hadn't locked the door.

23

I grabbed the nearest suppressed handgun and went straight for the bedroom door, flicking the lock closed and pressing my ear against it. Already the voices outside had fallen perfectly silent, a predictable result of the door being discovered unlocked.

It was a stupid, stupid mistake on my part. A dead give-away. I should have considered the possibility of the Chinese returning before I departed. Now they knew somebody had been inside—might still be inside.

Idiot.

From beyond the door I heard footsteps, very soft. They were probably moving on the balls of their feet. Stalking forward, taking their time. Clearing the living area and the kitchen.

Then they would check the first bedroom.

I backed away from the door, sidestepping to the bedroom's closet. It was a walk-in, not big but big enough. I eased the door closed and pressed my back against the bare wall. A case of water bottles and some dry foods rested on the floor—fuel for shut-ins—but the rest of the space was empty. In the near perfect dark, I pocketed my phone then rotated the commie handgun in my right palm. A gentle manipulation of the slide chambered the first round, and I found the safety from memory.

The suppressor was heavy on the handgun's nose. I imagined the snap of a shot, the twitch of dampened muzzle flip. The instant crimson hole drilled between a pair of wide eyes, just as a hole had been drilled between Rui's eyes.

I heard the footsteps again, entering the hallway. Holding my breath, I detected the gentle click of the door-knob being tried, followed by an unintelligible murmur.

Locked.

Maybe they were now thinking that this room could be safe. That they had simply forgotten to lock the apartment's exterior door on their way out. Maybe there was nothing to be concerned about.

I imagined their confused thoughts and could only hope that they were working in my favor. The slide of a key was followed by the twist of the knob. I looked instinctively right, even though a wall stood between myself and the door. I pointed the pistol double-handed at the closet's entrance and waited.

More murmurs. I could make out words, even though I didn't understand them. There were two men...maybe three. They shuffled around the room, items shifting, keys clicking. Somebody grunted. I didn't so much as move. I barely breathed.

Leave the closet. Just leave the closet.

But they didn't. The footfalls drew nearer and my muscles tensed. My finger constricted around the trigger, tightening a gritty quarter-inch. The door shifted, knocking against its frame. The knob twisted. I clenched my jaw and lowered my head.

Then the door swung open, all at once. I saw the hand, but I didn't see the body. The guy was smart—he stood off to one side. His buddy was farther back with a partial view of the closet's interior, enough to confirm its occupancy or emptiness. He had a pistol ready—it was pointed right at me. He was primed for a shot.

But I shot first. My pistol cracked, the muzzle twitching just as I had envisioned. I drilled him in the forehead, and he went down, just a dead tree slumping against the wall. Then it was all shouting and slamming, bodies crashing against the wall and a table overturning. The hand disappeared and I kept firing, pivoting my point of aim and driving rounds through the closet wall just to one side of the door frame. Bullets bit through two layers of drywall and a scream rent the room.

More shouting—I was still shooting. I was headed out of the closet, leaned low and directing my fire in a sweeping motion that drove the occupants toward the door.

Away from that table-load of rifles.

The ploy worked, if only just barely. One guy flailed for a submachine gun on his way to the floor, but he was out of time. I was shooting through the table and he was crawling desperately toward the door. I exploded out of the closet and turned just in time to catch his legs sliding through the gap. I swung the gun after him and yanked on the trigger.

My shot was rushed. It flew wide, and there was no time for a second attempt. Return fire was raining in from the hallway—it was the third guy, the one who had opened the closet door. The one I had shot through the wall. His gun sounded just like mine, a whispering snap of death that penetrated the drywall and showered me with dust. I scrambled backwards, bracing for cover behind the closet corner even as the bullets rained in. It was a perfect storm of suppressed fire—a full magazine dump.

But magazines run dry, and pistol magazines aren't large. I recognized the sudden hesitation of a slide locking back over empty, and I slung myself away from the wall, landing on the table full of guns. It collapsed sideways, submachine guns and pistols crashing to the floor alongside case after case of ammunition. I struck the floor also, landing on a crate of breaching charges that bit into my ribs and drove the air from my lungs.

But one of the MP5-like sub guns lay free against my arm. It rose into my shoulder even as I snatched the charging handle. One flick of the safety. The first snap of the Chinese guy opening fire after a reload.

And then I was returning fire, full auto. A blaze of hot lead voiced as a chain of tightly suppressed pops—blowing through the drywall and spraying the hallway, the kitchen, the living area. Another shout and then a heavy thud signaled the collapse of a body as my magazine ran dry, the room rank with a haze of gun smoke.

I was back on my feet, stripping the mag and gathering a second off the floor. Dropping the bolt. Kicking the door out of the way and stealing a glance down the hallway.

It was chaos. Carnage. Splintered wood and drywall dust and one body lying twisted and bullet-ridden on the floor. He was Asian, but he didn't have a scar running down his face.

And the door beyond him—the door into the breezeway outside—was open.

I ran back into the bedroom. Back over the pile of fallen

weapons, all the way to the window that was covered over by blackout curtains. I ripped them aside and found a window-pane secured by two latches. I had a clear view of the parking lot beyond—all those black sedans and SUVs lined up in neat little rows. One black sedan in particular was parked in slot 928. It was a Mercedes, jet black and dusty, headlights blinking as somebody keyed the locks.

Then the last Chinese operator appeared from the bottom of the apartment stairs, sprinting for the car. Jacket snapping in the wind, face twisting as he looked back toward the apartment, back toward me.

Blue eyes. A snaking scar. A tiger's snarl.

It was *him*.

I flipped the window latches and grabbed the pane by its lower sill. One heave and the window was up. Sticky Washington air rushed through, filtered by a screen. The tiger reached his car and tore the door open. He was throwing himself inside. The high-performance German engine rumbled to life.

And then I was firing, squeezing off shots straight through the window screen. One, two, six. Bullets slammed into the Mercedes' hood and burst through its grill. The radiator fan rattled against its housing and one headlight shattered. Tires spun and the car started backward, a wisp of blue rubber smoke already rising from the hood. The driver turned. He was halfway out of the parking space, running for his life.

But I was still firing. One zipping-fast pistol-caliber slug after another, slicing out of the second-floor window and striking the car at barely eighty yards. The smoke intensified. The car jolted to a stop, its one remaining headlight flashing.

Then the engine cut off.

I dropped the sub-gun, the bolt locked back over another empty magazine. Spinning on my heel I was fishing through the mess, grasping another suppressed handgun. Thrusting it into my pants and tugging my shirt over it. Rushing out the door, over the bodies. Across the living room and out into the breezeway. Catching sight of my prey as he dashed full-speed across the apartment complex, lunging for freedom.

But I was right on his heels.

24

I wasn't sure exactly when my grand strategy converted from mining evidence against my enemies to gunning them down. Probably somewhere around the moment they yanked the closet door open, ready to gun *me* down.

Whatever the case, the situation had escalated, and I bore zero regret for escalating along with it. By the time I reached the bottom of the stairs I had tightened my belt, cinching the pistol against my stomach in what is colloquially known as a "Mexican carry"—no holster at all. The handgun's safety lever bit into my skin but I didn't care. I barely noticed. I was stretching out my legs and hurtling across the parking lot, past the bullet-ridden Mercedes and past the property office. The club house. The pool. I saw him running with a phone clamped to one ear, and I knew I was almost out of time.

He was calling in backup. He was freaking. His entire universe was flying off the rails—his safe house compromised, his mission blown. Now he needed extraction, he needed QRF, he needed a miracle.

Because bullets aren't impressed by diplomatic immunity.

He reached the road and turned left. I found a rhythm and settled into it, content to gain on him by inches. I'm not a natural sprinter—given the choice, I'd rather swim than run at all. I'd rather pump out a hundred pushups than endure twenty minutes of traditional cardio. But the Army never cared about my preferences. They taught me to run with eighty pounds of junk strapped to my body. To keep going, no matter how badly it burned, no matter how terribly my head hurt or my feet ached or my mind screamed for me to stop.

There is no stopping in the Seventy-Fifth Ranger Regiment. Not until the very last inch of ground is claimed and secured. Whatever the cost, whatever the price, whatever the pain. Rangers lead the way, we said. *All the way.*

I breathed in cycles, matching my footfalls to the cadence of an old running chant in my mind. Remembering boot camp, remembering Ranger School. But most of all, remembering Phoenix. A bright fall day without a cloud in the sky. A chirp on my radio, a call to my fiancée's elementary school. A run I had not completed quite fast enough... and a cost I would bear for the rest of my life.

I would *not* bear that cost a second time.

We were out of the apartment complex and onto a golf course. The tiger tried losing me in a small thicket of trees but I predicted his stunt and circled him, gaining ten yards on his position and still coming strong. I swung wide again and crossed right over a putting green, followed him to a split rail fence with a split four-lane running beyond it— Fairfax Drive. It was chock-full of traffic.

He turned right toward the heart of town. I swung early

and shaved off another five yards. I leapt the fence and landed on my toes, still running. A rush of cars, a semi-truck, and a taxi blazed past. He waved his hand, frantically attempting to hail the cab—but this wasn't New York and cabs in Arlington don't work that way. The car hurtled onward, and the hesitation cost him another yard.

I was almost within shooting distance. Another few strides gained, and I could put a bullet in his spine. I didn't plan to do that—not here, not in front of all these people when my life wasn't directly threatened. But with every inch I gained he could feel me coming. At any moment he might panic himself, he might turn and draw, Old West-style.

I would be ready, regardless. I checked the grip of the captured pistol, my lungs really starting to burn as we reached an intersection and he blasted right across it. A horn honked and the light changed. I reached the same intersection and the cars were flowing across my path—not fast, but thick. They weren't watching for me. The sign across the road displayed a blinking red hand—*do not walk.*

I blinked. I saw Evelyn on the Chesapeake. I saw Evelyn in a hallway. And I kept running.

Horns and locking brakes. I skated past the front bumper of a minivan and lost some ground. A motorcycle locked its front wheel and slid sideways. The rider was laying the bike down at low speed, somehow managing to flip me the bird on his way to the pavement.

Back on the sidewalk at the far side of the street, I was still locked on my prey. One hundred yards, and he was no longer alone. Other pedestrians crowded around, some talking on phones, some pushing baby strollers. Some walking poodle-mix dogs. He was forced to slow, weaving and ducking and placing bodies between himself and me. I no longer had a clear shot even if I wanted it. Within seconds I was also fighting my way through the crowd, fuel stations and small strip malls rapidly evaporating as high-rise apartment towers took their places. We were well outside of downtown Arlington, but already the streets were narrowing. We were hitting intersections more regularly.

And I was losing ground. Inch by inch, not by lack of effort but by the sheer number of obstacles. The Army had taught me how to run, but not along sidewalks packed with innocent civilians. I could only ram ahead, stiff-arming some and sliding around others. Maintaining my pace the best I could even as he hooked a sudden left across the street—not a crosswalk, not even an intersection. Just a hard left.

I broke out of the crowd and followed, ignoring more horns and sliding tires. The next sidewalk was roped off with construction cones and tape, wet cement shining under the street lights. I skidded right to avoid it and found myself running the wrong way up a street full of oncoming traffic. A city bus was just crossing under a pair of swinging traffic lights and its horn thundered, deep and menacing.

I went left, blasting through the tape. Knocking over the cones. My left foot sank two inches in wet cement and the bus rushed by—a flash of glass and an injury lawyer's advertisement. It was gone as quickly as it came and I was back on the concrete, spinning toward my target. He had gained another twenty yards. He was turning left between two twenty-story apartment towers with glistening glass balconies. I rushed after him, turning the corner and crashing through a river of water pouring out of a drainage spout.

It wasn't an alley at all—it was an access drive for a pair of parking garages serving the towers. He could go left or he could go right. Either way he'd be fighting up levels of the garage with nothing waiting for him at the top. The calculation bogged him down for a split moment, his head swiveling, eyes wide.

Then he went straight, and I followed. Past the garages, gaining ground again. On toward the edge of the towers where a one-way street intersected our path. He dashed straight across, continuing down the access drive as it sliced between a pair of squat business complexes. He was only ninety yards out. On the open ground I was gaining again, head pounding and heart slamming. That Ranger cadence echoing over and over in my head.

Don't quit! Don't you dare quit.

I stretched my legs. His figure faded into the shadows between the business buildings, but I didn't lose sight. Zeroed in on him, I reached the edge of the apartment towers. I was one stride away from crossing into the one-way.

Then the engine thundered. Not a roar but a pure howl. Unleashed horsepower snarling through modified exhaust. My head pivoted left even as my right foot dropped into the street. I saw a charcoal-gray flash, the image of a hissing cobra etched into a scarlet-red shield. I recognized the emblem in a cryptical clear millisecond, staring the snake dead in its lifeless eyes.

Then the car hit me. Front bumper to my left leg, brakes locking, engine still surging. I was in the air, rolling left. Slamming into the hood, smacking my head against the sheet metal. Seeing stars. Rolling again, landing on the pavement with a crash of bone against asphalt. Seeing more stars —a blur of a sport rim and a skinny black racing tire. Blood in my mouth and the world spinning.

The car's door opened. A long leg capped by a black

dress shoe stepped out. I tumbled onto my back with a gasp and clawed at my gut, searching for the gun. I could barely see—everything was blurry, every object danced.

A face appeared above mine—only dark eyes and tight lips visible, the rest of the face covered by a ski mask. I found the pistol and wrapped my hand around the grip. A foot crushed down on my right elbow, locking it to the ground. Preventing me from drawing.

Then the face drew near. I jerked once before the bee sting sank into my neck—a bite, a flash of pain.

And then...nothing.

25

I awoke in darkness, but I knew I was awake because the nightmares had finally ceased. An endless sequence of predictable images played on repeat, a movie I could *not* stop watching.

The squeal of police tires on an elementary school parking lot. The click of my side arm snapping free of its holster. The thud of my boot slamming into the school's front entrance.

Then the gunfire, the gunfire. Pistols snapping, a shotgun pumping. Bullets zipping, slicing through the air. One slamming into my shoulder. Blood spraying the wall—I could actually hear it. Little droplets landing like meteors. Splashing in slow motion, echoing in my mind.

I was on the floor. I was stuck in a tidal wave of blood, desperately clawing my way forward. Desperately attempting another shot...

But too late. The shotgun thundered. The body slammed against the hallway wall with a soft thud. Almost an elegant thud.

Everything she did was elegant, like she wasn't even trying. Couldn't even help it.

But when the smoke cleared, when the spray of blood rained down and I could see...it wasn't my late fiancée resting against that wall, rapidly bleeding out.

It was Evelyn. Eyes wide, face twisting toward me. Jaw falling open.

"Why?" she rasped. "Why did you shoot me?"

Then I would blink. The vision began again, back at the car. Back at the squealing tires, the shouting partner, the crackling radio. Another cycle, another repeat. Another overwhelming rush of cortisol and panic and cataclysmic self-hatred...until at last, everything went black.

And then I knew I was awake. I blinked, but I still saw black. I tasted blood, both dry and fresh. I choked on my own breath, my mouth clogged by thick cloth. There was a bag on my head, and when I attempted to turn, my body wouldn't move. Pain erupted in my arms, in my back, in my left leg.

I was strapped in place. Bound, hand and foot. The panic was rising.

Calm down...don't lose control.

I clamped my eyes closed and repeated the directions over and over, blocking out the visions, the premonitions. Leaning on discipline and grit and maybe some real desper-ation. Not because I was afraid of being tied up with a hood over my head—I'd been there before. It all works out, or it doesn't. It might be out of my hands either way.

What really scared me was the vision. Something totally both in the past and now in the present.

Breathe. Just breathe.

My mind calmed very slowly, and my body relaxed.

Focusing on what senses I had left, I noted that I couldn't smell anything—the bag stifled that opportunity. But I could hear, and I thought I heard footsteps. Hard soles against a hard surface, maybe tile, maybe concrete. Swishing pants legs. The sound reminded me of slacks, of suit pants.

The figure was approaching. My return to consciousness had been detected. Now what?

I kept my body relaxed, working my wrists to identify my bonds. They were handcuffs—solid steel, standard police variant. The knowledge brought a little hope to my mind, warmth rushing through my chest. I keep a handcuff key in a hidden compartment of my nylon belt, right at the base of my spine. I'd used it before. I could unlock myself.

My fingers dropped. I felt my jeans, a rough seam. I worked upward...then stopped.

My belt was gone. I felt nothing but empty belt loops, then my shirt. The warmth in my chest faded, and then the footsteps stopped behind me. The room was dead quiet. I froze, half-expecting the muzzle of a gun to rest against my skull.

Instead I felt fingers. Quick, dexterous jerks. A rope untying.

Then the bag was yanked free in a rush. I gasped for fresh air, falling forward against the bonds that held me to a chair. I blinked and I saw concrete, I saw my own tennis shoes, I saw table legs and dirt and a smashed bottle cap.

The footsteps resumed behind me. I hauled my head up just in time to catch a blinding flood of light rushing straight into my face. Everything turned white and I twisted my head away. My mouth was *so* dry. My body ached from head to toe.

But also, I was pissed. I remembered the charcoal-gray muscle car howling out of nowhere. Exploding into me. I could still feel its sheet-metal hood popping beneath the impact of my skull, like the impact of a bowling ball.

Then the roll. The stars. The bee sting.

I turned back to the light, squinting. A figure was seated across a table from me. He—or she—was thin. Dressed in a black jacket with a black ski-mask. Staring and not blinking.

Then the figure raised a hand from their lap, exposing it above the table. A small silver object gleamed in the light. I blinked, my eyes slowly focusing.

It was a handcuff key.

"Looking for this?"

I recognized the voice. The figure set the key on the tabletop. Then he reached up and tugged the mask off, static carrying disheveled hair with it. He tossed it down and ran long fingers through black curls, sweeping them back. Mashing them in place.

He stared at me, jaw locked. Still not blinking. It was Alex Hudson.

"You've made one hell of a mess," he said.

26

The shock—whatever there was of it—was very mild. I sat squinting into the light, staring back at Alex, and not feeling much in the way of surprise that I had been run over, drugged, and abducted by an FBI agent.

It wasn't just because of who this particular FBI agent was, or because of the personal history, however brief, that I shared with him. It wouldn't have surprised me whoever sat in the chair. As both a soldier and a cop, I had all kinds of experience with three-letter federal agencies. I was well familiar with their methods.

And their methods, in my experience, were very pragmatic. Sometimes...very flexible.

"Is this how you make director these days?" I said. "Running over civilians in sports cars?"

Alex didn't answer. He did not smile. After a long minute, he tilted his head.

Then I heard additional footsteps, more claps against

concrete. A shadow appeared to my left. I tensed, attempting to twist.

Alex's cold voice cut me off. "Relax, Superman. It's water."

A straw was thrust into my mouth, and I was instantly reminded how dry my throat was. The water was cool and clean, cascading in a welcome torrent. I sucked until the cup ran dry, and then I was gasping for air.

The second figure walked away, invisible somewhere behind me. Water dripped down my chin and I wanted to wipe it.

It wasn't an option. Now that full consciousness had returned, I could identify additional bonds. Besides the handcuffs there was a strap lashing me to the chair. It was a ratchet strap, I thought—a trucker's tool. Something similar must be holding my legs to the chair legs, because I couldn't so much as twist them.

I was bound fast. Alex Hudson wasn't playing.

"What a story this will be for internal investigations," I said. "Talk about a Fourth Amendment lawsuit—I'll never work again. Seriously, I should be thanking you. I was almost broke."

Alex didn't smile. He didn't look away. Seated behind the glare of the lamp pointed at my face, I could only partially make out his features. Dark eyes, an angry jawline. He was fuming, but more than that, he was wrestling with something. Evaluating me, evaluating his own thoughts. I could sense it.

But I didn't care what his dilemma was. I was angry—livid, in fact. Because I had been *that close* to nailing the blue-eyed tiger. The man who had threatened Evelyn, who had started this whole mess in the first place. He was almost within my grasp when Alex and his howling muscle car turned up, and whatever the story behind his intrusion and my subsequent kidnap was, I didn't care.

Context still didn't matter. Only the objective of protecting Evelyn. Always, *always* protecting Evelyn.

"What is this, Hudson?" I snapped. "You gonna waterboard me? Threaten to dump me in the Chesapeake? Move your light already. I'm tired of squinting."

My tone was cutting. I didn't think Alex was intimidated, but to his credit he backhanded the light, sending it spinning on a swivel away from my face. There was still enough ambient illumination for me to see him, but I no longer had to squint. My eyes blinked back into focus.

"I *told you* not to endanger her," Alex spoke through his teeth.

It wasn't the statement I expected, although I really wasn't sure what to expect. I wasn't entirely sure why I was here, or why Alex was here.

But I was developing an idea. It was coming together in my mind, and Evelyn's security wasn't anything Alex should be worried about.

"Evelyn's safe," I said. "You can rest your faithless little mind about that."

"Safe in a hotel?" Alex said. "Say, the Skyways Inn and Suites in Chantilly? Room three-nineteen?"

I blinked. I couldn't help it, and Alex noticed. A humorless smirk twisted his lips.

"I know exactly what you did with her. I followed you there. I've got two plain-clothed agents on site as we speak."

It made me angry—instantly. Not because anyone was watching over Evelyn, but because *Alex* had put them there.

"You're pretty adept at creeping, aren't you?" I threw the words like a hand grenade. They landed much the same, Alex flinching. "Did you mount cameras in her bathroom, Alex? Did you tap her phone?"

A flush of red. His hand tightened into a fist. Then, very slowly, he lifted that fist. He extended a finger, pointed dead at my face, only inches away. He spoke in a growl.

"You're in a *heap* of trouble. You don't even know it."

"Oh, I know it. I'm quite aware, actually. I was nearly shot to pieces only minutes before you ran me over. Heck of a coincidence, actually. For me to be trailing Chinese covert operators and suddenly run into you. And this isn't the first time, is it?" I lowered my head—I couldn't quite lean forward thanks to the ratchet strap. My voice dropped. "Or do you think I haven't connected the dots between Delafield Place and Rui Huang?"

Again, his jaw tightened, and this time his gaze flicked over my shoulder and into the dark. Toward his comrade, whoever they were. Then back to me.

Alex folded his arms. He seemed to be deliberating again. Maybe warring with something. All the tell-tale signs were there—the pulsating vein in his temple, the clicking teeth.

He was vulnerable, whether he admitted it or not. He'd already lost the initiative in his own interrogation—or whatever this was meant to be. I pounced on the opportunity.

"Here's what's going to happen," I said. "You're going to cut me loose, and then you're going to get lost—you're going to get *out* of my way. If you don't, I'll scream like the loudest canary in the most polluted coal mine there's ever been. Your career will be the least of your concerns by the time I'm finished with you. Fourth Amendment lawsuits? That's just an appetizer. Don't forget, Alex. I know *all about you*. And just like I promised before, I will *bury* you."

Another flex of his jaw. The vein kept pumping, but despite the tension in his face, I couldn't help but notice that none of my threats seemed to be landing. None seemed to distract from his mental debate, whatever it was. He was hearing me—he simply wasn't concerned. All his focus was still bent on whatever conflict was raging in his mind.

I narrowed my eyes, and for the first time I looked away from Alex. I glanced around the room. It was dark—almost pitch black. Some kind of warehouse, I thought. There were vague, oversized shadows in the backdrop. Crates and pallets. Abandoned machinery. One vehicle, maybe an SUV. Two bulky figures leaning against it.

And behind me, one more person. I could sense them even though I couldn't see them. There were multiple witnesses to this little dance, and without any contradictory evidence, I assumed all of them to be Alex's fellow FBI agents.

Yet none of them were twitching. Nobody was running for the door, nobody was interjecting themselves into the conversation, alarmed at my promises of career doom and possible prosecution.

Why?

It was context, I knew it. It was that thing I had been deliberately ignoring for all of the past three days while I pursued my base priority of Evelyn's security. Because the bigger story didn't matter. It wasn't relevant.

Or was it?

I turned back to Alex. He still didn't move or speak. He sat with his arms folded, that vein pulsing in his temple

"What am I missing, here?" I said. "What are you really up to?"

No answer. His lips pursed. Once more he glanced over my shoulder at the individual behind me. Once more he looked back to me.

Then at last, he unfolded his arms. He leaned forward. When he spoke, all the anger was gone from his voice—all the bravado. He was calm.

"I am asking you—I am *entreating* you—for reasons bigger than both of us, you need to go away. Okay? I'm going to let you out of that chair. I'm going to take you to your truck, and then you have to leave. It's not about me, and it's not about you. It's not even about Evelyn. If you love your country, you will do it. Please—do it."

The room fell silent. Alex remained leaned against the table, eyebrows raised, waiting. His words sank in. I measured them against his body language and the veracity checked out. The sincerity, the earnestness was all there. There was nothing contrived or counterfeit about his request, and that last bit—that token about loving my country—struck home. It hit my chest and ignited that ember of patriotism that had carried me through one deployment after another. That had kept my life on the line serving as a cop in Phoenix. That had triggered so many impulsive, reckless decisions in recent years when my country had fallen under threat.

Be it a rural community, a big city ravaged by nature, a governmental conspiracy with American service members as its fodder, I couldn't help but throw myself into the mix. I was a patriot. I always would be.

But even deeper than that, I was Evelyn Landry's man.

Her lover. He protector. *Her* cannon fodder, and I didn't trust Alex Hudson as far as I could throw him.

Once a cheater, always a cheater.

"Not a chance," I said.

27

Alex rose out of his chair at my refusal. He marched out of sight, behind me. Other feet moved on the concrete and a conference was held. I couldn't hear words, only vague whispers. The discussion lasted several minutes. When Alex returned, he looked no less angry—also, no less resolved.

He sat.

"You are putting me in a *very* difficult position."

I grunted. "You can see that it's eating me up."

"You're endangering national security."

Alex's hands rested on the table-top, palms down. I could tell he was fuming—the debate was still there. But I also thought he might be reaching a breaking point.

"So explain," I said.

"What?"

"Explain how my country is being threatened."

"I can't do that."

"Sure you can."

"It's classified."

"And far be it from you to ever break the law."

He flinched. His gaze flicked behind me. My mind worked, filling in the gaps.

Then I decided to throw my cards on the table.

"How about this," I said. "I'll do the talking. You can just nod if I hit the mark."

No answer. I dove in.

"It all began with Rui Huang—this whole mess we're tangled in. I first encountered her on Delafield Place, your home street. She didn't live there. There are no restaurants, no entertainment venues or shopping. Besides, she was walking with purpose—with alarm, even before she knew that she was being followed. My guess? She was headed exactly where I was. To your townhome."

Alex didn't blink. He didn't so much as budge. I kept driving.

"The glaring question, of course, is *why?* A late-night liaison? Another notch for your bedpost?"

They were cheap shots, and they landed hard. The vein in Alex's temple pumped at an escalated tempo. I wasn't sorry.

"Maybe," I said. "But I've got another theory. It all orbits around the fact that Rui Huang was a clerk at the Chinese embassy. A low-level worker. A nobody, perhaps. At least to the Chinese." I lowered my head again, still unable to lean. "But what if she *wasn't* a nobody to the FBI? What if Rui Huang was actually an American asset, a spy buried right in the heart of the Chinese embassy? Maybe you were her handler. Maybe you'd been managing her, mining her for some time. Maybe she was headed to see you, that night, but she didn't quite make it."

Alex was silent. The whole room, in fact, was silent. I

couldn't even hear the other agents—or whatever they were —breathing. I lifted my head again.

"That's why you knew I was a witness to her murder. As soon as you heard that she had been shot, you were at the police station, investigating for yourself. That's also why you turned up in the tank after I was detained for illegal firearm possession...the night that Chinese operators broke into my apartment, attempted to murder me, failed, and then had their botched attempt scrubbed by *other* Chinese operators before the cops arrived. It was a quick, sloppy job. The DC police could have easily obtained witness statements from my neighbors. They could have found blood residue with black lights. They could have held me, but they didn't. Why?"

I raised both eyebrows. Waited. Alex didn't answer. I grunted.

"Because you asked them not to, Alex. You asked them to cut me loose and forget the entire thing. Pretend like it didn't happen, but not for my sake. You asked them to erase the event because you're neck-deep in your own investigation— you're hunting spies, and you can't afford for anybody to upset the apple cart before you finish the job. It's too important, whatever it is. Whatever Rui Huang was informing you about, it's big. It's *a threat to national security.*"

I repeated his words, then relaxed in my chair the best I could within the confines of the ratchet straps. I saw the jigsaw puzzle—the context—complete in my mind and I knew I was right, at least mostly so. The logic was all there, and it wasn't a complex puzzle, anyway. If I had cared, I might have put it all together some time prior.

I only cared now because I was done with Alex's games. Because the longer he kept me in this chair the longer

Evelyn remained at risk, however remote a risk it might be. Any danger was too much danger wherever she was concerned.

"You're a gifted storyteller," Alex said, at last.

"Oh, that's just the prologue. Wait until we meet our hero —a divorced, unscrupulous federal agent with an ax to grind, a mission to complete. He'll stop at nothing to get the job done. Three-letter agents are like that, but this guy is especially uncouth. He doesn't mind kidnapping civilians, drugging them up, tying them to chairs. Whatever it takes. It's a systemic practice with him, actually. There's a whole subplot about his harassment of his ex-wife, but we'll weave that in later. I guess he's not much of a hero, after all. Maybe more of an antihero. The important thing is, like all protagonists, he has a choice to make. And now is when he makes it."

Alex's lips twitched but he didn't answer. He was going to make me say it.

"It's up to you, Alex," I said. "If our country is really in jeopardy, you've got to explain how. I want every detail. I want to understand the problem in full. Otherwise, I'll blow this whole thing up. I'll blow you up, I'll blow your little band of merry men up. And I'll blow your investigation up, also. Because I really don't care about you. I don't care about your agenda. I only care about Evelyn—and in that way, I guess I'm a bit of an antihero myself. I'll do *anything* to protect her. Capisci?"

Alex flushed. "Bold words from a man tied to a chair."

"Indeed. And you're gonna have to keep me tied to this chair, unless you play ball. You're going to need to watch me, every moment, every second. Never take your eyes off me, because I'm slick as snot and—again—I *do not care* about you."

I finished. Alex's vein twitched. He muttered a curse under his breath and looked away...but he didn't get up. He closed his eyes and breathed once. He stooped to retrieve a water bottle and flicked the cap off. One long chug, another protracted moment.

Then he tilted his head. He wasn't looking at me. He was looking at the figure behind me. Footsteps tapped on the concrete, and small hands touched my arms. A key clicked in the handcuffs. The ratchet strap wrapped around my chest constricted, biting into my ribcage.

Then it popped loose, allowing a welcome rush of air into my lungs. My hands were free. I rubbed my wrists and rolled my shoulders. Popped my neck.

The strap around my legs remained in place. It would have been easy enough to disengage by leaning down to access the ratchet, but that would take time.

I couldn't spring up. I couldn't reach Alex. I couldn't run.

Alex tipped his head again, and the figure from behind approached from my side. I glanced up. It was a woman—middle-aged, blonde hair held back in a ponytail, hard gray eyes glaring down at me. She looked somewhat European, specifically Bavarian, with muscled shoulders and a strong jaw. She wore a trademark black FBI pantsuit, and she slammed a bottle of water down on the table without comment.

Then she backed away. I bypassed the water and faced Alex. I raised both eyebrows.

He said, "What do you know about Integrated Battle Networks?"

28

I t wasn't a phrase I was familiar with, but just the question was enough to confirm most of what I had guessed about Alex's investigation—his greater context. I decided to play it cool. "Assume nothing."

A grunt. "You were a soldier."

It wasn't a question, Alex already knew.

"And?" I said.

"You were overseas. You were in combat."

I was. Many times.

"Strategically speaking," Alex said, "what is any military's greatest battlefield challenge?"

This time it *was* a question, and it felt like a sincere one. I took a moment to consider.

"Shooting more of them than they shoot of us," I said.

Alex wasn't amused. "I'm being serious, Sharpe."

"So was I. But if you're looking for a technical answer, I would have to say logistics. Battles are won or lost based solely on moving the right materials, the right supplies, and the right people. All to the right place at the right time with the right information."

"Which is really more of a communications challenge, isn't it?"

I rocked my head. Shrugged. "If you prefer."

"So imagine this. You're downrange with a Ranger squad. Overhead support includes Airforce A-10s and Predator drones. Fifty miles off the coast the Navy has parked three missile boats and an amphibious assault ship. They're deploying Marines via V-22 Ospreys. CIA agents on the ground in your target city are feeding you intel on enemy movements, and strategic command is located in the Pentagon half a planet away. Four military branches, numerous assets and personnel."

"Sounds like a catastrophe waiting to happen," I said.

"So I'm told," Alex said. "Except, now imagine that your helmet is equipped with a headset that flawlessly links you with every other member of the battlefield. Real-time, one-hundred-percent reliable integrations with every soldier, every pilot, every ship commander, every senior Pentagon officer. Camera feeds, targeting data, exact positioning, instant communication. Even health stats—you'd know if a guy was dead or simply down. I'm talking total digital connection. Not just for people, but for machines. Those Predator drones, those A-10s? The pilots don't have to worry about committing friendly fire. Their targeting systems already know where all the friendlies are. The Navy can track the evolution of the entire battlefield on a computer screen, they can deploy Marine reinforcements and cruise missiles with moment-by-moment, pinpoint accuracy. All the most relevant information, all the most granular data.

Instant, accurate, dependable. Total dominance of the battlefield."

I grunted. "Now it sounds like a fantasy."

Alex nodded. He paused a moment longer, sipping his water. Then, "It's not a fantasy. At least...not for long. It's called an Integrated Battle Network. A supercharged digital computer system managed by artificial intelligence and calibrated to serve every combat element, every commander, every fighting machine at once. It's like..."

"A video game," I said.

Alex nodded. "Yes. It makes war look like a video game. Real people. Real weapons. But everything is totally...well, integrated. One cohesive fighting force. Unbeatable."

I pictured it and I knew he was right. I'd spent far too much time being shot at to not be tantalized by the idea. Instant, accurate communication. It was a better weapon than any rifle, any missile. All logistical challenges would be solved, all questions answered in real time.

In theory, anyway. All plans fly to pieces when the first shot is fired. Variables are introduced, the context morphs and evolves. Things go wrong. But still—what better way to overcome those inevitable challenges than with full, comprehensive communication? Total integration of every branch, every asset. It was indeed a fantasy.

And yet, I saw the problem. It hit me as soon as I retracted my mind away from a fictitious, futuristic battlefield and back to the present. This warehouse, this chair I was tied to, this FBI agent I was confronting.

And the Chinese.

"We have it," I said. "Or we almost have it, and the Chinese are trying to steal it."

Alex didn't answer.

"Rui Huang was monitoring the Chinese espionage efforts," I continued. "She was informing the FBI on their progress. There was some kind of bigger strategy at play. Some reason why you wouldn't or couldn't simply sabotage the Chinese operation. Something that you needed more information on..."

I trailed off. I squinted.

And then I saw it.

"There's another double agent," I said, looking up. "An American selling secrets to the Chinese. There's a leak someplace inside the Department of Defense, or whoever is developing this thing. It's somebody you haven't identified. Rui was helping you find him."

Still, Alex didn't answer. He sat with his arms folded, neither confirming nor denying, playing that age-old secret agent game.

But I knew I was right.

"The Chinese identified Rui before you could identify the American leak," I said. "The night she was killed, she knew she had been busted. That's why she was so agitated, even before she knew she was being followed. They shot her, but they knew that I was a witness. They came after me because of it, and even when I entrapped them at the Sleepy Days Inn, their government bailed them out. Declared their activities official and leveraged diplomatic immunity... because Beijing *can't* be caught. This mission is far too important."

I finished, staring at Alex. He studied me a long time, then said calmly, "You're a great storyteller."

I muttered a curse. "Stories, my ass. Am I right or wrong?"

"You know I can't answer that."

"So I'm right."

"I can neither confirm nor deny." Alex jabbed the table with one index finger, very purposefully. "But let's suppose, just hypothetically, that you're right. Do you understand now? Finally?"

I did understand. I understood why Alex had been aware of my involvement with Rui Huang's death from the start. Why he had turned up at the police station the night I was taken in for gun charges. Why, no matter which way I turned, I always seemed to collide with him.

I even understood why he had hit me with the car. Why I was here.

"You didn't want me killing that guy," I said. "The guy with the scarred face."

"Why not?" Alex prompted.

"You tell me."

He cocked an eyebrow. I considered again, staring at the table. I found the answer.

"Everything's flying off the rails. It started when the Chinese busted Rui. They know that the FBI is onto them, maybe close on their heels. But they still haven't pulled the plug on their operation—they're scrambling to finish the job, which means you're scrambling to get ahead of them. Everything has escalated. You're without an informant..."

I looked up. "So now you're tracking the Chinese operators directly, hoping they'll lead you to the American leak. You're working hard not to spook these guys any further, because if they pull the plug now, you're back to square one. Starting from scratch. You might never find the leak."

Alex grunted. "And what spooks a covert agent more than a gunfight in his own apartment?"

I heard him, but I wasn't really listening. I was thinking,

again. Twisting the parts in my mind, finally acknowledging the greater context and reaching another inevitable, crushing conclusion.

This wasn't about me anymore. It wasn't even about Evelyn. Much as I hated him for it, Alex was right. The situation was far bigger, the stakes much higher. If Alex's fantasy description of next-generation battlefield communications technology was anything close to a real possibility, the prospect of that technology falling into the hands of America's greatest political, economic, and—ultimately—military rival was blatantly catastrophic.

Best case scenario, both our armed forces and theirs were similarly equipped, which minimized the advantages of the tech in the first place. Worst case scenario, they ripped off our developments and implemented it into their military ahead of us...in which case the balance of power would dramatically shift in their favor.

It was, indeed, a nightmare scenario. The People's Liberation Army, totally integrated. China knowing all...just the way the tiger had said. It would be a massive win for our adversary—certainly large enough an advantage to justify the risk of a highly dangerous espionage operation. A cost-benefit analysis had been performed, and the Chinese had clearly made their choice. They wanted this tech, and if they obtained it, the results could be potentially apocalyptic.

All of that logic left me with only one relevant question. The question that Alex must be asking himself—the question all his bosses were asking.

How do we stop them?

Nothing else mattered. Not the death of Rui Huang, not the petty gun charges the DC cops could have leveled against me, or even the prospect of proving that Chinese agents had attempted to murder an American civilian in his own apartment. None of those details were significant. They were all small potatoes.

The *only* thing that mattered was identifying and plugging the American leak before it was too late. It was the only way to protect America, and what was more, it was the only way to protect Evelyn. Because I could keep dodging bullets, I could keep playing cat-and-mouse. But unless I was willing to abandon DC and abandon Evelyn with it—which wasn't happening—this problem would never fade away.

It had to be confronted, once and for all.

"I'm going to help you," I said, still looking at the tabletop. Mind still spinning.

"Excuse me?"

"You're clearly floundering. I'm going to assist."

Somebody snorted—it wasn't Alex, it was the female agent standing behind him. I ignored her, focusing on Alex instead. He was the boss, right?

"I'm not asking," I said. "I'm entangled in this now, for better or worse, and so long as I'm entangled, Evelyn is entangled. So whatever we've got to do to shut this thing down, I'm in for it."

Alex cursed. "Seriously? All that information—and that's your takeaway?"

"What did you expect me to say?"

"I didn't expect you to say anything. I expected you to climb back into that beater truck and *leave*."

"Wouldn't that be nice? But it's not an option. So either you can accept my help or you can accept my vigilante efforts. Knowing what I know, I might have a better shot at resolving this without you anyway. But then I'm on the outside, in the shadows. Who knows what apple carts I might topple?"

"Are you threatening me?"

"I don't know. Do you feel threatened?"

"Obstructing an investigation is—"

"Only a crime if an investigation is underway. Feel free to charge me whenever you'd like to acknowledge the investigation."

It was checkmate, and the twitch of that vein in Alex's temple told me that he knew it. Maybe he was wishing he'd never taken the bag off my head. That he had wrapped my body in a chain and dumped me into the Chesapeake.

Now I was a problem, and I'm not above exploiting myself as a problem.

"Hey. Jackass." It was the female agent. The voice was all Boston, all venom. "We don't *want* your help."

"Well, that's good," I said. "Because frankly, I don't want to help you. I need to help you, and you seem to need the help."

Alex stood. He grabbed the handcuffs from the tabletop.

"We're taking you back to DC. I'll rescind my request and have them charge you with illegal firearm possession. You'll spend the next six months selecting a prison wife."

I actually laughed. "Sounds great. You know, you get a phone call when you go to jail. Guess whom I'm going to call? The first newspaper I can think of, because *boy* do I have a story for them. Then I might bribe the jailer into a second call. I might call your bosses. I might call a congressman. Heck, I might call Hollywood. This could be a blockbuster!"

Alex slammed his hand against the table. The cuffs rattled, his mouth opened. Before he could speak, I was on my feet. My lower legs were still lashed to the chair, but I could stand, and as I did both the agents in the background and the stocky blonde woman moved at once.

Guns drawn. Closing in on me. But I was only focused on Alex.

"It's your choice, Alex. You cut me loose and I go right back to burning this town down. You lock me up and I blow your cover. Your only chance at maintaining any semblance of control is to work with me—do that, or shoot me in the head now."

I waited. Alex's hands trembled against the tabletop—the table trembled beneath him. He spoke in a growl.

"You are *endangering* your country."

"No, Alex. *You are.* I didn't make this mess, and I didn't dump Evelyn into the middle of it. There's no chance I'm going to entrust her life to the man who already betrayed her. I'm right in the middle of this, and I'm not leaving. So *deal with it.*"

I finished. Alex stared. His teeth were bared behind his lips like he was some kind of animal, his gaze fixated on me.

Then he shoved off the table. He turned for the distant shadow of the parked SUV, jerking his head at his associates. All the FBI people gathered for another conference, guns lowered but still drawn. I resumed my seat, watching them for a time.

Then looking away. Stooping to untie my legs and toss the strap away. Relaxing into the chair with a sigh and closing my eyes. My blood pressure was up—way up. But I had a pretty good idea what would happen next, and I needed to be ready for it. I needed a plan.

So I focused. I started back at the beginning and retraced the trail of my involvement in this web of chaos, stopping not at Rui's body or my own attempted murder, but at the convenience store. The one in Petworth with the overweight clerk behind the bulletproof glass.

The place where I had broken through when the FBI couldn't. The ace up my sleeve.

Five full minutes passed before Alex returned. When he did, his people came with them. They circled the table, facing me down. One woman and three men, counting Alex. Nobody spoke. They all looked like they wanted to strangle me.

"We're wasting time, Alex," I said.

He folded his arms. Breathed once. Then, "Pretend I'm a child. Explain to me just exactly how a vagrant bum is supposed to identify a leak the FBI can't find."

It was a good question. Luckily, I was ready with an answer.

"This new technology—the Integrated Battle Network."

"IBN," Alex said.

"IBN, right. It's being developed by the DOD?"

A hesitation. Then, "Yes."

"Third party contractors. DOD budget, DOD oversight."

"Yes."

"So the department that's managing the project would be located at the Pentagon."

"Maybe."

I raised my eyebrows. Alex sighed.

"Yes."

I nodded. I considered. Then I indulged in a tight smile.

"Well, then. I think I can help you."

29

"That will never work."

It was the woman who spoke—Special Agent Linda Kirsch, second in command of Alex's four-man task force. The other two members—the two men who stood in the shadows—neither spoke nor smiled nor interacted in any way. They just stood behind Alex and Kirsch, gazes locked on me, rarely blinking.

Like *The Shining* twins.

"So it doesn't work," I said, kicked back in my chair. "In that case you're no worse off than before, and I'll be the one carted off in handcuffs. Sounds like a petty risk to me."

Using a notepad and a pen, I had already sketched out my plan in basic bullet points, talking the special agents through my logic at each phase. The resulting list was very short, because it was a simple plan. Exactly the way I liked it.

"If we send him in there, he could spook the leak," Kirsch protested. "The guy could split."

"Or girl," I challenged, adding a smirk. Kirsch was not amused.

"Linda's right," Alex said. "If you spook this guy the game is up. He disappears. We never know how the information is leaking, or what other Chinese moles there may be. It's an all-or-nothing gamble—exactly what we've been trying to avoid this whole time."

"And where has that caution brought you?" I said. "Nowhere, Alex. With less time and fewer options. Treading water now is no better than rolling the dice and losing. The Chinese still collect their intelligence and your leak still disappears. Maybe he—or she—resurfaces two years from now in another department. Another critical intelligence breach."

I tossed my pen down. "Look. I don't pretend that it's a perfect idea. It's just the best option at hand. Clearly better than anything you've come up with."

"What's to stop you from being recognized?" It was Kirsch again. "The Chinese know your face. They could warn their double agent to be on the lookout."

"They could," I admitted. "But they won't, because that might spook him and spoil the good thing they've got going. It's too great a risk for them."

"So why can't one of us do it?" Kirsch continued. "Why does it have to be you?"

"Two reasons. First, because the Chinese already know that the FBI is hunting them, and the double agent probably expects that, as well. It would be very difficult and needlessly time consuming to attempt to mask any one of your FBI service records. One slipup, one forgotten document or one mutual acquaintance calling your name, and your cover would be blown, and this traitor is in the wind. Game over."

Kirsch gritted her teeth. "And second?"

"Second. Are any of you ex-military?"

No answer.

"Do you know how to salute?" I continued. "Know how to walk like a solider? What your back story is, what unit you served with, what installations you received training at? What MRE's taste like and what little candy packets they come with?"

Still no answer. I raised both hands, palm up.

"I rest my case. Once again you're busted in thirty seconds. It's got to be me."

I collected the pen again and wrote down a series of numbers on the pad. I finished, capped the pen, and stood.

"What's that?" Alex demanded.

"My sizes," I said. "ASUs, brand new. Have them pressed and the shoes shined. Make sure your DOD contact doesn't skimp on the paperwork."

I turned for the warehouse door, beyond the parked SUV. It hurt to walk—my head ached from the drugs Alex had injected me with, and my legs and hip ached from the collision of his muscle car with my unprotected body. But I wasn't about to let them see me in pain. I glided like a figure skater on freshly resurfaced ice.

"Wait!" Alex shouted, his voice echoing off the metal walls. "Where do you think you're going?"

I stopped. Looked back over one shoulder. Stared him in the eye.

"I'm going to check on my girlfriend."

MY PHONE, wallet, lock picks, Victorinox, MacroStream, and the keys to the rented Camry were all in the back seat of the FBI SUV—another black government Suburban. I collected them without permission and exited the building to find a black sky overhanging a gravel lot. Chain-link fences, rusted and sagging, enclosed the property on three sides. A gravel road provided access and egress, and the slow black snake of the Potomac River washed out into the Chesapeake Bay behind the warehouse. I could see the lights of DC some way beyond it, which meant I was still in Virginia. Someplace on the old industrial waterfront outside of Arlington, I thought.

I checked Google Maps on my phone, and I was right. The city lay southeast of my position, not all that far away. Well within cab range, certainly, but I elected to get a mile or two down the road before I called for any transport.

Alex and his buddies were still inside the warehouse, probably still deliberating. Perhaps there was an open argument. Maybe *The Shining* twins had found their voices. When the dust settled and the score was tallied, who knew what the final decision might be? Maybe Kirsch would talk Alex out of it. Maybe *The Shining* twins would cast their votes in favor of my audacious plan.

Whatever the case, it truly didn't matter to me. Alex had my number. He would either call to arrange a meetup or I would do what I promised I would do. I would go back to work against the Chinese, and he could deal with the fallout.

I walked over a mile to a convenience store and washed down two doses of extra-strength painkillers with a liter of water while I waited for my cab. Then I rode silently in the back seat, enduring full body aches and wondering why I hadn't driven Alex's nose into the tabletop for smashing me with his muscle car. Just looking into his dark, angry eyes, I couldn't help but recount Evelyn's side of their story. At least, as much of it as she had shared.

You know what they say about track runners? They get around.

I knew only general details of Alex's infidelity, but the pain of his treachery was evident enough in Evelyn's eyes, and still somewhat fresh. They'd only been divorced a short time when she and I reconnected in Iowa. I put myself in his shoes, and I wondered how any man could have discarded her so easily.

But really, wasn't that the rub? It was the part of Evelyn and Alex's story that didn't make sense to me, because Alex had clearly *not* discarded her. He was closer to obsessed than flippant. I could see the desperation in his eyes as clearly as I could see the pain in Evelyn's.

He wanted her back. Maybe he wanted control, something I'd seen before in all the worst sorts of men. The thought of that sort of obsession levied against Evelyn brought me full circle, back to Delafield Place. Back to a late night marching up to a townhome with a Clemson Tigers flag flapping out front...ready to kick some ass.

"Here you go!" The cab's brakes squealed. I paid him and stepped out at the apartment complex where I had confronted the Chinese. From beyond the gate blue police lights blinked—people were gathered by the clubhouse, pointing at the gun-blasted unit. The Mercedes sedan was gone, already towed. Yellow crime tape marked the bottom of the stairwell.

A full investigation was underway, it seemed. I reflected on the sequence of events leading up to my pursuit of the tiger, and remembered that I had removed the borrowed gloves *before* the gunfight, meaning that I had no doubt left fingerprints at the scene.

Would that be enough to charge me with conspiracy to

commit treason? With breaking and entering, manslaughter, or even homicide?

Maybe. If the next phase of my evolving plan was successful, perhaps Alex would be willing to pull some more strings and erase those problems—or perhaps he would lean into an opportunity to burn me. Regardless, I wasn't worried. What was the point?

I only wanted to see Evelyn again. To know she was safe. All other concerns could take a back seat.

I collected the rented Camry and headed south for Chantilly, making a brief pit stop at a grocery store along the way for a bouquet of flowers and a bottle of wine. I reached the Skyways Inn and Suites and parked in back, out of sight. I took a moment to straighten my clothes and run my fingers through my hair, using the visor mirror to check my appearance.

It wasn't great, but the painkillers had finally kicked in and my body was somewhat loose. I could resist limping.

I headed for her hotel room.

30

J ust standing outside Evelyn's door was enough to get my heart thumping a little faster. Flowers clutched tight, wine riding my arm like a football, I paused next to the little plastic sign that read *Room 319,* and the walls around me morphed in my mind. The doors became classroom doors. The floor no longer carpet, but tile. If I blinked, I saw the blood. My chest tightened.

And then I forced it all away, a wash of relief taking its place as I remembered and believed that this was not Phoenix, and I wouldn't let it become Phoenix.

I knocked. Moments passed. The latch slid.

Evelyn tugged the door open, standing in a bathrobe knotted tight around her waist, damp hair pulled back over her shoulders, face bright and clean without a trace of makeup—and all the more beautiful.

I smiled. She did not. She simply stared a long moment, gaze passing over the flowers and wine...then she stepped back, allowing me to enter.

The warmth in my chest cooled a little. I wasn't sure why

—something was wrong. She'd always smiled when she saw me before. Usually, she would throw her arms around my neck. Kiss me like we were both seventeen and this was the first time and it was going to last forever.

She didn't look angry, now. She didn't look cold. She simply looked...troubled.

By the time I reached the middle of the room the riddle was solved. The TV was muted, but a local newscast played. The camera feed displayed an apartment complex. Blinking blue lights, crime scene tape. A lot of cops.

The door closed behind us, but Evelyn remained out of sight. I turned back to find her standing with her arms crossed, eyebrows arched in a question.

I lowered the flowers but kept silent. What was I supposed to say, anyway? *Yeah, I shot up an apartment complex?*

"You promised me no shenanigans," Evelyn said. She didn't quite sound angry. More alarmed, maybe indignant.

"I promised to keep you safe," I said. "Six years ago, in Africa. I'm still keeping that promise."

"By shooting up the suburbs?" Evelyn jabbed a finger at the TV. I didn't answer, and she cursed. She collected the remote and switched off the newscast. She walked straight to the tinted window overlooking the parking lot and stood with her back to me.

I laid the flowers and wine down. I circled the foot of the bed and approached from behind. I touched her shoulder.

She didn't flinch. She didn't soften, either.

"I was jumped," I said. "I defended myself. That's all."

"Did you tell the police?"

"I told the FBI," I said. "They're sorting it out."

A long moment. Evelyn breathed deep...then she

relaxed, if only a little. She turned, head rocking back. Peering at me with wide, unblinking green eyes. I saw questions swirling there, but not doubt. I leaned down and I kissed her, and she kissed me back, and I held her close. She pressed her face against my chest and I ran my arms around her back. I thought I could stand all night in front of that window and not care. Never grow tired just as long as she was near.

"Did you...put on cologne?"

The question caught me off guard. I frowned. "No..."

Evelyn turned stiff again. She pulled away, frowning and staring at my wrinkled shirt.

"What is it?" I said.

She shook her head. Smiled at me—but not quite in the same way. Released me.

"I'm hungry," she said. "Let's order something."

Evelyn stepped around the bed, running fingers through still-damp hair. I could feel the disconnect, a sort of vague distance that I hadn't before, as though I were being held at arm's length.

I glanced down my shirt, brushing at some of the stains. Sweat, maybe a little blood...probably not my own.

Why hadn't I stopped by a Walmart to buy new clothes? *Stupid.*

Evelyn settled into a chair in front of the little hotel room desk. Her computer was there—notebooks and headphones, all her work stuff. She stared at them, gently picking at the edge of the desktop with one thumbnail. She seemed lost in thought.

Give her space, Mason.

I circled the bed and opened the nightstand drawer. There was a Gideon's Bible there, along with a menu of takeout places near the hotel. I scanned the selection, and my gaze landed on *Shanghai Palace*. I couldn't help but be amused by the irony.

"Want some Chinese?" I asked, glancing up.

Evelyn flinched. She looked back at me, but didn't answer. I lowered the menu.

"What's wrong?" I said.

No answer. She stared.

"Evelyn. Talk to me."

"Who did you see?" she asked.

"What?"

"At the FBI. Who did you see?"

My chest tightened. I tapped the edge of the menu against my leg, considering. I already knew I had delayed too long.

"I don't know all their names," I said. "Somebody named Kirsch."

"And Alex?"

The bomb landed. Evelyn swiveled in the chair, still fixated on me, gaze searching mine as though she could read my soul.

"Why would I see Alex?" I evaded.

"Why would you smell like him?" she said.

"What?"

"That's his cologne," she said, pointing at my chest. "He always wore it...I'd almost forgotten."

I squinted, genuinely confused. My thoughts raced backwards.

Then I remembered the muscle car. The moment my head smacked the pavement. How Alex had injected me with a sedative...then probably dragged me into his passenger seat. Body to body.

Enough to rub off some cologne, assuming he wore a lot of it.

I tossed the menu back into the still-open drawer. "Yes. I saw Alex."

"Why?" The question was sharp and demanding.

"It's complicated," I said.

"I have a doctorate," Evelyn snapped. "Try me."

I ran my tongue over my teeth, buying time and wondering what I could actually say—what I wanted to say. I didn't have all the facts. I only knew my part in them...and I knew Evelyn wouldn't like it.

"He's investigating an espionage case," I said. "I'm...involved."

"Involved *how?*"

I searched the pain in her eyes. The betrayal was undeniable. She *wanted* to trust me, but her guard was up like I'd never seen it.

"Evelyn..." I started.

"No." She raised a finger. "Don't you *Evelyn* me. I don't deal with men hiding things—I've been there before, remember?"

"This isn't like that."

"So *explain it to me*," she said. "Tell me the truth."

I hesitated again. I put myself in her shoes and I imagined what she might be feeling. The panic boiling toward paranoia—not at all unjustified. The scars of the past shaping present reactions, present judgement.

I understood. I had a few such experiences myself—one in particular. It was a reality I would not, *could not* relive. A line in the sand of my own, as unbendable, unbreakable as solid titanium. No exceptions. No compromise.

Not even here, in Room 319. Because if I explained to

Evelyn now, she would try to stop me. She would be involved also—any smart, self-respecting woman would be. She would be even deeper in danger.

I couldn't allow that.

"I can't explain," I said. "I need you to trust me."

I knew as soon as I spoke how the words would land, and I wasn't wrong. Evelyn's lips tightened. She stared a long time, not blinking, eyes growing red.

I thought she might cry. I wanted to rush across the room and hold her. To tell her that it would all be okay, that she would understand. I just couldn't explain now.

But I didn't, because she wasn't a child. She had her own choice to make, and pretty soon...she made it.

"You should leave," she said.

I winced. "Evie...please don't—"

"Don't call me that," she snapped.

My lips parted and I sat temporarily frozen, the breath sticking in my lungs. Then I simply closed my mouth. There was nothing to say—that line could still not be crossed.

I rose, leaving the flowers and wine where they lay.

"I love you," I said. "And I would never betray you."

Evelyn didn't answer. She was looking away, staring at the wall. I saw the tears gathering in her eyes, but she held them back. She was too strong, had too much pride.

And I loved her all the more for it.

"Sleep well," I said. "I'll call you in the morning."

Then I left, half-expecting her to call after me before I reached the door. Mentally begging for it.

But Evelyn had her own line, and she didn't cross it. I left the hotel and returned to the Camry, identifying both of Alex's plainclothes FBI agents as I did. They were sat in two separate unmarked black Fords, watching the hotel from opposing angles, speaking into radios as I passed.

Reporting my presence, no doubt. To each other and likely to Alex. My date night had run decidedly short—Alex should be pleased.

I threw the car into drive and spun out of the parking lot, turning north but not really knowing—or caring—where I was headed. It didn't even matter.

I could only think of Evelyn and how I had hurt her. With every passing mile traffic and road signs blurred out of my peripheral, and I cursed myself a little harder—my stupid, *stupid* self.

Why had I been in Petworth that night? Why couldn't I have gone just half an hour, just ten minutes later? Being there the moment Rui Huang arrived hadn't saved her life. It hadn't done anyone any good.

It had only endangered Evelyn in the end.

From my pocket the intrusion of an electronic buzz broke my stream of self-hatred. I drew the phone, hoping to find Evelyn's name but knowing I wouldn't. I found a blocked number instead, and my heart instantly thumped a beat faster. I looked over my shoulder, checking the vehicle behind me and half-expecting to see a jet-black Mercedes. I found a motorcycle instead, a fat guy on a Harley, his braided beard thrashed by the wind.

He didn't seem to be in a hurry. I changed lanes and he didn't follow.

The phone buzzed again, and my jaw tightened. I mashed the answer button.

"Hello?"

Long pause. Breath whispered on the other end of the line, a low rustle between teeth. Angry, clenched teeth, I thought. It was just a mental picture, just a guess—but I could imagine that long, snaking scar shining with agitated sweat.

"You killed two of my men."

It was the same voice as before. Perfect English with a light accent. No shortage of controlled rage.

"Only because I couldn't kill three," I snapped back.

A dry laugh. It took me by surprise—it was cold, like dead leaves skating over a sidewalk, but genuinely amused at the same time. Authentically sadistic.

"I'm going to find you," the voice said. "I'm going to find your woman. And when I do, I'm going to tie her to a chair. I'm going to take out my knife—it's a very sharp knife. Have you heard of *lingchi*?"

I had, and the mental picture was enough to make me sick. I kept myself together.

"Death by a thousand cuts," I said, flatly.

Again with the concrete laugh. "Yes. A thousand slow, agonizing cuts. *On your woman.*"

My hand tightened around the steering wheel. I wasn't blinking, but I was seeing the hallway again. I was seeing blood.

"That's so very Chinese of you," I said. "Now it's my turn. How do you feel about eighteen-wheelers?"

Pause. No answer. His rhythmic breathing stopped.

"It's a ten-ton American truck," I said. "And I'm going to flatten you with one."

I hung up.

31

I was blazing up I-395 as I ended the call, running hot straight across the Potomac and into Washington. I saw red—everything was red. The passing Washington Monument, the National Mall and the Capitol—just an endless landscape of bloody crimson as I drove with both hands wrapped tight around the wheel, pushed the rental well beyond the speed limit.

I was begging a cop to pull me over. I wanted the confrontation. I wanted somebody to yell at, even if they didn't deserve it. I wanted *something* to focus the frustration boiling in my chest against, however irrational that desire might be.

Most of all, I wanted a semi-truck and a blue-eyed Chinese tiger to crush with it. But no confrontation came my way that night. I made it all the way across DC and into Maryland without attracting police attention—a once-in-a-lifetime miracle, but such was my luck. I selected a random exit and dove into the community of Bladensburg, finally slowing as a knot of traffic mired my path.

I saw lights—blue and red, blinking slowly. There was an ambulance, a firetruck. An SUV with a caved-in driver's side.

And in the ditch, turned over on its roof...a black Toyota Camry. A few years older than my rental, and not a rental at all. There was a sticker on the rear bumper, visible under the glow of my headlights.

My Daughter is an Honor Student.

The windshield of the car was smashed in, all the airbags deployed. The driver's door was gone—torn off, with the mangled tooth marks of the jaws of life left behind. I could see the driver's seat inside, but there was no occupant.

The driver had been moved. He now lay on a stretcher just behind an ambulance. Paramedics were gathered around it, but nobody was tending to him. Only one figure crowded close, a young woman with tangled brown hair and a six-month baby bump. She leaned over the stretcher, sobbing. Screaming. Holding the limp body...

And receiving no answer.

I sat at the end of a line of cars, one foot on the brake, hands trembling as I released the wheel. I rolled them, looking into my palms. Noting grit and dried blood. Scratches from my collision with the asphalt after being hit by Alex's car.

My hands were shaking. Not badly, just a tremble, fingers aching as I opened and closed them. I realized my throat was dry, and I swallowed. I looked back to the ambulance.

I felt that woman's pain as though it were an iron rod stabbing through my chest. Instant, overwhelming, miserable. It thrust with a lot of reality, a lot of sudden and undeniable clarity. Like ice water to the face.

What's wrong with you, Mason? You're falling apart.

A sharp tap on my window jarred me out of the trance. I

looked left to find a Maryland State Trooper leaned low next to my car, tapping the window with a flashlight.

"Hey! Get it moving. You're blocking traffic."

He pointed and I dropped my foot off the brake. Glass crunched beneath my tires as I passed the smashed SUV— the best I could tell, that vehicle had pulled in front of the overturned Toyota. The dead guy had been in his lane, just doing his thing. Maybe headed home to see his honor-student daughter.

And then, just like that, it was all over. One lapse of focus. An eternal cost.

I passed the wreck and shook my head, hard. I jarred the rasping concrete laugh out of my mind, the betrayal in Evelyn's eyes, the rage clouding my own. I cleared it all, forcing it back. Bottling up anger with more anger.

Regaining control by brute force, because brute force had never failed me, and it wouldn't fail me now. I breathed deep and thought past the fog of emotional distractions to what actually mattered—the moment of focus that I could not afford to compromise.

I was running short on time, yes. Evelyn would leave the hotel soon, maybe tonight.

But if she did, Alex would know and his people would follow. There was nothing else I could do for Evelyn at the moment, and little I could do to target the blue-eyed tiger who haunted my cell phone. In the morning, I might rendezvous with Alex and embark on my admittedly reckless scheme. Alternatively, Alex might ditch me. I might be back on my own, hunting like I'd hunted before.

Whatever the case, both realities lay beyond the sunrise. For the moment, I needed rest, I needed food, and I needed to regain my edge.

I swung through a fast-food drive-through before selecting a cheap motel half a mile off the highway. A hot shower with a washcloth to my face and hands removed much of the grime I had accumulated. A stale burger and fries helped to calm my stomach and relax my body. The bed sagged and creaked under my tense muscles, offering a view of a water-stained ceiling crisscrossed by hairline cracks.

The parking lot outside wasn't quite silent. Somebody was playing country music on a radio. Two old friends, deep into a case of beer, were swapping war stories. One told a joke, the other howled in laughter.

It was the sound of blue-collar Americana. No fancy bellmen in white gloves. No sommeliers with six-page wine menus. Just long weeks and longer nights.

The cadence eased me to sleep, the visions of doom blocked out of my mind until my phone rang at just past seven a.m. I didn't recognize the number, but it wasn't blocked either. The area code was 202—Washington DC.

I placed my feet on the floor. I ran a hand over my face, rubbing my burning eyes.

"Hello?"

The voice that answered was familiar. It was Linda Kirsch.

"Ready to go to work, jackass?"

———

32

My rendezvous point with Alex's task force was the Crystal Gateway Marriott, located directly adjacent to Ronald Reagan International Airport on the Virginia side of the Potomac River. Not far from the warehouse where I had originally been detained in Arlington, but a great deal nicer an accommodation. I managed the drive in just under fifty minutes and pulled the Camry into the lot at nine a.m. on the dot.

I did not bring the coffee and donuts that Kirsch had demanded. I wasn't an errand boy, and despite my proposal of a partnership with Alex's team, I didn't want there to be any illusions about the balance of power. Even as we launched my proposed operation, I would keep one eye on an exit, one foot out the door. If things turned sideways or if I sniffed the first hint of treachery from Alex and his team, I would be gone.

I wouldn't let anything or anyone compromise my core objective of protecting Evelyn.

As I climbed from the Camry I looked down the sidewalk

to a slot marked *Elite Parking*, and noted a familiar charcoal-black silhouette resting right against the curb. Long in the nose and short in the trunk, the car hugged the ground with a low-slung body riding over glossy wheels. Twin, matte-black racing stripes streaked from the front bumper to the rear, fire-red pinstripes racing along their outside edges. The black plastic chin spoiler, hovering only inches over the ground, was stamped with the word "SHELBY", right in the middle. A cobra emblem etched into a bright crimson shield was mounted to the passenger's side of the grill, the head-lights narrow and angry as they stared out over the sidewalk. Like a squinting, snarling beast, at rest but far from asleep.

It was one of Ford's Shelby GT350 models, a late model variant of the Mustang equipped with a naturally aspirated 5.2L engine producing something north of five hundred horsepower…a truly insane number. I remembered the car from when it was announced only a few years prior. Gener-ally more of a truck guy, I was nonetheless enticed by the aggressive curves and angular edges, to say nothing of the sound.

What I was most fascinated with now, however, was neither the curves nor the edges. It was the ass-sized dent smashed between the racing stripes, right in the middle of the hood. Like a turd planted on a wedding cake, both grotesque and impossible to ignore.

It made me smile.

I ascended to the eighth floor as instructed, locating the correct room number by memory. Dirty breakfast trays resting on the carpet outside—enough for a small crowd.

Apparently, nobody was waiting for donuts.

I knocked. I stood back from the peep hole. The latch smacked, and the door swung open.

Special Agent Linda Kirsch stood just inside, looking precisely as she had the night prior. Narrow eyes, blonde hair tugged back into an aggressively tight ponytail. A strong jaw closed tight, a gray pantsuit wrapped snuggly around muscled shoulders.

And a glare hot enough to melt granite.

"Top of the morning to you, Agent."

I shoved past Kirsch without awaiting permission, entering a suite that was much as I expected. A wide living area with two couches, a dinner table laden with a garment bag, a minibar cluttered by multiple empty beer cans, and two doors leading to bedrooms.

I stopped alongside one couch and swept my gaze across the occupants. *The Shining* twins from the warehouse were there, both standing against the wall with coffee cups in their hands, neither drinking nor speaking. Then there was a new guy dressed in a plain black suit, same as the FBI agents, but he wasn't FBI. He wasn't a civilian either. I could tell that by his bearing, by the way he stood stiff-backed, chin up. His attire was cheap, but it fit better than the others. There was more attention to detail in the centering of his gig line and the perfectly symmetrical knots of his shoelaces.

He was military, or ex-military. And he was not happy to see me.

I shoved my hands into my pockets, sweeping my gaze toward the bedrooms, looking for Alex. The flush of a distant toilet was followed by a belt buckle clinking. Then a sink running.

Alex appeared, missing his jacket and tie, running one hand through his hair. Looking young and vibrant compared to the others, but no more enthused by my presence. He stopped just inside the living area and for a long moment nobody spoke. It was as though a film had been frozen, and everybody was just waiting for the tension to break.

I decided to break it.

"You guys ready or what?"

Alex glanced left, toward the newcomer. For his part, the military guy just eyeballed me, sweeping me head to toe. Then he shook his head.

"This'll never work. He looks like a bum."

"That's because I'm dressed like a bum."

"Maybe you *are* a bum," Kirsch interjected.

"Maybe I'd like to kick your bum," I retorted.

Kirsch bristled. Alex snapped his fingers. "Enough."

The room fell silent again. Alex approached me, folding his arms. We stood toe to toe, not speaking. I endured the scrutiny without comment, hands remaining in my pockets.

Still one foot out the door.

"I'm the youngest agent here," Alex said.

"Good for you."

"Do you know why I'm in charge?" Alex pressed.

I shrugged. "Because you're a clever cheat?"

He flushed. His jaw worked. He leaned an inch closer. "Because I am *very* good at my job. The best in my section— and it's not close."

Another protracted stare. I continued to stare back. Then Alex broke away and walked to the window. He interlaced his fingers behind his back and stared across the parking lot to the airport beyond. One jet lifting off, its nose pointed north. Another coming in on final approach, sunlight glinting on the windshield.

"You were right," Alex said, the bluster fading from his voice.

"About which part?" I said.

"All of it. The thing with Rui. The thing with the leak inside the Pentagon. The whole sorry mess."

I didn't say anything. I wasn't surprised to be right, but I wouldn't have been surprised to be wrong, either. It was an educated guess, nothing more.

"We can't stop the leak," Alex said. "Nearly twenty-nine months on the job, and no matter what I do the secrets keep flowing. Slower, sometimes. Faster at others. Rui Huang was my best asset inside the Chinese embassy—intrinsically motivated, and clever. She actually approached us about spying not long after the Chinese stationed her in Washington. Apparently, her parents back in Gansu were both old and needed advanced medical care. Chinese healthcare isn't so great. We agreed to provide green cards and asylum for both Rui and her parents in exchange for two years of her keeping tabs on the Chinese Ministry of State Security..." Alex glanced over his shoulder, locking eyes with me. "Those two guys you wasted at the Stone Creek apartments."

I still didn't answer, and Alex turned from the window, settling on a couch. He opened a bottle of water and sipped. He smoothed his pants. He seemed to be stalling—maybe working up the nerve for the next part.

Then, "The loss of Rui was catastrophic. Twenty-two months into her contract she had managed to worm her way into the MSS unit located at the Chinese embassy. We mined a lot of useful ancillary intelligence—the CIA was all over it. But what we really wanted, what we *needed*, was to identify and arrest the Chinese asset believed to be working inside the Pentagon—a character we simply call 'Benedict'. In the days leading up to her death, Rui was getting creative to connect the dots. She was sleeping with an MSS agent, actually. Some Chinese guy with a scar on his face. Rui thought he might have been Benedict's handler. She thought she could get a name, but..." Alex trailed off. Shook his head. "I guess she screwed up, somehow. They busted her."

I pictured the tiger—the guy with the scar on his face—and I imagined how desperate Rui must have been to secure green cards for her family if she was willing to sleep with a guy like that. It made me a little sick on her behalf, ashamed that my own government would leverage her need against her.

Ashamed, but not surprised. It was just another exhibit of mankind's depravity. The only thing I or anyone could do for Rui now was to finish the job she had started. Try to get her family out of China before they found themselves locked away in some prison camp.

"Whatever the case," Alex resumed, "without Rui we're... pretty much back to square one."

"Except you're not," I said. "Because you're also out of time. Right? I mean, that's why I'm here."

Alex's gaze turned hard, fingers crinkling around the bottle. But he kept himself together.

"An initial prototype of the Integrated Battle Network is nearing completion. The Pentagon expects to deliver test equipment to various military installations around the country by the end of the month. Beforehand, that equipment will be shipped to Pentagon offices for review by upper-level brass...kind of a show-and-tell thing. Some of it has already arrived."

"And?" I pressed.

"And our old friend Benedict is somewhere in the mix." It was the new guy who spoke, the guy I thought was military. His voice was cold, personally indignant. "Somewhere *inside* the Pentagon."

I considered, chewing my lip. I saw the problem as clear as anyone, but before I jumped to any further conclusions, I wanted clarification.

"Why can't you just cancel the demo?" I said. "Announce a security threat. Scrub everything. Change the passcodes, rotate the custodian staff. Move the IBN to a different base. Move it to NORAD if you have to."

No answer. I looked from face to face, even passing Kirsch. But it was the new guy who gave it away. The flush of his cheeks...the personal embarrassment.

"He's brass, isn't he?" I said. "Benedict. You think he's somebody way up the chain."

The new guy opened his mouth. Alex cut him off.

"We don't know what to think. Truth be told, this guy is a perfect ghost, but he does seem to have some unique access. Some astute spying ability. Without knowing his identity or his location, scrubbing the demo or relocating the equipment would only worsen the chances of exposure. We're not talking about a flash drive and a couple suitcases, here. We're talking about hundreds of engineers and developmental personnel. Coding laboratories in three states, hardware factories at two top-secret production facilities. You don't just *scrub* something like that. Not without cuing the sort of chaos that might worsen our existing exposure. It's too complex an operation, too great a risk."

I thought I knew what Alex meant. Not because I really understood anything about the sort of advanced, AI-powered tech that was at stake, but because common sense spoke volumes about Alex's arguments. It passed the smell test, leaving only one question remaining.

My gaze settled on the garment bag spread across the

table. "So your back is against a wall. You're running out of ideas...and you've decided to get creative."

I looked to the new guy. Alex rose from his couch.

"Meet Lieutenant Colonel Greene of Army Intelligence and Security Command," Alex said, gesturing to the new guy. "He's been tasked to liaise with the FBI on this matter. Colonel Greene has a number of friends inside the Defense Counterintelligence and Security Agency...the boys who can issue fake military credentials."

I extended my hand. Greene left me hanging for a long moment before slowly clasping his fingers around my palm. One solid, confident shake.

"Colonel," I said, ducking my head.

"Welcome back to the Army, *Major*."

33

I'd never been an officer. Discharging at the rank of E-5 —sergeant, in the Army—I served my entire military tenure as an enlisted man. A ground-pounder, a grunt, and then a leader of grunts.

But never commissioned, never the product of a college degree and DOD-approved "leadership" training that often left much to be desired. Truth be told, I never wanted any of those things. Like most enlisted guys, I maintained a certain level of disdain for officers of all sorts, but especially those without any combat experience. The desk jockeys and career office drones. The soldiers in name only who bounced from one air-conditioned post to the next, never touching a gun, never breaking a sweat.

Yet still holding lives in their hands. Climbing the ranks, one rung at a time. And maybe, if they were lucky, one reached the Pentagon.

All those thoughts and prejudices raced through my head as I stretched the Army Service Uniform over my shoulders and slowly buttoned the jacket. The name tag affixed to my chest read *Griffin*, a random name selected by the DCSA after Lieutenant Colonel Greene requested a temporary, covert military ID—and a commission to match it. A huge leap from my NCO heritage, right to the rank of O-4. Major.

The gold oak leaves felt heavy on my blue collar as I adjusted the jacket. When I gazed into the Marriott's bathroom mirror, I viewed a poor excuse for a soldier. Freshly covered in red welts from the cheap razor the hotel had supplied, my hair hastily and poorly trimmed into a high-and-tight with a pair of dollar store clippers. The shoes fit well and were shined to perfection, but I struggled to maintain a stiff back as I adjusted my belt to perfect my gig line.

It had been years since I'd worn an Army uniform, and I'd since become a totally different man. I was used to relaxing, now. The military stiffness I had perfected at Fort Benning had all but left me. I had to practice my stance as I adjusted the beret on my head—my "cover", as we used to call it. The flash positioned over my left eye, the excess beret material draping to the right of my skull. The shoulder sleeve insignia displaying a blue shield with an upright sword and crossed lightning bolts. It was the symbol of the U.S. Army Intelligence and Security Command, the unit my fictional identity of "Major Mason Lewis Griffin" was assigned to.

Mason Lewis Sharpe, of course, had never served inside INSCOM, but he had been deployed to Afghanistan. He had earned Ranger Tabs, a Parachutists Badge, a Combat Infantryman Badge, an Afghanistan Campaign Medal with multiple service stars, one Purple Heart for taking shrapnel across his calves, and one Bronze Star for an incident involving a lot of wounded comrades, a lot of dead Taliban fighters...and one very long hike through the mountains. None of those medals or accommodations were present on this uniform. What stripes and patches Greene had provided were meaningless to me, and I felt very fake wearing them.

Very uncomfortable.

Two raps on the door behind me, and then both Alex and Greene entered without further permission. I made eye contact in the mirror but didn't turn away from the counter. I pressed my heels together and stood at attention, hands at my sides. Measuring myself, getting comfortable with my own appearance.

Greene shook his head. "He's too stiff."

"So why don't you do it?" I said, adjusting my jacket.

Greene didn't answer. Alex remained quiet also. I nodded, snugging my tie.

"That's right, Greene. Because you *can't* do it. You're already a known quantity—an FBI liaison. But a guy like me?" I turned, relaxing my shoulders and instantly adopting my best, most condescending and yet totally indifferent fake-officer leer. "I'm just a nobody from nowhere Kansas. Major M. L. Griffin...here for an inspection tour."

Greene shot Alex a look. Both men turned back to me, but still, nobody spoke. The tension was palpable. I barged between them.

"A day's action is worth a lifetime of planning, eggheads. Let's roll."

I'D NEVER BEEN to the Pentagon before, but I knew something about it. The largest office building in the world was constructed in the shape of its namesake, and it wasn't really one building but five. Each was a five-floored ring built into a pentagon shape, just a little smaller than the one outside it, and a little bigger than the one inside it. Like Russian nesting dolls, with corridors connecting them and a courtyard in the very middle.

The smallest ring, known as A Ring, rested at the core of the complex and housed all the biggest of the big cheeses. The Secretary of Defense, the Joint Chiefs of Staff, and commanders of all the various branches. From there the structure sprawled to provide space for defense agencies, their logistical support structures, related civilian offices, and all the many things that were required to sustain the twenty-three thousand individuals who reported to the Pentagon each day.

Things like a gym, a library, and a litany of cafeterias and food courts. The Pentagon was less like an office building and more like a small city. An intensely busy, *incredibly secure*, city.

And I was headed straight into the heart of it.

"The IBN lab is inside the lowest basement floor of C Ring," Greene said, riding in the front right seat of a jet-black Suburban while Kirsch drove, Alex and I rode in the middle, and the still-silent *Shining* twins took the third row.

"Your orders are for a full inspection on behalf of Major General John Finkley, commander of INSCOM," Greene continued. "The on-site personnel should provide you full access to their facility."

"Does the good Major General know he ordered an

inspection?" I asked, flipping through the documents Greene had provided.

The LTC made eye contact with me in the rearview mirror. He was not smiling, and he did not answer the question.

I shuffled the papers back into a soft-sided suitcase along with a copy of the *Washington Post*, a wallet with a fake but high-quality Maryland driver's license, DOD identification card, and two debit cards, a box of chewing gum, a comb, and a John Grisham novel. Things that a legitimate officer might be expected to carry with him while traveling...all part of my cover, and nothing that would actually help me if the confetti hit the fan.

"What am I looking for?" I slid the suitcase between my uniformed legs, adjusting in the seat. Greene opened his mouth, but it was Alex who answered the question.

"Vulnerabilities. Somebody who doesn't belong. Somebody who's too willing to talk or refuses to talk at all. You were a detective, Sharpe. You should know what to look for."

"Actually, I was a track star at UGA," I said. "Big-time reader, big fan of European football and jazz music. I claim to appreciate fine bourbons and expensive wines, but my true weakness is anything sweet. I love old movies, but I hate Audrey Hepburn. I'm a clean freak and I sleep on my back like a corpse."

I looked left, making eye contact with Alex. "Also, I'm a ladies' man."

Alex didn't blink. A hint of crimson edged up his neck, but he controlled it well and remained quiet. Greene filled the silence without any clue of the underhanded communication that had just taken place.

"I'm already regretting this."

Kirsch pulled the Suburban into the Pentagon's South Parking Lot just off Rotary Road, edging to the curb and mashing her emergency flashers. The southwest face of the Pentagon's E-Ring was visible only a few hundred yards away, and just around the bend signs pointed toward the Pentagon Metro Station, where both the rail lines and multiple bus lines provide access to the complex.

"You go in through the metro entrance," Greene said. "You proceed past security and into the basement of C Ring. The officer on post at the research lab is an Army captain named Pike. He'll take your orders."

"And then?" I prompted.

Alex twisted toward me. "And then you *do your thing*, Sharpe. You deliver on your promises, and you don't blow your cover."

I reached for the door.

"Sharpe," Greene called, stopping me.

"What?"

"Don't mess with the PFPAs. They won't hesitate to detain you."

"PFPAs?" I questioned.

Greene shot Alex another look.

"Pentagon Force Protection Agency," Kirsch interjected. "Pentagon cops. Really spicy bunch." She eyeballed me in the rearview mirror, breaking her trademark stony-woman face for the first time since I'd met her. The replacement was a smirk.

"They'll eat you for breakfast, *Griffin*."

"I'll take that under advisement," I retorted.

Then I was out of the Suburban, onto the sidewalk. Adjusting my beret and turning toward the metro station, fading almost instantly into a swarm of other pedestrians.

Headed upstream through the crush toward the gate of a ten-foot black steel fence...and the nerve center of the most powerful military in world history standing just beyond it.

I was thinking of Evelyn, and I was headed into the Pentagon.

34

W hatever concerns I had regarding the civilian rust that had dulled the edge of my military training, they were long silenced before I reached the first security checkpoint.

Not dozens but *hundreds* of military personnel swarmed me on every side, dressed in the uniforms of every principal military branch—including the Coast Guard and the newly minted Space Force. The civilians that choked the spaces between those soldiers wore business suits and maintenance overalls, workout clothes and flip-flops. I even saw one individual in a red and white striped KFC shirt, headphones dangling from her neck as she presented an ID at the security checkpoint.

Just as I had read and just as Greene had promised, this place was nothing more nor less than a mini-metropolis, and literally nobody was paying any attention to me. I fell into line at the first security line, which reminded me a lot of a TSA checkpoint at an airport. There were horseshoe metal detectors, X-ray machines and a ton of personnel in dark blue uniforms, complete with bulletproof chest rigs and sidearms held on utility belts. Their arm patches read "POLICE", but on further inspection smaller letters were stitched in an arch across the patch.

Pentagon Force Protection Agency. They were the cops Greene had warned me about, and they certainly seemed to be running a tight ship. With each line proceeding neatly through a metal detector, bag inspection station, and ID scanner, absolutely nobody made it past that wall of blue uniforms without clearing all three hurdles.

That included an Army major with INSCOM patches on his arms. I presented my briefcase at the X-ray machine before stepping through the metal detector, which promptly blinked red and buzzed.

"Hold there, sir." A PFPA officer approached, a wand in one hand. "Do you have anything in your pockets?"

I dipped a hand into my front pocket, heart accelerating as I touched metal. I'd left my Victorinox and my Macro-Stream in my rental car, but in my fixation with the mission ahead I had neglected to leave the car keys with Alex.

"Just keys," I said.

"X-ray," the officer said, pointing with the wand.

I complied, backing out of the horseshoe and proceeding to the back of the X-ray machine to deposit the keys into the bin. Then I was passing through again, collecting my personal items, and proceeding to the ID scanner.

I presented the fake Department of Defense ID—it was tinted green, printed with my black and white photograph and so fresh that it reflected the overhead lights. The PFPA officer working the computer accepted it, scanned it, then spent a few moments clicking. Scrolling. Clicking again.

I glanced right and noted that everyone else was

proceeding right through the checkpoint and past the computers. I was being held back.

"What's the purpose of your visit today, Major?"

I glanced back. The officer wasn't looking at me, just the computer screen.

"Orders from Major General Finkley," I said. "I'm headed to C Ring."

A gentle nod. She scrolled again. My gut tightened as I watched another three military personnel and a blind civilian with a seeing-eye dog proceed past the checkpoint. The PFPA officer was leaning close to the screen, cocking her head.

"Where do you live, Major?"

The question caught me off guard. I blinked, instantly deadlocked. She looked up, arching her eyebrows. My mouth opened, but I couldn't get the words out. I couldn't think of something.

Where did I live? I didn't have a home address, not since abandoning my apartment. But no, this wasn't about me. This was about Griffin. Where did Griffin live?

"Home address?" the officer prompted.

"Anacostia," I managed. It was the first thing that came to mind.

"DC?" She seemed surprised.

I decided to own it. "Right. Cheap rent."

She looked back to the screen. Then she returned my ID.

"Your file is missing a home address," she said. "Get with your personnel officer and get that fixed for me."

I accepted the card with a simple nod, mentally cursing Greene for the oversight, but I didn't have time to dwell on it. I was moving again, down polished linoleum halls that clapped beneath my dress shoes. Low walls, suspended ceilings, a lot of fluorescent lighting.

The place felt exactly like every office building I'd ever entered as a Phoenix cop—every bank tower, every insurance complex, except with a definite military flare. Novelty displays of US Armed Forces artifacts and various historical plaques were mounted to the walls, the hallway crowded with more tourists than I would have expected. Ahead a seaman in full dress whites walked effortlessly backward as she provided a guided tour, gesturing to one side or the other while narrating a script of facts and trivia about the complex to a knot of wide-eyed, trailing civilians.

"Despite being six-point-five million square feet in size, the unique layout of the Pentagon allows for rapid travel," she bragged. "You can reach any room in the Pentagon from any other room in seven minutes or less."

The tourists undulated incredulity as military personnel and civilian worker bees sidestepped their party without a second glance, many carrying briefcases or laptop bags, some cramming down fast food as they jogged, but very few talking on cell phones. In fact, very few carried cell phones at all. It was like I had stepped back in time to a pre-digital period. I found the resulting order oddly refreshing—it was enough to clear my mind as I followed signs around the bend of E Ring, down corridors past D Ring, through another security checkpoint, and at last to C Ring.

The civilians had thinned out and the tourists were gone. The wide hallways persisted, but I could tell without being told that the ring I had entered was considerably smaller than the one I had left. Each turn of its five-pointed floorplan came more quickly, my shoes clopping on the polished floor, each door I passed advertising the department, agency, or office that resided within.

I was looking for stairs, maybe an elevator. One level down into the basement, possibly two. That was where Greene indicated the research lab would be. Whatever happened after that would be entirely up to my own wits. *Stay loose. Think fast.*

I reached another security checkpoint outside an elevator. I presented my ID, but this time the PSPA officer requested my orders before allowing access to the lower levels. He took his time reviewing them. He made a coded phone call. I stood waiting, body tense with constricting muscles as I remembered the error of my missing address.

"Do you know where you're going?" the officer asked.

"Not really. First time." I had already decided that honesty was my best policy, at least whenever it was possible. The bet paid off. The officer gave me directions. I entered the elevator, headed not to the first level of the basement, but the second. All the way down, the elevator gliding in perfect silence and easing to a stop.

The temperature dropped. A rush of cool air greeted me as I stepped out onto a concrete floor. Another gate blocked my path, but the guard was ready. I was admitted. I stepped under bright lights, taking a right. Passing one door after another—all solid steel with no windows, cameras staring down from overhead.

I was looking for room B2C121—B2 indicating the floor, C indicating the ring, and 121 being the actual room. I passed them in sequence and reached 121 to find it matching every other door in that hallway.

I was alone. The hallway was nearly quiet, nothing but the buzz of a climate control system somewhere overhead. I rapped with my knuckles on the door, looking into the camera.

Moments passed. A lock buzzed, then a voice spoke through an invisible speaker. "Proceed, Major."

The door swung on silent hinges. The floor beyond was also concrete, painted white. A short hallway opened beyond, with more doors on either side, these with reinforced glass windows that offered a view of wide laboratories stocked by plastic tables.

And those tables were loaded down with military equipment. Helmets, rifles, chest rigs, battlefield laptops units. Things I was familiar with from years downrange, but even from a distance I could tell that they were modified.

I caught myself staring as the door swung shut behind me. Footsteps tapped on the floor, and a pair of figures rounded the corner—one tall, one short. The tall one was dressed in an Army Service Uniform that matched mine. His collar bore captain's bars. His face was set in hard, unbending lines. All business.

The shorter guy was his companion's polar opposite. Long hair reached nearly to his shoulder blades. A scraggly beard, a big smile. His attire was a shirt and tie overhung by a white lab coat, screwdrivers and an electrical meter protruding from his pockets.

I stiffened at the sight of the captain—an instinct from my enlisted days that had apparently not died. The captain didn't seem to notice. He stopped at salute-distance, but extended a hand instead of saluting. We were indoors.

"Major Griffin?"

"That's me." His handshake was confident. One squeeze, then a release.

"I'm Captain Pike, Army Futures Command. With me is Dr. Greg Sparks, chief civilian director for this project."

I shook Sparks's hand. It was a much more enthusiastic experience.

"I understand you're here to inspect our progress on behalf of General Finkley at INSCOM?" Pike said.

"That's right."

Pike eyeballed me, and the room grew still. I could sense some hesitation, and I didn't immediately understand it. Then I remembered that I was no longer a sergeant—the man before me was no longer a corporal who was expected to speak his mind if something bothered him. All the rules were different in the officer ranks. The virtues of free speech were restricted, the costs of challenging a superior vastly increased.

It was one of the things that exhausted me about the Army, one of the things I didn't miss. I decided to make things easy on Pike.

"Would you like to see my orders, Captain?"

"If you don't mind, sir."

I produced the envelope containing my manufactured orders. While Pike read, Sparks seemed ready to wet his pants. He was shifting on his feet, hands entering and then retracting from his pockets, eyes twitching. That big smile remaining plastered across his face.

"Do they let you out much, Doctor?" I asked.

Sparks laughed but didn't answer. Pike returned the orders.

"I appreciate that, sir."

I dumped the envelope into my briefcase. Raised my eyebrows. "You have something to show me, Captain?"

35

I wasn't sure what I expected inside those laboratories. In truth, I hadn't given it much thought. Years spent in the Seventy-Fifth Ranger Regiment where all the best toys were usually first available had somewhat jaded me toward the concept of "cutting-edge battlefield technology." People think that *military grade* means the toughest, the best, the most bulletproof.

What it actually means is a piece of equipment that was purchased en masse by Congress for the lowest possible price. Sometimes it's quality, many times it's not. Whatever the case, new stuff is almost always fraught with unresolved imperfections, with front-line soldiers used like guinea pigs to work out the kinks of massive purchase orders that were already guaranteed by contract. Whether it was the Air Force's latest fighter jet or the Navy's latest electric can opener, the message from the DOD was always the same: *We bought this, we paid for it, now stop complaining and make it work.*

That sort of message might make sense in the Pentagon, but it wasn't well received by front-line soldiers taking enemy fire. Accordingly, most of the guys in the Seventy-Fifth tended to reject the latest tech in favor of what was proven to work, never making substitutions until they were absolutely forced to do so. I'd learned to be the same, which was maybe why I preferred a 1967 GMC pickup to a brand-new one. I don't trust new. I don't trust flashy sales brochures.

But all those biases, all those reservations flew right out the window the minute Sparks went to work demonstrating the equipment spread across the first lab. It was all calibrated for infantry use, which was a perfect place to orient me to the applications of the IBN. Sparks was a nervous, distracted tour guide—he clearly suffered from extreme levels of ADHD and was medicated accordingly—but his enthusiasm and expertise were unquestionable.

"The IBN basically has three key functions," Sparks explained, lifting an M4 rifle off the table and pointing to a small computer module mounted to the forward rail. "Collection of data, interpretation and organization of data, and dissemination of data."

I frowned. Pike rocked his head in an impatient, overtly familiar gesture. Sparks held up a hand.

"Right, right. So, it's like this. The things you need to know on the battlefield, the location of troops, the location of the enemy, the position of obstacles and obstructions, the weather, the location of civilians...all these things are collected via multimedia sensors mounted to all equipment. Rifles, chest rigs, vehicles, aircraft." Sparks pointed again to the sensor mounted to the M4. "Encrypted via microprocessors, these data are transferred to a forward command computer localized to the battlefield. It's roughly the size of a small refrigerator and can be easily transported on a truck. That computer works wirelessly, networking with similar computers around the region, and transmitting via satellite to a central command center at a military installation stateside. It's inside these computers that the AI works."

"You let AI run it?" I made no attempt to conceal the unease in my voice. I'd had some recent experience with weaponry enhanced by artificial intelligence, and I hadn't enjoyed it.

"Absolutely," Sparks said, unperturbed. "It's kind of our secret sauce. You see, there's very little new about this concept of an Integrated Battle Network. It's something we've been messing with for years, but we always hit a roadblock when it came to information processing. When you talk about collecting data points from hundreds, maybe thousands of sensors spread across a complex battlefield, that sheer volume of information is...is...it's *stupendous!*" Sparks threw his hands up, eyebrows arching. Both his tone and volume had gradually escalated during his spiel to the point that he was nearly screaming by the time he finished.

"Slow down, Sparks," Pike muttered. "Summarize for the major."

Sparks blinked, seeming to come back to earth. "Right— so the AI. That's the big breakthrough. Artificial intelligence acts as a smart filter working not only at the central command computer but also in all the forward command computers. It sorts the incoming information, making real-time, split-second decisions about which data is useful and relevant, and which data can be ignored. It condenses, interprets, and collects the relevant information through a series of digital checkpoints, scrapping the clutter at each stage. This allows the entire network to operate at break-neck speed, never bogging down, never delaying. The flow of information is instantaneous and always relevant."

"You mean for central command?" I asked.

Sparks grinned. "I mean for *everyone*. Every soldier, every pilot, every artillery officer. That's the beauty of the AI. It's trained to provide the most relevant information to whoever needs it—instantly."

The open-mouthed grin returned, eyebrows seemingly frozen in their upward arc. Sparks looked from me to Pike, then back again. He blinked.

"Give us a practical example," Pike prompted.

Sparks nodded like a bobblehead in an earthquake. "Right, example. So...let's say you were a ground soldier. Like, a special operator."

"A Ranger," I suggested.

"Sure, that would work. Now imagine you've got a headset that is supplying you with data from not only every soldier on the battlefield, but also from every aircraft. I'm not talking about distant, grainy imagery. I'm talking about *AI-processed imagery*. It's a blend of every available data point collected by battlefield sensors, with clever inferences added by the AI to fill in the gap. So, like...you could see through walls, in some cases. You could instantly calibrate your grenade launcher for a perfect shot through a small window. You could call suppressive fire from a helicopter gunship on your own command—as though *you* were sitting behind the trigger."

I continued to stare, still not impressed and definitely not sold. It sounded amazing—it sounded too good to be true.

Sparks detected the suspicion, and his smile only broadened. He poked his hands into his lab coat pockets, eyebrows finally relaxing.

"Skeptical?" he asked. "How about a test drive?"

36

Two hours later I was exiting E Ring and returning to the metro station. Fast-walking to the curb, heart thumping and sweat still streaming down my back from the exhilaration of an extensive simulator combat sequence.

So real I found myself ducking bullets. So visceral I could taste the blood on the air that wasn't even there.

And so cutting edge, so totally unparalleled by everything I'd ever experienced overseas that by the time I peeled off the gear and replaced the training rifle in Sparks's hands, I was no longer talking. I didn't bother to say goodbye.

I was only focused on one thing—getting back to Alex. Getting the point across. Getting this entire circus shut down, immediately. Without question, without deliberation.

Because what I'd seen in the basement of the Pentagon was the kind of monster that only emerges every few generations. A thing like gunpowder. Like the machine gun. Like the fighter plane, the guided cruise missile, the hydrogen bomb.

It was escalation in the most extreme sense of the word. A devourer of mankind.

I dialed Alex as soon as I was outside the building. He picked up immediately and I directed him to the South Parking Lot. By the time I reached the sidewalk the jet-black Suburban was there. I was inside, slamming the door and tugging my tie loose. Tossing my cover onto the seat next to me. Jabbing a finger forward.

"Drive."

Alex twisted to face me. "What?"

"*Drive.*"

He exchanged a glance with Greene. Kirsch eyeballed me in the rearview mirror. Then Alex nodded and Kirsch dropped her foot off the brake. We exited the parking lot and hit the highway, my gaze locked on the Pentagon as we orbited it. Then the building was lost behind Virginia trees, that lethal secret buried deep inside lost along with it.

For now.

"What happened?" Alex said. "What did you find?"

They were questions I myself was struggling to answer. More context, I thought. More big picture.

Did they even matter? The conclusion was the same, regardless.

"Shut it down," I said, simply.

"What?" That was Alex.

I turned from the window. "Shut it all down, the entire project. Everything you're developing. Lock it all up, interrogate every member of any team that has so much as sniffed it. Identify the Chinese operators and track them. Deploy wet teams if you need to—neutralize them. Whatever it takes—shut it *all* down."

"Have you lost your mind?" Greene joined the conversation, more than a little irate. He tore his seatbelt off and ratcheted around to face me.

"Far from it," I snapped. "I may be the only sane person left on the planet, and I'm telling you, *shut this down.*"

Greene just stared. Alex seemed caught without words. Ironically, it was Kirsch who broke the silence with the most relevant question.

"What did you see, Sharpe?"

I looked into my hands, not replying immediately. Closing my fingers into fists, then opening them again. Imagining that training rifle in my hands—except, paired with the helmeted headset Sparks gave me, it was so much more than a rifle. So much more than a weapon.

I was so much more than a soldier.

"I saw the future," I said. "I used their simulator, and saw next-generation warfare like we've never experienced. Complete, total cohesion of the battlefield. The ultimate advantage."

"That's the point," Alex said. "That's what we want."

"No, it's what you *think* you want," I said. "Just like we thought we wanted the nuclear bomb. The artillery cannon. The machine gun. The Colt Peacemaker. We always think these things are going to save lives, and maybe they do for a while. But the end is always the same. Before it's over, everybody gets one, and then more people die than ever. The risk of tyranny, of rampant genocide multiplies by orders of magnitude. It's almost inevitable."

"That's hyperbole," Greene snarled. "You're out of your depth, Sharpe."

"No, we're *all* out of our depth."

"It's really that powerful?" Kirsch said. She was starting to sound genuine for a change.

"Imagine..." I hesitated, struggling for a simile. "Imagine advanced fighter-jet technology in World War Two. F-35 stealth fighters against Axis fighter planes."

"Like that movie." It was one of *The Shining* twins from the back seat, speaking for the first time in my presence. "What was it? *The Final Countdown?* From the eighties."

"Yes," I said. "Exactly like that. A complete overhaul of the battlefield. Not all at once, of course. It'll take time to work the kinks out. But when they do..." I shook my head. "It'll make combat like a video game."

"That's what we *want*," Greene echoed Alex's earlier sentiment. "It's called unfair advantage, Sharpe. Good grief, weren't you a Ranger? How do you not understand this?"

"It's *because* I was a Ranger that I understand this. It's desk warriors like you who are missing the point. You think I ever felt like I had an unfair advantage against the Taliban? I had a rifle, they had a rifle. I had guided bombs, they had IEDs. That's how this *works*."

"And what if you had an IBN?" Greene's face flushed crimson. He jabbed a finger back toward the Pentagon. "What if that simulator was real life in Kandahar? What then, Sharpe?"

"Then I would have killed them all!" I shouted. The blood was hot in my own face. My heart hammered. I didn't care. "I would have killed every one of them—and you know what? It wouldn't have mattered. One war won, the next one already kicking off. Always the escalation. Always the next conflict. That's life, Greene. That's *humanity*. All we're doing is stacking bodies until it's our turn to get stacked."

I was still screaming as I finished, my body quivering.

The Suburban fell suddenly still at the end of my tirade and Alex looked forward—toward Greene. The Army officer didn't speak. Nobody spoke.

Then Alex snapped his fingers and pointed over Kirsch's shoulders. She responded by hauling the Suburban off the road—a harsh turn into a gas station. The SUV slid to a stop at the edge of the parking lot and Kirsch ratcheted the shifter into park. The engine continued to hum. The A/C churned.

Stillness. I looked out the window toward the convenience store only fifty yards away and I imagined I could see through its block walls the way I had seen through block walls with the headset back in the simulator. Powered by the infrared imagery of a circling drone, with AI technology to fill in the gaps and draw a compelling graphic of what lay inside.

Target locations. Recommended angles of fire. The best route of approach. That helmet had turned me into a killing machine.

"We're all soldiers, Sharpe." It was Alex who spoke, his voice barely above a whisper, but perfectly clear in the silent SUV. He sat with both hands riding his kneecaps, face pointed at the floor. "'Theirs not to reason why...Theirs but to do and die.'"

It was Tennyson—I recognized the verse and I wanted to throat-punch him.

"You're not a soldier," I said. "And frankly, neither am I. I don't take orders from anyone—not anymore. I'm done with this."

I reached for the door handle. Alex's voice stopped me short.

"And what about the Chinese, Mason? What happens when they steal this thing?"

My fingers closed around the handle. I clutched the plastic, muscles tensed.

But I couldn't pull it.

"They're not going to stop, Sharpe," Alex continued. "They never will. And if you think this technology will cause a war..." He snorted. "That war is already here. It's been here for years. If you'd seen what I've seen—the espionage activities, the trade sabotage, the internal disruptions..." He trailed off and I looked over my shoulder to meet his gaze. The man I saw looked ice cold. "We're already at war with China, Mason. Just like we were at war with the Soviet Union last century. It's a cold war, and the only thing keeping it from going hot is Chinese uncertainty. They don't know if they can win, but if that ever changes, if they ever gain an edge...I don't have to tell you what happens."

He didn't. I could picture that reality clearly. All I had to do was remember my worst firefights in Afghanistan and multiply that horror by hundreds of thousands of soldiers. Add drones and artillery. Maybe a few nukes.

"There's no stopping progress," Alex said. "There's only the dim hope of controlling it. Capisci?"

My gaze flicked left. I gritted my teeth and shook my head in disbelief—not at what a mess this was, but at the fact that I had yet again stumbled right into the heart of it.

And no matter how badly I wanted to walk away, no matter how insane this mess felt...I knew I couldn't disengage. It wasn't in me to stand on the sidelines.

It never had been.

I released the door handle. I spun my finger in the air as I collapsed back into my seat. Kirsch shifted back into gear and powered us out of the lot. We pulled into a drive-through for burgers. We all ate in silence on the way back to the Pentagon, where I donned my beret and smoothed the wrinkles out of my dress jacket.

Then, without a word, I was back out of the Suburban. Back through the metro station, the briefcase swinging by my leg. Back through the doors, sweeping my cover off and tucking it automatically beneath my left arm.

Up to the X-rays, the metal detectors. I remembered to dispense my keys into the tray this time. I presented my ID as before, and it was scanned. Same officer—I didn't expect any resistance about my address. She couldn't have expected me to fix it over lunch.

But I was not waved through. Seconds dragged by. The officer glanced sideways at me—there was something in her eye. A twitch in her right hand. She was looking at the computer but not doing anything. She was buying time.

Then I saw them. Three men in PFPA uniforms, two with their hands riding their sidearms. One leading the way, making a bee-line straight toward me. My body tensed, and I instinctively closed my right fist. I shifted my weight onto my back leg, my gaze snapping left and right, searching out any possible route of escape.

But it was already too late. There was no option to fight. They were on me, splitting and circling behind me, grabbing my arms and wrenching them behind my back. I dropped the suitcase. A murmur of alarm rippled through the crowd around us. The officer at the computer was stepping back, giving the arrest team room.

And then the lead guy—a beefy, bulging bulldog who seemed to erupt out of his uniform—was barking at me.

"Major Griffin, you're under arrest."

"Under what charge?" It was the only question that mattered. The bulldog didn't hesitate to answer.

"Conspiracy to commit espionage," he snapped. "Come with us."

_____

37

I t was all wrong—I knew it within seconds of my arrest. Not just because I'd been a cop myself and understood something about police protocol, but because of where they took me. Not deeper into the Pentagon, into a detainment facility. Surely, there was one. This place had a Taco Bell; there had to be a lockup.

But instead, we headed out. Beyond the security checkpoint, turning right along E Ring. They frog-marched me with one guy on either side, arms hooked, and the bulldog pushing from behind. Right down the middle of E Ring's main hallway, past gawking civilians and more than a few wide-eyed service members.

And then hooking right, away from the core of the building. Down a short corridor straight toward an exterior exit, where a black Ford Transit van sat waiting by the door.

Then I was certain. Not of the what, the when, or the where. I certainly didn't know the *how*. But I knew the who —and I also knew that I wasn't headed to any sort of lockup.

The Transit's side door rolled open. They shoved me onto a bare metal floor, knees biting the stainless steel. The two escorts climbed in along with me. The door slammed and I was hauled onto a bench seat with my arms pressed against the wall. One guy sat next to me, his hand riding his sidearm. The other sat across from me, drawing his weapon and aiming a gaping 9mm muzzle at my gut.

And not speaking.

The bulldog got behind the wheel. The shifter clunked into gear. We were off, but I couldn't see where. There were no rear windows at all, and when I twisted my face toward the windshield, the guy sitting next to me slammed me back against the metal wall.

"Face forward!"

My shoulder blades bit into the steel and I winced, growing genuinely irritated for the first moment since the handcuffs snapped around my wrists. Not only for the brute force, but mostly for the brazen gall of it all.

Right in the middle of the Pentagon, under the noses of the watchdogs of freedom, here these guys were.

Unbelievable. And yet, totally believable. I'd walked right into it.

"Aren't you going to read me my rights?" I addressed the question to the guy pointing his pistol at me, more than a little sarcasm in my tone.

He didn't reply. He only smirked, finger riding just above the trigger guard, the muzzle rock steady. He had some training. He was cool under pressure.

He was an American traitor.

"What did they pay you?" I said.

No answer.

"Ten grand?" I prompted. "Fifty? How cheap a whore are you, anyway?"

His jaw tightened. The van jolted as we crossed a bump, tires humming. We were gaining speed, headed up a ramp, I thought. Onto the highway—away from the city.

Someplace secluded and quiet. And then...

My wrists twisted in the cuffs, fingers dipping beneath the edge of the ASU jacket. Fishing for my belt but not touching nylon as I was used to. I touched leather instead, and my chest tightened.

I'd already forgotten. It wasn't my belt—the belt with the handcuff key hidden in a pocket at the base of my spine. This was the dress belt that came with the uniform. There was no key at all.

New problems.

"What if I told you..." the guy with the gun started, then stopped. The smirk grew into a broader smile. "A hundred grand."

"A hundred grand?" I didn't care about the number, but the conversation was good. It gave me precious seconds to survey his uniform in subtle, lightning-quick glances. Searching for a bulge in his pockets. A hook on his belt. Anyplace where the handcuff keys might reside.

"Or five hundred grand," the fake officer suggested. "Maybe...a *million*."

"A million?" I arched my eyebrows in mock interest. I'd completed my search and found nothing. I was glancing left, now. Making eye contact with the guy next to me, feigning interest in his input.

He fell for it. He chuckled, not immediately ramming me back against the wall. I looked once through the windshield

—I saw bright blue sky, traffic, and a bridge barrier only yards ahead to our right. The digital compass built into the rearview mirror read *N*. We were about to cross the Potomac. Then my gaze twitched down. Across pockets. Down to the belt of the guy next to me. I found what I was looking for hanging from a clip. A ring of door keys and one handcuff key.

"A million dollars?" I said, turning back to the guy with the gun. Raising my eyebrows. Smiling. "In that case...I'd say you're a *really* cheap whore."

His smile melted just as the van hit the bridge. I felt it as a bump, followed almost immediately by harsh braking. The vehicle jolted. The guy next to me swung toward the front of the van—away from my body. The guy across followed suit. The pistol's muzzle arced six inches to my left.

And I sprang. Off the bench, launching across the van like a charging bull. Head down and shoulder braced. He saw me coming but it was already too late. He was caught off balance. I passed inside his gun arm and body-slammed him to the wall, neck to neck, shoulder to cheek. His spine struck metal. He shouted.

And he fired. It was a chain-link reaction, one movement triggering the next. It all happened within two blinks, two lightning-quick seconds. The gun cracked and my ears rang —we were both toppling sideways, and somewhere behind me a choking cry signaled the bullet's impact. The van braked again, the bulldog shouting from the front seat.

And I was hurtling to the floor, bouncing off my target and crashing backward onto my handcuffed hands. Pain shot up my arms—I slid on a floor slick with blood. It was spurting behind me, coating the walls and the ceiling. The guy who had sat next to me was also on his back, also flailing, grasping at a wound in his clavicle as the blood just kept spurting.

The bulldog shouted again. The guy with the gun had lost it and was flailing on the floor. And then I drove both cocked and locked feet straight into the side of his head. Hard enough to bust bone, smashing his skull against the wall. The sheet metal popped, and he choked out a desperate cry. He slipped on the bloody floor and fell from his knees, one hand grasping for the misplaced Glock.

I kicked again. A third time. One foot found his face, another struck his chest. They were desperate, poorly aimed shots, but the force was there. The dress shoes were military standard, polished leather and slip-resistant rubber soles. The heels were sharp, and they tore his face. He shrieked and fought to escape, but the floor was too slick. The van swerved, knocking him off balance as horns blared from outside. The bulldog was fighting to throw me off balance. He was laying on the brakes again.

I kicked once more, and the gunman's neck snapped. I heard it as a crunch of collapsing vertebra. His eyelids froze open. His mouth went wide, but he didn't breathe. It was all over for him in that split second, and then I was rolling again. The bulldog was yanking the wheel, throwing me sideways on the floor. My hands scraped corrugated metal slick with blood. I spun and slid forward, toward the front seats. He yanked the wheel right and I bounced toward the driver's side. My head smacked the wall and my vision danced. I blinked in the glare of sunlight passing through the windshield. I saw the bulldog flailing for his sidearm— another Glock held fast in a hip holster, difficult to access beneath his seatbelt.

And then I found the fallen weapon—the one so recently

pointed at me. Coated in blood, resting right in the middle of the floor between the two bodies. It was three feet away. I looked up and caught the bulldog's gaze in the mirror—wide, angry eyes. His fingers closed around his pistol.

And I rolled. Kicking off the front seats, tumbling backwards. One revolution, then two. Past the gun-shot guy. Past the guy with the broken neck. I landed chest-down on the bloody Glock, metal and polymer biting into my sternum. The bulldog had his gun out and was arcing it backward, an awkward, underhand motion followed immediately by the ear-splitting crack of a nine millimeter. A bullet smacked the floor only inches from my side and punched right through.

I rolled once more. Onto my back, hands grasping. Fingers touching sticky checkered polymer. Closing around the grip, landing on my side with my face pointed toward the back doors. I couldn't see him—he couldn't clearly see me. I found the trigger. Another shot from the driver's compartment zipped over my hip and smacked the rear door.

Then I opened fire. Nothing aimed, nothing precise. Just a desperate mag dump, the muzzle pointed generally in the direction of the front seats. The van rang with each report, brass pinging off the walls and raining over my body. I clamped my eyes closed and kept yanking the trigger, twisting to alter my aim. Seeking the target in my mind.

And finding it. There was a scream. The van jolted, swerving hard. I braced myself against the passenger's side wall, but then we were yanking the other way. Right hand, hard. The engine surged. Horns blared. A sudden, bone-jarring jolt ripped down the chassis. Smashing metal and exploding airbags. The gun flew out of my hand. My head slammed into the metal flooring and blackness encroached.

Then I felt it. That unmistakable, weightless sensation. A

moment of hanging in free space, like the predicament of a cartoon character who runs straight off a cliff. The engine howled in sudden, unrestricted freedom. Wheels spun.

And then we were headed down—plummeting. The bulldog still shouting.

Diving straight into the Potomac.

38

The van struck the river hard enough to rattle teeth. Nose down, windshield first. I was sliding toward the driver's seat only a moment before a flash of sunlight vanished into a morass of instant, overwhelming darkness. Metal contorted, glass buckled, my breath was choked by airbag dust. Light vanished. The bulldog was thrashing but no longer screaming nor firing. Black water surged through cracks in the doorframe and bullet holes in the windshield. It was bubbling through matching holes in the cargo floor and the back door. I tumbled backwards as the rear end fell, the vehicle leveling off in the darkness. For just a moment sunlight broke through the upper half of the windshield—a promise of salvation, a last hope.

Then we were sinking. Not slowly, but rapidly. Water gushing in through every hole, every crack. Surging from beneath the front dash, churning up to the top of the windshield. The van dropped like a rock beneath the river's surface, and within seconds we were back in the dark. Water washed over my hips as I rolled, fighting to reach my knees.

It was shockingly cold, worsening the breathless sensation already clamping down around my lungs.

Adrenaline overwhelmed my system. I blinked, but I only saw blackness. I only heard churning water and the thrashing of the bulldog, wild and desperate.

Keys. The singular thought cracked through my mind like a gunshot. *Find the keys!*

I thrashed through the water, kicking with both legs and thumping against the van's floor, its walls, its wheel well.

And then a body. It lay to my left on the driver's side. Maybe not the guy who had his subclavian artery shot out, but I didn't have time to deliberate. Even on my knees the water was up to my ribcage. It was still rising. We were *still* dropping.

I tumbled left, turning my hands toward my target. Yanking against the cuffs, I kicked backward to pin the body against the wall. My tailbone struck the floor, and a wash of water surged right up to my chin. Raw panic flooded my mind, and for a moment I was deadlocked. Frozen in physical terror, temporarily overcome.

Focus! Get those keys or you'll never see her again.

It was enough. I jammed one boot against the base of the front passenger's seat and shoved myself backwards. The body behind me smashed against the wall, and my fingers clawed past a saturated shirt. I touched buttons and clammy flesh. I clawed downward as the water lapped up to my shoulders.

Then the van landed. I felt it as a gentle tremor. Tires sank into mud, metal groaning, and still the water surged in. From the front seat the rushing sound was mixed with a desperate gargle, water sloshing backward in a tidal wave that crashed right over my head.

I was losing my balance. I was losing my footing. I nearly lost the guy behind me. My legs floated up and my head went down. I was underwater, choking. My fingers clawed and found leather. I fought to get my feet back under me, but it was too late. Buoyancy was sucking my body upward. The wave passed over me, breaking over my head. I could breathe, just for a moment. I sucked down a lungful, and then I heard it.

The crash of glass. The bulldog breaking through his window. And then, only a split second behind, the final tidal wave.

I went under again, deliberate this time. I grabbed the dead guy's belt, and I hauled myself to the floor, back-first. I found his buckle and traced left. Past a multi-tool case. A spare magazine holster.

And then I found it—the key ring. My fingers hooked it, and I yanked. It wouldn't break free, and my lungs were already burning. I braced my feet against the floor, bunching sore muscles and balling myself into a fetal position. Rotating up—uniform shoes kicking down. Finding the floor. Knotting my fingers around the key ring.

And then driving upward as hard as I could. The clip snapped and I rose all the way to the ceiling of the van. My head smashed against the ceiling and my face broke through the surface. There were two inches of air left in the back of the van, barely enough to suck down one last desperate breath. Then that too was gone. The van was fully flooded, and I was fumbling in the dark. Touching house keys, padlock keys. Knowing that if I fumbled the ring now it would be over. There would be no second chances.

I clamped my eyes closed. I embraced the burn in my lungs and forced my mind to focus. One key at a time, tracing its outline. Looking for that familiar round barrel and simple hook. A key I'd carried for my entire tenure as a Phoenix cop. A unique key, unlike anything else on that chain. Barely an inch long. Easy to miss.

Focus. Find it.

I touched the smooth barrel, and my heart pounded. My fingers encircled it, I pinched it between a thumb and fore-finger. Twisting, searching for the handcuff keyhole. I didn't need both halves—one would do.

Then I fumbled. The key slipped, nearly falling out of my hand. I caught them by the ring, hooking my pinky at the last moment. Fresh panic surged my body, my heart working overtime. I was desperate for a breath, desperate to open my mouth. I wanted to swallow water—anything to satiate the hunger.

I found the key again. I twisted it and jabbed. Metal brushed metal, and I jabbed again. I felt a hole. I was twisting even before I fully mashed the key into the cuff. It clicked and loosened. I shook my wrists and twisted again.

Begging. Longing. *Praying.*

The cuffs broke loose. I tore my right hand free, and the keys dropped into watery darkness. I was kicking off the floor again, headed toward the van's ceiling. My head struck metal, but there was no pocket of air left. The vehicle was fully flooded, and I turned momentarily forward. I touched the driver's seat, reached for the wheel, and found the bull-dog. He was caught fast, wrapped in his seatbelt. Drowned in place next to a busted window.

And I was about to drown with him. I could feel it. I didn't have minutes, I had seconds. Maybe not a lot of them. The window was blocked, and I didn't have anything close to hand to bust another one.

But there was one virtue to the van being flooded—the pressure inside and outside the vehicle had equalized. I might be able to get a door open.

I shoved off the driver's seat and kicked. Over the two dead guys, straight to the back of the vehicle. With the cuffs dangling for my left wrist, I reached the back doors. Metal panels, no window. My lungs screamed as I clawed for a handle.

I found it. It was locked. I flailed for the lock. Each beat of my heart pulsated in my head, turning my already black vision into darker shades of midnight. My mouth slipped open, and I swallowed water—I wanted to choke. The desperation was getting to me.

I found the lock. A quick flip of the manual latch and another snatch of the door handle. It clicked in my hand. I braced one waterlogged boot against the floor and rammed my shoulder into the door. It swung open in slow motion, water swirling all around my head. Darkness. Grit passing between my teeth, the icy clutch of the Potomac rushing over my back, tearing at my eyes.

Then I was out. Kicking up—I hoped it was up. The van's roof brushed past my leg, and I clawed for the surface. I couldn't see the light, I had no idea how far down I was. In a moment of mental clarity, I imagined the claws of death closing around my body only inches before I reached the surface.

An ultimate triumph of irony. The last thing I remembered before eternity collected me. And I thought—what if I never made her smile again?

Then I broke the surface. A rush, a splash, and all at once the sun was blazing down. I was heaving, going under again. Choking. Thrashing. Breaking the surface once more, unable to see. Everything was a yellow blur. My eyes stung and I was gasping and turning in the water—I heard noises from not far away. Shouts and sirens. Unintelligible clamor.

I went under once more, but I was better prepared this time. I struck out with both arms and returned to the surface with a gentle heave, not an explosive rush. I blinked and I could see.

Open air, river water sloshing against my body. The shoreline passing on either side, maybe three hundred yards away. One bridge to my left, upstream, a shattered metal guard rail jutting out over the water. Another bridge, heavy with traffic, passing directly over my head.

And breaking down between gaps in the concrete, slicing into the water and cutting across my face were glorious, glorious beams of sunlight.

I breathed. My body relaxed, just a little.

I gave thanks, and then I struck out for shore.

39

Oone long, dripping cab ride later, I arrived at the Crystal Gateway Marriott. With my left hand tucked into my pocket to conceal the handcuffs still attached to that wrist, and muddy water streaming from the pants legs of my ASUs, I paid the driver in soggy cash, then marched directly through the front door and straight to the elevator.

People stared. People whispered. I knew I looked like a Class A washcloth freshly ejected from a washing machine. I didn't care—the twenty-minute cab ride had given me time to think, and now that the euphoria of survival was beginning to subside, the *pissed-off* phase was in full effect, its teeth digging in. I was burning under the collar by the time I reached the eighth floor, swiping a master key off the maid's cart and granting myself access to the FBI suite.

Three shots of Jack from the minibar, along with a Danish and two candy bars. I was starving, my stomach eating itself up. I crashed in a chair, tearing my jacket open, and went to work on the junk food. Washed down with the whiskey, the two candy bars were gone in seconds. I reached for the nearest phone and punched in a number from memory.

The phone rang three times. Alex Hudson answered with a curt "*What?*" to which I responded "Hotel. Now."

Then I hung up and tore open the Danish.

Alex and his entourage arrived twenty-five minutes later, by which time I had guzzled two bottles of water to join the whiskey and was halfway through a bag of chips. I was still wet. The chair I sat in was wet. The floor was soaked beneath my dress shoes.

I didn't care. It was comfortably cool in the hotel, both the chill of the Potomac and the muggy heat of northern Virginia safely in my rearview. Alex barged in like a storm, Kirsch, *The Shining* twins, and Greene right on his heels. The door smacked shut. They reached the sitting room and ground to a stop, standing momentarily slack-jawed as I crammed chips into my mouth, staring right back at them.

"What..." Alex started and stopped. "What *happened?*"

"The Potomac happened," I said. "Real lovely this time of year. Highly recommended."

Alex exchanged a look with Greene. The lieutenant colonel's brow wrinkled into a scowl, and he turned on me.

"*What?*"

I crumpled the chip bag. Tossed it to the floor. "Your pal Benedict has friends. Three double agents dressed as PFPAs. I was arrested and thrown in a van. Then we went for a swim."

"Wait." Now it was Kirsch who spoke. "That was *you?* Off the George Mason Memorial Bridge?"

"I didn't catch the name," I said. "Was kinda distracted by the gunshots."

"Gunshots?" Alex blinked again. For a self-proclaimed special agent genius, he was slow on the uptake. "What did you do, Mason?"

I snorted. Reached for my water and guzzled. It tasted worlds better than the Potomac.

"Who arrested you? You're *sure* they weren't PFPAs?" It was Alex again.

"They barely pretended to be."

"And now?"

"They're dead," I said. "One shot, one kicked to death, one drowned. All three in the river. Flip on the tube; I'm sure it's made the news."

Alex clenched his teeth. Kirsch went for the remote. A quick cycle through sports and soap opera television, and she found it. A local station, a helicopter view. One shattered guard rail and a lot of police boats circling. Divers jumping in. Civilians lined up on the banks to watch.

Alex cursed. "What were you *thinking?*"

I snorted. "I don't know, Alex. Let me see if I can remember. It was something like—*don't freaking drown.*"

Alex ran his fingers through his hair. He turned for a bedroom and stomped out, drawing his phone on the way. The door slammed shut while Kirsch and *The Shining* twins remained fixated on the TV. Only Greene turned back to me.

He was still scowling, almost boiling with rage. But unlike Alex, that anger did not seem fixated on me.

"Start from the beginning," he said.

So I did. Beginning with the moment I was detained at security, then proceeding to the van. The struggle. The three dead guys and my swim to shore.

"You're *sure* they weren't legitimate cops?" Greene pressed. Alex still hadn't returned to the room.

"Would they have removed me from the Pentagon if they were?" I asked.

Greene didn't answer, but I saw the truth in his eyes.

"They bragged about a Chinese payoff," I said. "They weren't cops, they were double agents. Three of them. Which means—"

"Which means we're dealing with a lot more than an isolated leak," Kirsch said, switching off the TV. "It's a whole network."

I nodded but didn't say anything more. There was nothing more to say.

Greene chewed his lip and commenced to pace, staring at the carpet and irregularly kicking at it. *The Shining* twins were trademark quiet. Kirsch was glaring at me.

Then Alex re-entered the room, slamming the door. His phone was clutched in one hand. He was red-faced as he jabbed a finger at me.

"You're done. I want you gone."

"Seriously?" I half-laughed the question.

"You were burned," Alex said. "Benedict knows we're onto him. You blew the whole thing."

"The guys who burned me are *dead*," I retorted. "And you say it like I screwed up. This wasn't me. They knew I was coming."

"So you *screwed up*," Alex said. "You tipped your hand, somehow."

"Or my cover was blown for me. Somebody leaked it."

"Excuse me?"

"You heard me. Somebody snitched. Somebody who knew I was coming."

I swept an open hand around the room, and Alex turned

crimson. Greene did not. He stared iron-jawed at me, and before Alex could explode Greene cut him off.

"He's right," Greene said. "We could have another leak. Somebody who sniffed him out and reported to Benedict. Maybe Pike...maybe that whacky civilian."

"Dr. Sparks," I said. "It wasn't him. The dude is so lost in his own world he wouldn't recognize a bribe if it were paid in gold coins."

"And Pike?" Greene said.

I shrugged. "He felt normal to me. We didn't talk, much. That's why I was going back in, remember?"

I turned back to Alex again, eyeballing him, speaking a silent challenge. The message was received, loud and clear.

"Get out," Alex snapped.

"What?"

"You heard me. I want you out—out of this hotel, out of this whole town, or I swear I will bury you *so far* beneath the prison they'll be chipping your bones out of fossils two millennia from now."

It was an empty threat, and what was more, Alex knew it. But before I could tell him just where to go, one of the twins was taking a call on his government cell phone. Stepping back, covering his ear. Asking for clarification, then snapping toward Alex.

"It's from the surveillance team," he said. "There was a fire at Dr. Landry's hotel—half the building is burning."

The words left his lips, and my heart nearly stopped. For one crystal-clear moment I sat frozen, just staring at him, the phone pressed against his chest.

Then I was exploding out of the chair. Alex was spinning on the carpet. And together, we were bolting for the door.

40

A lex and I took the stairs and reached the parking lot together, exploding out of the Marriott's front entrance. The first car in line sat in the *Elite Parking* slot—that charcoal-gray swoop of crafted metal and glimmering glass, headlights flashing as Alex mashed the key fob. Without asking I broke into a sprint, sliding around the same nose that had rammed the legs out from under me barely a day prior.

I reached the passenger's side and fell into a hard racing seat. Alex slammed the door next to me. Clutch in, finger pushing down on the start button. The engine howled and the tachometer needle bounded off its peg. I smacked my seatbelt into the latch and shouted for no particular reason, "*Go!*"

Alex was already going. Slapped into reverse, and the Shelby spun out of the slot. A horn blew. Alex smashed the brakes and found first gear. The wheels spun and the motor howled, and then we were lurching ahead. Out of the parking lot, onto the street, hauling like a freight train out of hell. With each gear shift I was thrown back, spine slamming into the seat and breath exploding out of my throat. Alex ran the car like it was a rental and this road was a racetrack, blasting past minivans and exploding up a highway ramp at eighty-five miles per hour.

A thousand yards farther and we hit triple digits on the speedometer, the world around us blurring into slow motion as vehicles moving at highway speed seemed to be standing still. It was all thunder and vibrations and *so* much power. With each surge of the engine the wind crushing down on the car pressed it closer to the ground, locking us to the pavement and converting the asphalt into rail lines. We ran hot and straight, blinking past exits and swerving around slower traffic. The mile markers came every few seconds. A sign advertising Chantilly rose out of the highway's shoulder, and I heard Alex whispering.

"Please, God, let her be okay."

There was an earnestness to his voice, a raw desperation that I recognized. It sank into my chest and rang authentic. I looked left and saw him, one hand riding the wheel and one hand riding the shifter. Zeroed in, eyes semi-bloodshot. Not blinking, just praying the same plea. Over and over.

I prayed it too.

Long before we reached Evelyn's hotel I could see the smoke rising above Chantilly's housetops. Thick, black, and boiling. A line of cars clogged the streets leading up to the parking lot entrance, fire trucks surging by and a picket of Virginia cops blocking off access to the turn.

Alex roared right up, sliding the car to a stop and cutting the engine. We were both out, headed for the barricade. The cops closed in as we approached, and Alex deployed his ID wallet, presenting it like a weapon.

"FBI! Let me through."

They parted. I followed. Past the barricade and around the turn. A short walk between trees, and then we reached the parking lot. I could see the hotel.

The three-story structure boiled with black clouds, smoke erupting through top-level windows as flames broke through the roof. One team of firemen assaulted the blaze with jets of water while another sprinted for the building's main entrance, clad in full protective gear.

Hotel guests and staff were stumbling out, choking on smoke and gathering near an armada of ambulances. Cops were directing, paramedics were passing out oxygen masks.

Everything was chaos. As we broke past a fire engine and slid to a stop near the portico, a chorus of shouts from a team of firemen was followed by a crash of splintering timbers. A section of the hotel's roof, about the size of a school bus, collapsed into the third floor and unleased a fresh storm of red flames and thick smoke. The fire was spreading—it was tearing toward the middle of the building.

Toward Room 319, where I'd left Evelyn.

I ran—and Alex ran alongside me. Across the lot, shoving past the firefighters. Headed for the hotel lobby, already choking on smoke, my eyes watering against the haze. I stumbled, catching myself on Alex's shoulder. He threw me off. Cops shouted for us to stop. We reached the portico and thrust past a firefighter who was guiding evacuees into the parking lot. He shouted for us to turn back. I was crossing the threshold, just about to enter the lobby.

And then I heard it. Breaking high above the clamor around me, a familiar tone, an unmistakable voice.

"Mason!"

I spun on my heel. Alex ground to a stop with me. We

looked back through the smoke, and there she was. Seated on the bumper of an ambulance, wrapped in an emergency blanket and huddled under the care of a paramedic. Her skin was blackened by smoke, her hair disheveled and tangled. One sleeve was ripped off her shirt. She was shoeless.

And she never looked better in her life.

I sprinted, clearing a line of survivors and crashing past a cop. People shouted, sobbing, mumbling into cell phones, but I didn't hear any of them. I reached the ambulance just as Evelyn reached her feet. I wrapped her into a hug and clamped her body against mine, burying my face into her shoulder. Sobbing—and not ashamed of it. Pulling her face away, kissing her. Pulling her close again.

She was alive. By happenstance or luck or miracle. She was *alive*.

Evelyn pushed me back, gazing up into my eyes with her own wide and watery. She blinked, she smiled. Then she swallowed hard.

"I don't know what happened," she managed. "There was an alarm, and then everything was just...burning."

My jaw closed, the heat returning to my chest. I simply nodded. There was no point in clarifying her confusion, even if I already had a pretty good idea what had happened here.

Evelyn's gaze passed over my shoulder and she stiffened. I looked back and found Alex standing one pace behind, sweaty and still panting. Hair out of order, tie yanked loose, and not looking back at me. He was fixated on Evelyn. I saw the same desperation in his gaze I'd seen before, the same fervent longing.

"Are you okay?" he said.

There was no hint of challenge in his voice. No hint of the creepy control complex I expected. Just a compulsive need to know.

Evelyn simply nodded. She looked away and I pulled her into a hug again. Evelyn hugged me back, but it wasn't as passionate an embrace as before. I felt her pulling away, and I let her go. She settled back onto the ambulance bumper, still wrapped in the emergency blanket. Suddenly shivering despite the warmth. Shaking her head.

I glanced to Alex. His jaw tightened, and I thought he might push past me. Instead, he simply turned away, hands in his pockets. Looking at the hotel, shoulders rising and settling in short, tense breaths.

I left him to it. I squatted next to the ambulance and took one of Evelyn's hands. It was soft between my fingers... smooth and familiar and warm. She squinted in the sunlight.

"Why are you dressed like a soldier?"

I laughed. I leaned forward to kiss her.

And then the first bullet sliced over my shoulders and slammed into the ambulance.

41

I t was a long shot. I knew that immediately, because the bullet struck before I actually heard the crack of the rifle. A slam of copper-jacketed lead into sheet steel, streaking through the airspace my head had occupied only seconds before. The bullet hole appeared as my eyes were closing, my lips only inches from Evelyn's.

And *then* I heard the shot. Sharp but already echoing, ripping from behind. An instant signal with an instant, compulsive response.

My hands closed around Evelyn's shoulders and I pulled her to the ground. Off the bumper, onto the asphalt. She shouted. I landed on top of her. Around us the chaos of only moments before seemed frozen in place—all voices falling silent, all running figures grinding to a stop. Everyone seeming to be stalled out by the same question—*Was that a gunshot?*

I was already moving again. Keeping my body between Evelyn and the general direction of the gunshot—somewhere behind me. I estimated the line of fire based on the impact point, but it was still only a guess. There was no time to be sure, no way to guarantee that another shooter wouldn't spring out of thin air from a different angle.

We had to *move*.

We were halfway around the bumper of the ambulance as the second bullet skipped off the pavement only inches from my feet. The second crack was just behind, and that was enough to break the freeze. In an instant, everyone was screaming. Everyone was running twice as fast as before. All the cops and first responders were shouting into radios. Evelyn was screaming, also.

Then I had her by the arms and was hauling her up, lunging forward just as Alex appeared out of nowhere, taking Evelyn by her right side while I instinctively took her left. We worked in silent, unspoken tandem, lifting her feet off the ground and sprinting around the ambulance. Weaving through people and parked cars and not stopping until we reached the bulk of a hook-and-ladder fire truck sitting in the back of the parking lot, engine chugging.

It was forty feet long, bright shiny red and surrounded by firefighters. But the part I liked best had to do with its solid steel construction. It was bulletproof.

As we skated around the tail of the truck Alex tripped over a firehose and went down hard, catching himself on his right wrist. Evelyn shouted and reached for him. I tugged her arm just as a third bullet shattered the truck's rear taillight.

"Move her!" Alex called.

I was already moving her. We were behind the truck. Alex was scrambling for cover on his stomach, army-crawling. We all reached shelter behind the truck's axle, and I let Evelyn down to the asphalt. Alex rolled onto his butt and slammed backward into the engine, grimacing and clutching his right wrist. I spun on my heel and was headed back around the engine, squinting into the sunlight, shielding my eyes.

"Did you see him?" I said.

"Parking garage due north of the hotel," Alex shouted, not requiring any clarity on the question. "Muzzle flash, fifth level."

I saw the garage. It was three-hundred-yards distant, and I thought I saw a car rolling across its top. Moving much too fast to be a responsible civilian, breaking for the exit.

And still, I hesitated. I looked back, face lifted in a question.

"I've got her," Alex said, drawing his service Glock from beneath his jacket. "Go! Take the car."

He flipped me the key. I caught both it and Evelyn's gaze at the same moment. There was fear in her eyes—a silent plea.

I simply smiled—a brief, projected confidence. Then I was back around the tail of the fire engine in a split second, barging through the knots of humanity and first responders. Choking on the smoke and leaping fire hoses. Breaking for that short, tree-covered drive. Hurtling around the barricades to where the Shelby sat—both doors open, lights still gleaming but the engine silenced.

I threw myself into the driver's seat, snatching the door closed and punching the start button. The engine thundered and the tachometer bounced. A chiming alarm warned me that the passenger's door was open. A cop shouted for me to hold up.

I ignored it all. I floored the racing clutch, rammed the short-throw shifter into first, cut the wheel to the left, then dropped my toe off the clutch pedal. The reaction was instantaneous. Tires screamed and the back end of the car broke traction. It swung hard and wide, front wheels remaining anchored in place as I rode the brake. The inertia was stupendous, the torque overwhelming. The passenger's door slammed closed, and I couldn't hear the cop anymore. I was still spinning, mirrors clouded by tire smoke, a news crew scrambling to get out of my way.

And then I was pointed away from the hotel. I released the brake and the Shelby launched like a rocket, exploding off an invisible checkered line and blazing between rows of parked cars. I leaned on the horn and people scrambled out of the way. The car reached a stop sign and I hauled hard left, instinctively headed in the general direction of the parking garage.

Not because I had a plan, or any sort of confident target. Simply because somebody on that deck had just cracked off not one, not two, but *three* shots at Evelyn Landry. They might have been aiming at me. They might even have been aiming at Alex.

But those bullets had come within inches of extinguishing Evelyn's life, and I couldn't let that go.

The Shelby reached sixty miles per hour, the tight wings of the racing seat hugging my ribcage as I blazed through curves and hurtled up a hill. I approached a blind turn and I leaned on the horn with my forearm even as I worked the wheel hard right—clutching to disconnect power from the rear wheels, braking to engage a slide.

Then dumping on the power again. I could see the parking deck, barely half a mile ahead. It was surrounded by trees and condo buildings, a dog park spilling out just across the street. Five floors and an exterior elevator shaft. I couldn't see the car I'd noted on that top level—the gaps between each floor were dark and narrow, nothing but glimmering windshields visible.

But I remembered what it looked like. Without needing to close my eyes I could picture it splitting across the fifth floor of the deck, low and fast and dark. It was a sedan, jet-black with flashing chrome wheels.

Like a Mercedes.

My gaze glanced across the face of the garage, down one level and on to the next. Right to the entrance of the garage where a lime-green Kia was nosed up to the exit, its driver fighting with the parking fee machine. As I slowed near the entrance, I thought I saw a dark shadow behind the Kia—a long, sloping silhouette. I leaned low beneath the Shelby's roofline, squinting into the sun. Drawing another hundred yards closer, that shape clarifying.

Then a horn blasted—loud and long, from inside the garage. The parking gate rose. The Kia rolled out.

And an inky dark Mercedes sedan exploded out directly behind it, wheels cutting hard to the right, the gate dropping down and scraping its roof.

The Kia honked back. The Mercedes buzzed past its rear bumper. Then I rammed my foot into the accelerator, and the race was on.

42

The driver of the Mercedes wasn't screwing around. Under the full authority of its supercharged engine, the midnight sedan exploded away from the parking garage, reaching highway speeds in the blink of an eye and blasting straight toward a red-light intersection.

Traffic was gliding across our path of travel, but the Mercedes didn't slow, and I knew he wouldn't stop. His horn blared again, the car's back-end dipping toward the pavement as the engine surged. He hurtled onward, swinging into the empty turn lane to circumvent a line of stopped traffic.

I followed. Up a gear into second, American horsepower howling from beneath the hood. I cut the wheel, and the back end broke loose—I was drifting before I could relax my foot off the accelerator. Gliding left into the turn lane, correcting the drift and grabbing pavement again. The Mercedes blazed through the intersection amid a crescendo of horns, and I stayed with him. Right on his tail, only yards behind. We both swept right out of the turn median and into the lane of forward travel, exploding past a schoolyard. A hospital. Another apartment complex and a strip mall. They all passed in a continuous blur, rolling Virginia greenery fading out of my peripheral vision as the driver of the Mercedes struggled to shake me.

He swerved left, faking a turn. A sudden flash of brake lights was followed by aggressive acceleration, then a snatching right turn that nearly drove the heavy sedan over a sidewalk and into the glass doors of a bank.

He tried everything to lose me, but nothing worked. I was able to guess his maneuvers and compensate for momentary losses of ground with the overwhelming wrath of the flat-plane crank V8. It was ravenous, insatiable. Like an asphalt-devouring beast, fully unleashed and out of control. I'd never driven anything like it—the suspension was so tight and perfectly tuned that it felt like I was running on rails. Every turn was effortless, every tap on the accelerator generated instant, overbearing torque.

The Mercedes, as elite a driving machine as it was, never stood a chance. By the time we cleared the edges of Chantilly and reached the junction of I-66, the driver knew it. He faked another swerve right, cutting across multiple lanes and sweeping as though he was going to take the ramp onto the interstate, but I didn't buy it for a second. He would have to be a raging fool to challenge the GT350 on an open highway—dumber than I thought he was. Sure enough, at the last possible second, the Mercedes swung hard left again. He departed the ramp and tore through a narrow strip of dirt before launching onto Sully Road. I accelerated and drew to within a yard of his rear bumper, laying on my horn. I jabbed a thumb at the side of the road—a warning.

He ignored me, dumping on more power. We screamed

beneath the I-66 overpass, a mess of elevated bridges and sweeping junction ramps. The Shelby backfired beneath the concrete, a sound as loud as a shotgun blast inside a house. Then we were clipping past a sign labeled *CENTERVILLE*. He was taking the exit, turning west on Highway 29, out of town and into the country.

Enough.

If this went on much longer somebody was going to die. A pedestrian, a college kid on a moped, a soccer mom in a minivan. The risk was building toward a certainty. I had to let him go or bring his amateur street racing days to an end.

And I wasn't letting him go. Not after he'd nearly shot Evelyn.

We hit Highway 29 and ripped through a knot of retail. Strip malls, hotels, restaurants. One intersection with a light that turned red just as we crossed through. The highway was a split six-lane with plenty of room to maneuver on either side. Traffic thickened temporarily, but the Mercedes cut around it, swerving and accelerating, riding hot on bumpers before breaking through the swarm.

I followed only yards behind. The highway constricted to a split four-lane, and we passed under I-66 a second time. The retail faded. Strip malls were replaced by churches with large parking lots, open fields spilling toward distant tree lines. The traffic thinned, broader gaps opening between each vehicle. Wide, shallow ditches sprawled to either side of the highway.

And I knew—this was it. The game was up. It was time to make a move.

I cut around a pickup truck and dumped fuel to the engine, blazing to the top of third gear at ninety-five miles per hour. The Mercedes was directly ahead but stuck behind a slow-moving SUV. A passing semi-truck blocked his access to the left lane. He was pinned in a box—only for a moment, but with the deranged power of the Shelby at my disposal, a moment was enough.

I closed to his bumper, sucking to within inches of plastic smashing plastic. I looked through the tinted rear window of the sedan, but I couldn't see him. I jabbed my thumb toward the shoulder again. One final warning.

Once again, he ignored it. The semi cleared the SUV, and before the Mercedes could slide left to fill the open gap, I beat him to the punch. Dumping power to the tires, snatching across the dashed line, and gaining twenty miles per hour—all in the blink of an eye. I raced past the Mercedes' rear bumper, drawing the nose of the Shelby level with his left rear wheel. I glided left, riding to the outside of my lane.

Then I popped hard right.

It was a perfect PIT maneuver—at least, in all measures except speed. At the Phoenix Police Department, I had been trained to never attempt a PIT maneuver at greater than thirty-five miles per hour. We were now moving at seventy, dramatically increasing the opportunity for the Mercedes to spin straight into a ditch. Buck across the median. Slam into a secondary car. Slam into *me*.

But I'd given him an option, I'd calculated the risks. I knew this had to end.

The Mercedes lost control the moment the front right corner of the Shelby's nose smacked the back left corner of the sedan. His back wheels broke traction and his front end swung around.

Then the car was spinning hard counter-clockwise, not

stopping even as it continued to hurtle down the highway. Sliding to the right, its nose pointed backwards, the driver's side wheels of the sedan dropped off the blacktop. I saw him through my righthand window and then I saw him in my rearview mirror. I was past him, laying on my brakes and swerving onto the shoulder. Gravel popped beneath my tires, and I slid to a stop. I looked over my shoulder, breathing hard.

I was just in time to see the Mercedes flip. Grass and dirt exploded from beneath its wheels, and it rotated in midair for one perfect, slow-motion moment. Then it slammed into the ditch on its roof. Metal collapsed and glass detonated— and *still* the car was spinning. It ate up grass. It hopped out of the ditch and continued to slide, ripping through dark Virginia soil.

Then it hit a power pole, smashing the timber sideways and driving against taut power lines before the car finally came to a slamming halt.

I left the Shelby in gear and mashed the start button, cutting the engine off. A cloud of dust had risen from the highway shoulder, consuming my view of the Mercedes as cars swerved by. Some honking. Some flashing lights.

I leaned over the center console and reached for the Shelby's glove box. It was unlocked and dropped open under the illumination of an LED light. Inside there was a map, a flashlight, a road flare—and a handgun. A Glock Model 26 chambered in nine-millimeter.

I drew the weapon and checked it. No round chambered. I worked the slide.

Then I was out of the car and jogging through the waving late-summer grass. Breathing easily, closing on the wrecked Mercedes and already viewing a tangible explanation of why the PPD had never allowed PIT maneuvers at high speeds.

The black sedan was history, resting upside down with all airbags deployed, all windows shattered. The roof was more than half caved in, one bumper hanging off, one wheel twisted and smashed into the well. The car looked like it had been run over by a bulldozer, and there was little chance that anyone inside had survived.

I approached with the Glock at the ready all the same. Circling the tail of the sedan, leaning low. Keeping the car between myself and the highway. Nobody had stopped yet, but I knew I was running out of time. The cops may have already been called.

I neared the driver's window. My view of the driver's compartment was obstructed by a dangling curtain of airbag, but I could see into the back seat. It was empty of humanity, but a long black rifle case was jammed against the collapsed roof. Evidence of the driver's identity.

I closed another five yards, twisting toward the windshield. Bending nearly to the ground and gaining a glimpse inside. I saw one body pinned in the driver's seat. It didn't move.

I thought about Evelyn and my chest tightened. I neared the A-pillar and thrust with the gun, ripping the curtain airbag aside with my finger already on the trigger, just a flinch away from firing.

But I didn't need to. The guy was dead beyond any question. Resting in the driver's seat, his head jerked awkwardly to one side with blood covering his face, he was small, with dark hair and dark eyes—an Asian, presumably Chinese. Dressed in all black, just like the men I had confronted in

Petworth. In Anacostia. At the Sleepy Days Inn and the Stone Creek apartment complex.

But it wasn't the man with the snaking scar on his face. It wasn't the blue-eyed tiger, or anyone I'd ever seen before. It was just some guy with a rifle in his back seat...the crush of a collapsing roof smashing his head sideways and snapping his neck.

Lights out.

I leaned forward and jabbed with the pistol, just to be sure. The body didn't respond, and one finger to his neck confirmed the lack of a pulse. Lowering the pistol, I fished through his pockets. First the pants, then the jacket. I located an ID wallet in an interior pocket, only one card housed inside.

It was a diplomatic ID issued by the People's Republic of China. Depicting his face and a name in both English and Mandarin, the card was brand new and reflected the sunlight without any scratches...

Just like the fake ID I had used to access the Pentagon. I pocketed the card and stood, regarding the smashed car and allowing my mind to work. Weighing the events and evaluating the resulting carnage.

The high-speed PIT maneuver had done its worst, and I was yet again without a witness.

43

I left the Mercedes where it lay and returned to the Shelby. More gravel popped as I returned to the highway, the distant blink of emergency lights visible in my rearview.

It was highway patrol. Excellent response time, all things considered. They were to be congratulated, but I wouldn't stick around to be the one to congratulate them. I didn't want to deal with the questions.

I needed to get back to Chantilly—back to Evelyn.

The car ran hard but not nearly as fast as I reversed my course back under I-66 and through Centerville. I dialed Alex and he picked up immediately. Without protest, he granted me the name of the hospital where the ambulance had taken Evelyn for a precautionary exam.

Maybe he was tired of arguing with me. Maybe he'd finally accepted that I couldn't be controlled. Or maybe he simply wanted his car back.

Parked in the garage of Inova Fair Oaks Hospital, I almost returned Alex's Glock to the glove box...but then I changed my mind and tucked it into my uniform waistband instead, concealed by the filthy ACU jacket. Given the events of the last few days, it felt like a good idea to be armed, and the G26 was easy to conceal. Simple insurance.

Looking like the commander of a military unit in an alien invasion film, I entered the hospital and found Evelyn behind a curtain, sitting on an ER bed. Alex was with her— Evelyn wore a hospital gown and was hooked to an IV. Alex wore a black brace around his right wrist and forearm.

As soon as I saw Evelyn the warmth in my chest returned. More than joy, it was profound relief. I pulled her into a hug and kissed the top of her head, trembling a little as my arms circled her back.

She was real. She was alive. She was safe again.

"I can't breathe," Evelyn mumbled. I released her with another kiss and blinked through misty eyes. I wasn't embarrassed.

When you've lost once, you never again apologize.

"They check you out?" I asked. "Are you okay?"

Evelyn shrugged, tilting her head toward the IV. "They put me on fluids. They say I have some smoke inhalation."

I nodded, once more breathing a silent prayer of gratitude. It was only then that I glanced to Alex and the brace.

"Break something?" I said. I wasn't sure if I cared.

"Sprained my wrist." Alex's voice was flat—not as angry as it usually sounded in our interactions, but then he wasn't looking at me. He was looking at Evelyn, his gaze distant and somewhat...gray.

I watched him watching her, and for the first time since I'd met Alex, I tried to imagine what was going on in his head. What had *been* going on in his head—what was driving this disconnected, illogical obsession. I remembered the stalking, all the times he had appeared in the same rooms and venues as Evelyn, hiding in plain sight and doing a terrible job of it. Almost as though he'd failed Quantico...

Or as though he wanted to be caught. I wasn't sure. I hadn't given it a lot of thought at the time. I only knew what he'd done to her, how he'd hurt her. She had made the choice to move on, and that was her right. The door was closed. He shouldn't be knocking on it, let alone endlessly loitering just outside.

Suddenly, I didn't like him staring at her. This way or any other way. I straightened from the bed and tilted my head toward the curtain.

"Let's talk."

Alex didn't object. He simply nodded, and I kissed Evelyn on the head again and promised to return. Then I followed Alex out of ER to a small, vacant waiting room with a pair of vending machines. Neither of us spoke as he fed quarters through a slot and selected a Mt. Dew. One long pull later and he shook his head like a dog fresh out of the rain, grimacing and settling into a chair. He held the soda against his forehead and closed his eyes, just breathing.

He was in pain. I could see it written in his face... I just wasn't sure what kind of pain it was.

"You gonna die?" I asked.

A grunt. "You'd like that, wouldn't you?"

I didn't answer and Alex swigged Mt. Dew. He rested the bottle on his knee, stared at the vending machines a long time, then finally looked to me.

"Well?"

"I didn't wreck it," I said, simply.

"And the other guy?"

"He's no longer with us."

Alex didn't say anything. I wasn't sure if he was angry, frustrated, or just flat, but whatever the case he certainly didn't look surprised. I settled into a chair, interlacing my fingers.

"He was Chinese. Looked just like the others—an MSS agent, I would guess. I found a diplomatic ID in his wallet. His rifle was in the back seat."

I produced the ID card and passed it to Alex. He squinted at it, rotating the card in his fingers. Not talking.

I waited. I already knew what would happen next—with or without Alex, with or without the FBI. I'd made that decision on the drive back from the overturned Mercedes. I only needed to see whether Alex would reach the same conclusion, or whether I would go it alone.

"What are they *doing?*" Alex muttered.

I knew what he was thinking. I'd thought the same thing. The burning hotel, presumably ignited via arson, may have been nothing more than an elaborate distraction designed to lure the two of us into the sniper's crosshairs, but the sheer audacity of the stunt was off the charts. It was the kind of thing that would make the news and trigger additional federal investigations which would very likely lead back to Beijing. A massive, catastrophic diplomatic crisis.

And yet the Chinese had plowed straight ahead. No hesitation.

"They don't care," I said. "When it's all said and done, when the smoke clears, it doesn't matter if we *know* that the Chinese stole the IBN. They simply have to have it, and they must be running out of time. Now they're pulling out all the stops—fires and snipers and double agents dressed as Pentagon cops. Whatever it takes to keep us away from Benedict."

"That's insanity."

"No, it's a calculated risk. An aggressive risk, certainly, but do they really have a choice? Imagine that it's nineteen fifty, and we discover that the Soviets have developed the intercontinental ballistic missile a decade ahead of us. Suddenly, Los Angeles is within range, and they never have to launch a plane. We're still screwing around with gravity bombs. Don't you think we're going to pull out all the stops to steal that technology?"

"But this could lead to *war*," Alex said. "Don't they realize that?"

"I'm sure they do, which is part of the risk. They still have to act, and I imagine they're hedging their bets. If they fail to obtain the IBN, they'll likely blame the whole thing on some rogue faction of their Ministry of State Security. Make some concessions, talk us off the ledge. It's very unlikely that we'd kick off World War Three over a failed espionage operation, and they know that. If, on the other hand, they succeed in stealing the IBN, our militaries will be evenly matched. It'll be mutually assured destruction again, which is a much better option for Beijing than allowing us to obtain a dominant military edge unchallenged."

I shook my head, staring at the floor. Examining the situation in my mind, imagining all the possible outcomes. I'd hunted bad guys before, both as a soldier and a cop. I'd followed right on their heels, working them into a corner.

I could sense the moment my prey became desperate. The moment they started going crazy, turning rabid. Becoming savages.

The Chinese were there. I could feel it. And that raised the stakes for everyone.

"I'm going back in," I said.

"What?"

"Back to the Pentagon. You're going to send me."

"Are you crazy? They busted you."

"The double agents busted me. Those guys took a fatal bath in the Potomac."

"But the Chinese will know what to expect, now. They might have alerted Benedict, moved him someplace."

"Maybe. It depends on how easily he might spook. Regardless, they're pulling out the stops, which means they're closing on their target. We have to escalate along with them. We don't have a choice."

Alex shook his head. "No. It's not an option. This is bigger than us, now. Bigger than a counter-espionage investigation. I've got to push this up the chain. The Bureau will deploy a larger task force—involve the brass, other agencies. There's a protocol for this."

"And how long will that protocol take, Alex? A day? A week? You do whatever you have to do, but I wasn't asking your permission. They set Evelyn's hotel on fire. They nearly killed her. They keep trying to kill me. My instincts tell me that I'm close—that *they're* close. There's no way I'm turning them loose now. I don't work like that, and I don't work for you."

I rose and turned for the door, leaving Alex sitting in his chair with teeth grinding, the bottle crinkling. I was halfway out of the room before he finally called after me.

"Wait."

I turned back, raising both eyebrows. He still wasn't looking at me. The Mt. Dew bottle looked ready to collapse between his dirty fingers.

"I wouldn't even get authorization," he said. "Not a

second time. I cashed in all my chips on your last hair-brained scheme."

"So don't ask," I said. "Call Greene directly. Have him make the arrangements. If things go sideways—"

"*When.*"

I stopped but didn't look away. I let the silence hang for a moment. Then, "*If* things go sideways, I'll take the fall."

Alex snorted. Shook his head. His jaw was still working —I could actually hear his teeth grinding. He glanced out of the waiting room, back toward the ER, and I had the sudden impression that he wasn't thinking about the mission at all. Not about the Pentagon, the Chinese, or his career on the line.

That desperation was back in his eyes. That question I couldn't answer.

Before I could consider it, he stood. He drew his phone and marched toward the door, snarling as he passed me. "This is insane."

Alex was gone for barely five minutes. I heard him in the hallway outside, raising his voice on the phone. I couldn't make out the words, but I could guess. When he finished, he was smacking his good hand against the wall. He stood outside for a while longer.

When he returned, he was less flustered but still red-faced. The door clapped shut behind him.

"Well?" I said.

"I was right," he said. "My bosses are pulling the plug. They're shutting down my task force."

I kept waiting, because he still hadn't answered my question.

"What happens if I cut you loose?" Alex said.

"You know what."

A snort. A shake of his head. I kept thinking he was about to say something, about to explode in some way. But the detonation never came—he continued to pack it in, chugging from the Mt. Dew.

And once more, it made me wonder.

Before I could raise the question, Alex was chucking the remainder of his soda into the trash can. He was digging his phone out once more.

"Go clean up. I'll call Greene."

I grunted. Alex pointed at me with the phone. "I'm throwing away a career, Sharpe. The only way any of us survives is if we make the bust."

"And yet you aren't hesitating," I said, cocking my head.

Alex's jaw tightened once more. He marched past me, shoving at the door with his good arm.

"Meet at the Marriott in three hours—don't make me come looking for you."

"I'll be there," I said. "And Alex?"

He looked back, angry again. "What?"

"I'm not walking out of there in handcuffs again. If we're going to do this, let's go all the way. Let's steamroll them."

"Meaning?"

"Meaning I'm gonna need some extra bling on my collar. Tell Greene that I want a promotion."

44

I spent a half-hour with Evelyn, sitting alongside her ER bed. After a full medical evaluation, she was back in her street clothes and ready to be surrendered to an FBI security team that Alex had tasked to escort her to another hotel—a property that Alex assured her was much safer than the last.

Maybe she was rattled, maybe she was simply saving her independent indignation for a later date. Whatever the case, Evelyn didn't argue about the security escort or the hotel. As a senior officer of a government agency herself, her own people were concerned. They were agreeable with the FBI's interest in ensuring her security, even if they had no real concept of what the actual threat was.

It was a temporary solution. The only permanent fix would be to pin the Chinese under a ten-ton American truck —and I was more than happy to make that happen.

"Mason?"

We stood in the hospital lobby, a government Tahoe idling just outside. As I watched the pair of burly FBI agents waiting to receive her, a sizeable part of me questioned my own sanity. It was like a screaming alarm, a barrage of red flags.

Don't let her go. Don't let her out of your sight. You can't trust anyone.

"Mason?" Evelyn called my name a second time, and I blinked out of my stupor. Tearing my gaze away from the FBI escorts, I faced her.

"Yeah?"

"Sometime soon...I want to know."

"Know what?"

Evelyn gestured to my wrinkled and muddy Army Service Uniform, the jacket unbuttoned and hanging open, my beret long gone. A disgrace to my heritage, honestly.

"I want to know," Evelyn repeated. "Everything. I have to know."

I nodded. I understood. It wasn't paranoia, it was high standards, lessons learned. She had a right.

"I'll tell you," I said. "Soon."

Evelyn forced a smile and wrapped me in a hug. She did not kiss me.

I watched her climb into the SUV, my stomach churning as the door closed. The engine chugged. The Tahoe pulled away. I couldn't see her through the heavily tinted windows —I didn't know where she was going, and as much as I hated it, I had to agree that my ignorance was to her benefit. It was safer this way.

And yet I couldn't shake the feeling that somehow I was watching her roll away for the last time. Not out of this life. Just...out of mine.

I shook my head, driving the thoughts away and cursing myself for the distraction, the overload of emotion. It was compromising my focus, and just then I needed every ounce of focus I could muster.

Get back to the Marriott. Gear up. This is the death blow.

I borrowed the hospital receptionist's phone and called for a cab—my own phone, knife, keys, and rental car were all back at the Marriott, but I did have a little cash on me, hopefully enough for a one-way ride.

The cabby was Irish, black-haired and quiet. He had the radio playing a broadcast of a European football match, and I didn't mind the distraction. We rode without conversation, and I gave him every dollar remaining in my pocket. It seemed to be enough.

Then I was up the elevator. Knocking at the door to the FBI suite, listening as footsteps tapped, then the peephole darkened.

When the door opened, I was unsurprised to find Linda Kirsch standing alone in the gap. She stared me down without comment, not so much as blinking. Then she simply turned and left the door open, marching back into the room.

I followed her inside to find fresh pizza laid out on the table, water and soda stacked beside it. *The Shining* twins were gone, as were Alex and Greene. Kirsch took her seat on a couch and went to work on a laptop while I peeled my jacket off and went to work on the pizza.

I was starving. Still mentally distracted, still physically exhausted, but the food was hot and amazing.

"You better not screw this up."

Kirsch's statement was sudden and icy. I looked up from my plate to find her staring over the top of her laptop, as solemn and unsmiling as a granite statue. Just as cold, too.

"I don't intend to," I said.

"He's a good man," Kirsch pressed. "Whatever you think of him. You don't know everything."

"I don't pretend to."

Kirsch didn't answer. She didn't look away, either. I squinted, setting my plate down as those questions bubbled up again. Those missing pieces slowly drawing into focus.

"Is there something you want to say, Special Agent?"

More silence. Kirsch's palms rested flat on the laptop, her back rebar-rigid. Then she looked away, back to her screen.

"Not mine to say," she said. "Just know that if you screw this up, I'll kill you. It's a guarantee."

"So noted."

I returned to my pizza and Kirsch returned to her keyboard. Neither of us spoke for the next hour, by which time I'd polished off six slices and scrubbed myself clean in the shower, re-dressing in the street clothes I'd worn before I donned the ASUs and tucking Alex's G26 into the small of my back.

I was just returning to the sitting area when the door lock buzzed. Kirsch slid her laptop aside but didn't stand. A pair of footsteps entered.

It was Alex and Greene. Alex wore a fresh suit, and Greene carried a fresh garment bag. They stopped in the middle of the room, Alex in the lead. He looked to Kirsch, then to me.

"I ran it up the chain," Alex said. "My bosses are forming another task force, just as I predicted."

I nodded slowly, my gaze switching to the garment bag. To Greene. Then back to Alex.

"And in the meantime?"

Alex's lips pinched tight together. "I've been ordered to stand down."

I suppressed a burp. The pizza was giving me heartburn—I wasn't twenty-one anymore.

"Any chance that's going to happen?" I asked.

"What do you think?" Alex's voice carried some edge—also, some exhaustion.

I remained quiet, and he pocketed his hands, looking to the floor. When he spoke, his tone had softened.

"You were right, before. The Chinese must be close, and whatever my bosses are doing, it won't be quick enough. I argued my case, but nobody is listening. Too many layers of authority to work through, too much procedure. The Chinese will be long gone before a plan is assembled. They'll have the IBN."

"Not an option." Linda Kirsch sounded like she looked—stone cold.

"I know," Alex said. "That's why I had Greene pull another uniform. Because as much as I hate it, I can't think of a better idea. We still need Benedict. We still need some idea of what the Chinese are planning next."

"So let's go," I said, simply.

Slowly, Alex turned to me. He held my gaze before speaking. "This could cost you everything, Sharpe."

"I know," I said, and I meant it. But Alex didn't break eye contact. I felt that he was trying to say something he wasn't willing to put into words. Something subtle, something conflicting. For a long moment I looked past his polished government bravado, his prep school southern charm, his stress and his angst and all his attitude. I looked deeper.

And finally, the picture clarified in my mind. I saw it...I believed it. It fell to earth like a boulder, a solid and irrefutable reality. The link in an invisible chain...now complete.

My chest tightened, but I didn't say anything else. I didn't voice the knowledge. Because whatever was or wasn't true, the reality remained the same.

I had sworn to protect my country. I had sworn to protect Evelyn Landry. And those oaths hadn't expired.

They never would.

"All right, then." Greene's voice was gruff and emotionless. "Let's get to it."

"You received my special request?" I said.

Greene didn't answer, he simply stepped across the room and presented me with the garment bag. I spread it across the clear end of the table and unbuttoned the top. Pulled the zipper down, exposing a brand-new, perfectly pressed and clean ASU uniform in my size. Dark blue with the same campaign bars, name plate, and medals as before.

Only this time the gold oak leaves were missing. In their place were a pair of silver eagles, wings spread apart, olive branches and a cluster of arrows held in each of their claws.

"Congratulations, Colonel," Greene said. "Your career runs on jet fuel."

I touched one of the eagles and smiled a dry, lethal smile.

Here goes nothing.

45

———

Same SUV, same driving formation. Kirsch and Greene in the front, Alex riding to my left. Only *The Shining* twins were missing, and nobody spoke as we pulled into the Pentagon's South Parking Lot. The sun was just beginning to sink over the Virginia countryside, and already the lot was emptying out.

Not that the Pentagon would close. This building never closed, not at midnight and not on Christmas. The lab would still be there, and under the authority of the eagles on my collar, I would be granted access. If anyone argued, I had orders. If anyone protested my legitimacy, they were welcome to run my credentials. The home address problem had now been fixed—Greene's friends at the Defense Counterintelligence and Security Agency had taken care of everything.

This arbitrary, rank-skipping promotion wasn't a trick we could repeat, but it wasn't really a trick at all. It was a battering ram, smashing through the laboratory buried under C Ring. We would find the truth, or we would go to jail.

All or nothing, cards on the table. I liked it.

The Suburban stopped along the curb and Kirsch shifted into park. Reaching beneath my brand-new ASU jacket, I subtly removed all the metal items that wouldn't make it through Pentagon security from my pocket, and slipped them into the open storage compartment of the Suburban's back door. Then I reached for the handle.

Alex's voice stopped me. "Mason."

I looked back. He wasn't facing me. He was looking out the window, suspended in the moment. And then finally, just above his breath: "Good luck."

I ducked my head. I stepped out, donning my brand-new beret and dragging a hard-sided, locking briefcase against my leg. No more soft-sided satchel—I was a full-bird colonel. There were secrets in this bag. There was no yield in my step.

I marched right to the front door of the Pentagon like I owned the place. An Airforce E-4 saw me coming and snapped to attention, holding the door. I flatly ignored her, headed straight for the X-ray. Moving into the senior officer line. Smacking the suitcase down, sweeping off my cover, flipping open my ID wallet.

And then freezing. It was the *same* PFPA agent from my first visit. Twenty-something, female, Italian heritage. I recognized her name—Spinelli—and she recognized me. She blinked. Frowned at my ID. Was suspended in space the same way Alex had been, although for different reasons. I cleared my throat.

"Is there a problem, Officer?"

I spat the words, looking down my nose at her. I adopted

every affectation of every officer I ever hated in the Seventy-Fifth—an admittedly short list, but you never remember the good ones. Only the clowns.

"Uh...sir..."

"Am I clear?"

She looked to the screen. Smacked a key. I saw my own face displayed in black and white, my own credentials spelled out just as before. The home address box was filled —it wasn't an Anacostia address, but what colonel would live in Anacostia, anyway?

"Uh...yes, sir. Of course."

She returned the ID. I took my briefcase. I saw her reaching for her phone as I departed but I didn't care. I was at least ten years too young to be a colonel, but that wasn't the point.

She hadn't been able to argue with me. Nobody could without definite proof of my illegitimacy—that was the power of the twin eagles pinned to my collar.

From E Ring to C Ring. All the tours were gone, as were most of the civilians. I reached the elevator for the basement only five minutes after clearing front door security. No alarms had sounded, no PFPA officers—legitimate or otherwise—were scrambling to confront me. The elevator checkpoint officer was a fresh face, and he cleared me without protest. I descended two levels and stepped out into the corridor of windowless doors. I was alone, just as before. I marched left, reaching room B2C121 and knocking twice.

Nobody answered. I waited ten seconds, then knocked again, louder this time. Again, there was no answer. I looked into the camera mounted over the door and snapped my fingers.

Still, nobody answered. I was just about to knock for the

third time when a door opened from down the hall and an Air Force first lieutenant appeared, face twisted into a scowl that quickly melted when he saw me.

Or, perhaps, saw the eagles on my collar.

"Can I help you, sir?"

"Where's the Army Futures Command officer in charge of this facility?" I shot the words as a demand, not a question.

"Captain Pike?"

"That's right."

"He didn't make it in today. Some personal matter. My office managed the shipment."

"Shipment?" I squinted. "What shipment?"

The lieutenant hesitated. "The...lab shipment, sir."

He said it like I should have known—or maybe like he wasn't sure if he was allowed to talk about it. I wasn't sure what he meant, but there was a sickening feeling boiling deep in my gut, gaining momentum. Warning me that I didn't have time to deliberate.

"Open this door," I said, snapping my fingers.

"Sir?"

"The door!" I shouted. "Open it."

He hesitated a moment longer, then stepped to B2C121 and flashed a keycard. The lock buzzed. He opened the door, and I barged into the same hallway where I'd initially met Pike and Sparks. That corridor lined by laboratories stacked with IBN gear. All the rifles, chest rigs, helmets...

Except they were now gone. All of it was gone. The tables visible through the reinforced glass windows of the labs were empty, bare. No boxes, no scraps, no personnel on site.

"What happened?" I demanded, spinning back on the Air Force lieutenant. "Where is it?"

"It's...gone, sir. It was shipped."

"Where?" I demanded.

"Sir?"

"Where was it shipped?"

This time the lieutenant—his nametag read *White*—didn't answer. Suspicions creased his face, and he shook his head. "I'm afraid that's classified, Colonel."

"Not to me, it isn't."

"I'm afraid it is."

I dropped my briefcase on the floor of the hallway. It smacked as loud as a gunshot, and White flinched despite himself. I ignored him, spinning the combination dials on the briefcase, snapping it open and producing the fabricated orders that Greene had secured. They featured the same pseudonym as before complete with an updated rank. White accepted the document and read quickly, twice more glancing over the top of the pages to eyeball me. He was starting to sweat. I didn't make it any easier on him, staring him down.

At last, "Sir...I'm going to need to make a call—"

"Look at me," I snapped, cutting him off.

He did. I leaned close, speaking in barely above a whisper. "Do you know who I am?"

He swallowed—he actually swallowed. "Sir—"

"M. L. Griffin, Lieutenant! The youngest commissioned colonel in US Army history. Do you know what that means?"

He quaked—didn't answer.

"It means I'm in a hellfire hurry! Take me to your commanding officer. *Now!*"

White was only too eager to comply. He stumbled back through the door, and I followed. Down the hall and around the corner into a suite of admin offices. Past junior officers and enlisted desk drones who snapped to attention as we walked by. We reached an office. A major was there, speaking into a phone. White barged in, and the major hung up.

Then I was popping off again, thrusting my printed orders at the major and barking demands. The major fumbled with the documents while White sweated bullets. I was in full character now. Like Jack Nicholson on the witness stand, I was just begging for somebody to demand the truth. I kept my voice near a shout and my motions short and abrupt. Before it was over I had half the office working the phones, the major popping off emails and digging through digital file systems.

Top-secret status melted amid the manufactured chaos. The act was working—and yet I could feel the clock in my head, ticking incessantly. Warning me that I was running out of time, and not just with my act. I could feel the pressure building, hammering inside my chest.

And then the major's head popped up from behind his computer. "Colonel?"

I returned to his office. He spun the computer monitor around.

"What's this?" I said.

"Transfer orders, sir. For the research project you asked about. *Project Unity.*"

I leaned low, squinting. Scanning. Speed-reading past the headlines, down to the bottom.

Post: Order for immediate transfer of all hardware, computer equipment, and research material related to Project Unity. Dispatch to Naval Support Activity Annapolis, Maryland.

My gaze snapped up. The major stood behind his desk, a little wide-eyed and flustered.

"Who ordered this?" Jack Nicholson was gone from my voice. It was me again—just a simple, blunt question. The tone shift caught him off guard.

"I'm not—"

"Find out!"

He was back at the keys. Clicking. Typing. Producing another document.

"It looks like...Army Brigadier General James Trace? The orders were dispatched two hours ago. It's signed."

Another spin of the monitor. A quick glance at the signature, but it meant nothing to me. Neither did the name, but that wasn't unusual. I'd been out of the Army for years, and there are a couple hundred O-7's in active Army service at any given time, anyway.

"You know him?" I asked.

"Uh...no, sir. Never met."

"Run his ID."

"Sir?"

"His UIN! Run it."

The major pivoted and was back at the keyboard. He accessed a Department of Defense personnel database and input Trace's ten-digit Unique Identification Number—a blend of his social security number and his DOD ID number. Every soldier has one. I could still quote mine from memory, a permanent fixture of my psyche.

Trace's file finally loaded, and I quickly scanned it from top to bottom. The brigadier general was fifty-two years old, born in Maine. A graduate of West Point and a thirty-three-year veteran of the Army. He'd served in multiple combat deployments, and now worked for Army Futures Command, just like Captain Pike.

The file checked out. It was all in order...except for one tiny detail that caught my eye and sank into my chest like a bullet. A blinking red beacon. The missing piece I'd been searching for.

"Print that file," I snapped. "Quick!"

The major smacked keys. The file was four sheets long. I snatched the pages off the printer tray and then I was out of the office. Down the hall, ignoring the major calling after me about my abandoned briefcase. Up the elevator, tearing my tie loose. Down the corridors from C Ring to E Ring, half-running the entire way. Heart pounding. Mind racing.

Annapolis. Why Annapolis?

I didn't know, but it might not matter. Another thought was already forming in my mind, the crystallization of a clarifying image. A theory quickly building steam into a conviction.

An idea of just who the American traitor was.

I closed on the security station and noted Officer Spinelli approaching from across the room. She was accompanied by two older men in PFPA uniforms. They were carrying tablet computers—they saw me, and one of them called out.

"Colonel! A word, please."

I didn't slow. I passed the security station, rushing the wrong way through a metal detector. The Pentagon Force Protection agent shouted again, louder this time. Feet smacked the tile. I reached the doors and exploded into the parking lot. The sun was gone. Only the parking lot lights remained.

But the Suburban was there.

"Colonel! Halt where you are!"

The voice persisted from behind, but I was already at the Suburban. Back door open, I landed in the rear seat behind Greene. The door slammed closed.

"Move," I snapped.

Kirsch saw the PFPAs coming and she didn't hesitate. The Suburban dropped into gear and we were off, out of the parking lot even as the agents stumbled to a stop and watched us go—suspicious, but not bold enough to trigger an alarm.

I breathed heavily from my half-jog and slouched into the seat. Brigadier General James Trace's personnel file was crumpled in one hand, stained with sweat. Alex stared from the seat next to me.

"*Well?*"

"It's gone," I said.

"What? What's gone?"

"All of it. The demo equipment, all the lab testing material. They put it on a truck, and it's headed to Annapolis."

"Annapolis?" Greene interjected. "Why Annapolis?"

I didn't answer. All eyes were boring into me.

But I was only looking at Greene.

"How long have you known Alex, Greene?"

No answer. Greene frowned.

"How'd you get hooked up with his investigation, anyway? Did he call you? Or...did you call him?"

A tinge of red appeared beneath the edge of Greene's collar. His face hardened.

"What are you getting at, Mason?" Alex said. "Why did they move the IBN?"

"That's a great question. Maybe we should ask James Trace."

The name left my lips, and Greene stiffened, just barely. But I noticed.

"*What* are you talking about?" the lieutenant colonel barked.

"I'm talking about Brigadier General James Trace," I said, thrusting the print-off forward. "Commander, Army Futures Command. You know him?"

Greene took the personnel file. He studied it longer than he should have. I could see the wheels spinning behind his eyes.

And I knew.

"This must be some mistake," Greene said. "Why would Army Futures Command send the IBN—"

"To a Navy base?" I said, cutting him off. "That's what I was wondering. But then I thought...what if it's not headed to Annapolis at all? What if this isn't a transfer at all, but a heist? What if the Chinese *already have the IBN?*"

Greene shook his head, waving the paper. "Are you accusing a brigadier general of treason?"

"No more than I'm claiming to be a legitimate colonel," I retorted.

"What does that mean?" Alex was interjecting. Kirsch was glancing into her rearview mirror.

"It means there isn't any Brigadier General James Trace," I said. "It means somebody made him up. Manufactured his file and his signature and then used that fake identity to steal a lab full of next-generation goodies right from under the Pentagon's nose."

Greene had stopped blinking. He was twisted now, eyes locked on me. I leaned forward, lowering my voice. Speaking through my teeth.

"Wanna know how I know, Greene?"

Everyone was still. Greene forced a single word. "How?"

I pointed at the sheet. "Because it seems that James and I are roommates. One-thirty-one Maple Street, Alexandria, Virginia. The same residence that appeared on my file after the blank was filled. What a coincidence."

I finished. Nobody spoke. Greene's gaze was flicking between me and Alex, then back again. His hips had subtly twisted. His right arm had moved off the armrest. It was in his lap.

It was as good as a smoking gun.

I leaned a little closer, dropping my own hand out of my lap. To the right of my seat. Into the door pocket of the back door.

My face was only inches from Greene's. I smiled. "Remind me. Who was it who arranged my fake DOD file? Wasn't it...*you?*"

The words landed. Greene's gaze turned titanium-hard and his right hand twitched. It fell off his lap. Alex saw it coming and shouted. Kirsch stiffened and yanked the Suburban left, driving her body against the doorpost in a futile attempt to find cover.

And then the first gunshot detonated like a thunderclap.

46

I shot Greene five times through the back of his seat with Alex's Glock 26. The little pistol snapped in my hands, pumping nine-millimeter rounds through cloth and foam and more cloth before smashing into Greene's back. Long before he could aim his concealed SIG P365 at me, even before he could fully wrap his finger around its trigger, his body was jerking and the Suburban was reverberating with the gunshots, Kirsch swerving and Alex shouting.

I stopped at the fifth shot only because Greene had fallen face-first into the dash, half-suspended by his seatbelt, his gun sliding to the floor. He was dead—not a single doubt about it.

And not soon enough.

"What the *hell?*" It was Alex, bellowing from the seat next to me as Kirsch swept the Suburban into the emergency lane and we ground to a stop. There was blood all over the interior of the windshield—blood running down Greene's ventilated back and pooling in the seat. A couple of my bullets had passed clean through his body at point-blank range and penetrated the dash.

The whole vehicle smelled like a battlefield. I tasted it on my lips.

"*Proditores pereunt*," I said, lowering the Glock.

"What?" It was Alex again, still looking wide-eyed from the body to me.

"Traitors perish," I said, simply.

Then Kirsch was barging in. She had her bureau-issued Glock 19 out, twisting around the seat and aligning the muzzle with my chest.

"*Give me that.*"

I didn't protest. One press of the mag release and a polymer-coated magazine hit the floor. I tugged the slide to eject the cartridge still housed in the chamber, then calmly placed the pistol in the seat next to me.

"Where did you get that?" Kirsch barked.

It was a pointless question. Alex answered for her.

"It's *mine.*"

"That's right."

"From my *car.*"

"We're wasting time here, Alex. Or maybe I need to clarify—Greene was Benedict."

I jabbed a finger at the limp body. Alex tore his seatbelt off and swore. Then he was kicking the door open, stepping out into the emergency lane.

And puking.

I listened in silence while Kirsch kept her sidearm on me. After Alex had finished, he reached a hand into the door pocket of the Suburban and tore out a wad of napkins. Most of them ended up strewn across the asphalt.

Then he was circling the vehicle, arriving at my door. He snatched it open. He stared me in the eye.

"*What happened?*"

Another pointless question. He should have been up to speed. I recounted the events anyway—my third trip into the Pentagon, the empty lab, my confrontation with the Air Force officers who ran that floor.

And my discovery of a transfer order signed by a man who shared my fake residence.

"He screwed up, Alex," I said. "A simple slip of the mind. The Defense Counterintelligence and Security Agency forgot to put an address into my fake file, and when I complained about it, Greene fixed it himself. He fed them an address, and his mind defaulted to a fake he'd used before, on a different file. Brigadier General James Trace's file. People do it all the time, defaulting to the same names and numbers when they're lying. It was as honest as a dishonest mistake can get."

"That doesn't prove that he was Benedict," Alex snapped. "It could have been any one of his buddies at DCSA."

"But it wasn't."

"What made you so sure?"

"Well, he tried to shoot me, for a start. But if that's not enough evidence for you, consider Exhibit B—he was *here*."

Alex said nothing. Kirsch narrowed her eyes. I sighed.

"You sent the twins away, right?"

"Twins?" Kirsch said.

"The big guys. The ones who were here before. You dismissed them when your bosses canceled your task force. Why? Because you were about to go off the books. Against protocol, against orders. I stuck around because I don't care about protocol, I'm protecting Evelyn. Kirsch stuck around because she's loyal to you—unquestionably. Kinda like she owes you something."

I looked at Kirsch when I said it, and her eyes narrowed, but she didn't blink. I let the moment hang, and then I let it go. As badly as I wanted to, it wasn't the right time to clarify the point—we would circle back later.

"All that leads us to Greene," I continued. "Why did *he* stick around? Why wasn't he concerned about participating in an illegal operation? I didn't consider it, at first, but I should have. We all should have. The answer?" I shrugged. "Greene wasn't concerned because Greene was Benedict. He was working for the Chinese all along, keeping his thumb on us, shuffling us around. He knew there was an FBI investigation into the Chinese mole operation, and he could hardly shut it down. The next best thing was to stick close to it, to manage it and sabotage it if he could. No doubt it was Greene who sent fake PFPA officers after me—the ones who died in the Potomac. Greene who told the Chinese where to find Evelyn, setting us up for a sniper ambush. Greene who sent me *back* inside the Pentagon as a fake colonel. Why? Because all efforts to eliminate me had failed, and he had to keep pretending that he was on our side. He knew the Chinese were clearing out the warehouse while I was busy chasing their sniper in your car. Maybe he thought the best way to keep himself safe until he could escape to China was to stay involved. Certainly, he never expected me to pull James Trace's file, and why would it matter if I did? He didn't know he screwed up the address."

I finished, and Alex said nothing. Kirsch said nothing. They both stared in semi-disbelief before at last Kirsch lowered her weapon, and Alex turned away from the Suburban, cursing.

I didn't call after him. I only looked at Kirsch, not speaking my challenge but circling back, nonetheless. She held my gaze for a moment, and then she was the first to look away, gaze dropping. Shoulders sagging, just a little.

Not speaking a word...but saying a lot.

Alex reappeared at the back door five seconds later, Greene's blood speckling his right cheek. In his black suit with wide, crazed eyes, he looked like a white-collar serial killer.

"You saw the lab?" Alex said.

"I did."

"And it's empty?"

"Totally."

"And there's no chance Trace is legit?"

I shrugged. "Make a phone call. Shouldn't be difficult to verify."

Alex fell quiet. We were all thinking the same thing, but it was Kirsch who voiced it first.

"So...they already have it."

47

A lex resumed his seat and Kirsch peeled her jacket off, throwing it over Greene's lifeless corpse before she powered out of the emergency lane.

There was nothing to do with the body. It didn't even matter. The only thing that *did* matter was the veracity of my story, and Alex was busy investigating that question with a series of phone calls.

To the FBI. To the DOD. To contacts he had inside Army Futures Command. He asked a lot of questions, but nobody had any answers, not about a transfer order for the IBN and not about anybody named James Trace.

Because he didn't exist...and neither did Maple Street.

We returned to DC just in time to catch rush hour, four lanes bogging down to a crawl. Kirsch switched on a system of concealed LED emergency lights, and some cars pulled over to allow us to pass. Many more couldn't move, and others simply refused to. It was just over three miles from the Pentagon to the J. Edgar Hoover building, head-quarters of the FBI, but the drive consumed nearly half an hour. By the time Kirsch finally swung the Suburban to the curb at the main entrance, Alex was just hanging up with a command officer of the FBI's Hostage Rescue Team —the closest thing the bureau had to an armed assault unit.

I couldn't hear both sides of the conversation, but I gathered the gist. The IBN was assumed to have been stolen right out from under the noses of Pentagon security, just as I said. There was a transfer order, and the destination was indeed the Navy base in Annapolis. But Annapolis knew nothing about an incoming top secret shipment, and the truck had never arrived.

The truck had disappeared.

"There's no official record of the shipping contractor or a manifest of the equipment moved," Alex said, ending his latest call. "And Captain Pike is missing."

"Somebody at the Pentagon told me he missed work for personal reasons," I said. "What about the civilian? Dr. Sparks."

"Also missed work today," Alex said. "Also for personal reasons. Nobody can get either one of them on the phone."

"More of *his* handiwork," Kirsch snarled, jabbing a finger at the dead Greene. Then she was climbing out of the Suburban, shouting to a nearby FBI agent on his way out of the building. She pitched him the keys as though he were a valet. "Find a place for this! And do something with the body."

The agent fumbled the keys. Kirsch was already halfway up the steps to the Hoover building's main entrance. Alex pushed his door open. "With me, Sharpe."

I cocked an eyebrow. He looked back over his shoulder. "You just gunned down a US Army officer, and there's still a lot of holes in this story. If you think I'm letting you out of my sight, you're insane."

I didn't protest—I wanted to be inside FBI headquarters nearly as badly as Alex. Marching up the steps toward the door Kirsch held open, we passed under a row of hanging American flags with J. Edgar's name printed above the main entrance. Then we were swallowed by the historic epicenter of America's preeminent law enforcement agency as though we were being swallowed by a whale. One moment it was rushing DC streets and the smell of blood still hanging in my nostrils, and then it was all cold tile and bland wall hangings. A row of horseshoe metal detectors standing at a security checkpoint. Agents behind a credenza, phones ringing. A bank of elevators and a *lot* of bustling men and women clad in black suits.

Maybe it was always this way. I'd never been to FBI headquarters before, neither as a soldier nor a cop. But something about the tension in the air told me that a sense of emergency had permeated this place. Word had leaked—or maybe been broadcasted. Even people who didn't seem to understand *why* they were in a rush were in a rush. We bottlenecked at security, then Kirsch was taking the lead again. Shoving people aside with muscled, stiff arms, ushering Alex and myself onward and daring the security officer standing next to the X-ray machine to defy her.

Kirsch and Alex's IDs beeped against electronic readers, I signed a clipboard that was thrust into my face, and then we were off to the elevators. Up to the seventh floor after a key-card swipe by Kirsch. The ride was uninterrupted, the destination heralded by a ding. I marched out across industrial carpet into a landing area surrounded by floor-to-ceiling glass walls. Kirsch pushed the door open.

Then the chaos really began. The seventh floor was an open bullpen, occupied by long rows of five-foot cubicles with walkways in between and glass-faced offices built into the perimeter. The space was maybe a hundred feet wide and twice as long, illuminated by row upon row of tube lights, with tinted windows overlooking the city.

And the floor was packed with people. No less than a hundred agents, all bustling from one cubicle to the next, some taking calls and others shouting to one another from across the room. Printers hummed and keyboards clacked. The place smelled like sweat and stale takeout food and really cheap cleaners—a cocktail that took me in a flash right back to the Phoenix PD homicide bullpen.

It was so much better than smelling Greene's lifeless corpse.

"On me," Alex snapped. He led the way through the maze, Kirsch right on his hip, myself only a yard behind. We cleared the body of the room amid the endless churn of semi-unhinged alarm—a noise that reinforced my worst fears about the missing equipment from the Pentagon lab.

Then we reached a glass door framed in metal amid a larger glass wall. Blinds hung closed behind it. Kirsch rapped twice with hard knuckles, and the door swung open.

"*Finally*," somebody exhaled. "Where have you been? Get in here! The Tripple-D is headed down."

Alex and Kirsch were ushered in. I slipped in behind them, the door smacking shut and blocking the bulk of the tumult outside. The space we entered was a large conference room, complete with a stretching table surrounded by short-backed leather chairs and a swarm of what I assumed to be FBI brass. Men and women in the same cheap suits with an aura of command swarming around them.

Command...and anxiety.

Alex took a chair near the end of the table, and Kirsch sat along the wall. I stood awkwardly near the door, not sure what to do with my hands. Kirsch snapped her fingers and pointed to the chair next to her. I sat.

Everyone was talking—murmurs and sidebar conversations. An endless, unintelligible garble that was terminated instantly by a second door opening into the room—a door located in the back corner. In an instant everyone was on their feet, and I rose with them. The chatter evaporated. A woman dressed in a conservative pant suit entered. She was early fifties, dark-haired and serious. Her face had one of those concrete fixtures to it that made it seem like she had never smiled.

Like Kirsch.

"Sit," the woman said. She took the chair at the end of the table. She didn't introduce herself—she didn't seem to need to. Certainly, I didn't recognize her, but the term "Triple-D" was semi-familiar. Usually, it meant *Assistant Deputy Director*. Like a vice-vice president.

Way up the food chain for the FBI. This investigation had just shifted into high gear.

The woman guzzled water. She set her glass down with a smack and faced the room. Then she said, "What happened?"

48

I t was a simple question, but the answer was predictably complicated. Three people began speaking at once, and the ADD snapped her fingers. She pointed to one guy. He resumed.

"It's concerning Project Unity, ma'am. It's a DOD developmental program involving Integrated Battle—"

"I'm familiar," the ADD cut him off. "*What happened?*"

"We..." The guy stopped. Lost his nerve. A glare broke him loose. "We believe the technology was stolen, ma'am. By the Chinese."

The ADD waited, face blank. Her eyebrows rose in a question, and my stomach sank as if operating on the plummeting end of a see-saw.

I could see it already. I'd been here before, so many times. Never with the FBI, but how different could the bureaucracy of a large police department or the US Army— the world's largest bureaucracy—be from that of the FBI? The story was the same anywhere leadership was sliced and sub-sliced a thousand times between the guy on the ground and the guy—or woman—at the very top. The problems were the same, also.

America's greatest military secret had just been snatched from right under the noses of the DOD, and the assistant director of the FBI wasn't even aware of the counter-espionage program Alex had been running to prevent that disaster. It was tribal miscommunication and *non*communication at its finest. A persistent, tenacious problem that had haunted every mission, every investigation I'd ever pursued as a soldier or a cop.

And I was watching it again. From a chair jammed against the wall, listening as precious minutes were wasted and the ADD's questions were answered, one at a time, largely by people who were so far out of touch with the facts of the situation that their information was days old at best. Nobody consulted Alex—I could see him nearly boiling at the end of the table, shoulders tensing and fingers digging into the arms of his chair. Resisting the urge to interrupt, to make himself the enemy of the entire FBI command hierarchy. To bring this wandering flight back to earth.

Well, screw that. I wasn't FBI.

I stood even as Kirsch scrambled to stop me. Jerking free of her grip, I closed on the end of the table, wheeling the stenographer in her office chair out of my way and rapping my knuckles twice on the tabletop.

"Look. Here's what matters." Every head in the room swiveled toward me, including that of the ADD. Jaws fell open. Brows wrinkled in confusion—a condition no doubt worsened by the fact that I was still wearing the uniform of a full-bird colonel. I was beginning to like it.

"The Chinese stole sensitive, next-generation warfighting technology from the Pentagon no less than three hours ago. The location of that equipment and their eventual destination is unknown. We don't have time for everybody at this table to fully understand the nature of what they stole, or how valuable it is. Just pretend the Chinese don't have nukes and they just stole the blueprints to build them. That'll put you on the right track. Obvious next step? We gotta find them. Now, is everybody on the same page?"

Nobody spoke. Everyone was still staring at me. It was the ADD herself who broke the silence. "Who are *you*?"

I almost answered with my best Jack Nicholson impersonation, but Alex answered for me. He stood, clearing his throat.

"Ma'am, Special Agent Alex Hudson, counter-intelligence operations. I was the SAIC for the investigation launched to identify a potential Chinese mole operating within the Pentagon."

"Well, it seems you've failed, Hudson."

There was no shortage of heat in the ADD's tone. Alex took it right on the chin.

"It seems so, ma'am. Standing at the table here is Mr. Mason Sharpe. He's former US Army and was a consultant for my task force. He was working with us to identify the Chinese mole—code name, *Benedict*."

"His nametag says Griffin," somebody barked, speaking about me as though I wasn't in the room.

"He was undercover," Alex clarified. "It's a long story. With respect—"

"Did you?" the ADD said, addressing the question to me.

"Did I what?" I said.

"Did you *find Benedict*?"

Alex shot me a panicked look. I could see the flashing signal in his gaze—the desperate *no, no, no*. I ignored it.

"Sure," I said. "He's lying dead in your parking garage."

That was enough to unleash the next round of consternation. Resumed sidebars, murmurs of shock, snarled curses. It was exactly what I expected—an opening for Alex to press ahead. He took it.

"Ma'am, I agree with Mr. Sharpe. We really don't have time to bring everyone up to speed on all the details. The most important thing is to recover this equipment, ASAP. With every moment we waste the Chinese slip farther from our grip. We need agents on the ground, *now*. This has to be a full emergency manhunt."

Nobody had anything to say about that. The ADD asked the next question—and she asked me.

"Do we have any idea where they might be headed?"

I didn't—at least, not specifically. But it wasn't hard to rationalize a partial answer, and at this juncture I figured that my opinion was just about as valid as anyone else's.

"They'll head for the border," I said. "The first border they can find. I'm sure you've already got people reviewing Pentagon security tapes and locating the crew that removed the equipment. The Chinese would expect this, and they wouldn't wait around for a manhunt. They'd get out now—before it gets hot."

"That's complete conjecture!" It was a senior special agent who spoke—I knew by both his age and his physical proximity to the ADD. "For all we know they could be headed to ground. A safe house, an apartment in Roanoke. They could be headed west. They could be hiding in their own embassy!"

"Have you put hands on that equipment?" I challenged. The guy spun on me—I kept going before he could interject. "I thought not. I have. The material they cleaned out of that lab is substantial. Bulky enough to fill an SUV, and that's assuming they only kept the smaller items. They'll need advanced research facilities to break it down and replicate it, which is why they won't take it back to their embassy. They need that tech in China, and the longer they wait to make a run for the border, the harder it will be to escape at all. I'm *telling you*, they're moving now. You're wasting time."

The guy I had challenged turned red-faced. He flustered. "Why are we even *listening* to you? We don't know who you are! Do you have a security clearance?"

Here we go.

The table dissolved once more into a near-instant squabble, some agents arguing my point, others protesting it. Most were tossing out wild, unfounded theories of their own—everything from Russian involvement to the groundless hope that this was all a huge mistake. That the material was simply misplaced.

I caught Alex's eye and pointed to the door. Then I was gone. Pushing back into the bullpen, leaving them to the meltdown. I didn't care whether he followed. There was no further use in me talking sense to bureaucracy.

But Alex did follow. So did Kirsch. They both met me outside, and before I could speak, Alex did.

"You're right. They're heading for the border. It's the only thing that makes sense."

"And they're not going to catch them," I said, lifting a chin toward the conference room. "Not in time."

Alex didn't answer. Both he and Kirsch were watching the bullpen, gazes darting, Kirsch chewing her lip. Then I spoke again.

"Do you have a map? I may have an idea."

49

A lex did have a map—it was in a map room, no less. Connected to the primary bullpen, the windowless chamber was hung with white projector screens and equipped with a computer terminal, several chairs, and a high-wattage projector that could display any portion of the world in high-definition detail.

Alex swiped his keycard and powered on the computer. Kirsch locked the door. The first map to display across the eight-foot screen at the end of the room was that of metro DC.

Highlights included all key government buildings, including the Capitol, the White House, and the J. Edgar Hoover Building.

"Expand," I said.

Alex zoomed out. I saw the East Coast—the Chesapeake Bay, Virginia, Maryland, Delaware, New Jersey. Mountains rolling inward over West Virginia and Pennsylvania.

I breathed deep—I pictured myself as a terrorist getting out of Dodge with a labload of heavy equipment to move.

Maybe multiple personnel. I would have started with a truck, of course. Whatever I used to transfer the tech out of the Pentagon in the first place.

Then I would change vehicles, quickly and maybe more than once. Would I stick to highways? Turn inland like the FBI brass in the conference room had suggested?

"Can you highlight airports?" I said.

Alex snorted. He clicked with the mouse. A split second later every airport in the region was flagged in bright red—not just the major ones but everything as small as a private dirt strip in a rich guy's backyard. Literally *hundreds* of options. Too many to quickly count, with a cluster the size of a red fist gathered around DC.

Kirsch breathed a curse. "They could be anywhere."

"Not anywhere," I shook my head. "They'd need a larger plane. Something big enough to carry an SUV load of tech and multiple personnel. Filter out the smaller strips."

Alex tapped and clicked again. Roughly a quarter of the red flags disappeared.

It was still an overwhelming number of prospects.

"Okay...let's think about this," Alex said. "We can unpack it."

Kirsch nodded—but nobody spoke. We stared at the map, arms crossed, blocking out the din of the bullpen outside. Focusing. Begging for a break.

And I squinted. Something was nagging at me—something in the back of my mind. It wasn't logic. It wasn't even rational. It was a gut feeling. A nearly silent voice, just a whisper. I was fighting to focus on it, to tease it onto center stage as Kirsch and Alex began to exchange ideas.

All about planes. Range. Fuel.

And then I shook my head.

"It's not a plane."

"What?" That was Alex.

I turned from the map. "They won't use a plane. It's something else."

"Why? A plane makes perfect sense."

"Exactly. And it's exactly what we'd look for. Just like I said before, in the conference room, they *know* what to expect. Whether by their own intelligence or Greene's inside information, they know your playbook. Put yourself in Chinese shoes. You've got to think outside the box—think of something the FBI won't think of."

"There's a thousand airports," Kirsch said. "Just because we'd check them doesn't mean the Chinese wouldn't try one."

"True, maybe. But the planes themselves are a problem. Flying out of the country requires a flight plan, air traffic controller check-ins, and fuel stops. The bigger the plane, the harder to fly under the radar. The smaller the plane, the shorter their potential flight range. It's a catch twenty-two— and it's a *long way* to China. It's a long way even to a Chinese-allied nation who might give them shelter. Fleeing Washington aboard a plane is just the first step. Then you have to flee Columbus. Milwaukee. Denver. Seattle. Wherever you stop for fuel. It's a leap-frog game all the way to the Pacific, with the full might of the FBI and the FAA running right on your heels."

"So what if they flew east?" Kirsch gestured to the map.

"*Where?*" I said. "Bermuda? Western Europe? It's even farther to China that way, with a whole bunch of America's best allies standing in the way."

"So maybe they fly to Africa," Alex suggested. "China has been developing partnerships in Africa for years.

Corrupt governments and warlords. People they could exploit."

"And people who might also sell them out," I countered, shaking my head and turning back to the map. "It's too complicated. Too many moving parts. Too much that could go wrong."

We lapsed into silence again—all of us studying the map. All thinking the same thing.

What, then?

I closed my eyes, shutting out the map, shutting out Alex and Kirsch's muttered arguments about my logic. I put myself in Chinese boots, picturing every radical step of their plan. How they had murdered Rui. Attempted to murder me. Pulled diplomatic immunity when I ambushed them. Exploited double agents at the Pentagon and even set a hotel on fire. Deployed a *sniper*.

It was a full-blown, no-holds-barred, Beijing-sponsored operation. Total commitment. Every available resource...and everything planned in advance.

Yes. They would have planned this escape well in advance. Put the pieces in motion days, weeks, maybe months prior. Been ready for this moment, like the Japanese deploying warships against Pearl Harbor even while they pursued peace talks in DC.

Warships.

My eyes snapped open. I saw it.

"They'll go by sea."

Kirsch and Alex broke off their argument. I turned on them. "What do the Chinese do better than anyone?"

Kirsch snorted. "Manufacture junk?"

"Exactly. And they deliver that junk via *ocean shipping*. Container vessels. Thousands of them, every size and type.

Flying under Chinese flags and the flags of three dozen smaller nations. Tracked but generally not submitted to the same levels of regulatory inspection as aircraft. Moving invisible from country to country...an entire, forgotten society."

"What?" Alex was squinting.

I pointed to the projector map. "It's barely forty miles from DC to Port Baltimore. Only a couple hundred miles to Norfolk. They probably wouldn't use either—it takes too long to reach international waters. But what if..."

I lifted a laser pointer from the computer stand. I traced a line across the Chesapeake. Across the Maryland Eastern Shore, beyond Delaware.

To the open Atlantic. I stopped there.

"What if they drove a truck to Delaware. They offload the tech onto a light, fast boat and they head straight out to sea to a waiting container ship in international waters. Board the ship, turn east. Wait for a good storm—something to obstruct satellite view. Then they surface a Chinese attack sub alongside the container ship. Transfer the men and the gear. Disappear beneath the waves." I turned back to Alex, lowering the pointer. "And take their time getting back to China...because they're already home free. By the time anyone thinks to board that container ship, it's squeaky clean."

Both Alex and Kirsch fixated on the map, considering. I could see the wheels turning behind their eyes. I knew my logic was sound.

But there was still one massive, glaring problem.

"You said there are thousands of container ships," Kirsch said. "How many are sailing off the Eastern Seaboard right now?"

Too many, I thought. Which was only further confirma-
tion that I was on the right track. The sheer volume of potential ships was an advantage to the Chinese, a smoke screen of
the ordinary.

"We've got to have more," Alex said. "We can't search
every ship in the Atlantic—we might as well search every
truck in DC."

I chewed my lip, and we all fell quiet. I closed my eyes
and listened to that nearly silent voice in the back of my
mind. It was speaking again, whispering to my subconscious.
There *was* something more just out of reach.

They have to know. The Chinese had to know. Just like
twentieth-century Japanese aircraft carriers, container ships
are slow. This one would have been dispatched weeks ago.
The Ministry of State Security agents working out of the
Chinese embassy had to know which ship it was. It wouldn't
be last-minute information.

So...

My hand flew to my uniform pocket, and I dug past the
rental car keys. Past the MacroStream. Right down to my
latest burner phone. It was nearly dead, but it powered on. I
jabbed in the passcode and flicked straight to the photos
application. I called up an image of the back side of a
Kentucky Fried Chicken receipt.

"Do either of you read Mandarin?" I said.

Both Alex and Kirsch appeared blank. I twisted the
phone so that they could see.

"*Mandarin*," I repeated.

That jolted Alex out of his confusion. He snapped to
Kirsch, "Get Lang."

She was gone. Alex took the phone and zoomed in.
Squinted.

"Where—"

"The apartment I broke into," I said. "It was written on a receipt, like a note from a phone call."

The door blew open and already Kirsch was back, a young Asian-American woman in tow. Another FBI special agent, or maybe an analyst.

"Can you read this?" Alex passed her the phone. Lang squinted behind oval glasses, studying and using her fingers to adjust the photo.

"It's not...it's not really a sentence."

"So what does it mean?" Alex's voice crackled with impatience. Lang lifted a hand.

"I think it's two parts. The handwriting is bad, but the first part is a name, I think. The second is a number."

"What's—"

"How many digits?" I cut Kirsch's question off. I didn't care about the name. I already had an idea what the number was.

"Uh...seven. Yes, seven. Nine six five four seven eight... two. Yes, two."

I spun to the computer desk. The laptop was still unlocked. A web browser was powered by secure internet access. I input a web address in the top bar: *vesselfinder.com*. It was a service I once used as a Phoenix beat cop while assisting with a narcotics investigation.

Mexican cartels and Columbian cargo ships.

The website loaded. It was a blue and white map of the world, with thousands of dots and little triangles spread across every sea lane, every port and coast around the planet. I didn't bother zooming on the US Eastern Seaboard. I went right to the search bar and jabbed in the seven-digit number that Lang gave me. The website loaded slowly. The other three crowded in.

Then the screen zoomed—sucking in straight toward Delaware. Just fifteen miles off the coast, inside international waters. It was a Chinese container ship.

"*Jade Star?*" I said, turning to Lang.

She nodded. "Yes. That's the name."

"That's them," I said, facing Alex. "That's your ship."

Kirsh shook her head. "No way they would just write that down. They should have had it locked up—on a computer or something."

"Paper notes can't be hacked or traced," I said. "Or maybe they just got sloppy. Whatever the case, we're not lucky yet. We need boots on that ship. Do you have a helicopter?"

I addressed the last question to Alex. He hesitated, glancing back toward the door—back toward the conference room. I shook my head.

"There's no time, Alex. If this is the ship, the Chinese are already outside of American waters—outside FBI jurisdiction. You go in there and it'll be deadlock with DOD. They'll wait to get the president on the line. They'll want to plan a Coast Guard inspection. The State Department will be involved. The Chinese will pitch a fit. *Nothing* will happen."

He looked back to me. He still didn't speak.

"We go now, and we can end this," I said. "We just need a helicopter and a crate of ammo."

Steel entered Alex's gaze. Something besides bureaucratic protocol took over. Something more personal.

"There's a chopper at Reagan," he said. "Ten-minute drive."

"And a pilot?"

Kirsch took that one. "He owes me a favor."

"Get him on the phone," I said. "Let's roll."

50

The FBI weapons locker at the Hoover Building was a gun nut's wet dream. Everything required not only by the bureau's standard field agents but also by the Hostage Rescue Team was available in spades—row upon row, one rack stacked on top of another, all encased inside a vault that demanded both keycard and biometric access.

Alex took the lead, swiping his ID and pressing his eye to a retinal scanner. The door lock buzzed, and then we entered a cramped lobby. There was a custodial officer there, and he had a lot of questions. A lot of paperwork, also.

This wasn't like a special operations weapons cache at Fort Moore, where Rangers checked out weapons and ammunition to their heart's content for field days at the range. Much more highly regulated, with a lot more paperwork, that custodian wanted to know everything. What we were taking, where we were taking it, and who was authorizing the weapons release.

Alex answered three shotgun questions in a row, then he

passed the situation off to Kirsch and he and I barged past the desk into the locker.

"SMGs on your right, handguns below," Alex said. "Body armor in the rear lockers."

I didn't need a second invitation. The HRT stuff was good—much better than the mass-manufactured DOD gear I wore in the Army. The chest rig I tugged over my shoulders actually fit, with state-of-the-art chest and back plates sucking tight against my skin. H&K MP5 magazines stacked into slots over my stomach, and I hung smoke and flash-bang grenades above them—there were no frag grenades.

Then I was selecting a helmet. A drop holster with a Glock 19 and three spare mags. An MP5 fully equipped with an EOTech EXPS3 red dot optic, a Surefire X300 Ultra weapon light, and an L3Harris laser module.

All the best toys compliments of all the best taxpayers.

"Kirsch!" Alex shouted. "Gear up!"

The custodian was still protesting. He wanted serial numbers. He wanted more explanations. He wanted to know why an Army colonel was checking out FBI combat equipment.

"Alex Parker Hudson," Alex said, cutting him off and drawing his ID. "SAIC of counter-espionage Taskforce Romeo. Blame it on me."

The ID card hit the counter, and Alex's career smacked the counter with it. No matter what happened in the next two hours, no matter whether the day was saved or we wound up rotting in the North Atlantic, nothing would ever be the same. Alex would forever be viewed as a maverick, a wild card.

Bureaucracies *hate* wild cards.

Our gazes locked. That question I'd been wrestling with

all afternoons sank in all the deeper. There was no doubt left
—he might as well have said it out loud.

"Let's move!" That was Kirsch. She slapped a helmet
onto her blonde head as she thundered past, her stocky
arms and legs protruding from a set of body armor that,
unlike mine, didn't quite fit. She was equipped with a
sidearm, a bandolier of shells, and a Remington 870 pump-
action shotgun.

Not an ideal weapon for ship boarding, but I wasn't
about to tell her that. Alex led the way and we jogged out of
the weapons locker, the custodian shouting from behind.
Down the elevator to the ground floor, out the door to the
street. An FBI Suburban was just pulling up to the curb with
two special agents climbing out.

Kirsch tore the keys out of the driver's hands with a brief
"need this", and then we were loading up. The agents were
shouting. The tires spun.

We were hurtling through downtown DC with grill-
mounted emergency lights blazing. Alex's phone rang, but
he didn't answer. He mashed a button to send the call to
voicemail instead, muttering a curse.

And avoiding my gaze.

"The pilot will meet us at Reagan," Kirsch said. "He's got
a Bell 412 fueling up now. We'll be airborne as soon as we
arrive."

"Did you give him the ship's location?" I asked.

"No need," she said. "There's a computer on the chopper,
like a car's GPS. It'll lead us."

I wasn't familiar with a Bell 412, but I was familiar with
Bell helicopters in general. The Phoenix PD used Bell 206s
and 407s in times past. They were agile, versatile, effective
traffic monitors and surveillance craft.

But they weren't combat grade. They weren't fast enough, armored enough, and couldn't fly far enough. Hopefully the 412 was better.

"We can't just...board this thing," Alex said. "We'll need some kind of excuse."

"We're breaking enough laws already," I said. "Might as well add piracy."

It wasn't a joke. Nobody laughed. We hit the highway and just as we raced across the Potomac a sudden flash of brilliant blue illuminated the western sky, followed shortly thereafter by a crash of thunder. Specks of rain bounced off the Suburban's windshield, and I exchanged another glance with Alex.

No turning back now.

Reagan International lit the Virginia sky just east of the Pentagon, right along the southern banks of the Potomac. I briefly wondered about crashing into a major airport so heavily armed, but Kirsch had that covered. There was a secondary entrance, exclusively reserved for the use of law enforcement and government agencies. One flash of her badge and the guard let us through. We roared straight across the tarmac, the Suburban shuddering as a 747 exploded off the airstrip only a few hundred yards to our left. Kirsch had the windshield wipers going, fighting a steady spray of rain that blew sideways under a driving wind. It was a late-summer storm, the kind that boils up out of nowhere and, if you're lucky, fades away just as fast.

I wasn't sure if I felt lucky.

"There," Kirsch said, steering us toward the end of a row of hangars where a jet-black helicopter sat on the tarmac, the tips of its four rotor blades flexing in the wind. It was bigger than I expected and looked to be part of Bell's Huey family of helicopters. A distant relative of the UH-1, the helicopter that bore brave young men barely out of high school into the jungles of Vietnam.

Just the thought of that faithful old workhorse was enough to dull a little of the edginess plaguing my mind. The next flash of lightning and a louder burst of thunder, however, muted that small comfort.

Kirsch turned the Suburban in at the end of the hangars, and then we were all bailing out. I slid my helmet on and affixed the chin strap as rain bounced off the Kevlar in a steady chorus of taps, like small-caliber bullets pinging off the Humvee armor. The shower was growing into a downpour, and my ASU uniform was already soaked.

I followed Alex and Kirsch to the helicopter, where a young guy dressed in sweatpants and a Nationals ball cap stood just outside the open rolling door of the aircraft, tugging on a vape pen. He shook his head as Kirsch approached, pointing to the sky.

"No go, Linda. Storm is gaining steam. ATC recommends we wait."

"Recommends or orders?" Kirsch barked. There was zero patience in her voice.

"Well...uh. I guess it's not technically an order, but—"

"Then *get in!* This isn't a joke."

"I'd really feel more comfortable—"

"Pissing in a cup?" Kirsch challenged. The guy froze. His nervous gaze flashed from Alex to me, then back at the bullish Kirsch. She raised both eyebrows, and he caved.

"Okay, okay. Sheesh. Don't say I didn't warn you!"

We all clambered inside. The kid—he couldn't be older than early twenties—took the left stick and slipped a headset on. The interior of the helicopter was compact but not cramped. Two rows of forward-facing, high-backed bench seats filled the main body. Kirsch and Alex took the front, and I slid into the back, reaching for my seatbelt as the engines fired. A slow *whoop, whoop* of the rotors beginning to turn, and a sensation I hadn't felt in years trembled through my tailbone.

The first vibrations of pre-takeoff, mixed with the flush of pre-combat jitters. It wasn't fear. It wasn't anything, really. Just a physiological reaction borne out of so many memories from inside a chopper, taking off at night, pointed east.

Focus, Sharpe. Breathe in, breathe out. This will be quick.

Alex rolled the side door closed as the pilot spoke with air traffic control. The ATC authorized takeoff. A flight plan was logged for Cape May, New Jersey, the nearest point of land to our target. After that it was just open water.

I got the belt cinched down and leaned forward to tap Kirsch on the shoulder. She glared back at me.

"What?"

"He has a drug problem?" I shouted.

"Huh?"

"The pilot! You threatened to make him pee in a cup."

Kirsch squinted. "Oh, right. Just weed! Helps with his nerves. He contracts with the bureau—nobody knows. It's no problem! He's super good."

Right. A pothead behind the stick...no problem.

I settled back into my seat, reminding myself that I'd seen worse. Then the kid was looking over his shoulder, shooting a thumbs-up. Working the collective. The engines howled.

And we were off.

51

When you fly through rain in a utility helicopter everything gets wet. Even with the rolling doors closed, water lashed the windows and blew in through the cracks, slashing our visibility to mere yards as the kid turned us east, nosing the chopper down and unleashing power through the collective.

It was a twin-engine craft. I could just make out the air speed indicator built into the dash. The needle hovered around one hundred forty knots, just a touch over one hundred sixty miles per hour. It was rocket-fast compared to a boat or a car, but as lightning periodically illuminated the ground some five thousand feet beneath us, I couldn't help feeling like we were crawling.

Out of DC. Across Maryland, and eventually to the Chesapeake Bay. The water was torn and dark far below, so much less inviting than the day Evelyn and I had visited the beach and I had snapped that favorite photo. Her hair torn, her eyes alight. That gorgeous smile.

The memory filled me with aching longing, and I

couldn't help but glance forward. Not to Kirsch or the potentially stoned pilot, but to Alex. He was strapped into his seat, arms wrapped around his MP5 and fingers closed into fists. Eyes clamped closed, lips moving. Shuddering with each blast of unexpected turbulence.

Kirsch saw me looking and she grinned. It was the first time I'd ever seen her truly amused.

"He hates flying!"

Alex may have heard her, but he didn't respond. He just sat there, lips moving rhythmically, and I realized he must be praying.

A good idea.

I closed my own eyes and followed suit. I kept it simple, just the way Sol prayed every morning before work at the mission, and each afternoon before lunch. It was a new practice for me. I'd only ever prayed for the first time the previous year, and I was never sure I was doing it correctly.

But as a God-fearing woman in Arkansas once told me, *Just talk to Him, child.*

So I did. I asked for safe passage. I asked for Evelyn to be kept safe back in DC, for us to be right about the *Jade Star.*

Most of all, I asked for a target.

"Hey!" It was the pilot, shouting from the cockpit. I opened my eyes to find him opening and closing his hand— five fingers each time, a sequence of two signals.

"Ten minutes!" Kirsch called.

Ten minutes?

I checked my watch. It was forty-eight minutes since we'd departed Reagan. I'd prayed for most of that period, not even noticing the passage of time. With the prospect of only moments remaining until the inevitable collision of reality aboard the *Jade Star*, whatever that reality might be, the adrenaline came pumping in.

A steady, controlled surge. No panic, just calm readiness. Energy held in reserve, focus honed to a razor's edge. I was ready.

Was Alex?

I leaned forward, tapping his shoulder. His eyes snapped open, and he glanced backward.

"How's your combat training?" I said.

I was pretty sure I knew the answer.

Alex hesitated. "I qualified at the range."

"Handgun?"

"Yeah."

"And the MP5?"

Another hesitation. "I shot it a few times."

Right.

I considered my next words carefully. It was a balancing act of control and ego. Alex had come this far—he was hellbent on finishing this thing. I didn't want to think about why. I only needed to consider if his motivation made him an asset or a risk.

"If we board her, I'll take the lead," I said. "You just fall in behind me and make sure you know exactly what you're shooting at before you press the trigger. Everything will be made of steel—that's a lot of things for a small-caliber round to ricochet against. Bouncing bullets kill. Alright?"

Alex simply nodded. The bravado was gone from his face. He didn't look scared, he just looked dialed in.

"I'm fine with a gun, by the way," Kirsch barked. "Grew up on a dairy farm. Shot groundhogs for fun. Don't worry about me!"

I smacked her on the shoulder. "I wasn't worried about you."

She smiled again—just very little.

Then the pilot was shouting once more. "I've got her on radar...she's dead in the water."

I leaned over the front seat, craning for a view through the windshield. It streamed with rain, the sky pitch-black beyond. The storm that engulfed us at Reagan might be a small one, but it was moving east right along with us. Not as fast, but as soon as we landed the body of it would catch up.

It would be raining for the entire operation...whatever that operation might be.

"I see her!" The pilot pointed, and I saw her too.

Dim navigation lights, nearly dead ahead. By the location of the green and red lights marking her starboard and port sides, I knew we were flying straight at her nose. It was too dark to see much else, the rain and low-hanging clouds obscuring my view.

We would need to be closer to confirm the identity of the vessel. Maybe circle behind for a look at her stern.

Then the kid was shouting again.

"Smaller vessel inbound from the coast! Five hundred yards off her starboard side, headed dead for her."

My hands dropped immediately to my lap belt, and I snatched it free. The next jostle of turbulence sent me sliding toward the left side door of the chopper, but I was headed there anyway. Bracing myself on the seat backs, I leaned toward the window as the kid banked the Bell left, offering a clean view of the torn ocean far below.

Sure enough, there it was. Long and sleek, fully illuminated by the next flash of lightning, it was some kind of racing craft—like a cigarette boat, but built for rougher seas.

An ocean racer with massive inboard engines churning power out of its stern, shoving it straight toward the *Jade Star*.

"Is that them?" It was Kirsch who shouted the question. Nobody answered, and I called to the cockpit.

"Get us lower—we need a better view."

The pilot spun the chopper again, tracking the vessel with ease and bleeding off another thousand feet of altitude. Despite the weather, he kept our view steady the entire time —the boat was perpetually visible through the lefthand windows of the Bell's sliding rear door.

And now I could see people. Visible in the boat's open cockpit—two figures, maybe three. The distance and poor visibility made it impossible to be sure. I was restricted to infrequent flashes of lightning to see them at all, but in the next sky-blazing burst of blue I thought I saw one point.

No—he wasn't pointing. He was *aiming*.

"Up! Up! Up!"

I shouted, grabbing Kirsch by the shoulder and snatching her right into Alex. We all crashed sideways. The kid jerked the Bell's nose upright.

And then the bullets struck. I never heard the gunshots —the roar of the helicopter's engines was too loud. I only heard the ping of lead smashing into steel, bullets ricocheting and whining. Glass cracking but not breaking.

The pilot was cursing. The helicopter raced skyward. We leveled out some thousand feet higher than we were, driving straight into a bank of storm clouds so thick that even the next flash of lightning barely registered through the smog.

"They were shooting at us!" the pilot shouted. "They were *shooting at us!*"

"We know!" I retorted. "Bring us around."

"Wait." He looked over his shoulder. "You wanna go back?"

"What do you think we came here for?" That was Kirsch. "Do your job!"

He did. The helicopter broke back through the clouds in a blaze of temporary blue. I saw the *Jade Star*. I saw the race boat slowing, pulling up alongside the freighter amid rolling waves. I thought I made out little ant-like figures racing back and forth across the ship deck.

And I looked to Alex. "You wanted an excuse—you just got one. What's the play?"

Alex peered through a window as muzzle flash blinked from the boat, but nothing hit the chopper. They were too far out of range.

Then Alex turned to Kirsch. "Call it in. Container ship, *Jade Star*, with multiple armed militants believed to be in possession of stolen tech."

Kirsch was already reaching for her phone. Alex was gazing back into the blackness. As the lightning faded, only the *Jade's* navigation lights were visible, obscured by rain but still shining.

"No signal," Kirsch called. "Sharpe—check yours!"

I did. My burner phone was dead, its overworked battery finally giving out.

"No dice. Radio?"

Kirsch smacked the kid on the arm and communicated her request. He mumbled something and shook his head.

"He's working off New York's air route traffic control center," Kirsch said. "They're breaking up. It's the weather."

"We could fly back," I suggested. I already knew it was a bad option. There was no way to know how close a Chinese stealth sub might be lurking. With this cloud cover they might make the transfer tonight, if my guess was correct. And I thought it was.

"We're going in," Alex said. "Kirsch, you stay with the kid and—"

"No chance! I'm going with you."

Alex cursed, turning from the window. "Or maybe you should *listen* for a change! Sharpe and I will hit the boat. We may not be able to take them all, but we can at least hold them in place. You fly back to cell signal and call in the cavalry. We'll be waiting for your arrival."

"I'm not letting you—"

Alex's hand closed around Kirsch's shoulder. His fingers tightened, turning white. He shook her, just a little. His voice softened.

"Linda. We're square. Okay? We're square."

Their gazes locked. Kirsch's mouth slowly closed. Her eyes rimmed suddenly red.

Then she grabbed Alex by the shoulder and pulled him into a hug. She smacked his back like they were two old football bros meeting at a bar. She released him and was immediately shouting at the kid—cussing him out. Giving him specific directions. Threatening urine tests and vaporized careers if he didn't do exactly as she said.

Alex, for his part, tore the Velcro straps of his wrist brace with his teeth and shook the cumbersome device to the floor. He tugged the charging handle of his MP5 and flexed his fingers around the grip. Then he looked to me.

"You ready?"

Now I saw the fear in his eyes. His face was pale, his breath a little quick, but he wasn't hesitating for a second... and just like before, I knew why.

"Right there with you." I smacked him on the arm and turned to the pilot. "Take her down, kid! Fast as you like."

52

The pilot may have been young but he understood my rationale for speed, and he was smart enough to not need to be told where to fly. The *Jade Star* looked to be about eight hundred feet long, built in the typical container ship style with a towering superstructure rising out of the stern, the middle and forward sections of the ship stacked high with three and four layers of steel shipping containers. I made them out under the next blast of lightning, one thousand yards away and four thousand feet down. There was a block of containers near the bow that looked to be about four units wide—three pastel greens and one very bright red. Their roofs sat about thirty feet off the main deck, ribbed metal slick with rainwater.

It wasn't much of a helipad, but it would have to do.

"There!"

I pointed and the kid nodded. Alarms flashed from his dash, alerting him of an unsafe descent speed, but he ignored them as he kept one hand on the cyclic and one hand on the collective—managing power, guiding us straight down toward the *Jade's* starboard side before sweeping right.

It was a brilliant strategy. Our angle of approach kept the steel bulk of the *Jade* between us and the bobbing race boat on the far side, minimizing our exposure to small-arms fire —at least temporarily. But by the time the Bell had descended to a hundred feet above the containers and was slicing sideways to meet them, the attack resumed.

Gunfire streamed in from the *Jade's* main deck, from in between the containers, and from the railed walkway that circled the top of the superstructure. I marked each point of attack as bright orange stars—I still couldn't see the gunshots.

And then I heard the bullets. Pinging against the Bell's metal skin as before, skipping off her sides and ricocheting off the whirling four-bladed rotor. Glass shattered in the right sliding door and a bullet slammed into the roof of the aircraft. I glanced up—it was a narrow hole, about the size of a 5.56 NATO round but maybe a touch larger. Something Chinese.

Something lethal.

"Stay focused!" I called. "Put her down, down, down!"

Already I was out of my seat, allowing my MP5 to hang by its two-point sling. Closing to the right side of the chopper where Alex sat with his hand on the door. Another burst of distant bullets smacked metal, and lightning blazed. I saw the containers—fifty feet down, a hundred yards to the right. The *Jade Star* was rising over a swell, a hulking mass of illogically buoyant steel that groaned so loudly I could hear it even through the wind and engine noise. Waves passed beneath its keel and the bulbous bow nearly broke out of the water.

Then the ship was headed down again, fast and hard, and so were we.

"Hold on!" The pilot leaned back in his seat, feet jammed into the pedals, sweat streaming from his young face as he worked the cyclic. The pastel surfaces of the containers soared toward us, and I knew we were headed down way, way too fast. I grabbed the back of the seat in front of me and retracted my tongue away from my teeth, ready for a bone-jarring impact.

But Kirsch had been right about the kid. He *was* good. At the last possible moment he dumped on power, lifting the nose and deftly converting our plummet into a near-hover. We started to rise away from the containers again, lifting ten feet off their roofs.

And then the next swell washed beneath the *Jade*. The containers were rising toward us, reaching their apex just a couple feet beneath the chopper's skids. The kid was shouting, "Go! *Go now!*"

Alex tore the door open, allowing a hurricane of rotor wash to break into the cabin even as gunfire popped in the distance. I couldn't see the deck—I couldn't see most of the muzzle flashes. But I could hear the ping of bullets bouncing off the rotors, whizzing into the night and slamming into containers. It was like a storm of hail, just one metallic pop after another, and the kid was still shouting.

"*Move!*"

I did. Alex went first, and I was right behind him. ACU dress shoes landed on the ribbed roof of a container—it popped and rang under my feet. I crouched and rolled, hitting my stomach under the storm of rotor wash, and then the chopper was lifting away. Jet engines howled. Bullets whistled overhead and I could at last hear the pops of those gunshots. It was a perfect storm, coming from every angle and bearing down in one specific place.

Right on top of us.

I kept my face pressed against the container roof and swept my arm sideways, toward Alex. He was scrambling toward the container's edge, no doubt planning to return fire. But it was too soon for that. There were too many of them. The effective range of their assault rifles, whatever specific models they might be, had to be far greater than our lighter MP5s.

And I had brought smoke.

"With me!" I called, yanking his sleeve. Alex turned. The *Jade* groaned and descended beneath us, a crash of water breaking high over the bow and raining over our legs. I'd been outside the Bell less than a full minute, and already I was soaked to the bone. The rain was pounding down. I rocked my head toward the sky and couldn't see the helicopter.

I assumed that to be a good thing. I shot off a prayer for Kirsch's safe travel—for backup to be swift and lethal.

And then I was grabbing Alex by the arm, drawing him near me. The gunfire was still raining in, but it was more sporadic than before. They couldn't see us from deck level, and the night was too dark to snipe from the superstructure walkway nearly three hundred yards away.

Now they would be closing, I knew. Headed for the bow, ready to flush us out.

"Listen carefully," I hissed straight into Alex's ear. "We can't stay here—we'll be sitting ducks. I'm going to throw smoke, then we climb down the forward face of these containers and get to the deck. We fight our way through the access aisles. Okay?"

"Smoke?" Alex called. He was shouting—his ears must be as numb as mine from the roar of the helicopter.

"Grenade!" I said, shaking a canister loose from my chest rig and shoving it in front of his face.

"Oh. Right. Okay!"

"Scramble back." I pushed him behind me, and he began to army-crawl in reverse toward the *Jade*'s bow. I hooked a finger through the grenade's pin ring and took a moment to breathe. A pair of bullets pinged against the container to my right, but I didn't so much as flinch.

What was the point in being afraid? They say you never hear the one that hits you.

From the deck below I thought I did hear shouting. Voices in Chinese growing louder. Boots thumping. They were coming.

Here we go.

I pulled the pin. I dumped the spoon. I dropped the grenade straight over the edge of the container stack and into an exposed section of deck about the size of a semi-truck. The grenade landed with a bounce. Somebody shouted.

Then it was pumping smoke, a persistent rushing hiss, and I was scrambling backward, working my elbows and dragging my legs, headed for the bow.

"Go!" I called. "Go now!"

53

Alex reached the forward end of the container stack ahead of me but paused to allow me to catch up. The moment I reached the edge alongside him and peered downward, I understood why.

There was no ladder. Nothing to cling to, nothing to shinny down. Just three eight-plus-foot containers stacked on top of each other, creating a twenty-something foot cliff with a slick steel deck at the bottom, and save a low railing blocking a further drop over the bow and into the ocean. With another wave dropping out from beneath *Jade*'s keel, that bow sank in the waves and the churning Atlantic rose toward us in a boiling swell. Containers creaked and shifted, and the ship groaned like it was about to break apart. My legs slid around and before I could stop myself I was overhanging the edge with one leg, fighting to maintain my purchase on the container roof with the other. Alex was already dangling by his hands, feet shredding the air, MP5 hanging by its strap.

"Wait for the swell!" I called. "Then drop!"

The swell came. I could feel the *Jade* heaving over it, lifting the deck. I allowed both legs to fall over the edge of the top container and smack against its ends. I was hanging by my fingers. The ship was groaning and headed up.

"Drop!"

We both released. The ship met us on the way down, reducing our actual fall by six or eight feet. I landed with a thud and proceeded into a roll. Alex's impact was somewhat less graceful. He grunted and slammed sideways into the slick deck, sliding a few inches as the Atlantic shoved the *Jade* sideways like a rubber duck in a bathtub.

"You good?" I called.

Alex didn't reply, but he was scrambling upward. I could barely see him under the illumination of the ship's bow light, little more than ambient glow. Drifting smoke further clouded my view, footsteps pounding toward us, a voice shouting in Mandarin.

The Chinese were almost on top of us.

I lifted the MP5 and blew water off my lip. The EOTech was already live, the halo reticle hovering just over the weapon's front sight post. I disengaged the safety but left the sub gun on semi-automatic. I returned to the end of the containers and pressed my side against the metal.

I looked back once more—Alex was on his feet. He was stumbling a little, but he reached a matching position two containers down. I listened as the boots drew nearer—the Chinese were approaching down a corridor between tall stacks of containers. Their shouts had dropped to whispers. I could barely hear them over the pound of the rain against so much steel, wind howling over the railing and sweeping water off the deck.

I breathed and calmed my mind. I focused on the moment. Then I swung out around the corner.

There were three of them. Breaking out of a cloud of grenade smoke, they were all Chinese, all dressed in full black, and all armed to the teeth with side arms and quirky-looking bullpup assault rifles that pivoted toward me as soon as our gazes locked. One of them shouted in Mandarin.

And then I was firing. Quick shots aimed straight for their faces—no body armor. I double-tapped the trigger once per man before sweeping the MP5 to the next target, the ear-splitting cracks of each nine-millimeter shot echoing off the surrounding containers. To my left I heard Alex engaging, also. A full burst of automatic fire returned by the thunder of bullpup rifle.

My second guy was down. My third guy was leveling his rifle, opening fire. I threw myself sideways and squeezed off three shots, stitching holes through his neck, jaw, and fore-head as heavier rifle slugs ripped over my left shoulder.

I slammed into a container, breaking my fall as his life-less body collapsed. Bullpups lay scattered across a deck now running with blood, but I didn't have time to even consider collecting them. There was fresh gunfire from Alex's sector—and even more flashing from somewhere far astern above the containers. I couldn't make out the precise location amid the smoke, but I thought it was coming from the ship's superstructure.

I had to move. I had to *stay* moving. I had to collect Alex and together we had to press the attack—keep them on their heels. It was our only possible hope of maintaining a fighting edge against a vastly larger force.

I started down the corridor. Not back the way I'd come, but over the bodies. Keeping the MP5 riding against my shoulder, reaching the next intersection three containers down and checking both ways before turning left. The gunfire from Alex's position had ceased—I couldn't hear anything except the vague rush of rain through my ringing ears.

I passed through the open space I had tossed the smoke grenade into. I could still taste the acrid flavor of cover smoke on the air, but the visual obstruction had long since blown away. Creeping along with my back half-turned to the containers, I was forced to sweep one-hundred-eighty degrees on the ground while also monitoring the container tops. It was far too much vulnerability to keep up with—a terrible place to fight. I needed to get out.

I needed to find Alex.

I reached the corridor I thought might be the one his attackers had approached down. I slowed at the corner and blinked my weapon light once, risking exposure in the hope that he would call out. I wasn't quite ready to shout. The containers would shelter the weapon light, but my voice would carry.

One LED blink, and no answer. I shrank against the container wall and listened, desperate for the thump of steps along the deck. I thought I heard them, but they were far too stealthy to belong to a confident friend. These sounded more like a stalker drawing steadily nearer. Only yards away, around the bend to my left.

I shrank into a crouch, cutting my height in half. One finger on the trigger, I pressed myself as close as I could to the end of the rain-dripping container, breathing easily. Listening for the approach.

I could no longer hear it. Only the patter of the downpour broke through the persistent ringing in my ears. But then, maybe...

He moved in a rush, opening fire the second he rounded the corner and shooting straight over my head. Had I still been standing, he would have unloaded straight into my chest, maybe my face. As it was, as soon as I saw the flash I was pivoting my MP5 up into his groin, just beneath his body armor. Constricting on the trigger, about to fire.

Then stopping.

"Alex!"

He stumbled and nearly fell. I shoved him off me and kept my muzzle on him. Alex caught himself on the edge of the container and blew rain off his lips, heaving like a winded bull. He was wide-eyed and chalky pale.

"Mason?"

"Who did you think it was?" I shoved him in the chest. Alex didn't answer. He swallowed and looked left toward the superstructure. I had heard it also—a distant shout. The howl of a motor...or several motors. A shrieking surge.

It was the race boat breaking free of the *Jade Star*. I could only conclude that meant the transfer of the stolen hardware had been completed, in which case the *Jade* would also soon be underway.

As if on signal, a rumble broke through the deck. I looked down as metal squealed. The ship was rising again, cresting another wave, but now it felt like the water was hitting us sideways. Rolling us starboard, forcing me to slide past Alex and catch myself on the next container wall.

We were turning.

"Listen," I hissed. "They're going to sweep the deck and try to flush us out. We've got to take the fight to them. If we stay here, we're cooked. Okay?"

Alex was still wide-eyed, still breathing too hard. I shook him by the shoulder. He blinked.

"Hey!" I snapped. "You're a federal agent. You can handle this. Right?"

He closed his mouth. He nodded.

"You stay on my six and only shoot to my left or my right —*never* over my head. Got it? Not over my head."

Another nod. I squeezed his waterlogged suit jacket sleeve. "Let's go."

The wave broke from beneath the *Jade* and the ship groaned in the dark. The deck leveled beneath our feet, and I shouldered the MP5.

Then I led the way through the containers, turning aft. Toward the Chinese.

54

Ten yards. That was all we made it before the gunfire resumed. A barrage of rifle rounds exploded from half a dozen points of attack. Bullets bounced off steel containers and ricocheted off the deck, twisting and whining, lost in the darkness. I could only track the shooters by their intermittent muzzle flash. It came from directly ahead, both on deck level and from the top of the next row of containers. It was just as I feared—they were climbing to gain overwatch, and that shooter from the superstructure was still a problem.

"Keep moving!" I hissed, leading the way around a bend and unleashing a quick four rounds down a corridor. It was enough to silence the shooter there, and the next corner we turned led us to the starboard rail of the ship. One long corridor, barely wide enough for us to run single file. There was a waist-high steel-cable railing that separated the deck from the churning black water far below, but the ocean was only an academic reality. I couldn't see it—the night was too dark.

And then muzzle flash blinked ahead, blazing from fifty yards and unleashing a fresh storm of lead. I yanked backward, nearly running Alex over as we both crouched into partial cover against the wall of containers. The bullets kept flying, and from somewhere overhead I thought I heard a thump between the gunshots—a body landing on a container. The sniper I had feared was racing toward our safe haven, eager to shoot fish in a barrel.

Move. We have to move!

I pulled the first grenade I could put my hand on. I thought it was probably smoke, but it was a flash-bang, and that was even better. Pinky through the ring, a yank of the pin. Then I slung it as high and as far as I could over the top of the container wall—somewhere near the bridge; it didn't really matter where. It landed with a clang, and then it went off. An ear-splitting blast and a bright flash of light that would have been blinding in an enclosed space.

As it was, the flash was little more than a diversion, but maybe diversion enough.

I lunged back to my feet, shouting for Alex to follow and flicking my MP5 to full auto. We cleared three out of five container lengths, half-staggering for balance as the *Jade Star* rolled to starboard.

Then the nest shooter appeared at the end of the corridor, and I unloaded on him. Whatever remained in my mag sprayed right into his face. His body pitched backwards, and his weapon flew out of his hands. I tore a fresh mag from my chest rig and used it to knock the last one loose. Locked in, bolt dropped, then we were at the end of the corridor and swinging right just past the last container.

We had reached midships—no, we were somewhere just behind midships. If the *Jade* had been a football field, we would have already crossed the fifty-yard line. This was enemy territory, and the point was quickly underscored by the next storm of rifle fire. Popping to my left, from straight ahead, from twenty degrees to my right, and once more from the superstructure walkway. I ducked back behind the container as lead pinged off its end. Alex tried to lean past me, sub gun at the ready, but I shoved him back.

"Wait! They'll run dry."

And they did. Not all of them, but better than half, and that half together. The thunder of enemy rifles choked, and I was back around the corner. Aiming first at the ship's superstructure, dumping nine-millimeter slugs at the last place I'd witnessed muzzle flash. A scream broke the night, and something flew from underneath the walkway railing—maybe a weapon. I didn't have time to wonder as I pivoted right. Somebody else was shooting, but this time I never had the chance to cut him down. From behind me Alex fired, spitting lead over my head and toward the muzzle flash. The noise of his unsuppressed MP5 was deafening, so close to my skull that it felt like a shotgun blast straight into my ear drum. I staggered, half-falling. My balance was thrown off, and I slid to my knees behind an equipment fuel drum mounted to the deck.

I tasted blood—it was running out of my ear. I couldn't hear anything from my right side, not even the gunfire. Lightning flashed and Alex appeared, sliding to his knee next to me. Screaming something.

"Not over my head!" I bellowed.

He only frowned, then flinched. Ducked. I couldn't hear the bullets, but I saw them sparking against the edges of the fuel tank, skipping off the steel and blazing into the dark. My gaze flashed across a red sign with an open flame and a red X over it—a universal warning against fire. It was enough to drive me back to my feet. I sprinted left to the end of the tank, moving deeper into enemy territory. Circling the tank's edge and engaging a figure standing near the *Jade's* port railing, a shadow sweeping a rifle into his shoulder.

He never completed the motion. My bullets caught him in the face, and he pitched backward, cartwheeling over the rail and simply disappearing. Two of his buddies popped up from the roofs of shipping containers farther forward, madly dumping rounds not at us but at the tank—a solid hundred gallons raw fuel, maybe gasoline.

I remembered the sparks of copper-jacketed slugs skipping against steel and I grabbed Alex by the sleeve, yanking him. Blasting out from behind the tanks and hurtling straight for the bridge. A door stood open at its base, a circle of bright yellow light shining through a porthole window. It was thirty yards away—then ten. A hot rifle round tore past my leg and I nearly tripped. The next slug slammed into the heel of my ASU dress shoe and blew it away.

I kept running, staggering on the broken shoe. We reached the door with the porthole window. I shoved Alex ahead. I pivoted right.

Then the fuel tank went up. I felt it more than heard it, a concussive earthquake that ripped across the deck and slammed into the superstructure's walls. The ship shuddered. I was stumbling down an interior corridor, catching myself on a bulkhead. The deck pitched beneath me. Smoke blasted through the still-open door, and I choked on it.

Fire alarms were already blaring. White lights blinked from the ceiling of the corridor and a long, whooping wail split the night from someplace outside.

Then the gunfire resumed—bullets slicing through the

door and ricocheting off steel walls before whining past my head. I ducked, turning to find Alex scrambling backward across a pitching corridor floor. Blood streaming down his face, his gaze locked on the still-open door.

"Get it closed!" he shouted.

He was right. The door swung toward me; it was chained open against my wall. I sprinted, dropping the MP5 against its sling and reaching the chain. One thrust of my right arm against the door produced slack in the chain, then I had the door loose. I shoved it closed as rifle rounds pinged against its exterior and ricocheted into the night. The water latch spun easily, and the lock slammed into place. I could still see outside through the porthole.

The muzzle flash had ceased. Without any lightning I couldn't see beyond the brief illumination of exterior alarm lights blinking once every two seconds. It was all shadows, all dark shipping containers and rain and an indeterminate number of Chinese commandos.

Still coming for us.

I heaved to recover my breath as I removed the MP5's partially spent mag and locked in a fresh one. I turned from the door to check on Alex. He was staggering to his feet, spitting blood and gasping. I couldn't tell if he was shot or had simply broken his nose.

Glancing over my shoulder I noted that the corridor ended in a locked watertight door on the port side of the superstructure. To the starboard side, behind Alex, the hallway turned a blind corner—a corner that a gunman might explode around at any moment.

I swung the MP5 back into my shoulder and hurried past Alex, reaching the turn and leaning quickly around the corner—just a glimpse.

It was another hallway, a hundred yards long. Stairs leading up, additional doors opening to the right. A morass, a labyrinth of potential passages, all foreign to me. I'd never boarded a container ship before. I wasn't sure what to expect inside the superstructure.

But I still knew where to go. It was a simple plan, brash and direct. The only way two guys with a rapidly dwindling supply of ammunition could hope to out-gun a small army of Chinese soldiers.

"You hit?" I called over my shoulder.

Alex spat again. I looked back and he shook his head.

"Fell and bit my lip," he said. "I'm good."

"Ammo?"

He swept a hand across his chest rig. "Two full mags left. Plus whatever's in the gun."

"Combat reload."

"Huh?"

"Swap the partial mag for a full one. Hurry!"

He complied, and I checked my own loadout. I'd fired a little more judiciously than Alex, and had two-and-a-half mags remaining in my rig, plus thirty-one rounds in the MP5.

Enough? That all depended on how the next five minutes proceeded.

Alex closed on my shoulder, wiping blood from his mouth and smearing it across his right cheek. I still saw the fear in his face, but he was zeroed in despite it. He was focused, breathing calmly, maintaining trigger discipline as he shouldered the MP5.

"What next?" His voice was calm.

I stole another glance around the corner. The hallway was still empty. I wasn't sure if that was a good thing.

"We get to the citadel," I said. "It's an armored portion of the superstructure where the ship's control center is located. There will be lockout bars on the exterior doors—security against piracy. We barricade ourselves inside, then we point the bow west and we drive for American waters. We wait for FBI backup."

Alex nodded. He spat blood again.

"And what if you were right about the Chinese attack sub? What if they torpedo us?"

It wasn't a crazy question. I made eye contact for a long moment, considering. Then I shook my head.

"One problem at a time, Alex. Let's move."

55

I didn't need to be a maritime expert to know that the ship's bridge would reside near the top of the super-structure, someplace with a lot of windows and a clear view over the masses of shipping containers spread across the deck. We were still at deck level, so wherever we needed to go, we needed to go up, and *up* meant *stairs*. A confined space with nowhere to take cover should we be ambushed along the way.

A near-certain death trap.

"You walk sideways," I said. "No matter what happens you keep your gun pointed behind us. Understand? If anything twitches, you blow it away."

Alex nodded his understanding. He leaned closer to my shoulder, his MP5 pointed three feet to the left of mine. I glanced sideways.

"Alex. *Now.*"

"Oh. Right, right."

All the polished southern prep school charm was gone from Alex's voice. He rotated sideways and directed his sub gun to my six. Then we were off, turning the corridor corner and moving low, our bodies pressed close together like some kind of disjointed crab. The wall to our left was solid steel, but the wall to our right featured a series of closed metal doors. I crossed the first door ducked beneath its porthole window, slapping my non-trigger hand against the latch.

It was locked. So was the next. I kept moving toward a skeletonized set of metal steps that shot upward, disappearing through the corridor ceiling. With each step I was conscious of the rain beating against the exterior wall to my left and the howl of wind ripping against shipping containers outside, but there were no voices—no pounding feet, no more gunshots.

The Chinese were regrouping. How many had we killed? Maybe six, maybe eight. Dozens more could remain—or at least as many as we'd already shot. The time for pray-and-spray had passed for the Chinese. They were playing smart, now.

And somewhere in their midst, lurking in these stale steel passageways, was a blue-eyed tiger with a scar ripping down his face.

"Five yards to the stairs," I said. "Keep covering my back. Don't turn for any reason."

Alex acknowledged my directions and we reached the steps. I kept my body in a crouch and cocked my head upwards. The stairs led directly to another corridor, illuminated by bright white light. Then they switched back on themselves and were headed up again, another level. Another distant hallway.

Bridge level?

"Up," I hissed.

I put one sopping dress shoe on the stairs—and then all hell broke loose.

Gunshots from behind, gunshots from dead ahead, gunshots from *overhead*. Muzzle flash lit the corridor and Alex was shouting—he was dumping automatic fire. A bullet ripped past my thigh, and then I was sprinting. Up the steps, dumping rounds toward the blink of muzzle flash from two levels overhead.

"*Go!*" I shouted. "Run now!"

Alex didn't need to be told twice. We cleared twelve steps to the second level two at a time, small-caliber bullets pinging off steel and whining past my ear. Just as we reached the second-floor hallway, a door swung open. I saw the shadow moving and I unloaded on him, pumping nine-millimeter slugs through the gap and blowing his body to the floor. He never even shouted.

Then we were turning again, headed up the next set of steps. Moving to the third level even as boots pounded from below. The Chinese were close. They were pressing the attack. We had an opportunity.

I burst onto the third level where a new, shorter corridor opened to my right. It was barely ten yards long with only one door—this one solid steel and windowless—opening out of it. No visible combatants, but that single door stood six inches open, and the moment I rotated out of the stair-well gunshots resumed.

Pops from directly ahead, the familiar signature of a handgun. A whizzing whine ripped past my ear, and then the next shot caught me straight in the sternum like the punch of a giant. The breath raced from my lungs. I was choking as I looked ahead to that half-open door and saw the sign. Plastic, written in logograms that I couldn't read, but the symbols stamped in a lefthand column were universal. Familiar.

A lightning bolt signaling an electrical control room.

A bold red cross indicating a medical bay.

A ship's wheel promising the helm.

I saw it all in the same split second that I saw the handgun poked through the gap in the door, dumping fire on me. I knew that it meant we had reached the citadel.

And I also knew that if that door ever closed, this whole party was over. We'd be stuck in an iron box with no route of escape, Chinese commandos headed up the stairs behind us.

"*Go!*"

I shouted, but I didn't wait for Alex. I charged ahead, aiming at the gap in the door and frantically squeezing off shots. I hit the pistol, the hand that fired it, and the arm beyond. I couldn't see anything else, but somebody screamed. The pistol dropped, landing with a clang across the doorsill. The door was swinging closed just as I reached the halfway point of the corridor. Heavy steel slammed into the pistol, smashing it against the jamb and leaving a two-inch gap. Somebody shouted from the room beyond. The door opened a little and a foot kicked at the pistol. I shot again, pouring bullets into the gap. The pistol spun out of the way, skittering across the floor of the corridor.

Then I was there. I was dropping the MP5 to let it hang across my chest and I was grabbing the door, yanking it toward me. Whoever stood on the other side was also yanking, pressing their feet against the door jamb and heaving. They were strong—they had the leverage. My feet were slipping as Alex caught up to me, still running sideways. Still popping off shots at the stairwell behind us even as voices grew louder from the floors below.

"Grenade!" I shouted. "*Hurry!*"

Alex was still guarding my back just the way I'd ordered him to, but he understood the new directions. He twisted and found the last of my three grenades on my chest rig. I wasn't sure if it was smoke or flash-bang. Maybe it didn't matter. The gun fell from his hands, and he struggled with the grenade pin, nearly dropping the weapon.

My hands were slipping. The force on the other side of the door was growing stronger. I dug my toes in and clenched my teeth, focusing every muscle. Willing myself to overcome. Barely four inches remained between the door and the jamb—just enough to pass the grenade through if Alex hurried.

The pin broke free. The spoon fell. I ducked and Alex swept his arm over my head, ramming the weapon through the gap. My hands slipped just as the grenade disappeared. The door clanged shut.

But before the bolt could drop, a shout echoed from the room beyond. Maddened panic. Tension left the door, and I snatched it open just as a popping hiss signaled the release of smoke. I saw a white floor—a wide room with slanted windows pointed down toward the *Jade Star's* deck directly ahead. A control module with levers and screens and switches. A hallway opening to my left with additional doors visible beyond.

And smoke—so much smoke. Billowing off the floor and fogging the windows. Rolling toward us in a cloud, obscuring my vision. Already the control panels were fading from view—but there wasn't a doubt in my mind that I was crossing that threshold. From behind us the voices had grown louder. Boots hammered up the stairs. A pistol snapped.

I hurtled through the door and into the *Jade's* citadel, Alex right on my heels. As I spun to slam the door gunshots were cracking from the stairwell. Bullets slammed against steel. Behind me Alex was engaging someone through the smoke—maybe one of the Chinese sailors who had fought to get the door closed. Pistols were snapping at each other. A body hit the floor, and I choked on a cloud of gray. I got the door closed and slammed the bolt home, barring the citadel shut.

I turned toward Alex, already raising my MP5.

Then I heard the shout. Not an intelligible sound, not any precise word. It was the voice of sudden, absolute desperation. Of mortal reality. Of certain, irrefutable danger.

The shout came from Alex. I heard him just as I turned from the door, the air around us already swirling with gray. My visibility was slashed to under ten feet. Alex stood to my right, his Glock sidearm extended away from his body as his MP5 dangled helplessly from its sling, the bolt locked back over empty. He was facing away from me, into the smoke. He was looking toward a dark shadow that morphed toward us like a demon apparition—like a monster in a nightmare.

I saw the shadow. I saw Alex. I saw the silhouette of a handgun sweeping up and toward me.

Alex fired as he threw himself sideways, his body crossing over mine. His gun snapping, the slide locking back over an empty magazine, muzzle flash reflecting against the smoke.

Then the demon fired, and Alex's shout died as he fell.

56

Even before Alex hit the floor I was firing. Snatching the MP5 up to chest level and clamping down on the trigger. Alex's body dropped below my waist and the FBI sub gun chugged into the smoke. His shoulder blades slammed into the floor and a geyser of blood splashed against my thigh—not a spray, not a stream, but a surge. I recognized the signature of a breached artery even as my target vanished into the smoke. It was now so thick that I could barely breathe. I couldn't see more than two feet. I couldn't see Alex.

And I couldn't hear him, either. No more shouts. Not even any gurgling. Just sickening silence as his warm blood ran down my leg...unleashed by a bullet that was meant for me.

I kept firing, hitting my knees and flailing for Alex. I found the source of the blood loss in his neck, a nasty jagged hole that had cut his common carotid artery just to one side of his windpipe. Sticky warm blood was still spurting out,

Alex's hand flailing uselessly against mine as he fought to reach the wound.

I grabbed his fingers, dropping my MP5 as the bolt locked back over an empty magazine. I found his index finger and I found the bullet hole. I rammed the first into the second and then I was back on my feet, reaching for my sidearm.

Just in time to catch another bullet to my ribcage. It struck the layers of Kevlar protection wrapped around my body and I actually thought I heard bones cracking, but it was impossible to tell in the enclosed space. Every gunshot rang like a grenade blast against the walls. My ears were numb, and I couldn't see my enemy. I only saw his muzzle flash from fifteen, maybe twenty feet away near the bridge's control panels. He was firing blindly through the smog with a handgun. His next round whispered past my ear.

I raised my Glock and returned fire, launching away from Alex. Charging through the smoke. Not certain whether my bullets were hitting him or hitting anything. Glass shattered somewhere around us, but it could have been his bullets as easily as mine. He shot me again, this time just a few inches below my right shoulder, barely striking body armor. The force was so sudden and over-whelming that it ripped my shoulder back, snatching my point of aim to the right. My next three shots zipped some-where toward the front of the bridge, and more glass shat-tered. An alarm sounded. I saw my target materializing out of the smoke only two yards away, just a silhouette at first, then a clarifying shape. He saw me, also. Our gazes locked.

Blue eyes. A snaking scar ripping down one entire side of his face. Lips lifted in a snarl. Hands fighting to reload his gun.

And then I hit him. Full speed, never breaking stride. With my right shoulder screaming in pain, my body twisted and my gun pointed uselessly to one side, there was no chance to reacquire my target and shoot him in the face. There was no time. I saw him too late. I was already too close. His pistol was almost reloaded.

So I smashed into the tiger the same way I'd smashed into his buddy, back at my apartment in Anacostia. I drove him to the floor of the *Jade Star's* bridge amid the smoke and sirens and distant shouts of Chinese operators locked in the hallway outside. His shoulder blades struck stippled steel and the breath rushed from his lungs. The pistol flew out of my hand. His weapon was trapped beneath my left leg, his body already contorting as all those writhing martial arts muscles bunched and prepared to sling me off. To dislodge me, to outmaneuver me just the way he'd outmaneuvered me in the alley near Petworth.

Only this time, I was ready. And this time, I was gonna hit him with a truck.

My right fist smashed into the tiger's face just as his hips were jerking sideways, ready to hurl me off. Knuckles bunched, driving straight for his nose and targeting the floor behind his head, I threw my whole shoulder into it. Every roofing muscle, every ounce of bottled rage and battlefield ferocity, and more than anything—love.

Love for the country he threatened. Love for the global peace he jeopardized.

And above all else, love for the woman he had endangered.

The tiger's head slammed into the steel floor with a crack, blood exploding from his shattered nose, eyes going wide. He choked, his body went rigid, but I wasn't done. I wasn't even started. I hit him again, raw-handed. More smashing bones and collapsing cartilage. His body was thrashing, but the jerks were no longer calculated, no longer calibrated. His training was gone, lost in a deluge of panic as the hits just kept coming.

A ten-ton truck rolling and smashing and crushing. My own body aching and throbbing and screaming. His blood spraying my face. His cries dying in a gargle.

His body finally, slowly, falling still...and then falling silent.

57

I spat the tiger's blood as I finally toppled off him. Head spinning, swirling clouds of smoke still obstructing my view, the world around me seemed to dance. I could barely tell which way was up. My stomach was convulsing and every breath was misery, pain erupting from the three individual points where body armor had prevented penetration but could do little against the freight-train force of an oncoming bullet.

I saw Evelyn. Just out of reach in the smoke, my oxygen-starved body hallucinating as I landed on my hands and knees. I saw her reaching for me, heard her calling to me. Face contorted, voice pleading.

But not for me. For Alex.

Alex.

I inhaled thinning grenade smoke and hacked on the air. Drawn by the distant shout of voices and the banging of a sledgehammer against the locked citadel door, I crawled across the steel floor, leaving bloody handprints behind. I'd lost my Glock. The MP5 dangled uselessly from my chest.

Broken windows from the front of the bridge were supplying ventilation for the smoke, but I could still barely see six feet. I slipped and nearly fell.

And then I reached him. Alex Hudson lay on his back in a lake of his own blood, face chalky pale and eyes closed. With his right-hand index finger jammed into his neck, a stream of blood still ran down his neck. Not the geyser of before, but still a trickle.

He was motionless, barely breathing. I clasped his shoulders and shook him, but Alex didn't respond. Only after I made a fist and conducted a sternum rub with my knuckles did his eyelids flicker, but that was all the physical reaction I received. His arm was falling limp, his hand sliding from his neck as blood flow worsened. I scanned the bridge for a medical kit, but didn't immediately find one, and resorted to ripping the bottom of my t-shirt instead. One long strip that I packed into his neck wound finger over finger like poorman's hemostatic gauze. It wasn't the same—I needed Quik-Clot—but it was all I had. I packed the entire wad as the pound of a Chinese sledgehammer persisted against the bolted door, just a distant metallic thunder that rang meaningless in my mind.

I was only thinking of Alex. Only remembering him fearlessly hurling himself in front of the bullet that would have caught me right in my own neck. Only thinking in terms of the blood he'd already lost, the blood remaining, and the minutes—if not seconds—that Alex had left on this earth.

Medical bay.

I remembered the symbol displayed just outside the citadel door. A bright red cross, a universal sign of hope. I hadn't passed the entrance of the medical bay on my way into the bridge…so it must lie behind me. From the direction the tiger had come.

I hauled Alex over my shoulder with an agonized heave of my gunshot torso. Pain exploded from my ribs, from my sternum and my shoulder. I used my right hand to maintain pressure on the t-shirt-packed wound, but it might have been wasted time.

Blood was still seeping out—very slowly, but every drop was precious. I was running out of time. I might already *be* out of time.

And I still heard Evelyn calling. Pleading. Begging.

Back on my feet amid the thinning grenade smoke, I staggered over the dead sailors Alex had killed and the face-smashed tiger I had flattened. Across the bridge as *Jade Star* rolled in the waves and the Chinese kept hammering on the citadel door. Around the bend, guided by overhead lights, the MP5 still slapping against my chest.

My broken ASU shoes slipped in the blood. I caught myself on a doorframe as I reached another hallway. A row of doors ran along its lefthand wall. Eyes burning, I stumbled past a storage closet, an officers' mess, an electrical control room.

And finally, at the back side of the citadel, I found the medical bay—a windowless door marked with a red cross. It swung open with a groan of metal hinges, bright fluorescent lights illuminating the space beyond. I nearly tripped over the threshold, Alex's legs slapping against my gut. I gasped for air and made it through. I hauled the door shut and slammed the bolt closed to block out the smoke—and to add one more barrier between myself and the surviving Chinese.

Then I turned to the pair of medical beds standing against the wall, only a couple feet apart. The nearest accepted Alex's body with a hiss of air escaping a thin mattress. His arms flopped off the edge and blood dripped from the saturated t-shirt bandage.

Move. Oxygen!

I sucked down smoke-free air and snatched an oxygen mask off a rack near the bed. It was already attached to an H-cylinder which was in turn chained to the wall. I fit it over Alex's face and spun the tank valve on. I didn't have time to set the exact flow rate—I just wanted something to help combat his smoke inhalation. Then I was scrambling across the room. The nearest row of cabinets was filled with medications, bandages, disposable medical implements. All the labels were written in Mandarin—I couldn't read a thing. I tore through one cabinet after the next but still couldn't find what I wanted. I moved to the drawers, snatching them open, ripping through the contents.

Hurry. Hurry! You're out of time.

I finally found the surgical tools in the last drawer, housed in a plastic case. Medical scissors and forceps spilled across the floor, pinging and sliding beneath a countertop before my fingers found the vascular clamp—a six-inch, stainless-steel tool with flat jaws and a locking grip. I took a scalpel along with the clamp and located an electric suction device mounted to the wall next to Alex's bed. It powered on with a hum when I flipped the switch. A Yankauer disposable suction tip was wrapped in plastic, and I tore it open with my teeth.

I wasn't trained for this—not really. The Army had taught me how to use tourniquets, and Afghanistan had provided plenty of opportunities to put that knowledge into action. I understood blood vessels; I understood how quickly blood loss can end it all.

But you can't use a tourniquet on a person's neck. You can't access a sliced artery via a bullet hole. And nobody else was coming to save Alex—not nearly soon enough. What I had in mind might just push him over the edge into eternity.

But if there was a chance, even a one percent chance, of saving his life, I had to roll the dice.

Crimson coated my fingers as I stretched the skin around the packed t-shirt in Alex's neck. His body, now limp on the table, was unresponsive to the pain. I held the vascular clamp in my teeth and went to work with the scalpel first, slicing two inches of skin from the bullet hole outward to open Alex's neck.

It might be too deep. I might worsen the existing injury or open another blood vessel. I didn't have time to wonder or worry. I needed to locate the compromised artery, and for that I needed more room to work.

I peeled the skin back, fishing beneath the wad of saturated t-shirt with two fingers. The current of red draining from Alex's neck now dripped to the floor. It speckled my shoes and the pant legs of my ASU uniform. I couldn't tell whether Alex was still breathing.

Using the Yankauer tip, I began to suck blood from the open wound. Thumb covering the control hole, moving in small circles as I leaned low and breathed in tense gasps. With the excess blood removed I could identify individual neck tendons. Muscles. The edge of his windpipe.

None of that mattered. What I needed was the damaged artery, and I finally found it on my third application of the Yankauer. Buried in his neck, torn by the passage of the bullet but not fully severed. It was still leaking blood—I could see it clearly.

I dropped the suction device and grabbed the vascular

clamp from my teeth. I got it opened and fished through the wound with the jaws, hands trembling.

Come on...come on. Don't miss!

The thoughts raced through my mind like bursts from a machine gun. I saw Alex beneath the glare of the medical bay fluorescents, lying motionless and pale on the hospital bed, and then in a blink he was seated beneath red and green umbrellas at the Greek restaurant in Penn Quarter. Another blink and it was Foggy Bottom, Saturday night and a theater by the river with a replay of an Audrey Hepburn movie that I knew he hated. Evelyn *told* me he hated it even as I sat next to her, only one of us aware that her ex-husband was with us in the room, seated in the theater's back seat with a box of M&Ms.

All those places I found Alex. All those times I knew he was stalking us. Working from the shadows, so desperate to reach her. Desperate to close this case. Desperate to push me out of the way.

And I knew why. Even as I gently slipped the jaws of the clamp around the artery, praying that I wouldn't tear it, I remembered that wedding photo I'd stumbled across at Evelyn's townhome. A single printout she hid in her night-stand—a memento of the marriage she ended. The same shining smile in that photo as the one she gave me that day at the Chesapeake.

Love. Real love. The kind that won't die no matter how many bullets you drive through its chest.

I got the clamp in place. The grip clicked as I ratcheted down, and the steady stream of blood terminated. I withdrew my hands, covered in blood, and fumbled for Alex's wrists. I was checking for a pulse, pressing with the tips of my index and middle fingers.

Give me something, Alex.

I felt it. So weak I might have imagined it, so slow I thought his heart might be skipping beats. But it was there.

"Hang on," I said. "Just hang on."

I released his hand and crashed back to the medical supplies. Ripping past gloves, cleaning supplies, gauze and stitching equipment.

I found what I was looking for buried in the back of a cabinet—emergency IV kits, two of them, complete with plastic bags of rehydration fluids and coils of plastic tubing, capped on their ends with IV catheters.

Bingo.

I spun for the white metal appliance bolted to the floor at the end of the counter, the door printed with a red rain-drop symbol—*blood*. I reached the door, heart still slam-ming, but even before I got it open I knew I'd hit another roadblock.

The appliance wasn't a refrigerator but a freezer. It contained blood—stacks of it in red packages. But all that blood was frozen solid, unusable without hours to thaw it out.

Useless.

I looked back to Alex, lying so still on the medical bed, so chalky white that he already looked dead. Maybe he was. Maybe I was already too late.

And I couldn't accept that.

I grabbed a second IV kit, a roll of medical tape, and a tourniquet on my way back to his bedside. I tore the IV pack-aging away, allowing the fluid-filled IV pouches to drop between Alex's legs. My fingers smeared blood as I unwrapped the IV lines, slicing one free of its fluid pouch with the bloody scalpel, but leaving the other in place. I lifted the IV pouch still attached to an IV line and cut an incision in its top—a one-inch slice.

Fluid gushed out over the floor as I squeezed the bag, talking to Alex again as much for my own sanity as for any hope that he might actually hear me. "Just one more minute. Hang with me!"

Alex didn't answer. I finished squeezing out the IV fluid, then retrieved the sliced IV tube and stuck it through the hole in the pouch. What resulted was a single long IV line with an IV catheter on either end, and an empty IV pouch serving as a kind of improvised connector in the middle.

Workable? I didn't know.

I circled between the two medical beds. Bracing myself against the wall, I shook the CAT-style tourniquet open with a practiced flip and slid it over my own left arm, up past my elbow, then spun the windlass until it tightened. With my elbow locked, a bulging vein popped to the surface. Wide and blue, an easy target. I've always had good veins—back in my younger Army days I used to run rehydration IVs on myself to combat cataclysmic hangovers. It wasn't a sanctioned activity, but neither is pounding a case of beer inside of four hours. I knew I should swab the skin of my arm with an antiseptic wipe before inserting the catheter.

I didn't have time—I had to keep moving. One prick of the IV catheter and I winced. The pain was nothing like the throbbing misery in my chest, but my muscles constricted anyway. I dropped my arm toward the floor and thumped the catheter, breathing between my teeth. Popping the tourniquet loose and praying.

Come on...come on...

The blood began to flow. It ran down the length of one IV line and into the empty IV bag, quickly pooling. Then it ran into the second IV line, gaining inches with every thump of my racing heart. The crimson edged toward the opposing IV catheter, and I let it go all the way, pushing the air out of the line. Dripping, then streaming from the end. A precious red pencil-lead, splashing to the floor and quickly spreading.

I leaned. I found Alex's left arm and got the tourniquet over it. I ran the windlass as tight as I could and probed his taut skin, but I couldn't locate a vein. There was simply nothing there—all the blood vessels in his arms were too empty to bulge, and I knew I couldn't afford to keep searching.

I had to roll the dice again. I stretched the skin of his inside elbow with two fingers and breathed a short prayer.

Then I stuck the needle in.

Alex didn't so much as twitch as I released the tourniquet. I staggered backward to the second bed, watching the solid red line draped between us, half a pint of blood already filling the IV bag. I couldn't be sure the blood was flowing into his body...but I thought it was.

I grabbed the IV bag and pinned it to a hook on the wall —below my body, above his. I fumbled with the roll of medical tape and ran several lengths of it around both my own arm and Alex's, securing the catheters as best I could. I threw every blanket piled beneath Alex's bed across his body, bundling him against the onslaught of hypothermia.

It was all sloppy, but already my thoughts were wandering away from the crisis at hand. Alex's body was wavering in my vision, coming in and out of focus. Blurring and then seeming to levitate.

I staggered backward against the thin mattress of the second bed and blinked. I was getting a little light-headed. I felt a little short of breath, a little dizzy. I leaned slowly backward, careful not to inadvertently pull the IV line from the bag. The mattress crushed and crackled beneath my weight. My head rested against a pillow. I rolled my face toward him, checking Alex's catheter to make sure the blood wasn't bubbling out of his arm.

It had oozed a little, but not much. I pictured it channeling into his veins, and I thought of the Army doctor back at Fort Benning who had performed my first-ever military medical eval.

"Well, well, Private Sharpe. O-negative. You're gonna be a popular guy."

His words faded from my mind as I suddenly felt very calm...very tired. I relaxed my shoulders against the mattress, and I just breathed. I let the blood drip out of me, down that makeshift miracle highway, into Alex's drained body.

I closed my eyes, and I thought of her. By the Chesapeake. A brilliant smile and so very much happiness.

Like her wedding day. Like the look she gave Alex. A woman in love.

I understood. I opened my eyes, and I found Alex's eyes open also. He stared at me, his mouth and nose still covered by the oxygen mask. I thought I saw a touch of color in his cheeks...just maybe. The briefest of hints.

I managed a weak smile. A brief nod.

Then I closed my eyes and embraced the growing darkness.

58

I never heard the Coast Guard choppers land. I never witnessed the white and orange cutters racing up to the sides of the *Jade Star*, swarms of USCG Maritime Enforcement Specialists climbing aboard and engulfing the ship. Engaging what few Chinese remained—shooting two, detaining the rest.

I would read about that later. Linda Kirsch and the two *Shining* twins, whom she had called back into service after dropping Alex and me on the *Jade's* bow, would recount the tale in matter-of-fact detail.

Well, Kirsch would. *The Shining* twins just...shined, I guess. Stiff-backed as they stood against the wall of the New Jersey hospital room I awoke in, hot sunlight streaming through the windows. I'd slept for nearly fifteen hours, although the drugs the docs had pumped into my system may have helped with that. They hydrated me. They patched up my scrapes, wrapped my ribcage, and placed splints on the index and middle fingers of my right hand.

I'd broken those fingers while pounding the tiger to

death. I'd also suffered a pair of cracked ribs and a fractured sternum, compliments of Chinese gunshots. The Kevlar body armor had saved my life just as it was intended to, but it would hurt to breathe for a long time. You can't do much about cracked ribs...just brace them and deal with it.

I dealt with it while I learned the details of the events following my "reckless and moronic vigilante activity"—the words of the FBI, not mine. Specifically, I learned that the Coast Guard had seized *Jade Star* and accounted for each and every item of missing Project Unity equipment stolen from the Pentagon. That the FBI's assistant deputy director was managing the recovery effort and resulting investigation herself, that newspapers were boiling with rumors but the government was doing everything they could to keep the story under wraps.

Chinese operators were dead. A Chinese ship had been boarded and seized in international waters. And yet the Chinese, thus far, had little to say about it. No public protests, no accusations against the United States.

Just brooding silence...and the promise of darker things to come.

That was the big picture, but beyond the fact that the blue-eyed tiger was dead, and the IBN equipment had been recovered, I didn't much care about the big picture. For me it was all about the up-close image. The personal facts—two of them.

First, the fact that Dr. Evelyn Landry was once again safe. And second, the fact that Special Agent Alex Parker Hudson had survived. By the skin of his teeth, by the narrowest of margins. Just enough blood at the last possible moment. The Coast Guard lifted us both off by chopper and raced us to the nearest major hospital with a level I trauma center—

Cooper University Hospital in Camden, New Jersey, apparently. Alex needed emergency surgery and a doctor-approved blood transfusion. Even after the bullet was removed and his artery was repaired, it would be some weeks before he was fit to return to work—and that assumed that his bosses at the Bureau allowed him to return at all.

But concerns of career loss notwithstanding, Alex was alive. Kirsch informed me of the news with a wide smile and traces of tears in her granite eyes, appearing truly human for the first time since I'd met her. She squeezed my arm and promised that the government would cover my hospital bills. She was going to make calls, see about getting me a medal. Maybe even set me up with some kind of disability pension, some credit for my efforts.

I seriously doubted that the government would play ball with any of her promises, but I also didn't much care. I was barely listening, my head lost in a swirling daze. My chest constricted by the pressure of unspoken reality. Of certainty yet to be confirmed.

When Kirsch finally drew breath, I faced her and asked the question I had been waiting to ask for days. Her smile evaporated in an instant, and she just stared. She didn't answer—she didn't want to answer.

But I forced her to. She owed me the truth, and she knew it. Her gaze dropped, and she simply nodded. Another question from me and another nod from her—they were all nods.

I was right about everything. And I hated it.

I finished my inquiry and the pressure on my chest converted from a load of bricks to a cluster of stabbing needles. They bit deep, they stung like bullets. The reality set in as I stared up at the ceiling, watching the tiles blur out of focus as tears bubbled into my eyes. I didn't fight them.

I had earned them. They helped, if only a little. Kirsch released my arm and stood. She shifted on her feet, not seeming to know what to do with her hands. She muttered something about checking back on me, then she and the twins left.

I was alone in the room. I closed my eyes and took myself back to the Chesapeake. Back to a bright sunrise and early spring warmth on my skin. So much happiness. So much joy.

No matter what happened, that memory would be mine forever.

59

They discharged me the next day. I dressed in brand-new clothes that Kirsch brought me—she still remembered my sizes. All my personal items had been carefully cleaned—probably also by Kirsch—and arranged on the table next to my hospital bed. The Macro-Stream, my lock picks, my wallet and my Victorinox, which Kirsch had brought from the Marriott hotel where I'd left it. She also charged my phone, and one tap of the screen revealed Evelyn's picture, that broad smile and wind-torn hair.

I hadn't seen her yet. I still didn't know what to say to her. I didn't know whose job it was to tell her the truth...or what would happen once the truth was told.

I rode the elevator to the first floor and stepped out into glaring midday sunlight. I wasn't hurting—I was too hopped up on hospital painkillers for that. Pretty soon they would wear off and I would come to regret refusing a prescription for more, but until I knew for sure that Uncle Sam was picking up my medical tab, I wasn't eager to run it any higher.

For now, the pain was muted. My ribcage was wrapped tight in a brace, my fingers were stiff, but I could still mostly use my right hand. It was enough.

Standing on the sidewalk outside the hospital, I enjoyed the sun while pedestrians walked right by me as though I wasn't there. Cars packed the parking lot. An ambulance buzzed up to the ER and somebody called for a stretcher. A kid coughed as his parents carried him through sliding glass doors to the emergency room.

It was all the typical stuff. The world spinning on its axis exactly the way it had the day before...except not at all the way it had. Nothing close to the same. It was like a different planet. Like I was stepping outside for the very first time.

Like I was alone.

"Mason?"

The voice caught me from over my shoulder. I looked that way and found Evelyn standing on the sidewalk twenty yards away, a duffel bag dangling from one arm. Its top was open, clothes stuffed hastily inside. The bright orange pawprint of the Clemson Tigers was printed proudly along one side.

I stared, but I didn't answer. I just stood with my hands in my pockets.

Evelyn dropped the bag and she ran to me. She wrapped me in a hug and pulled me close—she was sobbing. She put her hand around my neck and kissed me hard. She smiled and shook her head.

"What happened? I tried to see you yesterday and they wouldn't let me in. They said you wouldn't allow visitors."

I didn't answer. I just looked into her perfect eyes and lost myself in the comfort of the familiar for a moment. The warm. The safe and comfortable.

It was home, so much more than any address ever could be. A resonant security. A sanctuary. A place to grow very old one Chesapeake sunrise at a time.

Home...yes. But was it my home?

"Mason," Evelyn whispered, smile fading. "What...what happened?"

I looked away. I swallowed and tried not to cry. I saw a bench standing near the sidewalk and I started toward it. Evelyn followed, arm clutched in mine, Tigers duffel bag forgotten. We reached the bench, and I sat. Evelyn sat sideways to face me. She didn't crowd in. She just waited. I rubbed my hands together and looked at the parking lot and desperately wished it could be anybody besides me.

Alex should be saying this. Or Kirsch, even.

Why does it have to be me?

I turned. I stared a long time. Evelyn looked shell-shocked. She could feel the disconnect, the problem in the air. Her lips parted, but she didn't speak.

And I knew I had to say it. There was no other choice.

"I need to show you something," I said. I dipped my hand into my pocket and found my burner phone. I punched in the passcode and called up my photos app. I found that picture of another bright, smiling face. A Sheltie dog.

A young woman murdered by a blue-eyed tiger.

I rotated the phone. "Do you know this woman?"

The horror in Evelyn's face said it all. The instant flush. The closing mouth, the swallow. All the little tell-tale signals of a woman fighting to hold it together.

"Where did you get that?" Evelyn managed.

I switched off the phone. "She was the woman who was killed in Petworth. The woman I failed to save."

"In Petworth?" Evelyn's lip quivered. She was staring at me. There was deep anger in her eyes, now. Accusation, confusion, and a lot of pain boiling up from a wound that refused to heal.

"I was headed to Alex's house," I said. "I was...going to confront him. About stalking you. About bothering you. Rui Huang was headed there, also."

"Rui Huang?"

"That was her name," I said.

Evelyn looked away. Her jaw locked, her fingers knotting around the tail ends of her cardigan. Twisting it, fighting to hold herself together.

"Why are you telling me this?" she managed.

I gathered my resolve. I set the phone on my knee.

"I'm telling you because...you think Alex cheated on you with Rui. And he never did."

Evelyn's face snapped back toward me. She squinted, something between shock and confusion and anger boiling all together at once and locking her down.

I didn't let her explode. I simply told the story from its very beginning. All the pieces I'd put together and all the details Linda Kirsch had confirmed. How Alex Hudson had been assigned to form a counter-intelligence task force with the sole purpose of identifying the American traitor, code name *Benedict*. How Alex had been advised of a Chinese national who worked inside the PRC embassy and had expressed interest in serving as an American spy. Rui Huang was willing to exchange information on Chinese Ministry of

State Security operations in exchange for both her and her entire family being granted United States green cards.

I told Evelyn how Alex had sprung on the opportunity. How he had developed the asset, built a relationship with Rui, and made an American mole out of her. I described the context of Project Unity in only the broadest of terms— Evelyn didn't need and probably didn't care about the details, but I needed her to understand the gravity of the situation. The massive risk to American security.

It was the key ingredient. The reason why Alex would not —could not—explain himself when Evelyn confronted him about Rui. Evelyn hadn't known Rui's name. She'd only known that Alex wasn't at the office when his partner, Linda Kirsch, said that he was. Evelyn knew because she had seen Alex in town, and the fact that Kirsch lied aroused Evelyn's suspicions.

So she dug. She watched. She found text messages and gaps in Alex's schedule and eventually she lied about a business trip to Atlanta and set Alex up. She took a cab to the airport—she took a cab right back later that night, only to find Alex and Rui sitting in the living room of her Petworth townhome.

It was her worst possible nightmare—her beloved husband with another woman in their own house. A rendezvous he couldn't explain, because it was all so deeply classified. To tell Evelyn the truth would have compromised the whole mission, threatening Rui's cover, and in the end, endangering national security.

The stakes were simply too high...and Alex Parker Hudson was simply too committed a patriot. He never admitted to cheating, because he hadn't. He begged Evelyn to stay—to trust him.

But she left. Who could blame her? She filed for divorce. They split with tears on both sides.

And Alex sank his teeth deeper than ever into the Benedict investigation, desperate to solve the case. Desperate to conclude the task force, to close out the mission. Even if it cost him his career, even if he had to color way outside the lines to get the job done.

Because getting the job done was his only possible hope of ever getting his wife back. A woman he loved more than his career. More than life itself. His home—a home he loved so much that when Evelyn began dating a drifting veteran with a history of loss and questionable mental stability, Alex began keeping tabs.

He began stalking, effectively. But he wasn't stalking Evelyn, he was stalking *me*—because if he couldn't have his wife back, he had to make sure she was at least safe. At least happy.

I finished the story and Evelyn just sat, stunned. She was crying, but silently. She'd stopped looking at me somewhere along the way and was staring at the concrete. People hurried past us and cars rushed by but neither of us noticed. It was all just a blur. We might as well be on other planets.

Separate planets.

"If you don't believe me, you can talk to Kirsch," I said. "She has proof...she kept proof. I guess she never got over the fact that she compromised her partner's marriage. She was willing to do anything to help Alex get you back."

As I said the words, I remembered how Kirsch had stuck by Alex's side, even after *The Shining* twins were ejected from the operation. Charging headlong, regardless of the personal risk, she fought right up until the moment Alex looked her in the eye and said, *"We're square."*

"What..." Evelyn trailed off. Her mascara was running, and I knew she didn't care. She shook her head. "What does this mean?"

I swallowed, closing one hand into a fist over my leg and tapping it. Lowering my face and breathing deep against the pressure of the ribcage brace. Fighting to get the words out.

"It means..." I started. Stopped. Resolved again to say what I must. "It means he loves you, Evelyn. Desperately. It means he was willing to let you go because he couldn't compromise his FBI oath...and it means he was willing to move heaven and earth to get you back. I guess it means..."

I trailed off again. I thought of all those moments that led to me marching down the sidewalk toward the townhome with the Clemson Tigers flag. I shook my head.

"He's obsessed with you. And I understand."

I nodded a few times. I fixated on my shoes and thought that Kirsch had done a good job picking them out. They were muted, simple colors. Comfortable. Walmart value.

But no petty distraction could break my mind away from the last thing I had to say. The real load of bricks crushing down on me, the thing I'd been dreading more than anything else.

The thing I loved Evelyn Landry too much to ignore.

"If I asked you something, would you promise to tell me the truth?" I said.

I looked up. Evelyn was still crying but the anger was completely gone. Now it was just confusion. Overwhelmed numbness. And maybe...a lot of relief.

Evelyn swallowed. I took her hand and squeezed it once.

"Do you love him, too?" I asked.

Evelyn's lip quivered. Her head rocked to one side and the tears bubbled up. She trembled and then she threw her arms around me, burying her face into my shoulder and quaking.

Not answering me, but that didn't matter.

She didn't need to.

60

Kirsch gave me a ride back to Washington in her FBI-issued Chevrolet Malibu. We listened to Scandinavian death metal on the way...which somehow didn't at all surprise me, and frankly, I didn't mind it. I had the window down, the fresh air rushing through, and we didn't say a word all the way to the Marriott hotel where I would collect my rental Camry. It was way overdue to be returned to the rental agency. My prepaid debit card was probably declining their late fees, and there would be some explaining to do.

I wasn't worried about it. I wasn't really worried about anything...or feeling much of anything. My whole body was numb, and not just from the waning effects of the hospital painkillers.

There was a much deeper ache in my mind. It cascaded through my chest—I thought it probably reached my soul. It was emptiness like I hadn't felt in months. Like I had so often hoped, so often *prayed* to never, ever feel again.

And yet, despite the pain...this wasn't like the last time. It wasn't like Phoenix, like that school hallway and that shotgun thunder. When I lifted my phone, the Chesapeake Bay picture was still there, and Evelyn Landry was still smiling like the first sunshine of a brand-new spring.

Happy, so happy. And safe. I could own that. I could claim it.

At least for now.

Kirsch pulled the car into the slot next to my Camry and shifted into park. She popped her gum and we both endured the thunder of a guy throat-screaming in Norwegian for another brutal sixty seconds before the track finally ended. Kirsch mashed the power button on the stereo, and I simply shook my head.

"Your musical tastes are dog crap."

Kirsch smiled at that. We got out of the car. She reached into her pocket and produced a card, sliding it into my hand. It was printed with her name and her phone number, the FBI logo emblazoned above both.

"If you ever need anything, Sharpe."

There was a sincerity to her tone that resounded with the brotherhood of soldiers downrange. Of cops who had taken fire together. Of service members of every stripe and uniform who never extended an offer unless they absolutely, one hundred percent meant it.

And Linda Kirsch meant it.

I took the card and pocketed it without comment. I stood awkwardly a moment next to her car, unsure what to say. I looked north toward the Potomac, toward the planes soaring over Reagan International. I thought of what lay beyond that river and it was almost more than I could take.

"Not one in a million would do what you did," Kirsch said.

I simply shook my head. "I'm still not sure I have done it."

A moment of silence. Then Kirsch sighed.

"No. But you're gonna."

The words landed easily, even though they should have crashed like tank shells. Maybe because Kirsch sounded uncharacteristically human when she spoke, but probably just because I knew she was right.

I offered my hand. We shook once, nice and stiff and awkward.

Then we parted ways without another word, and I took the Camry back to the rental place. I caught a cab to collect my truck. I drove it way out into the Maryland countryside and found an empty church parking lot surrounded by soybean fields. I inflated my air mattress and dropped my tailgate, lying on my back where I could watch the sun slowly set, and the stars slowly brighten.

I lay that way, all alone, for a long time. I marveled at how good it felt to not be surrounded by walls, to not hear any glass crashing or any drunks swearing. No police sirens, no muted gunshots.

And nobody looking for me. Nobody around the next corner, threatening to jump me in my own apartment. Nobody looking for the woman I loved, either.

It was comfort enough for me to ignore everything else on my mind and just sleep. I awoke to a golden sunrise and the worst body aches I'd ever experienced. I downed a double dose of extra-strength Tylenol and ate cold beans and sausage from a can. It was sticky, congealed, and abso-lutely delicious, reminding me of Georgia and Florida and Missouri and all the places in between.

I fired up the truck and drove back to DC, across the river

to Deanwood. It was a Friday and Sol and his crew were already hard at work on the roof of the last wing of the new rehab facility. They'd covered a lot of ground in the time I'd been gone, but Sol looked happy to see me. He broke into a big smile, straddling a ridgeline with sweat glistening on his forehead. A working man enjoying his day.

"Brother Mason! We was beginning to think you'd bit the dust. Gone clubbing again?"

I hoisted myself up the ladder, trembling with rib pain the entire way but refusing to surrender. My ears still rang, my body felt like it had been run over three or four times by Sol's old work truck. I needed rest, desperately. I needed good food, lots of water, a long vacation.

But what I wanted more than anything was a hard day's blue-collar work. I wanted to pound nails, even if I could only do so very slowly.

"Partying like it's nineteen-ninety-nine, Sol. Where's my hammer?"

61

I gave the FBI and the DC cops and whoever else was involved in the fallout of the Project Unity debacle two weeks to arrest me. Or interview me. Or subpoena me as a witness. Or whatever they were going to do in response to my involvement in the Chinese espionage operation.

But they never turned up. They never arrived at the Grace Church rehab construction site. They never appeared at Sol's house, where I was staying until I cashed a few paychecks—Sol offered the accommodations after catching me sleeping in my truck, and he never asked why I needed them.

I never even received a phone call from the federal government, and after ten days of bottling my body aches to pound nails, hang windows, and lay carpet, I thought I knew why.

This was a disaster, top to bottom. An FBI embarrassment, a Pentagon embarrassment, and mostly especially a US Army embarrassment, thanks to Greene and his treachery. Nobody came looking for me because nobody wanted

me around—nobody wanted the loudest canary in the most
polluted coal mine of all time to be singing his songs to the
media or hiring lawyers who might call legislators who
might in turn call for a congressional hearing.

What everyone *wanted* was to make this whole mess go
away, a default response that was right on brand for the federal
government. The FBI may or may not have accepted that I had
justifiably shot Greene, but nobody was going to question me
on the matter either way. It was too dangerous a question that
might uncover answers the federal government would prefer
to keep buried, and so I was left alone. Nobody came knocking,
nobody came calling, but I got their message loud and clear.

Leave us alone, and we'll leave you alone.

Maybe Kirsch had pulled some strings to ensure my
sanctuary. Maybe Alex had. Whatever the case, I was more
than happy to take the deal. I was no more interested in
being a squawking canary than I was interested in entering
any more polluted coal mines. It had been years since I'd
officially worked for Uncle Sam, and truth be told, those
ASUs hadn't fit at all, and not just because of the fake rank
pins.

I wanted to be left alone. I was content to be so. I wanted
to work at the mission and try, God help me, to do something I had spent long nights praying that I would never
again have to do.

Let go.

I met Evelyn for lunch on her request. We hadn't shared
any phone calls. We hadn't exchanged any texts. When we
dined in Georgetown overlooking the Potomac, I ignored the
sommelier and didn't care that the roast beef sandwich I
ordered was dry and bland. I looked at the river and I

thought about the three American traitors who had died in it.

Nobody was asking about them, either. Justified kills, all three. Quite literally water under the bridge.

Evelyn sat across from me picking at her pasta and avoiding eye contact. We'd exchanged awkward chitchat about the weather and the new ball cap I was wearing—a Grace Church hat Sol had given me—but we didn't talk about Chinese spies or exploding hotels or emergency battlefield blood transfusions aboard storm-thrashed container ships.

Most especially, we didn't talk about Alex. And yet I knew he was on her mind. I knew they had been together. It wasn't that I could smell his cologne or that she was back to wearing a ring on her left hand. Nothing nearly so obvious or sudden. It was a much subtler, much quieter signal. The kind of thing I remembered from my solo days chasing women at bars and Army dance halls.

It's the way good men can tell, if they care and if they're paying attention, that a girl is already taken. Even if there's no ring. Even if there's no mention of a boyfriend and no heart-shaped jewelry hanging from her neck with his initials on it.

It's a look in her eye, distant and distracted. A little whimsical, maybe a little conflicted. Maybe she's not even aware of it, yet...but it's there. Her heart is already gone. She's in love. She's all caught up in somebody else.

And for Evelyn Landry, I knew exactly who that some-body else was. It hurt to think about...it made me want to throw *myself* under a ten-ton American truck. Even worse, I knew why Evelyn wanted to meet for lunch. I knew what a terrible, awful position she was caught in. How conflicted and in pain she must be.

And I knew that it was my job to be her hero—one last time.

Wiping tart mustard from my lips, I looked off the elevated dining patio and out to the river. I swallowed deep. As deep as I could, as much air as I could. I planted it all in my stomach and then I constricted my abdominal muscles and opened my mouth and belched like an absolute cow. Loud and long and sudden enough to draw every eye on the patio.

The diners. The waitresses. That danged sommelier with his six-page wine menu. And Evelyn, too. They all stared. I shook my head and grimaced.

And then I said, "That was a truly awful sandwich."

Nobody spoke. Some of the women blushed. The sommelier snapped his menu closed and looked ready to string me up by my ears. Murmurs of disbelief and disgust and judgement circled all around.

But Evelyn? She smiled. A small, slow smile that gently spread into a broad, full-mouthed smile. It stretched her cheeks into dimples and reached her eyes and kept growing until she was laughing. Falling forward toward her plate. Setting her glass down and splashing wine. Giggling like a drunk college girl. Catching herself on the table but still laughing. Crying, also. Tears streaming down flushed cheeks. Not caring a whit that everyone was staring.

And I laughed too. We laughed for a long time. We pissed everyone off. I expected the manager to evict us at any moment.

But instead the chuckles dimmed, slowly and naturally. The tears in her eyes persisted but she didn't bother to wipe them. She didn't seem to care. I looked at her across the table and the world faded out, and I couldn't help but feel like the luckiest man on earth.

Not because Evelyn Landry was mine, but because she didn't need to be. She was *her*. She was alive and vibrant. I'd made her laugh one more time.

And I'd take that memory to the grave.

"You're such a bumpkin," Evelyn said, finally wiping her eyes with a cloth napkin.

I lifted my wine glass in salute, then rocked it up like a beer can and chugged. No sniffing. It was fantastic wine.

Evelyn finished with the napkin and sat staring at her abandoned pasta. Lip quivering now, all the smiles gone. She seemed to be fighting to hold herself together.

"I...I don't know what to say," she whispered.

They were the words I'd been waiting for since we sat down. The words that sealed the answer in my mind, stamping the situation with certainty. Closing a door that I longed to throw open.

But breaking and entering is a crime even when it isn't illegal.

"She was...like nothing in this world," I said, staring out over the Potomac and admiring the sun on the water. Happy to be safe and dry on the shore.

"Mia?" Evelyn had never said her name before. Not once. She knew I didn't want to talk about it—maybe couldn't talk about it. It was another kind of closed door, and Evelyn was no burglar.

But when she said the name now, I nodded. I smiled, and I didn't tear up.

"I knew it was forever from the first night," I said. "I didn't *know* that I knew. Not then. But looking back...it was inevitable. Just the way things were meant to be. Two people that fit perfectly together and would never be the same apart."

"Soul mates," Evelyn whispered.

I shrugged. "Maybe. I never gave it a title. I just...knew we belonged."

I looked to Evelyn. She was fiddling with her napkin.

"What are you saying?"

I leaned across the table and took her hand gently in mine. Watching her close her eyes to avoid crying again.

"I'm saying that he's a good man, Evelyn. I'm saying that I understand the difference between a great fit and the *perfect* fit. And most of all I'm saying...you don't need anybody's permission."

Her eyes opened and she was crying again, despite herself. Her fingers wrapped tight around mine and she squeezed. I squeezed back. There were knives slicing through my chest that she couldn't see, and there was no chance I was going to show them.

"I'll never forget you," Evelyn whispered.

I smiled. "And that's all I could ever ask for."

62

I watched Evelyn leave in her Mini Cooper, that psychopathic little turbocharged engine surging over a speed bump, and I knew I would never see her again. Not because I didn't want to, and not because I couldn't handle seeing her with another man. I wasn't that petty.

I just knew what she deserved, and as much as it hurt, I was resolved to see her have it.

Back in my truck, I drove to Deanwood where Sol and his crew were rolling paint onto fresh drywall. I shook his hand, and he pulled me into a hug. The hug hurt—my ribs still hurt—but I didn't complain. He prayed for me, and the gentle, confident words dulled a little of the pain in my chest. I collected my outstanding pay in cash and shook hands with every one of his other workers. I stepped back out into the lot and looked up into a blasting sun without a cloud in the sky.

It was a perfect day. Warm, not quite hot. I wouldn't need the aftermarket A/C unit built beneath my truck's dash. I didn't think I would need the GPS app on my burner phone either...or for that matter, I wouldn't even need the phone.

The open highway was calling. I didn't know where, and it really didn't matter. I only knew that I'd worn out my welcome in DC, or perhaps DC had worn out its welcome with me. It was time for new horizons, and I was contemplating someplace I'd never been.

Maybe west, into the mountains. Or northeast, up the Eastern Seaboard. Maybe I would flip a coin.

I rolled the Victorinox in my pocket and breathed deep... then I started for my truck. It was fully packed, my violin case and backpack and my late fiancée's Bible riding in the seat next to me. My air mattress inflated in the bed, ready for another quiet night in some field in the middle of nowhere.

The idea wasn't quite paradise, but it was peace. And peace was enough.

I lifted a hand in final farewell to Sol and was just reaching for my truck keys when a gleam of blue lights flashed from down the road. Exploding over a hilltop, a ripple of angry American thunder rumbling from the tailpipes, the Shelby GT350 bottomed out over a dip in the road and scraped its frame against the asphalt, but never slowed. The blinking blue came from a dash-mounted emergency light bar. The sun blazed right onto the windshield, and I couldn't see inside.

I simply stood by my truck with my hands in my pockets as the car ground to a halt in the church's gravel parking lot, dust rising in a cloud over a crushed right front fender and a dented hood.

The engine died. Then the door popped open, and Alex Hudson stepped out.

The cheap government suit was gone. He wasn't wearing

a suit at all, just jeans and a Clemson Tigers t-shirt. Dark sunglasses obscured his eyes, and his entire neck was encircled in bandages. I couldn't even see his windpipe.

Even after two weeks, I could only imagine that Alex was under a great deal of pain, or else was doped up on painkillers, and shouldn't be driving.

He shut the door and stepped toward me, walking stiffly with a hint of a limp. I still couldn't see through the lenses of his glasses, but nothing about the approach was threatening. I remained loose next to my truck until he was three feet away.

He stopped. He slowly lifted his hand and removed the glasses.

His eyes were streaked red. He stared at me a long time, and I stared at him. Neither of us spoke.

Then, slowly, Alex extended his right hand. Palm open. Waiting.

I accepted it. His squeeze was strong and confident, despite his recent wrist sprain. His shake firm, but not overbearing. Certainly not sarcastic—there was no undercurrent of *capisci* to be found.

Just a lot of silent gratitude.

"If you ever need *anything*, Mason Sharpe." Alex's voice was soft and hoarse and sounded as though it was still difficult for him to speak, but I understood every word.

He released my hand. I pocketed mine.

"I won't be calling you," I said, simply. Then I withdrew my right hand from my pocket and flashed a white paper card affixed with the FBI logo. "I've got Kirsch."

Alex smiled at that. I smiled back. I slid the card back into my pocket, opened the truck door and slid inside. The engine fired up with a smooth purr. Alex approached and put his hands across the open window frame. He glanced down the length of the truck and nodded in admiration.

"Not bad for an old junker," I said.

That brought another smile.

"Where...where will you go?" Alex rasped.

It sounded like a question he had to ask, but maybe not a question he really wanted to have answered. I looked out the window and rested one hand on the wheel, admiring that open blue sky. Then I turned to Alex.

"Somewhere," I said.

He nodded.

"Can I ask one thing?" I said.

He lifted his eyebrows. Didn't answer.

"Keep her smiling," I said. "Always."

Alex patted his hand against the door. He took a step back and I dropped the truck into gear. As I rolled out of the parking lot I glanced once into the mirror and saw him standing in front of the Shelby, watching me go. Lost in a cloud of dust...just like the rest of DC and everything that had happened there.

Then I looked ahead. I settled in for the hum of the tires on the pavement and the rush of the wind in my hair. I took a right turn at the first intersection, because right turns are easy.

And I just drove.

ABOUT THE AUTHOR

Logan Ryles was born in small town USA and knew from an early age he wanted to be a writer. After working as a pizza delivery driver, sawmill operator, and banker, he finally embraced the dream and has been writing ever since. With a passion for action-packed and mystery-laced stories, Logan's work has ranged from global-scale political thrillers to small town vigilante hero fiction.

Beyond writing, Logan enjoys saltwater fishing, road trips, sports, and fast cars. He lives with his wife and three fun-loving dogs in Alabama.

Did you enjoy *Full Force?* Please consider leaving a review on Amazon to help other readers discover the book.

www.loganryles.com

ALSO BY LOGAN RYLES

Mason Sharpe Thriller Series

Point Blank

Take Down

End Game

Fire Team

Flash Point

Storm Surge

Strike Back

Knock Out

Lethal Action

Full Force

Printed in Dunstable, United Kingdom